IN THE FLAMES OF
THE FLICKERMAN

IN THE FLAMES OF THE FLICKERMAN

HAYFORD PEIRCE

WILDSIDE PRESS

for **ARISSA**

*a curious story for a unique person
who might find it amusing in a offbeat way*

IN THE FLAMES OF THE FLICKERMAN

Published by Wildside Press LLC.
www.wildsidebooks.com

PROLOGUE

Not far from the star Lacaille 9352, some 3,400 Terran years after leaving behind the furthest outpost of the Silumiut Continuum, the scoutship Riestu *met disaster.*

Tre'ze had been on duty for nearly thirty hours now and was drifting slowly from his post in the propulsion room to the life center for his long-awaited turn with the sparse stock of Yas'elda available for the crew when he was stopped by Alns, his sometime soulcompanion.

In his agitation Alns' colors were flickering almost through the spectrum and his normal mist-like shape was expanding and contracting in quick pulsations. In an instant Alns imparted the news: all of the ship's Yas'elda were dead or dying of a sudden mutated virus that had raced through them without warning. In a fury the captain had summarily terminated the existence of both the ship's veterinarian and geneticist, but as a gesture this was more soothing to the soul than of practical use to those who remained alive.

As the news sank in, Tre'ze became aware of his own field pulsing now in erratic throbs. For brutally, and without warning, he had just been apprised of the certainty of his own forthcoming death. . . .

Of whichever religious bent you were, one thing was always certain: without Yas'elda even the hardiest Silumiut could not survive. Why this was so the Silumiut had never succeeded in finding a satisfactory answer. Perhaps it was some obscure and subtle need of the psyche for their long-discarded flesh that even the genius of the ancient geneticists had been unable to erase from the racial memory. But without at least occasional coalescence with their corporeal symbiotes, the supremely complex structure of particles that made up the Silumiut rapidly began to decay. Within two millennia at the most — the bare fraction of a normal lifetime — whatever force it was that animated Tre'ze would begin to dim and gutter out. . . .

Every member of the ship's company knew there was but a single hope — to locate a fresh source of Yas'elda, and quickly. Off to one side, a mere three centuries of flight away, hovered a G-type star that normally they would have ignored as unthinkingly as they would have passed by a red giant. For although stars of this type frequently gave birth to planets that were inhabitable and even salubrious, by a still-unexplained quirk no Yas'elda had ever been found in a G-type system.

But now, with nothing more promising for a dozen light years in any direction, the Riestu *slowly turned its course in the direction of that far-off glint. . . .*

CHAPTER 1

Still screaming, he landed painfully on his neck and shoulders. He lay there half-conscious with the wind knocked out of him, nearly blinded by the sudden impossible brilliance of the overhead sun. With a moan he raised an arm to cover his eyes and shield himself from the terrible radiance. As the throbbing pain began to fade he became conscious of the movement of his chest rising and falling as he drew in great gasps of warm air, and of the intense heat of the sun against his bare skin.

Grimacing, he pulled himself up so that he was supported on his elbows, and cautiously opened his eyes.

He stared in horror, and a terrible question battered at his consciousness: was he *insane?*

For brief moments his eyes lingered in astonishment on his naked body that instants before had been fully clothed, but this was a mystery that was inconsequential compared to what lay beyond the sight of his pale white feet and toes.

He blinked, and shook his head in shock, and blinked again, but still the placid blue waters of a great lagoon lay before him, while on the far horizon to his right he could dimly make out the dark green fronds of coconut trees diminishing into the distance. His eyes lifted briefly to the translucent gray sky that arched above him with its furnace-like sun, dazzling and blinding. Two white sea birds swooped and soared, and as he tried to follow them, squinting against the sun, far out to his left he saw a small dark object nearly at the horizon that was almost certainly a fisherman in a tiny wooden pirogue.

Disbelievingly, his eyes fell back to the familiar lines of what mercifully was instantly recognizable as his own body, the tanned brown skin of his wiry arms and legs and hard flat stomach set off by the pale white of his feet and midriff. The sparse blond hairs on his arms and legs glistened brilliantly in the sunlight, as did the thin line that ran from his navel down to the curly tangle on his pubis. As if to reassure himself, he reached out to clasp the soft warm comfort of his genitals in his left hand, before letting his head fall back to the heated sand with a moan of dismay and disbelief.

His neck still throbbed painfully, but now he became aware of the hot gritty surface on which he lay, and turned his head in bewilderment to either side of him. His hands clutched the coarse white sand convulsively so that it flowed like water through his fingers. A few yards away he could see the long gray trunks of innumerable coconut trees growing out of the harsh soil, and scattered between them the peculiar-looking pandanus plants with their sword-like leaves and multiple roots growing out of the ground to meet midway up the spindly trunk. Bright shafts of sunlight filtered through the gently waving fronds of the trees for the few dozen yards he could see into the forest. The only sound to be heard in the absolute silence that blanketed him was that of his own labored breathing. . . .

He squeezed his eyes shut until brightly colored rings and motes danced before them, and wished with all his being that when he awoke from this terrible dream he would once again be safe in the depths of his soft deep bed in Fatu Hiva with the comforting warmth of Kristin wrapped around him.

For unless he was in the midst of some unspeakably vivid dream, or, even worse, utterly and hopelessly insane, he, Ken Camden, was now completely naked on what seemed to be the white sand beach of an atoll island — he who a short moment before had been high on the green hillside of mountainous Rapa Iti!

He lay there for a long, indeterminable time while the sun beat relentlessly on his unprotected skin, his mind a jumble of strange fears and primitive emotions. At last he became aware of the burning sun on the tender white flesh of his midriff and slowly, warily pulled himself to his feet.

He stepped forward uncertainly — and burned his feet painfully on the searing white coral sand. Awkwardly he ran on the balls of his feet the few yards down the gentle slope of the beach to the cool relief of the almost motionless water. He stood ankle deep in it while gentle wavelets lapped around his feet and tiny electric-blue fish darted with quicksilver flashes about his shimmering white toes.

Now that he was on the edge of the shore he could clearly discern the white strip of sand with its jungle of coconut trees and undergrowth running off to either side of him to disappear over the horizon. To his right there was nothing but the placid waters of the lagoon; to his left the tops of coconut trees were still visible above the water as somewhere beyond the horizon the atoll began to gently swing back on itself. But then they too were nothing but a dark smudge where sky met sea, and there was only the soft glimmering of the water in the tropical sun.

Just before him, beyond the sand where he had so suddenly landed on his back, the density of the trees seemed marginally less, and the far-off glimmer of shimmering gray sky was visible here and there between the trunks. So the depth of the forest in that direction was clearly to be measured in hundreds of yards rather than miles.

His lips tightened. There could be no doubt of it — there was no other possible explanation that fit the circumstances: he *was* on a ring-shaped coral atoll. He shook his head in disbelief and felt drops of sweat spill from his forehead. He raised a hand to touch the glowing warmth of his skin. A few more minutes of the burning sun, he knew, and he would be risking sunburn or worse, exposed as he was to the added reflection from the blinding white sand and the transparent waters of the shallow lagoon.

Carefully he waded out into the warm clear water until it reached the middle of his thighs, then sank gratefully into its soothing buoyancy, lightly balanced on his toes, half squatting, half floating, passively letting the waters wash over his shoulders and around his neck. Pensively he stared ashore at the impossible image of coconut trees swaying gently in the soft breeze. . . .

But why impossible? he asked himself, at last feeling his mind beginning to clear from the numbness that had clouded it since he had landed here in the sand. Why was this peaceful scene more impossible than the events that had immediately preceded it?

He shivered at the memory and let his breath out with a sharp hiss. A sharp chill of fear ran through him as he recalled those terrifying moments — so mercifully short — as he had flown helplessly through the air to what had seemed his certain doom. He closed his eyes and once again saw before him the lustrous gray shimmering of the forcefield with its rainbow glimmering of other colors hovering just barely at the edge of perception, an unequaled source of wonder and beauty — unless one was being lifted high in the air by hysterical Rapa islanders and being hurled at its deadly beauty with fanatical strength and determination. . . .

Would he someday be able to forget that ghastly moment of weightlessness as he soared for brief instants that stretched out like centuries, his scream ringing in his ears, watching his doom approach, the despair as he saw his outstretched arm disappear into the shimmering luminescence, the final fatal rush of his face and being towards the mystery, and then —

— being here!

He surged to his feet with sudden energy, as if fearful of falling into another such field here in the midst of these placid waters, and strode quickly to the shore, heedless of his noisy splashing. Once ashore, he stood on the cool wet sand by the water's edge and wondered uneasily what to do next. If only Kristin were here, he thought with a sudden sharp pang. *She* would have a full plan of action ready to be acted on. He actually felt his lips twitch in a faint smile as memories of Kristin and her ways flooded him.

Those broad leaves of that plant growing over there in the shadows of that pandanus, she might say, *those* were used by the ancient Tahitians as towels when stepping forth from ceremonial bathing in the waters of the lagoon. Get some, he could hear her order, and use them to dry yourself.

And that curious brown fibrous substance almost like burlap that could be pulled from the trunks of certain coconut trees — surely that was what the Polynesians had used to make a humble sort of clothing. Or did they? He knew that some of them still made tapa cloth from the bark of various trees, and painted it with homemade dyes, and in the old days had worn it. That much he had learned from Kristin, whose specialty was tapa cloth and all its intricate Marquesan designs. How ignorant he was! And how much Kristin knew. Knowledge that now she might never be able to share with him. . . . His momentary spark of whimsicality flickered out and he shook his head in bleak despair.

How marvelous to be like Kristin, a Polynesian anthropologist, when unexpectedly dumped upon a desert island somewhere in the South Seas. . . .

But even he — a mere carpenter — knew enough to get out of the sun. He ran lightly across the hot sand to the shade of the trees. After a quick embarrassed glance around him he pulled one of the large rubbery leaves he had fantasized as Kristin's towels from the ground and awkwardly used it to dab at the water on his body. It made a terrible towel, and he threw it away angrily, grateful that no one was watching. How an ancient Polynesian would have laughed!

From far away he heard the faint demented wail of a rooster, and he knew with certainty that wherever he had been transported by the incomprehensible agency of the forcefield he was still somewhere in Polynesia. He himself had not traveled extensively, but to judge from the exasperated comments of Kristin and other Americans he had met in the past two years, nowhere in the rest of the world did roosters continue their manic crowing much past the traditional hour of dawn. But he had quickly learned during his life in the Marquesas that Polynesian roosters followed no such petty restrictions. If they felt like crowing at midnight or midday, crow they did, arousing the neighboring roosters until soon the entire island was a maddening cacophony of nerve-jangling shrieks.

But roosters, he knew, even in Polynesia, remained domesticated birds. Wherever there were roosters, sooner or later he would find Tahitians. Clothed or unclothed, he had best start looking for them.

It was impossible to judge from which direction the faint sound had come, so after a moment's scrutiny to locate a glimpse of sky through the trees, he started off towards what should be the other side of the narrow strip of land that composed the atoll. If a path or road existed at all, logic dictated that sooner or later he would have to cross it.

He was surprised by the unkempt tangle of the coconut trees growing in the harsh, sandy soil. Those he had seen in the plantations in the Marquesas or Tahiti had always been neatly aligned in long straight rows with equal spaces between the individual trees and shiny galvanized bands of metal around their trunks to keep the islands' voracious rats from running to the tops of the trees and destroying the nuts by gnawing large round holes through the thick husks.

But here uncounted thousands of old coconuts lay moldering on the rotting remains of long-fallen fronds, most of them with the tell-tale evidence of neat round holes in them. Many of the others had sprouted, or had taken root and were already trees in various stages of growth, oblivious to any order that man might have imposed on them. Even as he made his way cautiously in his bare feet over the sharp edges of the fallen fronds and the lumpy soil with its occasional small pieces of broken coral, he heard rustlings within the shadowy detritus and glimpsed quick, barely discernable movements.

At first he took them to be rats, but when he stopped in the shelter of the thick leaves and twisted limbs of a *bourau* tree that had managed to take root in the midst of the ubiquitous coconuts he soon discovered that what he had glimpsed were the large brown land crabs responsible for the thousands of holes and craters that pitted the landscape like half-remembered pictures of World War I battlefields. The crabs had scuttled away with their curious sideways movement at the sound of his approach to dart down their underground tunnels, but after a few minutes' stillness cautiously began to peer out from their shelters and soon were scurrying through the decay and rot on their incomprehensible missions.

For a long time he remained motionless, studying them with single-minded intensity, desperately absorbed by anything that could even momentarily relieve him of the hard necessity of having to deal with his own strange plight. Tupas had existed in the Marquesas, he remembered, but there they led a marginal existence, the target of wrathful farmers and householders who enthusiastically poisoned or trapped them to stop their depredations. Obviously nobody here — wherever *here* should turn out to be — cared whether their coconut plantations were turned into mine fields or not.

He snorted at the image, and walked slowly away from the cool deep shade of the *bourau* towards the ever-larger patches of sky he could see between the trunks of the coconut trees. If these were coconut plantations, it looked as if some twenty or thirty years had passed since anyone had tended to them. A small frisson of fear began to work its way up his spine. Many of the atoll islands were now deserted, Kristin had told him, their entire populations gone to enjoy the glamorous modern life that existed on Tahiti.

His knowledge of the coral reef atolls of the Tuamotu group was sketchy, but he knew that many of them were great rings of land twenty or thirty miles in diameter enclosing a central lagoon, hot and dry and flat and at the mercy of the occasional hurricanes that roared through the South Pacific. Even with the landing strips and regular airplane service that now linked them to Tahiti and the rest of the world, life on the atolls was monotonous and unrewarding, a subsistence existence based on fishing from the lagoon and tending the ubiquitous coconut trees. There were dozens of atoll islands that had supported populations in pre-European times, but now their numbers had dwindled radically and even some of the larger ones were home to only a few dozen Polynesians.

Suppose the forcefield had deposited him on one of those that had been deserted now for twenty years or more?

He leaned against the gray trunk of a coconut tree and let his breath out despairingly. How long would he be able to survive, leading even the most miserable existence? He was no Robinson Crusoe, and certainly no Polynesian, able to fish the lagoon in a pirogue fashioned from a coconut trunk and to nourish and clothe himself with the many products the natives wrested from the bountiful coconut tree.

Kristin, he had no doubt, would soon have had a dry shelter constructed from pandanus fronds lashed together with homemade rope and would be serving tasty meals scrounged from coconuts in eight separate stages of their development, but he was nothing more than an ordinary American carpenter, dependent on his chest full of power tools and precision instruments to tackle even the simplest design. As for catching fish with a homemade fishhook and climbing coconut trees barefooted to harvest the nuts. . . .

He shook his head despairingly and moved off again through the dappled sunlight that pierced the great canopy that swayed above him. He had heard a rooster — that much was certain. Where there were roosters there were chickens. Where there were chickens there were eggs. Even if the island had been deserted by its former habitants some traces of their generations of existence here would have been left behind. Besides chickens there would probably be wild pigs, and dogs. The sudden thought of killing, and eating, a dog brought the sour taste of bile to his mouth. It wouldn't come to that, he told himself firmly. There were plenty of fish in the immense lagoon, he could learn to —

He halted with one foot in midair. Had being thrown through the forcefield completely unhinged him? Here he was nearly hysterical with despair at the thought of being isolated on this uninhabited desert island, totally oblivious to the fact that the first thing he had seen upon opening his eyes had been the silhouette on the distant horizon of the lagoon of what was clearly a native fisherman out in his pirogue!

Cursing himself for a fool, he stepped forward with something approaching lightheadedness. However vast this lonely atoll, however sparsely populated, somewhere there were other human beings to tend to his needs. He was not alone!

Twenty feet further on he came across the footpath that his logic had so acutely predicted must exist, running directly parallel to both the shorelines. He stopped, and became aware at the same time of what he had been hearing now for sometime without being consciously aware of it — the unceasing rumble of the ocean's waves crashing ashore on the side of the atoll that he was approaching. The sound of the booming surf was somehow reassuring — perhaps because it had been so constant a part of his life with Kristin in their ocean-side home in Fatu Hiva — and he turned with an almost jaunty step to the right and whatever awaited him at the end of the trail.

After all, he asked himself as he marched along, how many men had ever survived an encounter with the flickermen or with their all-encompassing forcefield? As far as he knew, no one. Except himself, Ken Camden. His pace quickened and suddenly he found himself whistling the cheerful tune from the *River Kwai*. He, Ken Camden, was a match for the forcefield! What difficulties could a few days spent on an atoll coral reef possibly pose for him?

CHAPTER 2

An hour later the smell of smoke suddenly filled his nostrils and he stopped and cocked his head, but the only sound he could hear was the dull roar of the Pacific crashing endlessly against the shore somewhere to his left. He looked down and became aware of his nakedness. This was 2002, not the middle of the pre-European sixteenth century! Even in the far-off Tuamotus nobody ran around naked. Whatever settlement lay ahead, the people would be clothed and civilized, probably at home now in the heat of the tropical noon watching a movie on their VCRs. He grinned. There might even be a French gendarme ready to throw him into jail for *outrage aux moeurs publics*!

Thoughtfully he turned to consider the coconut trees that surrounded him on all sides. A short stubby one growing at nearly a 45-degree angle as the undoubted result of some great storm had its trunk enveloped by winding sheets of that peculiar brown substance that so closely resembled broadly woven burlap. It seemed to grow out of the trunk in the midst of the coconuts themselves and then drape itself around the trunk as it continued to grow. Feeling supremely foolish, he began to pull off a large piece of it and to fashion it into a *pareo* cloth to wrap about his middle. The material was tougher than it appeared, and difficult to fashion into the right size, but eventually, with the aid of a sharp piece of white coral unearthed from beneath some fallen fronds, he had it cut and wrapped around his waist to his satisfaction. He grimaced: it felt rough and itchy against his skin. He tossed away the piece of coral and continued down the path somewhat less gaily. How he would be laughed at!

He shrugged irritably. How did they expect someone to be clad who had survived the furies of the flickermen's forcefield? he asked himself sourly. Let them answer that!

Here the coconut trees were more regularly spaced, and they all seemed to soar gracefully above him to the same height. There were fewer nuts lying on the ground, and as he walked he could see that the undergrowth and fallen fronds that cluttered the forest were gradually becoming less and less in evidence. There were no seedling trees growing irregularly among the others, and what before had seemed a forest, or even a jungle, was now clearly a plantation that received at least a minimum of attention.

The light between the trees began to brighten, and he saw there was at last an end to this vast wilderness of coconuts he had walked through for so long now. He began to hear a dull, repetitive hammering like that he had come to associate with the endless pounding of breadfruit bark into tapa cloth in his village of Hanavavé on Fatu Hiva. Then there were faint voices, and his mouth suddenly watered at the savory smell of cooking fish.

He quickened his pace, and a moment later stepped into a small grove of breadfruit and chestnut trees with scattered pandanus plants growing amidst their great trunks. Just beyond he could see a large clearing that seemed to stretch across the entire width of the atoll. He squinted against the bright sunlight that flooded it, then shaded his eyes with his hand. Before him was a small Polynesian village that at first glance seemed peculiarly ramshackle, even for one in the depths of the Tuamotus.

A dozen or so naked children played noisily on the hard white coral soil that was carpeted here and there with sparse batches of wiry grass, while an equal number of scrawny dogs lazed indolently in whatever shadows could be found. Chickens trailing retinues of small yellow chicks scratched purposefully or waddled sedately about the clearing, oblivious to the half-dozen roosters who strutted arrogantly among them.

He remained hidden in the shade of a pandanus plant, observing a number of brown Tahitian women hovering around small cooking fires, while others squatted in the shade of paper mulberry trees pounding white tapa cloth with round stones and wooden sticks. A hundred yards to his right a dozen men in drab shorts stood idly on the shoreline of the lagoon beside a row of small wooden pirogues pulled up on the beach. Two skinny old men in light brown pareos played a game of *pétanque* in the merciless sunlight, thoughtfully tossing large steel balls at a small stone ten yards away. It was all supremely Polynesian.

He frowned uneasily, then raised his eyes to study the two or three dozen houses that made up the village. Most of them were low and rectangular, built of coral blocks from which the exterior plastering had fallen off to expose the raw blocks. The few wooden porches that remained in front of them were little more than unpainted ruins, while none of the open windows he could see had any glass in their shabby frames. Their roofs were a curious jumble of unpainted galvanized tin incompletely covered by plaited coconut or pandanus leaves held in place by intricate networks of ropes. His frown deepened, and he took a silent step backwards, deeper into the shadows of the pandanus. Why did everything seem so — *wrong?*

He cocked his head. There was the noise of the children and the occasional shrill Polynesian laugh from one of the women gathered around their fires. The boom of the surf was a dull presence he had almost forgotten. But —

Where was the blare of the ubiquitous Tahitian radio turned to full volume in competition with 200-watt stereo sets and portable cassette decks and ever-playing VCRs, all of them shrieking and hooting in mind-shattering uproar? It was this universal Polynesian love of ear-splitting noise that had bemused him more than anything else about the strangeness of life in the Marquesas, and the few weeks he had spent in the capital city of Papeete were different only in that Tahitians augmented the electronic din by thousands of unmuffled cars and motorcycles. There was something very odd, or very wrong, about a settlement of Polynesians in which amplified music booming from a dozen directions wasn't threatening to scramble his brains. . . .

He looked again at the women hunched over their fires, and realized with a start what his mind hadn't registered before. All of them were bare-breasted, and clothed only in shabby wrappings of tapa cloth that seemed equally as makeshift as the piece of coconut fiber that he himself wore.

He shook his head in bewilderment. Could he have stumbled onto a movie set, a recreation of an ancient Tahitian village? For a moment that seemed like the certain answer, and then the absurdities of this notion became evident: if movies were made of half-naked natives, they would be of beautiful young bare-breasted maidens, not ugly fat crones such as these. And these tumbledown houses were obviously of nineteenth or twentieth century design, certainly not the coconut frond dwellings of centuries before. And finally, most important of all, so obvious that it was something the mind seemed to almost automatically ignore: Tahiti was now in the age of the flickermen. There were no Hollywood movie companies disembarking from DC-10s and 747s at Faaa International in Tahiti to film their South Seas epics. There was no longer *anyone* disembarking. . . .

Just as there was no longer any gasoline for the inter-island planes that linked Tahiti to the outlying islands, any more than there was for the tens of thousands of cars and motor scooters that had once clogged the streets of Papeete. Which brought him back to the puzzling scene before him. Where were *this* island's motorcycles and scooters, or, at the very least, bicycles. . . ?

He was still pondering this, absently contemplating the half-naked women, when one of the scrawny dogs suddenly woke up with a start and began to bark furiously. Ken moved deeper into the shadows of the trees, unwilling now to step forth into this peculiar village without having considered the situation somewhat more fully.

The women looked up from their chores to turn in his direction, and after a moment's hesitation one of them began to scream shrilly. Another took up the cry, and in what seemed like seconds he found himself surrounded by angrily barking dogs and a dozen Tahitian males who had materialized out of the trees and village with an assortment of dangerous looking home-made arms that they seemed clearly ready to use against him. Uneasily he eyed the heavy stone adzes of various sizes, strapped to their intricately carved handles with neat twistings of coarse fiber, cutting and pounding implements made of sharpened shells from the lagoon, and a few curious knifes and machetes that were obviously deadly in spite of their clearly improvised character. The men's clothing was equally odd, nothing more than a variety of white and brown tapa cloths wrapped around their hips in the way Tahitians normally wore pareos.

This is absurd, he thought, half-panicked. Could he have been cast by the incomprehensible forces of the flickermen onto an island of half-wits, some remote settlement maintained by the government in Papeete to which the idiots of a hundred scattered islands were sent to commune in peace with nature, far from the stress of the modern world?

A short Polynesian tanned nearly black by the sun, with enormously muscled shoulders, stepped forward to prod him tentatively with the sharp end of a homemade spear. Ken looked down at what appeared to be a galvanized spike lashed to a piece of wood jabbing against the suddenly quivering muscles of his stomach and the sight of it was more terrifying than if it had been a knife in the hands of a mugger. He could feel his knees begin to shake. Anyone crazy enough to make a homemade spear was crazy enough to *use* it!

"Hello," said Ken in his careful Tahitian, speaking softly so as not to startle them. He held his empty hands wide. "My name is Ken. Can you tell me the name of this island?"

The islanders turned to look at one another with unfathomable expressions, then crowded in around him menacingly. "Why do you speak so strangely, Frenchman?" asked a middle-aged man with long stringy muscles and glossy jet-black hair combed back over his scalp in precise furrows. "How do you hope to deceive us?" He cocked his head inquisitively and stared curiously at Ken with rheumy red eyes.

His own speech was peculiar, and Ken had to pause to decipher its meaning. It was akin to the Marquesan dialect he had initially learned, but more closely allied to the dominant speech of Tahiti, with merely a shift in some of the consonants. In any case, Tahitian, and all its related languages, was mostly a matter of endlessly strung-together vowels that remained the same whatever the variations in the five or six consonants the islanders bothered to use. Obviously this was one of those Tuamotu dialects he had occasionally overheard, a language that fell into a neat classification, linguistic as well as geographic, midway between Marquesan to the north and Tahitian to the south.

"Deceive you?" asked Ken, uneasily turning his head to appraise the dozen men who hemmed him in from all sides. "In what way do you think I am trying to deceive you?"

The spokesman frowned. "That strange language you speak. It is Tahitian."

"Yes. That is what I learned. I speak Marquesan as well. Would you prefer that I speak that?"

The islander sucked in his breath with a loud hiss and fell back a pace. A tremor seemed to run through the crowd, and there was a low murmur of voices. "The Marquesas are beyond the sky-curtain."

"The sky-curtain?" Ken echoed.

The Tuamotuan gestured impatiently at the great vault of shimmering gray that arched above them. "The sky-curtain."

"Oh, the forcefield," muttered Ken in English.

"Forkfeel?" repeated the Tuamotuan. "Is that what you *faranis* now call the sky-curtain?"

"No. It's English. I'm not French." Ken smiled as winningly as he could under the circumstances. To the Polynesians, Frenchmen had been the colonial masters of Tahiti, who even now governed the islands under a cloak of local autonomy, whereas Americans for many generations had been rich friends come to frolic insouciantly with the Polynesians in frequent defiance of the dour French. Frenchmen had erected a set of so-called laws that enabled them to cast Tahitians into their stone and metal jails for strange, unfathomable reasons. Americans had merely come to uninhibitedly play music and drink beer and fondle the local women and spend their money generously. All of this Tahitians could understand. Polynesia was one of the few parts of the world in which Americans were still genuinely liked.

"No," said Ken with his faint smile. "I am American."

"American!" The word was repeated incredulously by the islanders. One of them shoved him roughly on the shoulder. "You lie, Frenchmen," he shouted. "There *are* no Americans! There are only Frenchmen like you. *Farani taioro!*" he spat angrily.

Ken drew himself up. *Uncircumcised Frenchman* was the ultimate in local insults, connoting as it did in Tahitian a gross inattention to personal cleanliness. "I am neither French nor uncircumcised," he said angrily. "If you like, you can see for yourselves."

"What. . . ." murmured the middle-aged man before him, but Ken was suddenly in the grip of an anger that overcame any fear he might have had of these ridiculous drugstore-Tahitians. He brushed the spear irritably away from his stomach and ripped apart the fibrous brown coconut cloth that circled his waist. He threw it furiously to the ground.

"Look!" he shouted, grasping his dangling white flesh and shaking it at the gaping islanders. "Is that the cock of a Frenchman? Tell me, is that an uncircumcised cock?" He waved it furiously. "Let me see *yours,*" he raged. "How do I know that *you* aren't all *farani taioro?*"

There was a great silence while Ken could feel the hot flush in his cheeks and the giddy shaking in his limbs of the surging adrenaline, and then it was broken by a loud guffaw behind him.

"Eh, Vetea," cried a gleeful voice, "let's see *your* cock! You're too old to use it anymore, maybe the white man is right, maybe you *are a farani taioro!* None of the women here would ever know!" There was a great burst of laughter, and heads turned towards the middle-aged Tuamotuan in front of Ken. He grinned and shook his head helplessly as he searched for a riposte.

"Bring me all of your daughters and women, you sperm-drinking whoremongers," he at last roared good-naturedly, "and I'll show all of you buggering ass-thumpers what a *man's* tool is like!" He glanced down appreciatively at Ken. "Even if it isn't as long and ugly as this skinny white sea serpent this so-called American is trying to frighten us with!"

There was another roar of laughter, and the islanders suddenly turned their eyes down to examine the motley collection of weapons in their hands with looks of astonishment, as if wondering how such peculiar objects had found their way there. Ken could feel his own tension suddenly draining away and he broke into a sheepish grin. A moment later he had joined the Tuamotuans in their boisterous laughter. Embarrassed now at the angry display he had so unexpectedly made of himself, he stooped to gather up his folds of coconut fiber and awkwardly began to wrap it around his hips.

Vetea watched his fumblings with tolerant good humor. "Where then do you come from, O white American with the wiggly white sea serpent?" he asked with a sly smile that indicated his fundamental skepticism. "And how do you come among us to astonish our daughters and women with your terrible weapon?"

Ken had always felt uncomfortable with the perpetual genial bawdiness of the Polynesians. "I am here because the sky-curtain threw me here," he said slowly. "What I am about to say is the solemn truth. A few hours ago I stood on the island of Rapa Iti, far to the south of Tahiti. There I . . . fell into the sky-curtain that splits that island. Rather than being killed, as I had supposed that everyone is who falls into the sky-curtain, I suddenly found myself lying here on your beach, somewhere back there." He turned to point. "I found your path in the middle of the island, and have been following it for the last two hours." He ignored their looks of confusion and incredulity to gesture at the small village before him and the large group of women and children who stood silently watching them from some distance off in the shade of an enormous breadfruit tree. "What is the name of your island?" A note of desperation crept into his voice. "Where *am* I ?"

For millions of years now the Silumiut had been slowly expanding along the rim of the galaxy in epic journeys that frequently lasted for dozens of centuries. Hardly more substantial than a twinkling glitter, the Silumiut were so long-lived as to be nearly immortal — so long as they possessed an unending supply of the Yas'elda, that short-lived race of non-sentient beasts who so disconcertingly still retained the awkward burden of their corporeal bodies.

As far back as they could trace their history — and that was hundreds of millions of years — the Silumiut had pressed further and further into the arms of the galaxy in search of a single rare treasure: the occasional life-bearing planet that harbored the degenerate remnants of what must once have been an even more ancient species of space explorers than themselves.

Why the Yas'elda had retained their corporeal bodies was a question that still preoccupied scientists, theologians, and philosophers. The Silumiut themselves had long ago become masters of the interaction of elementary particles and at some remote time in the past had divested themselves of the hideous constraints of their earthbound bodies. But now, eons later, the reason for this dramatic transformation had long since been forgotten and had become a question that profoundly affected their religious and philosophical thought.

The majority of Silumiut, the Aspirants of the Fourteenth Harbinger, believed that the great transmutation was but a natural step in that on-going evolutionary process set in motion by the Original One, and whose single goal was to lift the Silumiut to the level of His own ineffable Godhead.

The doctrine of a vocal minority, the Unifactionists, held that far from being on a path that led inevitably towards the Godhead, the Silumiut had been obliged by some now-forgotten cataclysm to transform themselves into immateriality as the sole and desperate means of preserving the race.

Doctrinaires of each point of view could find supporting evidence in the existence of the Yas'elda, a moderately large quadruped scattered erratically upon oxygen-based planets throughout this end of the galaxy. Both sides agreed that the Yas'elda had once been a sentient race of spacefarers, for there was no other way to explain their existence on hundreds of planets scattered over thousands of light years.

To the Aspirants the existence of the Yas'elda was divine proof that those species that did not take the next evolutionary step up to non-material life could only degenerate, regressing along the evolutionary ladder to the level of brute animals, where they existed now for whatever services they might render to higher beings.

All very well, argued the Unifactionists, but in that case why were we, the evolutionarily superior Silumiut, obliged to live in total symbio-sis with such inferior creatures, these gross corporeal animals? For all Silumiut now were such tenuously grouped arrangements of particles that their very existence was held by certain advanced thinkers to be philosophically dubious, and without the Yas'elda their bonds with life all too soon flickered away into eternal nothingness.

Of equal importance to the species, it was only in conjunction with their lowly symbiotes that the all-powerful Silumiut, conquerors of the stars, highest rung of evolution's towering ladder, could reproduce their kind. It was a strange type of superbeing, argued the Unifaction-ists, whose very existence was dependent upon brute animals. As a generally unpopular consequence of their doctrines, the Unifaction-ists urged a far greater humility upon the Silumiut when they looked out upon the Cosmos to consider their place in the divine scheme of things.

Neither Tre'ze nor most of the other members of the Riestu cared at all about this rather academic theological dispute as their ship moved slowly through the void, but the hard fact of their dependence upon the Yas'elda surrounded them at every turning in the cramped quarters of the scoutship.

For the Silumiut had been forced to expand through space for mil-lions of years now under the pressure of constant population growth on the hundreds of inhabited worlds that made up the Continuum. Without their fleet of scoutships incessantly scouring the galaxy for new worlds and additional Yas'elda, it was widely believed, the civilization built up over so many eons would eventually collapse upon itself from sheer numbers.

The role of the Riestu was essential, therefore, and the members of its crew were theoretically held in the Continuum's highest esteem. But they were far from being the most emulated, for the Silumiut were non-gregarious and unadventurous, and rare were those who would voluntarily leave the familiar comforts of their planet of birth for the cramped quarters and dangers of voyaging among the stars, no matter how great the rewards.

There was no question that the rewards were great — for those Silu-miut fortunate to return to the Continuum with the good news that yet another planet of Yas'elda had been found. But mere rewards, however great, were not considered by those who directed the fortunes of the Continuum a sufficient stimulus to always sustain the basically reluctant Silumiut in journeys that might last hundreds of centuries.

As an ultimate incentive, therefore, scoutships were sent forth with only a minimal supply of Yas'elda to fulfill the barest requirements of the officers and crew. As the centuries and millennia passed, these Yas'elda would inevitably sicken and die, or mutate unexpectedly into endless variants that were totally unacceptable for their natural role of symbiote, for they could no longer be bred to survive for endless periods of time in the close confines of space. If the unlucky ship should fail to locate a fresh source of symbiotes within a millennia or so after the death of the last Yas'elda its crew faced a bleak future with certain extinction at its end.

For to return to the Silumiut Continuum without a sampling of fresh new Yas'elda aboard was to return to a single drastic penalty: the auto-matic termination of the life processes of all those aboard. . . .

CHAPTER 3

Stunned, he sat dazed in the shade of an enormous breadfruit tree while he watched the islanders begin the preparations of a great feast, in the grip of an unspeakable emptiness. Even the terrible screams of pigs and piglets having their throats slit by giggling teenagers failed to rouse him from his half-conscious stupor.

Over and over the same inane refrain ran through his mind until he thought he would lose his reason. I shouldn't have asked "Where *am I?*" but "When *am I?*" I shouldn't have asked. . . .

Oh God, he cried in silent anguish, *Kristin!*

His beautiful Kristin, whom he knew he would never see again.

Dead these fifty years.

He buried his face in his arms and wept.

When the spasms had at last subsided he lifted his head and looked dully about him at the shabby world that would encompass the rest of his life. Even now that he was irrevocably *here* it seemed impossible to believe that such a sorry joke could have been perpetrated on him by the flickermen. A thousand times over he would have preferred to have perished in the forcefield, but for inscrutable reasons his life had been spared only to have his soul destroyed.

With unseeing eyes he watched the women cautiously dunking the carcasses of the dead pigs into an ancient enameled bathtub filled with boiling water to help them scrap off the tough black bristles, while off to his left great pits were being dug to be filled with rocks and fire. Excited children were arranging a long row of banana leaves on the beach next to the lagoon and adorning it with a multitude of red, yellow, and white hibiscus blossoms. This would be the banqueting table for the great feast.

He looked away, sickened by the sight of these frivolously carefree savages. How could they propose a feast in honor of a man who had just lost more than these ignorant beings could ever imagine? A man whose sole desire was to be left alone until he found the resolve to turn his back on the world with the same terrible finality as it had turned its back on him. Never would he be able to join with these over-grown children in their laughter and drunken revelry.

Even now, hours before the celebration would begin, he could hear the raucous songs and ragged shouts of the island's men as they passed around coconut gourds of homemade beer and alcohol while they readied their pirogues for a few hours' languid fishing on the broad lagoon. Eventually, he supposed, freed from those minimal constraints that church and state had imposed on the Marquesas islanders he had lived among, these — Takaroans? — would drink and debauch until the entire population lay stupefied on the beach under the evening sky.

He sighed despairingly. How could Kristin have *done* this to him. . . ?

Three small naked girls about four years old came over to stand before him and examine him solemnly with enormous brown eyes. They were joined by two little boys, one of whom sucked thoughtfully on his thumb while he stared unblinkingly at the strange white being sitting so motionlessly beneath the *uru* tree. Ken stared back at them with hopelessness and dismay. Welcome to Takaroa, he thought, welcome to Takaroa. . . .

Takaroa. . . .

A few ancient paper maps and charts still existed, cherished and carefully guarded by an older half-brother of Vetea's to whom the other islanders deferred in matters of navigation. They had been copied for practical use onto large white pieces of exceptionally fine tapa cloth using a dark brown ink made from the roots of the *tou* tree. Vetea and Tupi had begun to unfold a particularly large map and spread it out on a table made from roughly hewn coconut trunks while what seemed the entire population of the island crowded around them.

"There," said Tupi with assurance, placing a gnarled brown finger on a large irregular ring on the northern edge of the thousand-mile chain of atolls that composed the Tuamotus. "That is our home of Takaroa. Here is the pass of Teavanae, and here is the village of Teavaroa where we now find ourselves. On the other side of island, *here,* there is a smaller village called Paketaketa but it is not worthy of consideration."

"The women are leprous, the men pederasts," interjected a voice from the crowd around them to admiring guffaws.

"No matter," said Vetea impatiently, unfolding another segment of the map. "This, as you can see, is Tahiti, 375 miles to the southwest. Let me see now, it is from Rapa Iti that you say the sky-curtain transported you. . . ." Yet more of the enormous map was carefully opened. "Rapa is far to the south of Tahiti, south even of the Australes and —"

"To the east," interrupted Tupi. "There!" He produced a wooden ruler with elaborate markings and made a series of meticulous measurements. "Rapa would appear to be approximately 800 miles from Tahiti, which, so we are told, is the source of the sky-curtain that defines our world. You say that the sky curtain passes directly through the island of Rapa?"

"Yes, from east to west." Ken's lips tightened at the memory. "It forms a great circle in the midst of the ocean with Tahiti as its center. My . . . our home on Fatu Hiva was about 850 miles away from Tahiti. It was impossible to return there. If only I —" He broke off abruptly, unable to continue, and pushed his way blindly through the crowd.

If only I had done *this*. . . .
If only Kristin had done *that*. . . .
If only I *hadn't* done this. . . .
If only Kristin *hadn't* done that. . . .
If only. . . .
If! he thought bitterly, if!

He threw himself despairingly to the ground at the base of a breadfruit tree, oblivious to the large hard fruit that dangled dangerously among the leaves above him. If only he weren't *here*. If only Kristin weren't dead. If only five generations — a hundred years! — hadn't passed since he had been thrown screaming into that sky-curtain 950 miles away.

Late that afternoon, wearing a crisp white pareo of newly cut tapa cloth and a garland of red, orange, and yellow flowers intricately woven into a band of bright green leaves, he took his place next to Vetea on the carefully arranged banana leaves that had been set out for the celebration in honor of his arrival. As far as he could tell the entire village was there, all two or three hundred of them, including a dozen babies at their mothers' breast.

He looked listlessly at the great feast that had been set before them, food enough, he would have thought, for a thousand people or more. The cooking pits had been dug open and an endless procession of food brought forth from them: four steaming brown pigs with crackling skin, as well as two dozen piglets; four varieties of plantains and bananas; yams and sweet potatoes; hundreds of large round breadfruit; *poé* wrapped in leaves and baked with rich sweet coconut cream; chicken baked with *fafa* spinach; half a dozen fifty-pound fish. Hundreds of smaller fish had been grilled or boiled, and there were great bowls of raw fish marinated in lime juice, then mixed with tomatoes and hard-boiled eggs. As if all this were not sufficient, hundreds of purplish slabs of the daily staple, boiled taro, had been laid out in neat packages of wrapped leaves.

On the bright green banana leaves before him there were piles of shiny red lobsters, and gourds overflowing with varieties of snails and mollusks from the shallow waters of the reef, some cooked, others raw, and more gourds filled with various of the Tahitian sauces and condiments: *mitihué, taioro,* and the abominably foul-smelling *fafaru.* Four separate gourds were handed to him: fresh rainwater; coconut water; beer made from pineapples; and a fiery alcohol distilled from the hearts that grew in each of the island's thousands of coconut trees.

He sipped the sparkling sweet beer and was surprised at how pleasant it tasted. He took another sip and reached tentatively for a small piece of cooked banana. In a few minutes he had discovered how famished he was, and Vetea was clucking appreciatively and leaning over to solicitously offer choice morsels of fish and pork. He drank another gourd of the warm bubbly beer and sipped haltingly at the coconut toddy. It was unpleasantly harsh, and he exchanged it for Vetea's gourd of innocuous beer.

An hour or so later he slumped half-dazed, gorged with food, his hands and face thick with grease from the fatty pork, and watched with glassy eyes as the Takaroa islanders continued to stuff food into their mouths with both hands until it seemed they must burst. There were loud shouts and glad cries and unending shrill laughter, and the fat woman next to him had begun to whisper lewd enticements into his ear. She reeked of coconut oil perfumed with a sickening essence of some local flower, and as the sweet cloying odor filled his nostrils, it was all he could do to retain the enormous greasy mass that now sat so heavily in his bloated stomach. He shook his head and pushed her away roughly. For a long while afterwards his head seemed to continue to shake by itself, and he felt a curious numbness in the fingers of his right hand. Perhaps if I dip them in the coconut alcohol, he told himself, that will stop them from tingling like that. . . .

Night suddenly fell, and flickering torches were planted in the sandy soil around the banqueting area. By their smokey orange glow he could see that several dozen revelers had already fallen unconscious upon the heaps of discarded bones and skins of fruits and vegetables that littered the banana leaves, while others nodded blearily or stared vacantly into their bowls of pineapple beer. The fat woman's head fell against his shoulder and he pushed it irritably away.

Random chords of thin twangy music strummed on homemade ukuleles and banjos vied with one another from various parts of the feasting grounds until suddenly the voices of one group seemed to coalesce around a common theme and quickly drove all the others into silence. The tune was bright and lively and those islanders still awake joined in loudly on the refrain. Vaguely he understood that it concerned lovemaking on the beach but beyond that he was unable to follow the words.

His own head was beginning to seem strangely heavy on his shoulders now, and he took a long swallow of the still bubbly pineapple beer to refresh himself. The fat woman with the broad grin and three widely spaced teeth swayed against him, then fell backwards into the sand and lay snoring loudly. To rowdy shouts of approval from those nearby, Vetea reached behind Ken's back to solemnly pour a gourd of the foul *fafaru* over her head, but even this failed to awaken her. The cries of the singers were louder and faster now, and dimly he could see the shiny half-naked bodies of dancers gleaming and twisting in and out of the yellow light of the guttering torches.

A young girl with long flowing hair and a garland of gardenias around her head bent over and pulled urgently on his arm, inviting him to dance. He looked up blearily at the cheerful round face glowing golden in the torchlight and the firm breasts barely concealed by the tapa cloth wrapped around her lithe body and began to struggle clumsily to his feet. She giggled happily, and tugged at his elbow, overbalancing him so that he fell against the inert mound of the stupefied fat woman. The fetid reek of the noisome *fafaru* and the sickening stench of her coconut-oil perfume assailed his nostrils. His stomach lurched and he suddenly felt the sharp taste of bile in his throat. A moment later he had stumbled blindly into the lagoon and was kneeling in the shallow water, racked by painful spasms.

When at last the spasms had passed he moved further out into the lagoon to submerse his spinning head in the warm waters and to rinse the ghastly taste from his mouth. As he massaged the painful knots of his tender stomach muscles he could see the wild movements of the dancers in the flickering torchlight and hear the driving rhythms of the island music. Two plump young girls, he could see, had stripped themselves naked and were wading out in his direction. How many millions of men, he asked himself, would willingly have given everything they possessed, friends, family, country, even their very *time,* to exchange places with him?

He plunged his head underwater again and began to swim off blindly beneath the dark waters. When at last his aching lungs forced him to the surface he heard the voices of the two girls calling softly somewhere behind him. He submerged again and again, swimming until the lights of the feast were far down the shoreline and the music and singing were only a faint murmur.

He walked ashore by the light of a half-moon, shivering faintly as a cool breeze caressed his wet body. Haltingly he pushed his way into the thick undergrowth that spread along the shoreline until there was nothing but darkness to all sides of him. His head was throbbing painfully now, but his thoughts seemed again sharp and lucid. He found a coconut tree in the darkness and leaned against it as if to keep from falling to the ground, his forearms and forehead resting against the cool rough bark. He could still taste bile in his mouth, and his esophagus burned painfully. Great waves of desolation washed over him, and he let himself sink slowly to the ground, where he lay hunched and quivering. Oh God, he cried, as he looked back in the darkness at the simple chain of events that led with such inevitable finality to where he now lay huddled on this cold sandy ground, what did I do to *deserve* this?

Yet another beach had begun the chain, he saw, for it was there he had met Kathie Leitner, and if he had never known Kathie Leitner he would even now be no more than a small-time carpenter and handyman and failed actor living and working in Culver City, California, in the shadows of what remained of the MGM studios. Small-time was the correct word for him, he knew, a high-school graduate with half-hearted ambitions to be an actor that had eventually translated into seven roles as a non-speaking extra and one part as a two-line bit player in an obscure soap opera. After that he had returned full-time to carpentry with no ambitions to press on any further, but even a small-time carpenter was enough in demand in the wealthy enclaves of Westwood and Beverly Hills to permit a life of quiet independence in which the most pressing decision was whether the weekends should be spent surfing in the cold waters of Malibu or on the broad sandy expanses of the Santa Monica beach, lying in the sun and watching the golden girls of California frolic in the surf. But in the event, it was on the rocky shore south of Malibu that he met Kathie Leitner, a small bouncy blonde in a bright red wetsuit stumbling over the rocks with a long blue surfboard.

They rode the waves together until the chill of the Pacific waters penetrated even their wetsuits, then drove down the coast in their separate cars to a cocktail lounge that overlooked the endless rollers of the cold gray ocean. It was called the Forbidden Tiki, and was full of bamboo and fishnets and potted palm trees. They watched the enormous misshapen red sun sink slowly over the edge of the world while they drank first hot toddies and then maitais and finally zombies, nibbling all the while at microwaved eggrolls and shrimps.

"Haven't I seen you on television?" asked Kathie. "You're certainly handsome enough to be there."

Ken felt himself blushing. A major deficiency in egomania, he knew, had been the principal cause for his failure in the world of performing arts. "I once had a couple of lines in a soap called *The Times of Our Troubles,*" he muttered.

"I *knew* it!" Kathie clapped her hands in delight. "Now I can say I know a movie star!"

"I was a lousy actor." He grinned awkwardly and looked down into his drink. "That's the real reason I don't do it any more. And I was offered a job in a porno flick once but I didn't take it."

"You *didn't?* I thought that was every guy's dream job! To get paid for. . . well, you know. What's the matter? Didn't you think you could get it. . . well, you know, with all those people watching?"

Ken shrugged. "Yeah, I guess I did wonder about that a little. But. . . but suppose my *mother* found out?"

Kathie leaned closed on her barstool and wrapped an arm around him for a brief but enthusiastic hug. "You know? You're *sweet!*"

A while later, as she waved her glass at the varnished blowfish that hung from the ceiling, she said, "This isn't anything at all like the *real* South Seas, you know. This is just make-believe stuff, like Don the Beachcomber and Trader Vic."

Ken felt obscurely displeased. He had *liked* Don the Beachcomber's and Trader Vic's, back in the days when he thought that movie actors hung out in places like that, and a criticism of them seemed to be a criticism of himself. And if the real South Seas wasn't like that he wasn't sure he wanted to know about it. "I suppose you go there often?" he said, his voice sounding more sarcastic than he had meant it to.

She looked at him in surprise, and frowned. "No. Just once, with my family. My father does a lot of sailing. We sailed down there once — before I was married."

"I didn't know you were married. You didn't —"

"I *was* married. Now I'm not. Okay?" She scowled at him belligerently.

"Sure." He smiled apologetically. "Look, I didn't mean to sound . . . you know." He lowered his eyes bashfully, afraid to look at her. "I don't really hate people who can go to the South Seas, you know. How about, maybe, you'll let me take you to Trader Vic's for dinner?" He raised his bright blue eyes and ran his hand through his thick blond hair, bleached nearly white by the sun. "You can tell me all about the *real* South Seas." He looked across the small table at her earnestly. "Please?"

She popped a shrimp into her mouth and chewed it slowly. Her brown eyes considered him thoughtfully. "July 7th, 1999," she said finally. "That's three years ago."

Ken nodded, puzzled. "Yes?"

Her faint smile was barely perceptible. "That was the last time I heard my husband say *please.*"

"Oh."

She gathered up her bag. "It's not a word my father uses much, either." She rose to her feet. "If we're going to Trader Vic's I need a shower and a gardenia for my hair." Standing, the top of her short blonde hair came barely to his chin. "Newport Beach is a long way to go for a shower."

"I don't have a gardenia at home, but I do have a shower."

"That's what I thought. Just lead the way." She stopped at the heavy teak door and waited for him to push it open. "Another first," she said over her shoulder. "The last time my husband opened a door for me was —"

"April 16th, 1742," he finished, and they grinned foolishly at each other and stepped out into the night.

CHAPTER 4

He discovered a number of other things her husband hadn't done for her by the time they were ready to sail for Australia four months later. Among them was making love to her more than once a week. This at least Ken was able to remedy, along with offering all the tenderness and cheerfulness that she seemed to need. The decision to accompany Kathie on Charles Leitner's cruise of the South Pacific had been made without soul-searching. A carpenter could always take a year off and pick up again without difficulty. He sold his truck and his car, gave his landlord thirty-days' notice on his apartment, and carefully packed his hand tools and smaller power tools into a single large metal chest for delivery to the *Last One Left*. His personal items barely filled a small suitcase.

A carpenter was a useful adjunct aboard a ninety-three-foot yacht when setting out for a year's sail, he knew, and perhaps because of this Charles Leitner seemed to regard him with tolerant forbearing. Retired stockbrokers with multi-million dollar estates in Newport Beach didn't generally approve of their only daughters taking up with Culver City carpenters, he supposed, but the old man was reasonably polite about it in a rather distant fashion. Another reason may have been because Leitner himself had arranged to be accompanied on the voyage by a busty young brunette named Marti Fleischmann who was thirty years his junior.

Or he may even have genuinely loved his daughter. Certainly he made no attempt to conceal his hatred and contempt for the former husband his lawyers had successfully pried away from her, and Ken occasionally wondered if Leitner simply regarded him as a useful form of psychotherapy, to be dispensed with upon the patient's discharge.

It was not until the ship was well underway on its initial four-week run south from Los Angeles to the Marquesas that Ken discovered he really wasn't very comfortable in his enforced proximity to the very rich. Charles Leitner at first seemed politely amused that any young man Ken's age had not yet amassed his first million in the commodities market, or, even worse, showed no great interest in doing so. But as the trip wore on, his air of polite amusement grew increasingly exasperated, until finally his lips seemed perpetually set in a thin line of disapproval when Ken was in his vicinity.

For even on a ninety-three-foot boat it was hard to avoid his company, as well as that of his friends and guests, James and Aileen Erikson, a middle-aged couple from Santa Barbara with soft voices and careful eyes whose sole tropic of conversation was their 200-horse racing stable and stud farm, and the millions of dollars needed annually to maintain it. After the first week at sea they made no further effort to even pretend that he existed for them. He shrugged off their contempt, even as he was hurt by it, as well as that of Leitner's twenty-three-year-old girlfriend, a simple, basically good-natured girl from the Wisconsin diary lands, who was loudly and unabashedly thrilled to find herself in the midst of an opulent dream, and whose faint scorn was a sorry imitation of those she tried to emulate.

He sought companionship with Dave and Larry, semi-professional sailors his own age who were crewing in return for a year's free travel, but they were equally derisive about so-called crew whose only qualifications were a chest of carpenter's tools and a tool of a more personal nature for working on the captain's daughter.

For in spite of his Southern California beachboy good looks and bronzed muscular body, Ken knew himself to be basically introverted and self-effacing, and his lack of assurance in dealing with the other members of the boat soon communicated itself to Kathie.

"Why do you let her talk to you like that?" she asked in exasperation as they lay in her narrow bunk, referring to a remark Aileen Erikson had made that afternoon about Ken's lack of adroitness in tying reef knots. "You'd think a *knothead* would be good at doing at least *two* things," she observed with an arch smile at her husband. "Tying knots is one." She glanced slyly at Kathie, who was peeling potatoes in the shade of the afterdeck's awning. "I'll let *you* guess the other."

Kathie flushed a deep red and flung a half-peeled potato at the startled woman. "If you weren't such a foul-mouthed old bitch that you'd poison the sharks, I'd throw you overboard, you ugly piece of horseshit," she cried, and stomped off to the front of the ship, where Ken could see her expostulating bitterly with her father. He sighed softly and returned to the infuriating knots.

"What can I say?" he asked. "They're your father's friends. I'm just. . . ."

"Just what?" she asked angrily. "Just a deckhand? Just someone who screws the old man's daughter? Just a knothead who ties knots and gives head? Is that how you think of yourself?" She pushed herself away from him to huddle against the paneled bulkhead. "How do you think that makes *me* look?"

He shook his head miserably.

"Why don't you *defend* yourself, for chrissake? How do you think they'll ever respect you if you don't *make* them?"

It was a question Ken had often asked himself, but he was no closer now to finding the answer than when he had first considered it. "I can't be what I'm not," he said. "I can't . . . well, throw *potatoes* at people."

Kathie sat up violently, bumping her head with a loud thump on the upper bunk. "What's *that* supposed to mean?" she cried shrilly. "I can't defend myself on my own boat?" She shoved angrily against his bare shoulders. "Jesus Christ, what kind of a man are you, anyway? Leave me alone, would you? Get up in your own bunk and just leave me alone. Oh Jesus fucking Christ!" She buried her face in her pillows and began to sob softly. Ken stared helplessly at the warm honey-colored skin of her bare back and with a dismayed sigh swung out of the lower bunk. For a long moment he stood indecisively in the middle of the tiny cabin, then flicked off the overhead light and climbed up to his bunk, where he stared blindly into the darkness.

Eight days later Ken sipped his glass of ice-cold Hinano beer on the terrace of a small restaurant with five bungalows attached to it in the hills behind the town of Taiohae. From where he sat he could look down at the toy-like Last One Left sitting motionlessly on the great blue Bay of Taiohae. Two rocky arms thrust out into the Pacific, and it was through their narrow pass that the Last One Left had come to make landfall three days earlier. On the lip of the giant amphitheater created by the massive green mountains girdling the bay lay the small town of Taiohae, the administrative and social capital of the Marquesas Islands, and here he had forlornly come ashore.

Now he ordered another beer from the Hungarian proprietor, a former Foreign Legionnaire, who so improbably owned this small establishment in one of the most isolated corners of the world, and bleakly contemplated his future. He had a chest of tools, a suitcase of clothes, and a $1,000 deposit somewhere with the immigration services in the town below as surety for his airplane ticket from Papeete back to Los Angeles. Today was Tuesday; the next flight to Tahiti was on Saturday, a two-engined prop plane that left from an airstrip that could only be reached by a two-hour boat ride. Of so much he was certain, as well as the fact that he had a reserved bungalow until that time. Beyond that his future was cloudy. He had money in the bank in Los Angeles from the sale of his truck. He could use some of it to rubberneck in Tahiti while he had the opportunity, or he could catch the Sunday morning jet to Los Angeles and be in a hotel by evening.

And carpentering again the following week.

It seemed like a miserable end to a love affair, and to his great adventure in the South Seas.

"Do you enjoy drinking alone, or would you like some company?"

At first he took her to be a particularly attractive Marquesan woman, tall and slender and in her mid-thirties, for her glossy black hair was knotted into two long braids that dangled down between her smallish breasts and her face was the color of old mahogany. But now he saw that the coils of hair framed a fine straight nose and high Slavic cheekbones and that her face had the angular beauty of an Indian princess and not the soft contours of the Polynesian *vahiné*. Her eyes were a soft hazel-green and sparkled with a quizzical intelligence. Her accent was clearly American, and her pale lips were drawn into a faint, knowing smile that suddenly made him feel fourteen years old again and nervously preparing for his first date.

He rose to his feet and pulled a chair away from the table. "Please," he said. "I'd enjoy some company."

"Who wouldn't, up in this miserable part of the world?" She seated herself with easy grace, and with total self-assurance appraised him openly, running her eyes up and down his body as if he were some late-model android she was considering ordering for her home. Ken smiled uneasily and looked around for the proprietor, conscious of her eyes on him. When she had been served with a gin and tonic she raised her glass and clinked it against his glass of beer. "Chin," she said with an ironic smile on her broad, rather thin, mouth.

"Chin?"

"As in the hair of my chinny chin chin," he heard her say improbably but solemnly. "It's what the French say instead of *cheers. Chin-chin.* It seems to have been the name of an English musical of the twenties. For reasons best known to themselves, the French have turned it into a toast."

"You sound like a . . . teacher?" he hazarded.

"In a way. You have a neurosis about teachers? You were frightened by one in the cloakroom after school once?"

To his surprise he felt himself blushing. "No, no, I was —"

"Just making small talk." She gulped her drink, set it down, and produced a metal tin of small black cigarillos that she offered to Ken. "No? Sensible. But who wants to be sensible all the time?" Her knee brushed Ken's under the table as she turned to signal the proprietor to bring fresh drinks. "My name's Dellinger, by the way, Kristin Dellinger."

"I'm Ken Camden."

"You're off that boat down there, the one with the name of a book?"

"It is? The *Last One Left?* I didn't know that." He shrugged wistfully. "There are a lot of things I don't know, I guess."

"You're still young. There's plenty of time to learn."

"I was only on it for a couple of weeks," he said in limp explanation, obscurely seeking the approval of this peculiar, almost daunting woman.

"And now you're going to stay here in the *Marquises?*" Her already highly arched brown eyebrows lifted in surprise.

He stared down at the puddle of moisture his glass had made. "No. Only till Saturday. Then I go to Tahiti. After that I don't know. Back to the States, I suppose."

"Hrmph. That doesn't sound like much of a trip." She snapped the remains of her cigarillo in a long glowing arc across the terrace and into the orange hibiscus that grew below. "You don't enjoy sailing? You get seasick, perhaps?"

"No. I just . . . decided . . . to leave, was all."

"Ah so," she hissed in a ludicrous Japanese accent. "You have wife and family waiting for you in States, little mouths to feed, miles to go before you sleep?"

It was impossible not to be amused by what he supposed she considered her very special brand of humor, even though he wasn't sure whether she was actually making fun of him or not. But even if she was, so far it didn't seem very malicious. Probably she was just a lady tourist, lonely and hungry for someone American to talk to. He shook his head. "Nothing like that. There's just me."

"And your fine friends on that peculiarly named boat? They won't miss your many manly attributes?"

He looked at her sharply. Was she mocking him now? Did she *know* about Kathie and him? No, that was impossible, how could she? But she had a way of looking at him as if he was completely naked, as if she could see whatever was going on inside his mind. It was an uncomfortable feeling, but flattering at the same time, and he felt himself enjoying the obvious interest she was taking in him. And she was, after all, a good-looking woman, even if she was a little bit older.

"No," he replied with conviction. "They won't miss me."

"That's too bad," she said, gulping down half her drink. "Everyone should have someone who misses her. Or him, as the case may be." She lighted another cigarillo and leaned across the table, blowing a lingering cloud of smoke over his shoulder. "Well then, Ken, since you're here in the beautiful Marquises until Saturday, what are your plans for debauch until then?"

He looked around at the flowered terrace, the rocky crags of the mountains on three sides of them, the broad expanse of the bay below, as if seeing it all for the first time. "I don't know," he said. "I really hadn't thought about it, I guess. I've just been . . . well, sitting here thinking."

She smiled indulgently. "'Ale, man, ale's the thing to drink, for fellows whom it hurts to think.' Seriously, independent studies show that too much thinking can be an actual detriment to the health, especially for handsome young men who should be busy doing other things."

He raised his eyes to meet hers. They had high prominent eyelids and long black lashes. She really did look like an Indian princess, or actually, now that he considered it, more like a Hollywood actress made up to *look* like an Indian princess. In spite of their thinness, the pale lips of her constantly mobile mouth offered a promise of great sensuality. The more he studied her, the more he became certain he had never met so genuinely beautiful a woman even though she looked nothing at all like the countless starlets and bimbos that swarmed around Los Angeles and with whom he had enjoyed a certain amount of success. Certainly he had never met a woman who seemed so exotically exciting.

"Something pleases you?"

He felt himself blushing again, and the knowledge made him blush even more furiously. He shrugged meaninglessly, and drank his beer, casting furtive glances at her from under hooded lids. She wore a long-sleeved man's shirt of faded white and green plaids and equally faded blue jeans that tightly hugged her narrow haunches and long slender legs. She had something of the air and mannerisms of the few lesbians he had met, and he was turning this uncomfortable thought over in his mind when she unexpectedly pushed her chair back and rose to her feet in one easy movement.

"Come along," she ordered briskly. "If you sit there drinking beer and *kava* all day you'll turn into a vegetable like these wretched natives, and God knows *how* you'll end up."

"Come along where?" he asked as he followed her eagerly across the terrace.

"Not to my bungalow, you randy rascal, if that's what you're think-ing," she said without turning. "That comes later. Perhaps. Right now we'll rent some horses at a stable down the road and I'll show you the sights. You *can* ride, can't you?"

"I don't know, I've never tried."

She stopped abruptly and turned to grimace at him. "God! This younger generation is absolutely hopeless." She reached out to cover his mouth with the fingers of her long brown hand and he could feel his entire body tingle at the touch of the cool flesh. "Don't enumerate all the other things you can't do, my central nervous system could never stand the shock." She smiled fondly at him as if he were a favorite dog who had just performed his sole trick. "Now come along and stop all your talking. A couple of hours bouncing up and down on a couple of dumb Marquisian horses is just what we need to make us all loose and juicy."

To his horror he felt an almost instant erection thrusting against the tight confines of his pants, but she had already turned away. "Have you ever done it on horseback?" he heard her ask. "No, I suppose not. I did once, with an Apache in Arizona. At least he told me he was an Apache, *I* think he was just a Navaho sheepherder, but no matter, *c'était drôlement jouissif. . . .*"

He followed her haltingly, trying to push his unruly organ discreetly down his pants leg. Christine, Christina, whatever her name was, was like no one he had ever met before. Certainly no other woman had ever had so galvanizing an effect on him. He raised his eyes to the broad square shoulders, the slim waist, the long muscular buttocks of the woman striding regally down the road before him as if the entire Marquesas were her private domain. No, she was no lesbian, and she didn't really look mannish, even from behind, or even talk like a man, she was just . . . different.

Already, he knew, he was her slave.

CHAPTER 5

They honeymooned for two weeks in Tahiti and then returned to Kristin's small wooden house, hardly more than a shack, in the village of Hana-vavé on the island of Fatu Hiva. To reach it they caught the weekly flight of the DeHavilland Twin Otter from the airport at Nuku Hiva and flew southeast to the island of Hiva Oa, where Paul Gauguin had painted and died. They spent the afternoon in the tiny town of Atuona stocking up on provisions and dried goods at the local general store, an old wooden colonial structure that looked unchanged from the days of Gauguin, and the following morning loaded their cartons of pork and beans and canned bully beef along with Ken's chest of tools onto a small wooden boat for the three-hour trip to Fatu Hiva.

The captain and crew and seven other passengers greeted Kristin with rowdy shouts and much wet kissing of cheeks, as if she had been gone for three years rather than three weeks. She passed around icy bottles of beer from the ten cases she had purchased a few minutes before and proudly introduced Ken. He tried to merely shake hands but was quickly embraced and kissed by men and women alike.

Afterwards he caught the younger men looking at him with sly glances and sudden toothy grins, and he listened to them exchange loud banter with Kristin that drew gales of laughter from the plump Polynesian women. "You're too Westernized to hear," was her only comment when asked for a translation. "Ask me again after you've been in Hanavavé for six months." He hid his chagrin, and vowed he would learn Marquesan long before the six months were up — never again would Kristin have secrets from him, particularly those that obviously involved other men. . . .

The great jagged mountains of Fatu Hiva were even more impressive than Ken's first sight of Nuku Hiva from the *Last One Left,* for they seemed to rise directly out of the sea and were covered with a lush green vegetation that darkened into blue and purple high up in the inland ridges. As the boat slowly neared his new home he watched enormous gray rain clouds form in the deep blue sky over the interior peaks, and here and there he could see the glint of silvery waterfalls dropping hundreds of yards down the green sides of the mountains.

"Look," said Kristin as the boat chugged into the Bay of Virgins with its stupendous gray rocks thrusting up out of the shoreline, "see that wooden platform built on the side of the cliff, with the ladder running up to it from the bay?"

Ken squinted, and suddenly saw the ramshackle structure of faded wood nearly at the base of the towering cliff that was gliding past them. "That's where you hold your human sacrifices, I suppose?"

She squeezed his hand fondly. "A hundred years ago, maybe. The Marquisians used to spend their time being tattooed, killing each other as bloodily as possible, and occasionally eating the losers." She pointed to the small grove of banana trees waving in the sea breeze where the sheer cliffs softened briefly to slope into the sea. "Their descendants are a more peaceable lot. They take the bananas up to that platform to dry in the sun. They think the sea air gives them a special flavor."

"Why do you say Marquisian instead of Marquesan?" he wondered idly. "Aren't these the Marquesas? You're always saying the Marquises — 'Mar-Keys'."

"Am I ? They're *Marquises* in French."

"Oh. Marquises. Like that?"

"Exactly like that. You've never studied French?"

"No. A little Spanish in school. I was good at that."

"Were you now? Along with groping your lady Spanish teachers, I'll bet. Hmmm. Well, up here you'll certainly have plenty of time to brush up on your French. It sounds like you've got a good ear, you shouldn't have much trouble with it."

Ken had, in fact, a superb ear. To his own surprise, within three months he had mastered the Marquesan language as spoken by the 200 villagers of Hanavavé and was rapidly absorbing Tahitian from a retired Mormon schoolteacher from Papeete who had once attended Brigham Young University and who now talked to him ceaselessly in Tahitian while Ken rebuilt first the porch and then the living room of his small wooden house.

Kristin's days were spent among the villagers of Hanavavé and those of Omoa three miles down the coast. Omoa was inaccessible except by sea and by a single winding footpath high through the mountains, and in centuries past had been as isolated from Hanavavé as if it had been in the Tuamotus. Except, of course, for the endless bloody wars that the tattooed inhabitants of the two villages had waged against each other.

Now their sole rivalry lay in the design and production of high-grade tapa cloth from the barks of various trees, still beaten by hand and elaborately dyed and painted with inks painstakingly manufactured from leaves and roots. They were the sole communities left among the dozens of islands scattered over the millions of square miles of French Polynesia to practice this traditional craft, and for sixteen months now Kristin had been at work on her doctorate for the University of Chicago studying their artisanship, and supposedly relating it to the lives and rivalries of the two villages.

"What bullshit!" she cried scornfully as she slammed her notebook down on the rickety table that served as her desk. "Fifty years ago you could get your degree just by watching a bunch of islanders fucking each other and writing it all down using a lot of Latin words. Now we're reduced to watching them scribble inkblots on moldy pieces of bark and trying to find the cosmic significance in that!" She brushed the notebook irritably to the floor. "Comic significance is more like it!"

"Why do you do it then?" he asked diffidently. "I mean, isn't thirty-seven sort of late to be getting your PhD?"

She leered at him lewdly. "Maybe I happen to *like* fucking islanders. It's just writing about breadfruit bark that bores me."

"You . . . fuck . . . these natives here in —" he asked haltingly, hardly daring to voice the words.

She scowled and shook her head vigorously. "That would be *outrageously* unprofessional, unethical even. Of *course* I don't!" She caught his faint sigh of relief, and added, "I go over to Nuku Hiva to fuck the natives *there*. What do you *think* I was doing in that Hungarian whorehouse when I picked you up?"

He shook his head and smiled faintly. "I never know when you're serious or not."

She leaned forward to kiss him on the lips and run her hand through his hair. "That's because you love me. And because I love you. Now then, tonight you're reading this book by Suggs about his stay in the Marquises. After that we'll run over your verbs again, and then as a treat you can read out loud to me from the dirty parts of this French novel."

"I'm never going to be an anthropologist," he sighed. "Do I have to?"

"What else do you think you're going to have to talk about with all of those boring people back at Chicago or Harvard or Podunk U.? How you fucked all the happy Marquisians?"

"They smell too funny," he said, wrinkling his nose. "All that perfume and stuff they wear. Ugh."

She smiled at him grimly. "Just make certain you keep smelling them that way."If I ever catch you. . . ." Her smile faded until the set of her face was merely grim.

"Oh, Kristin," he said plaintively. "How can you —"

She reached across to place a finger against his lips. "Hush," she said softly. "It's time for your French verbs."

* * * *

All the other things Kristin tried to make him learn, anthropology and ethnology and social science and psychology and the elements of psychotherapy and parapsychology reminded him of high school and vividly brought back all the reasons he had never tried to continue on to even junior college. Whatever he learned for her in the course of an evening he had forgotten by the following morning. For a while this seemed to irritate her, and she snapped at him impatiently when he was unable to recall that the great New Zealand anthropologist Sir Peter Buck was actually named Te Rangi Hiroa, or maybe it was the other way around. But one day the impatience suddenly disappeared and she began to spend more time with the one thing he enjoyed and less and less with the others until eventually it became unusual for her to hand him one of her heavy academic tomes. What he enjoyed was the study of French, and Kristin began to shake her head as he mimicked perfectly whatever she said in French, whether or not he understood the words.

"That's fucking *unfair!*" she cried, glaring at him in mock menace. "I had to study French for nine years and then live two more years in Bordeaux, and in two months you speak it as well as I do."

Ken blushed with pleasure and drew her tall slender body to his. "Because you're such a great teacher," he murmured before suddenly pouncing on her delicate earlobe with his teeth and then thrusting the point of his tongue deep into her ear. He could feel her shudder violently against him, and her hands clawing into his back. He ground his tongue into the tiny orifice with its odd salty taste until she groaned incoherently, and then swung her up easily in his arms and carried her off to the lumpy double bed with the red and white pareo cloth cover. It was lunchtime, and any of their neighbors might have wandered by and peered in through the open door or windows, but neither of them bothered to pull the flimsy pareo curtains before they fell heavily on the bed and began ripping the clothes from the other's body.

Was she really eleven years older? he sometimes wondered as he looked down at her perfect body with its high firm breasts and smooth taut flesh free from wrinkles or any sign of aging. Of course thirty-seven really wasn't very old, he told himself, it was just the age when a lot of women were beginning to look their best. At least that was what he had sometimes heard, and with Kristin it was certainly true, for it didn't seem possible she could have been any better looking as a nineteen-year-old than she was now.

She was a woman mostly without vanity, but she was proud of the fact, he soon learned, that she enjoyed a radiant beauty that scorned all the creams and lotions and so-called beauty products to which the lesser women of the world had recourse. "Silly cunts," she snorted disdainfully. "All they need is a regimen of Dr. Camden's Hot Beef Injection three times a day and they'd have skin like a baby's. Can you imagine putting all that muck on your face before climbing into bed, and maybe some pin curlers the size of beer cans into your hair, and then expecting your poor schnook of a boyfriend to fuck you? Jesus H. Christ! It must be like fucking a garbage can!"

Ken fell back on the bed in helpless laughter, while Kristin flashed an enormous grin and sat back on her haunches, puffing on her black cigarillo and occasionally trying to blow smoke rings over the stiff penis she was languidly caressing. Finally she flipped the still-glowing butt out the window into the hot damp air of the night, and in the glow of the kerosene lamp he watched her straddle him and slide herself down over his rigid flesh with exquisite slowness.

He gasped with pleasure as she tightened her muscles around him, and reached up to clasp the hard little white breasts that seemed almost painted onto the glossy mahogany of her body. He kneaded them fiercely, as he knew she wanted him to, pinching and squeezing the dark brown nipples until he feared he must be hurting her. "Harder," she ordered, and he reluctantly pinched them between his fingers with all his strength.

"You look like you're wearing a white bathing suit," he murmured, his eyes on the narrow strip of pale flesh punctuated by the dark tuft of her triangle as she reached down to encircle the base of his penis with her long grasping fingers.

"It's from lying in the sun with all the horny teenagers on the island watching me from the bushes and jacking off," she murmured in breathless gasps.

"Is that all?" he asked, at once jealous and anxious. "All those Marquesan customs I've been reading about, *motoro,* and like that. You've never had trouble, never. . . ."

"Been raped?" She looked down at him from hooded eyelids. "It might be . . . fun," she gasped, the cords in her neck suddenly bulging and her breasts heaving. "Does . . . that . . . worry . . . you?"

"You *know* it does!" he cried, thrusting up deep within her, as if trying to establish his rights of sole possession. "All these guys crawling through the bushes at night, sneaking into people's houses, trying to fuck girls while their parents are sleeping. And nobody sees anything *wrong* with it! It's —"

"— the national sport of Polynesia," she muttered through lips drawn back as if in a snarl. "Just a little . . . *motoro.*"

"Well, it'll get someone killed if they try a little *motoro* around here," he said angrily, reaching forward to pull her damp glistening body down against his.

"You'd kill them?" she whispered into his ear. "If they tried to —"

"If they try any *motoro* around here, yes."

The next thirteen months were the happiest of his life. Kristin should have long since returned to her academic duties but flatly refused. "I'll tell 'em I'm writing the Gone With the Wind of tapa treatises," she snorted, crumpling an official looking letter and tossing it across the room. "What's the goddam hurry? I've got one PhD that's as useful as Ken Camden's left nipple, they think another will be useful as his right one?"

He learned that besides her doctorate in child psychology — "I discovered too late I couldn't stand the little bastards" — she also received a number of small oil royalty checks from Texas and Louisiana every month that enabled them to continue their endless honeymoon on this nearly uninhabited speck of rock at the ends of the earth.

Protector, mentor, mother, companion, Kristin was all of these, as well as wife and indefatigable lover. Occasionally she flew into towering rages at some failure of his to comply with the standards she had set for him, but these were like the terrible bouts of thunder that accompanied the downpours of the summer rainy season, noisy and even frightening, but brief and soon forgotten. Between their bouts of lovemaking she treated him, he often thought, with the wry affection she might bestow on a clumsy but lovable puppy.

Because it was now so obvious he would never attain her own level of cultivation, however much she tutored him? Or had she always considered him little more than the traditional Polynesian sex object that visitors to the islands were supposed to dally with before returning to the real world beyond the seas? Would she, in fact, discard him as lightheartedly as she had picked him up when at last she decided in her own unfathomable way that it was time to return to her own real world?

The thought troubled him occasionally during the hot sticky nights when the rain thundered down on the tin roof a few feet overhead and Kristin's sweaty body snuggled close to his as she slept soundly and peacefully, oblivious to the tangled sheets and pounding rain. It was the only cloud on an otherwise idyllic existence, that and the always nagging presence of the native Marquesans of the village, boys and men that he was certain Kristin had once made love to with the same lighthearted carelessness and spontaneity of the Polynesians.

She skipped easily over these brief encounters with airy dismissals. "They're nothing more to me than *godemiché vivants,*" she said lightly. "You know the word *godemiché?* Well, that's all they are, less even. At least with a good *godemiché* you just put in some new batteries and don't have to listen to them talk to you." She cocked her head in reminiscence and snorted derisively. "Although I will say in their favor, Marquisian men never hang around to bore you with their *post-coitem* chitchat."

If this was meant to comfort him it fell considerably short of the mark. "Hrmph," he muttered irritably. "What about these Marquesan women? Some of those books of yours have some pretty strange stuff in them. They say they —"

"— stuff their little pussies with fruits and flowers and God knows what else to make them hot and fragrant?" She sniffed contemptuously. "That's one thing I haven't bothered to investigate. We'll just have to let someone else report to us on the subject."

"That's what I don't understand. It seems like *you* can . . . well, do whatever you like with all of these men. To you it's just like sneezing, at least that's what you say. Suppose I was like that? Suppose I —"

"Men are so much more sentimental than women, at least *some* men are," she explained impatiently. "And you: *you* I know all too well. All you'd have to do is fuck one of these Marquisians just once and you'd be head over heels in love with her."

"That's not true!" he cried indignantly. "Just because they stuff themselves up with flowers and old mangos? Anyway, who cares about them? *I* don't! I was just saying —"

"And I was just saying that if I want a report on Marquisian pussy I'll get it from some bulldyke of an ethnologist, not a refugee from Muscle Beach." She glared at him with glittering eyes.

His lips tightened, and he turned away, baffled and hurt by the gratuitous cruelty she could use so readily.

The following Sunday they attended an afternoon feast in the backyard of one of the villagers that was made merry by several large demijohns of smooth red wine to wash down the whole roasted calves, and enlivened by the music of numerous guitars and ukuleles. Kristin was shouting out the lyrics and twisting her hips to the wild gyrations of the tamuré with a dozen admiring men surrounding her, while without quite remembering how he came to be there Ken found himself sprawled on the grass a few yards behind the musicians with a glass of wine in one hand and his arm around a tipsy Marquesan girl with long frizzy hair that spread out behind her like a peacock's tail.

Over and over she assured him solemnly that she possessed the best developed clitoris on all the islands of the Marquesas, the result of intensive and expert attention since the age of three. Ken was owlishly asking her about the baffling role of fruits and flowers in these ministrations when he became conscious of Kristin standing over them and looking down at him with a terrible wrath that instantly cut off his words. She opened her mouth, then suddenly let out her breath with a loud hiss and stalked angrily off to where the others were still noisily dancing.

A week passed in which Kristin made no reference to the scene, but Ken was uneasily aware of the tightness of her lips and of frequent oblique glances that seemed more foreboding than any overt reproaches she might have made to him. As the days passed and his sense of guilt intensified, he was startled to be told they would be leaving for a few days' vacation at the Hungarian's in the town of Taoihae on Nuku Hiva. "A second honeymoon," said Kristin without further explanation.

They arrived in time for lunch, then showered in their bungalow and made love languidly on the large comfortable bed under the slowly turning ceiling fan that quickly dried the sweat on their naked bodies. "It's pleasant to have a comfortable bed again," said Kristin with a cool smile as she pulled her blue jeans up over her naked buttocks and buttoned her shirt so that it barely concealed the small white mounds of her breasts. "I'll see you later," she said, and stepped out into the bright afternoon.

She returned in time for a candlelit dinner on the terrace and deftly avoided his questions about her afternoon. They drank brandy with ice cubes afterwards, then strolled hand in hand to their bungalow. They were naked on the bed when the lights of the hotel flickered and then went out for the night. Ken had just entered her from behind as she knelt before him when there was a gentle tapping at the door, and to his amazement she pulled away to pad naked across the room to push it open. Even more shocking were the words he heard her utter in Marquesan.

"Come in," she said softly. "Hurry."

In the darkness of the overcast night it was hard to see exactly what happened after that but Kristin left him in no doubt. "Don't say anything," she ordered, "just sit over there and watch. Later you can join in, if you like." She laughed deep in her throat and as if he were trapped in some half-comprehended nightmare he saw her silhouette pull a dark shape forward onto the bed. A moment later they were joined by another, and he heard the soft murmur of male voices. Unable to tear himself from the small wooden chair, he listened to the increasingly frantic sounds of passion as Kristin noisily climaxed and the two Marquesans approached theirs.

He heard muffled laughter and looked up to see two more of them silhouetted against the door, one of them with an enormous ball of hair that gave him the appearance of some grotesque alien. The bed was shaking noisily now, and first one, and then the other, of the two men was replaced by those at the door. His eyes had grown accustomed to the darkness, and now he could see the details of their coupling, but after a while he closed his eyes and for an interminable time sat listening to their mingled cries and groans. At last he heard doors opening and closing, and looked up to see Kristin's silhouette disappearing into the bathroom.

When she returned he felt the long cool fingers of her hand on his arm. Wordlessly she drew him to the bed and moments later had caressed him to an erection he could feel throbbing in her hand. She straddled him, then rolled herself beneath him, her arms and legs clasping him with a strength he had never known. He thrust into her with a fury that suddenly had her shaking her head wildly and moaning incoherently. He came with an intensity that left him gasping raggedly, but he continued to pound against the sharp bone of her pubis while she spasmed again and again.

"A lesson," she gasped into his ear. "For every time you are unfaithful to me, even in your thoughts, I will return the favor tenfold." Her arms tightened around his back. "Do you understand?" she whispered fiercely.

"I understand," he muttered into the side of her neck, pushing himself ever deeper into her flesh.

"Then fuck me, fuck me, *fuck me!*" Her teeth sank into the hard flesh of his shoulder and as he felt himself about to uncontrollably lose himself in her yet again he could hear her murmuring as if from a great distance, "Oh Ken, I love you, I love you, I *love* you. . . ."

CHAPTER 6

It was some days after its initial appearance over Europe before Ken and Kristin heard of the UFO that was drifting slowly through the skies of the world. Kristin sharply dismissed the notion as just the latest in an endless series of mythical sightings reported by untrained observers, misguided lunatics, or out-and-out hoaxsters. But at last the villagers' insistence that it was real, that they had heard about it on the broadcasts from Papeete, aroused her sufficiently to install a fresh set of batteries in her ancient Zenith shortwave receiver and carefully turn the dials until she picked up with sudden startling clarity the twangy accents of Radio Australia.

". . . .is being tracked by satellite as well as radar and millions of eyewitnesses, as the dully glowing object moves slowly from Madrid on a path that will apparently take it directly over Rome. Our correspondent Ron Jeffries of the BBC is standing by in Rome where a frenzied crowd from the Holy City has filled the enormous square in front of Saint Peter's and where the Pope is expected momentarily to address them from the balcony. Are you there, Ron?"

"Yes, I am, Ashley. Nearly half a million people are —"

"Half a million nitwits," said Kristin, spinning the dial until she found the static-filled but reassuring accents of the Voice of America.

". . . .ident is still meeting with the cabinet and senior members of Congress. We will switch to our correspondent at the White House at the first indication of any news. In the meantime, Tom Connors, our military expert, is standing by at the Pentagon, where he has Lieutenant General Leland Waters of the United States Air Force with him. Tom?"

"Yes, Arthur, this is Tom Connors at the Pentagon, where I'm talking with Lieutenant General Leland Waters of the Air Force. General Waters, is there any feeling among the military that this . . . well, I suppose unidentified flying object is still the most accurate description of it, is an actual *menace* to the world in general, and to the United States in particular?"

"Jesus," breathed Kristin. "It's *real*. Did you hear that, Ken? This UFO is *real!*"

". . . .have to assume that anything unknown of this nature is always a potential —"

"I *knew* I saw a flying saucer once," said Ken unexpectedly. "I guess I was right all the time."

Kristin looked at him sharply. "You saw one? You never told me."

"You never asked me. Everyone else I told about it just laughed at me."

"I don't blame them. Most of the so-called sightings are ludicrously mistaken."

"Well, I'll bet they not laughing now," he said with a certain satisfaction.

Her lips twisted in the ghost of a smile. "Not unless this particular UFO turns out to be a giant ball of swamp gas secretly launched by the Uruguayan Air Force."

For the next three days, to Ken's growing puzzlement, Kristin remained fixed to the radio, hushing him impatiently whenever he tried to interrupt whichever of the world's shortwave services she was tuned to. On the third day he returned for lunch from the repairs he was making on a villager's termite-infested corner post that threatened the collapse of his entire house to find his suitcase lying open on the bed and Kristin's standing by the door. His heart lurched with mingled dread and excitement as the memories of their last visit to the Hungarian's flooded back. Was this to be another of Kristin's peculiar ways of declaring her love for him?

"We're leaving for the States," she said as she came into the house from the lean-to kitchen at the back, an eagerness in her voice he had never heard before.

"The States?" he faltered. "How come? I thought —"

"The hell with it!" she snorted. "You think the world needs another book about tapa cloth when there's an alien civilization about to make contact?"

He looked around in bewilderment at the shabby but cheerful little room flooded with bright Marquesan sunlight that he had come to think of as his home. Leave this? For the routine drudgery of life in the States? For an apartment in *Chicago?* In the wintertime? For academic conversations he wouldn't be able to understand with Kristin's snotty egghead friends?

For sharing Kristin with anyone else?

"This has something to do with . . . this *flying saucer?"* he asked incredulously.

She stared at him with equal wonderment. "Are you feeling well?" she asked in mock concern. "We're witnesses to the single most important event in the two-million-year history of mankind, and you're asking if leaving has anything to do with that? You think we're going to sit here in the metropolis of Hanavavé while the rest of the world is —"

"That's bullshit!" he heard himself unexpectedly shouting, stung by her sharp sarcasm. "You're telling me you're going to let a flying saucer ruin our lives? What do *you* care about flying saucers? What does *anyone* care about flying saucers? You're just looking for an excuse to leave me so you can go back to all your fine friends with their PhDs and —"

She gaped at him as if he had struck her, and to his astonishment he saw tears well up and glitter in her eyes. He reached out for her in sudden anguish, aghast at the words some inner demon had uttered through his mouth, but she slapped his hand away brutally. "You really are a beachboy," she breathed softly, as if seeing him for the first time, "just an ignorant fucked-up Hollywood actor. . . ."

She stared at him a moment longer, while he beseeched her with imploring eyes, desperately searching for the words that could bridge this hideous chasm that suddenly yawned between them. The tears rolled unheeded down her cheeks, and her lips trembled with a terrible indecisiveness he had never seen before. He stepped forward to pull her to him, but she swirled away and disappeared out the door into the dazzle of the sunlight, where he watched her slender form skitter frantically across the bright green grass before disappearing into the black shadows of the nearby forest.

When he awoke at first light and dragged himself from the rumpled bed with anguished trepidation to peer blearily through the pale gloom of their tiny house he saw what he had known with awful certainty he would find.

Kristin's suitcase was gone, and with it Kristin.

For three weeks he moved through the village in little more than a stupor, still dazed by the calamity that had befallen him, unwilling to allow his thoughts to dwell on anything more than the marginal business of eating and sleeping enough to keep alive. He could have followed her, he told himself over and over, should have followed her. He could have kept her from getting on that boat to Hiva Oa, or the plane to Nuku Hiva, or the plane to Papeete, or even the plane to Los Angeles. Any of these things he could have done. Instead he had been rendered incapable of action by this overwhelming lassitude that seemed to immobilize him as if he were trying to push his way through some thick ocean pressing in upon him from all sides. Even now, he knew, he could follow her to . . . where? Chicago? Surely the University of Chicago would have some knowledge of her.

But. . . .

Suppose he followed her to Chicago. Found her. Pledged his eternal love, his undying obedience.

And she refused him. Denied him. Sent him away.

The dreadful possibility was more than he could bear to think about.

The village policeman found him sitting listlessly in a canvas chair on his tiny porch staring blankly at nothing. "A letter," he said jovially, holding out an airmail envelope. "From Kristin, eh?" He stabbed a thick brown finger at the address in the upper lefthand corner. "She's in Chicago, eh? What does she say, is she already missing all her friends in Hanavavé?" And he sat down on the sunlit steps to patiently await the news.

With hands that trembled Ken pulled open the envelope. He realized that in the strange daze through which he had been moving the possibility Kristin might *write* to him had somehow never occurred to him. He unfolded a large sheet of university letterhead that was folded around the red cover of an airline ticket. It was dated nearly three weeks before and his spirits plunged as he saw there were only a few brief lines written in Kristin's neat hand in the middle of the page. At last he willed his eyes to them.

> *My Dearest Ken,*
>
> *I see now that I am unable to live without you. I beseech you to forgive me. Please come. Please.*
>
> *Hurry, although if need be I will wait for you forever.*
>
> *I pledge my eternal love.*
>
> K.

"I pledge my eternal love."

The words he had meant to say to her.

His heart leaped up with joy, and suffused with an almost unbearable happiness he thrust the letter at the startled Marquesan policeman. "Look," he said, as tears suddenly bleared his vision, in a voice that sounded strangely hoarse, "I'm going to Chicago. I'm going to meet Kristin."

Three nights later he was in Tahiti, impatiently waiting for the morning and the DC-10 that would carry him to Los Angeles and Kristin. It was only as he lay in bed at his hotel that he realized he could have telephoned to tell her he was coming, that he would be in her arms in only a few more hours. How could he be so stupid? Too much time in the Marquesas had rotted his brain. Kristin was right: he was an ignorant beachboy. . . .

He swung out of bed and groped for the lamp on the nightstand. He was frowning over the instructions for the use of the phone when another thought occurred to him. Chicago was in a different time zone from here. But was there four, or five hours, difference? And was it earlier or later? The more he debated it, the more confused he became. Certainly Kristin would not appreciate being awakened if it was three in the morning in Chicago.

Groaning, he stepped into his pants and pulled his shirt around him. Someone at the desk could tell him about the time zones. As he made his way through the dark gardens of the hotel towards the Tahitian-style building that housed the restaurant and reception desk he raised his eyes through the scattering of coconut trees to the myriad of stars that sparkled brightly in the clear night sky. Would Chicago be like Los Angeles, he wondered, eternally covered by smog? Would he ever see the stars again?

The great peaks of the island's mountains, far higher than those of the Marquesas, loomed before him, an impenetrable blackness against the starry tropical sky. Even as he noticed them, their tops were suddenly illuminated by a glow of bluish-green light. An instant later the sky above the mountains began to flicker with the same strange light, as if someone had turned on a tremendous fluorescent light somewhere deep in the interior of the island. He stared at it for long moments, conscious now of the sound of barking on all sides as the Tahitian dogs awoke and began their nightly chorus, then shrugged his shoulders in bafflement.

Some strange form of tropical heat lightning? he wondered.

He shrugged again, and went on into the reception desk, where he learned that in Chicago it would be 3:17 in the morning. Back outside there were three or four other people now staring up at the eerie glow emanating behind the mountains, but after a few minutes in which nothing seemed to change he went back to his room and tried vainly to shut his ears to the dogs and roosters who were apparently howling from all corners of the entire island.

The following day he learned the true meaning of despair. He stopped short on his way to breakfast as he suddenly realized that the early morning sky above the mountains was not overcast with rain clouds but was an eerie pale gray that seemed to shimmer and flicker with undertones of green and other subtle colors locked deep within an opaque gray that was as shiny as the interior of the local pearl shells. He stared at it uneasily, and wondered if it could have something to do with the strange glow he had seen in the mountains a few hours before. It was, he suddenly thought, as if someone had lowered an enormous glass bowl over the world. . . .

He went in to breakfast, to be told that his flight to Los Angeles had been delayed indefinitely and that the airline would pay for his room and meals until he was able to leave. A crowd of forlorn-looking tourists was standing by their suitcases near the reception desk and buzzing noisily. From them he learned that apparently the plane that was to carry them to the States had not yet left Los Angeles. He looked at his watch. It would be noontime in Chicago. He would call Kristin. Just the sound of her voice would be enough to dispel the empty feeling of dread that was beginning to build inside him. He hurried back to his room, trying not to look up as the pearly gray sky that was the cause of his unease.

Half an hour later he was at last convinced by a harried operator that for the time being it was impossible to telephone the United States. His uneasiness, now an almost physical constriction around his chest, continued to build. It was impossible to remain any longer within the confines of his room, so he walked through the hotel gardens to the road and a few minutes later flagged down one of the homemade jitney buses that the locals called *le truck*. The blare of Tahitian music piped in from the driver's compartment at the front of the two long wooden benches that stretched the length of *le truck* prevented him from hearing any conversation, but he noticed that like himself none of the Tahitian passengers were able to keep from casting anxious glances up at the ominous glassy sky.

Fifteen minutes later he alighted at the Papeete market and began to stroll aimlessly through the crowded streets along the waterfront. Groups of people, Tahitians, Chinese, Europeans, and obvious tourists, were clustered at random, staring up at the sky and talking excitedly. By late in the morning there was some reassurance to be drawn from the fact that, whatever might have happened to the sky, the sun at least was up in its accustomed place, while fluffy white clouds were beginning to form over the peaks of Moorea, the sister island across the channel from Tahiti. But even the harsh tropical sun seemed curiously diffused by the glassy gray bowl with its iridescent glimmer that was now an overwhelming physical presence, brooding, foreboding, menacing.

He visited the airline office, and then sat in the shade of three waterfront cafés, drinking a cold Hinano beer in each and becoming increasingly apprehensive, as the voices he heard around him seemed to be becoming increasingly strident. He joined three worried-looking Americans for lunch after exchanging speculation with them at the bar of the Vaima Café. One of them was the friend of a friend who worked at Air New Zealand. "There's no more planes coming in," he said flatly.

"There's *nothing* coming in. She wasn't supposed to tell me this, so keep it under your hats, but she said the telephones and telex and fax and Internet lines are down all over the Pacific. They can't even *talk* to Los Angeles or New Zealand to find out what's going on."

"Like sunspots," said another, nodding wisely. "I hear that sunspots can knock out all sorts of communications."

"With satellites sending everything these days?" said the third incredulously. "How can sunspots interfere with satellites?"

"I didn't say it *was* sunspots, I said it was *like* sunspots." He gestured to encompass the small patch of sky that was visible from the covered terrace where they sat. "Sunspots are 93 million miles away. Whatever that stuff in the sky is, it's sure a helluva lot closer than 93 million miles. If *it* can't blank out radio traffic, tell me what can."

"UFOs," said Ken immediately, surprised by his sudden insight. "They can . . . do what you say. Stop cars, stop radios, at least that's what —"

"Jesus," breathed one of the others. "I'd forgotten about that UFO. Isn't it over Bangkok, someplace like that?"

"No, South America," said another. "It was in Argentina the last time I heard, yesterday, or was it the day before?"

"Jesus, Argentina's pretty close to here, you really think —"

"Hell no, Argentina's further away than the States," said the third. "You gotta stop off on Easter Island on the way. Christ, it must be 7,000 miles from here."

"Flying saucers are pretty fast, what's 7,000 miles to —"

"We'd have seen it if it was here. I saw it on TV before I left the States. It's *enormous!* It lights up the whole goddam sky!"

"Like up in the mountains last night," said Ken, now almost desperate with anguish. "That flying saucer was the reason Kristin went back to the States, the reason she. . . ." He lurched to his feet and stood staring glassy-eyed out across the harbor at the jagged peaks of Moorea. "And now it's here," he muttered. "Trying to keep me from Kristin."

For twenty-nine days now the Silumiut had slowly quartered the planet in the glowing oblate sphere that was the Riestu. To their mild surprise the planet teemed with intelligent life, apparently harbored within corporeal beings. This was not the first time the Silumiut had come upon other sentient species in their millions of years of expanding throughout the galaxy. Some still retained their bodily form, others had evolved in the direction of the Silumiut. None had ever constituted a possible threat, or even competition, to the mighty Silumiut, nor had many of them possessed anything the Silumiut would have found worth taking. The Silumiut were not an aggressive race by nature, and the idea of warfare was initially alien to them, but over the course of eons battles had been fought and even entire worlds destroyed. Finally defenses had evolved that were impervious to any conceivable attack, and thereafter the Silumiut had simply bypassed those systems or sectors of the galaxy that contained intelligent life in any form.

But now as the Riestu drifted slowly from city to city studying the inhabitants of this planet, those on board increasingly posed themselves the same tantalizing question: could they have at last stumbled upon an outpost of undegenerated Yas'elda?

At first glance there was little outward resemblance between these gaunt, hyperactive bipeds and the placid round quadrupeds that until so recently had occupied the ship's life room. But as the second officer pointed out with massive corroborative detail from the ship's memory banks, there were a number of eerie similarities between these bipeds and their civilization and what the general consensus of thought held the original Yas'elda to have been.

For a short time a growing jubilation swept through the ship, infecting officers and crewmen alike, as the possibility they had stumbled across that mythical planet of the original Yas'elda took hold. For the value of such a find to the scientists of the Continuum would be incalculable. The ship that returned with evidence of such a discovery would be quickly forgiven its failure to locate a new source of those more mundane Yas'elda for which it had been sent.

Gon'ut the geneticist, the man most qualified to speculate on such matters, had been terminated centuries before by the captain's ill-considered whim, along with Aroto, the ship's veterinarian. Now, to the general surprise, Bylangu, the second officer, revealed himself to be an unreconstructed Unifactionist of deeply held convictions. The more information he drew from the memory banks the more he became convinced that this pleasant watery planet in an obscure G-type system was indeed a home of original Yas'eldas.

Hippelon the captain was normally a man of stern authoritarian mien and swift implacable decision. But for seventeen days he had drifted indecisively through the ship, listening attentively now to Bylangu, turning then to Kundo'oni the ship's chaplain, a severe Aspirant of the Fourteenth Harbinger, to hear his sharply contradictory views. On the eighteenth day he at last came to a decision.

"There are two overriding factors to take into account," he told the ship's officers, although until now it had been unheard of for him to justify any decisions he made. "First, the divergence between these beings and Yas'elda is far too great to be ignored. Any chance similarities are merely that: chance. Second, in the general excitement, it appears to have been totally ignored that the Riestu is still some 3,700 years of travel from the Continuum. There is not the remotest possibility that any of us would survive long enough to reach Koshi'ongo. Therefore, gentlemen, you will inform the crew to begin preparations for leaving this system in the shortest possible time. Our only hope lies in continuing our search."

"Before we do that," suggested Bylangu, "why not at least examine some of these natives more closely? Physically, at first hand. It may well be possible that —"

"That Silumiut would sully themselves by bestial contact with animals?" exclaimed Kundo'oni the chaplain, who harbored a deep animosity for the Unifactionist officer.

"Only in the spirit of scientific inquiry," replied Bylangu coldly. "What have we to lose? Already two members of the crew are clearly in their final decline. They will never live to seen another planetfall. If, as I still maintain, these are remnants of the original Yas'elda, it is conceivable that an intensive breeding program could —"

"The chances of success would be minimal," declared the captain. "In any case, we would need the services of both the geneticist and the veter —"

"And whose fault is it we no longer enjoy their services?" flared Bylangu recklessly, conscious only that his life was terribly foreshortened whatever the future held.

There was a stunned silence. At last Hippelon spoke. "We will deal with your insubordination later. In the meantime —"

"In the meantime let me make one further suggestion. That whether the natives of this planet are Yas'elda or not, we set down ship and end our days here in peace and spaciousness. The crew —"

"— will not be led into desertion!" roared the captain. "For that is what you are suggesting!"

"We are doomed to die in the near —"

"We will die doing our duty!"

"Perhaps there is a higher duty. I believe we should put it to a decision of the entire ship's complement to —"

"Guards! Seize that man!" The captain turned to the other officers, who had been following the debate with horrified attentiveness. "You will procure the texts that deal with the proceedings for attempted mutiny. It may take some time: I doubt if there has been one now for at least ten million years."

Two hours later Second Officer Bylangu was tried before his peers, convicted according to the relevant regulations, and duly sentenced to

termination by Captain Hippelon. The sentence was carried out imme-
diately by the ship's two policemen, aided by six crew members chosen
at random. As the assembled ship's company watched in shock, the eight
unfortunate crewmen mingled their fields with that of the helpless By-
langu and, following the captain's directives, slowly and excruciatingly
stripped it away from his tortured persona. At last the deed was done and
the rebellious Bylangu was no more.

That evening, just as the captain was preparing to lift the ship through
the planet's atmosphere, he was brusquely seized by four crewmen and
thrust into the Riestu's *emergency lifeboat. Moments later he was joined*
there by Chaplain Kundo'oni and the sixteen remaining officers. The
hatch was dogged shut and the lifeboat precipitated into space.

The remaining Silumiut brought their ship to ground on a barely in-
habited speck of land lost in the tracts of the planet's mightiest ocean.

CHAPTER 7

There were enormous photographs the next morning in the two local newspapers of a large glowing disk lying improbably on the Crest of Teivimarama just behind the island's highest peak of Mount Orohena. The disk was light in color, perhaps seventy-five yards across, and seemed broader than it was high, but these were the only details that could be elicited, for the entire shimmering disk, and particularly its edges, seemed curiously lacking in resolution.

The photos had been taken from light planes and the newspapers distributed before the residual vestiges of the French government in Tahiti had decided how to handle what was obviously a UFO in their midst. For the past twenty years the French High Commissioner had been little more than a figurehead while the day-to-day business of governing the islands had increasingly been taken up by the local inhabitants and their elected Assembly. But as private fears and speculations began to turn to public panic it was soon obvious that the sole authority capable of dealing with the emergency was that of the High Commissioner, de facto commander of the French military forces with its 1,200-man brigade of Foreign Legionnaires, and of the state police force of gendarmes on every island.

Ken watched the address of the High Commissioner on the color television set in the small lobby of his hotel. "We have no means of knowing how long this emergency will last," he said, addressing the scattered islands of the archipelago from his office. "As you are aware, French Polynesia is entirely dependant upon imports for its entire supply of oil and gas, which in turn are the basis of 95 percent of all electricity generated in the islands. These stocks are now our single most precious resource." A draconian rationing of gasoline and petroleum products was decreed. Private automobile traffic was banned in favor of *les trucks,* and air travel to the outer islands was indefinitely postponed except for certain military flights. Anyone found in violation of these edicts would be tried under military law and in all probability incarcerated in a military prison.

To round out his proclamation of martial law, he declared a strict curfew and an even stricter rationing of all items of imported food. "For unfortunately," he added sardonically, "the inhabitants of our islands have become almost totally dependant for many years now on two basic staples: imported rice, and bread baked from imported flour. Might it not have been wiser for those in the recent past who clamored most loudly for an end to dependance on France to have cultivated their own taro patch somewhat more assiduously?" Even as he was speaking, soldiers and gendarmes were taking up their posts in the islands' stores to distribute ration cards and prevent hoarding.

Forty-five years earlier, in a sleepy Polynesian society overlaid with a thin veneer of French colonial culture, where barely 500 cars chugged around the island and most of the population still devoted its time to fishing and agriculture and lighted its homes with kerosene lanterns, these measures would have passed largely unnoticed.

Today they were highly unpopular with a population that was remarkably affluent and thoroughly Westernized. Thirty-five percent of the work force labored in some way for the government or in the public sector, receiving a salary paid by the faraway French government equal or greater to what was paid for the same job in France. Tahitians ate steaks and vegetables flown in from France, New Zealand, and the United States, while forty-seven shops in town rented video cassettes, and more 120 thousand cars now clogged the island's single road.

The two local newspapers trumpeted the resentment and outrage felt by Tahitians and French alike at these dictatorial measures, until on the third day they were brusquely replaced by a two-page paper published by the office of the High Commissioner and the French military.

On an island in which the coconut radio disseminated its rumors and gossip at nearly light-speed, it seemed to Ken senseless to try to censor anything, and in any case it was impossible after the first day to deny the obvious, that Tahiti, and with it a large part of French Polynesia, was now entirely cut off from the rest of the world.

Perhaps the High Commissioner was trying to avoid speculation as to whether the large French military base and atomic testing grounds on the atoll of Mururoa 750 miles to the east had fallen within the forcefield or not. But as soon as the first armed legionnaires took up their posts in downtown Papeete it was obvious even to the tourists at Ken's hotel that Mururoa was indeed within the limits of the forcefield.

Since interisland radio and telephone service still functioned within the limits of the forcefield, it was not much longer before it was equally certain that Ken's home in the Marquesas, a scant fifty miles further from Tahiti than Mururoa, was not.

He clenched his teeth in fury. If only he had delayed his trip by another three days! Whatever it was that was happening here in Polynesia because of this flying saucer, he would have been safely outside the circle of the forcefield. And however great his isolation in the Marquesas, at least *there* he would be in the same world as Kristin's, where one way or another he could make his way to her.

At the thought of Kristin he sagged weakly to his bed. At least *she* was safe, he tried to tell himself. Thank God she'd left when she had. But he soon realized that this was thin comfort, for without Kristin, however safe she might be, he himself was nothing. . . .

If only, if only. . . .

His fury gave way to despair and black depression at the bitter realization that it was only his own stubborn folly that had separated them, that except for his childishness he would even now be in her arms somewhere in Chicago. . . .

As the days slowly passed with nothing else to do than arise in the morning and eat three increasingly skimpy meals at the hotel's restaurant, Ken began to piece together from rumor, speculation, and official news releases a picture of the UFO and forcefield that had so shattered his placid existence.

Although no one had actually seen it in the skies over Polynesia, it was taken for granted that what now glowed nightly in the mountains of Tahiti was that same silent UFO which had so tantalized the rest of the world for the better part of a month. By whatever means it had come to Tahiti, it was undeniably there, high on the Teivimarama Crest, apparently impervious to either civilized appeal or military attack.

Civilized appeal had consisted of delegations of civilian and military authorities being flown by helicopter to the crest, where they attempted in vain to establish communications with the huge, nearly spherical object that glowed so brightly and yet so coolly, or with any of its hypothetical occupants.

Disconcertingly, the closer the mysterious object was approached, the less solid it appeared to be. It was still entirely opaque, but the edges shimmered and flickered with no clear definition of exactly where they left off and the air around them began.

Other baffling features were rumored throughout Papeete, and were never expressly denied by the small daily news bulletin. A stick, or other small object, it was said, could be poked into the curious glowing field with increasing difficulty, and pulled back out again. But past a certain point, a matter of several feet, the end of the stick would abruptly disappear, cleanly sheared off.

Test animals could also penetrate a certain distance, but were brought back lifeless. Any living matter that intruded into the field, it seemed, instantly ceased to function down to the molecular level and became nothing more than dead meat. A number of fingers, and even arms, were rumored to have been destroyed this way, eventually to be amputated by military surgeons for further study.

The great forcefield that now isolated them was officially stated to form a perfect circle 1,274 kilometers from the object in the mountains. Ken made the glum calculation: 796 miles, just a few miles short of Hanavavé on Fatu Hiva.

The rumors were vaguer concerning the forcefield, for it enclosed little more than trackless ocean, but it appeared to be of a similar nature to whatever it was on the crest. It began apparently at the ocean floor and rose in awesome beauty from the waters of Pacific, a mighty wall of glimmering color that extended at least up to the ionosphere and perhaps higher before beginning to arch inward on itself.

Opinion was divided as to whether air, clouds, and water could pass through it. Sunlight obviously could. Apparently nothing material such as airplanes or ships, or immaterial such as man-made radio waves could. No one knew yet about fish. It was rumored to intersect at least two of the Tuamotu atolls, although just which ones were hotly debated, and the mountainous green island of Rapa Iti far to the south of Tahiti.

Like many of the other 220 thousand trapped inhabitants of Polynesia, Ken wondered if a tunnel driven through the soil of Rapa could lead under the forcefield and out to safety on the other side. . . .

An article in one of the local newspapers by a retired physicist from France speculated that if sunlight could pass through the forcefield then other visible light ought to do so as well. In which case communication with the outside world by laser beams should be eminently practical. If not lasers, then old-fashioned heliographs, which reflected sunlight by mirrors. There were, said the physicist, a couple of them in the *Musée de Tahiti et des Îles....*"

"What do you think of that?" asked the Australian stockbroker who shared a table with Ken at the Vaima Café as he put down the day-old copy of *Le Journal de Tahiti* from which he had just finished a halting translation of the story. He snorted skeptically. "Why not *smoke* signals?"

"It sounds logical, I suppose," said Ken after a while. "I certainly *hope* so. At least then we could. . . *communicate* with whoever's out there, let them know that. . . that we were thinking of them. . . ."

Of Kristin. . . .

The seventh day after the skies had turned a shiny gray Ken watched with jubilation as French military jets shrieked back and forth around the island, to suddenly dart out of sight behind the peaks of the interior. Long seconds later there came to him the sound of muffled explosions, and he knew the French army was subjecting the object of his intense hatred to whatever punishment they could devise short of using the atomic bombs they had stockpiled on Mururoa.

The bombardment continued for an entire day, but at its end the glassy gray skies were as before and that evening a faint glow of greenish-blue was clearly discernable behind the peaks of the mountains.

Early the next morning while it was still cool he walked slowly along the main road into town along with thousands of others. The island's trucks were far too few to transport the entire population, and it was now rumored that even their gasoline would shortly be rationed more strictly. He wondered bleakly how much longer the airline would continue to subsidize him and the other miserable tourists at the hotel, and how much longer the hotel itself could continue to operate. He wouldn't starve, he supposed, skilled carpenters were always in demand, but he had better see to acquiring a set of tools while his remaining money still had meaning. A pity he had had to sell his own in Hanavavé. . . .

It was while he wandered through town, inspecting and pricing tools in a number of stores, that he became increasingly conscious of a slight defect in his vision, an occasional blurring of some small part of his field of vision. Too much sunlight, he told himself, blinking his eyes, and moved over to the shadows on the other side of the street.

It was only when a barely perceptible wraith appeared directly before him on the crowded sidewalks by the downtown market that he realized the fault might not lie in his eyes, but — in his mind? He stopped and stared in consternation at what seemed little more than a distortion in the hot thick tropical air drifting slowly through the concrete wall of the Chinese store beside him. He tried in vain to focus upon it but it had already melted into the interior of the building.

He shook his head as if to physically deny the possibility that he had been hallucinating. Was this the first step, he wondered fearfully, of the terrible descent into madness? But people who were going mad — did they *know* they were losing their minds?

Hesitantly he looked about him. None of the hundreds of people who crowded around the market seemed to have been aware of whatever it was he thought he had seen. He let out a soft sigh of dismay, and turned towards the waterfront.

A fire had been built in the barbecue pit in the hotel's garden from coconut husks and odd pieces of wood, and lunch that noon was baked fish accompanied by slabs of boiled taro. A few more days, he saw, and the entire population of the island would once again be eating and cooking as the old-time Tahitians had. He wondered how the two elderly American tourists who shared his table would enjoy that? He had to admit: he himself had little relish for the heavy, doughy taro.

He looked up to see a faint flickering in the shadowy corner of the restaurant, a fuzziness in the air that partially obscured the plaited bamboo wall. It seemed to be four or five feet high, a foot or so across, and hovered perhaps a foot off the ground. Unable to tear his eyes away from it, he watched it slowly drift forward across the room, nearly disappearing as it moved into shafts of sunlight, reappearing more distinctly in the shade.

He looked around in desperation. Surely he wasn't the only person to see this —

A Tahitian waitress dropped the tray she carried with a resounding crash and began to scream shrilly. Heads turned to see her staring terror-stricken at what appeared to be empty space, but that on examination revealed a shimmering pattern of flickering light. There were other screams now, and the sound of chairs being knocked to the floor. A few moments later the entire restaurant had emptied in panic.

By the end of the day it was apparent that these peculiar apparitions had appeared everywhere on the island, but particularly in the urban center of Papeete. The government news bulletin made no mention of them for two days, and then stated categorically that whatever the nature of these drifting wraiths they were totally innocuous and in no way to be feared, although a discreet caution might well be observed in their presence.

As Ken slowly began to accumulate his tools he kept a wary eye on the mysterious specters as they drifted unobtrusively in total silence through the streets of Papeete, passing unimpeded through the seemingly solid barriers of buildings and abandoned automobiles. He was not the only person to shy quickly away from their apparently random approach, unwilling to place much confidence in the government's assurances of harmlessness.

Late that afternoon he made his way slowly along the waterfront, returning from the industrial zone of Fare Ute with a heavy sack gripped in each hand. To his left was the sweep of the waterfront, with its stores and restaurants and dark green shade trees arching out over the road. Off to his right was a mostly deserted parking lot and beyond it the small harbor of Papeete with the jagged silhouette of Moorea looming above the customs sheds on the far side.

A rusty Korean trawler was moored at quayside, with dozens of shark fins hanging from guy wires to dry in the sun. Even from here their stench was atrocious. He was wondering why the port authorities permitted such a nuisance in the middle of town when he was unexpectedly jostled and nearly thrown off his feet.

He looked up to see the back of a muscular little sailor running at full speed first across the grass border and then the asphalt parking lot in the direction of the trawler. A soft wail of terror could be barely heard, and now Ken could see that floating just above his shoulders as he ran was the nearly invisible outline of one of the flickering creatures from the flying saucer. He dropped his bags with a gasp, and watched horror-stricken as the short brown legs of the wiry Korean churned towards the safety of his battered trawler.

Now there were screams coming from others who had stopped to watch the sailor's desperate flight. For a moment it seemed he might reach whatever sanctuary the trawler might offer, but as he neared the lowered gangplank the wraith-like presence seemed to sink and then merge with the sailor, enclosing him within its barely discernable shimmering.

For long horrible seconds the sailor danced and twisted within the flickering blur as if he were a puppet on the ends of jerking strings. Ken found that he was running mindlessly towards the awful scene, a hammer clenched in his hand. A terrible scream issued from the throat of the bedeviled wretch and for a moment the shimmering field around him seemed to intensify in the sunlight.

And then the sailor lurched forward in a hideous convulsion as the flickering around him suddenly disappeared. He spun around, his face taut with agony, then with muscles that seemed as rigid as if they had been carved from stone toppled to the pavement at Ken's feet. His sightless eyes stared up at Ken's uncomprehending face.

Horrified, Ken backed slowly away, his eyes glued to the horrid spectacle. He felt himself brush against someone behind him, and slowly turned his head to find himself looking into the equally appalled gaze of Kathie Leitner, the small blonde girl with whom he had sailed from California to whatever great adventure awaited him in the South Pacific.

Soon after landing, the mutinous Silumiut began to float out across their new domain. With the ship now drawing the necessary energy directly from this system's sun, their defenses were fixed in place and it was inconceivable that any threat could be mounted by those natives of Water who found themselves outside the perimeter established by the ship's forcefield. The region within that would now be theirs for the rest of their days was mostly water and the name of their new home had suggested itself swiftly. Most of the natives were huddled here on the largest of the many islands, while the rest were scattered about in small groups on the others. But distance was of little consequence to the Silumiut once within a planet's gravitational field, for they could shift their tenuously grouped particles as swiftly to the visible horizon as they could to the other side of a ship's cabin.

With the forcefield in place the sky took on a strange glossy sheen charged with surging colors that cast a peculiar color over their new world, but in the relief that followed the long centuries of confinement aboard the Riestu *Water's* essential alienness quickly began to fade from their consciousness. By nature most Silumiut were of solitary disposition, cherishing their privacy save for the occasional company of their soulcompanion for mating games. Here, the towering mountains and rolling blue seas of an entire world promised them more than ample room for solitude and tranquil introspection.

But Silumiut required more than mere solitude and tranquility. As the martyred Bylangu had speculated, close proximity to these peculiar gaunt beings who moved so clumsily across their world revealed a neural field that in many ways was similar to that of their vital symbiotes the Yas'elda. It was, in fact, strikingly reminiscent of those that mutated variants aboard a scoutship might be expected to produce. On a ship with genuine Yas'elda available, it would have been unthinkable of course to even consider coalescing with such an unsavory oddity. But here on their new home, where there was no other choice, the frustrated crewmen yearned desperately for the sense of well-being and life-giving invigoration that came only from coalescing with their symbiotes.

In the few brief days since they had taken control of the ship a third crewman had sickened, and then a fourth. The crew members were dispersing among the native population, following them closely as they went about their incomprehensible activities. Now in desperation first one and then another of the crew could no longer restrain themselves. They sought to coalesce with these gaunt creatures — with tragic results. The field of the unlucky crewman quickly absorbed that of the native — as well as all of the hidden overload that lurked within. With ghastly suffering the crewman's field was torn to pieces and his life snuffed out forever. After the third such experience the 279 remaining Silumiut retreated despondently to the Riestu, wondering if perhaps the wiser course might not have been to follow their captain back into space after all.

CHAPTER 8

Do you really think we'll be able to break out at Rapa?" asked Kathie Leitner as they stood on the afterdeck, idly watching the wake left behind by the *Last One Left*. Her voice was subdued and cheerless.

"I don't know," said Ken bleakly. "Your father seems to think it's possible."

"He thinks anything's possible. If he yells at it loud enough."

Ken smiled faintly. "As good a way as any, I guess. So you've been in Australia ever since. . . ."

"You jumped ship in the Marquesas?" She sighed in resignation. "That, and sailing from one island to the next. What a drag. Thank God those awful Eriksons left when we got to Rarotonga, I couldn't have —"

"You came back again through Rarotonga, didn't you? It's inside this forcefield, isn't it?"

"I don't know. Just barely I guess. We were three days out of there on our way back when . . . this thing happened. It seemed easier to just keep on going than to go back."

"I'm glad you did."

She looked up at him. "You are? Really? Not because of. . . ." Her voice trailed off.

"Because of you?" He shrugged minutely. "I told you, I'm married. But I'm always glad to see —"

"To a lady professor. And you want to get back to her."

"Yes."

"It's nice to have someone you miss, I suppose," she said listlessly, unknowingly echoing Kristin's words at that first unforgettable encounter on the Hungarian's terrace and instantly plunging Ken even more deeply into gloom. "I was kind of hoping that . . . well, you know. . . ."

"That's all over," he muttered, his eyes fixed on the rushing green water of the wake.

"Is it?" She raised her head to scowl at him. "Right now you're just lucky Papa needs some extra hands, and likes speaking English to them."

"It's very kind of him to —"

"Oh goddam it! That's just what's the matter with you, Ken, you're just too fucking *nice!* Someone craps all over you and you just make excuses for them. He needs you more right now than you —"

"I'm *not* too nice," he said. "I'm *scared.* Did you see what that . . . *thing* did to that Korean sailor?"

She shuddered visibly and turned away. "I heard . . . that . . . after that. . . ."

"There were another three people killed the same way? They're beginning to panic in the streets back there. You got this boat out just in time. *Now* do you know why I wanted to be on board?"

She bowed her head to let the light blonde bangs of her forehead come to rest against his arm. "And what if we *can't* get out at Rapa?" she whispered breathlessly. "What if we're *stuck* here? Stuck here in Tahiti for maybe the rest of our lives?" She looked up at him with eyes that welled with tears. "Then will you be glad you came aboard? For . . . for some other reason?"

He patted her awkwardly on the shoulder, trying to avoid her eyes. "Don't even *think* such a thing," he said grimly. "We'll get out, all right. Your father knows what he's doing."

Besides Kathie and her father and the old man's girlfriend, Marti Fleischmann, the only other person on board was a middle-aged New Zealander named Peter Brooke. He at least was a professional sailor, although after more than a year at sea all the others were far more capable than Ken could ever hope to be. But at least he could do what the others ordered him to, he told himself as he left the forward cabin he shared with Brooke to take the midnight watch. And crewing on a boat was better than doing nothing in Papeete, brooding about Kristin and wondering if he would be the next victim of the . . . flickerers? Was that what he had heard Charles Leitner call the deadly phantoms?

He checked the compass as he had been taught, carefully examined the softly glowing dials of the autopilot system without touching anything, and sat back in the darkness with a sigh. It was a long way till morning.

"It's me," came a soft voice. "Can I join you?"

"Sure. What are you doing up? It's awfully late."

"Boats have such stupid hours, with all these watches and everything. I *never* know what time it is, except I'm always sleepy when I'm not supposed to be, and vice versa."

"Me too," said Ken. "These watches are so boring. Or else the mast breaks in two, and then they're *too* exciting."

He felt Kathie snuggle closer to him on the padded settee, and automatically his arm went around her shoulders.

"This professor lady of yours," said Kathie. "Is she very beautiful?"

"Yes. You're beautiful too, but she's . . . well, different."

"And you're faithful to her all the time? Even . . . even when you know you may never see her again?"

"I don't know," said Ken miserably, his voice thick with anguish.

She turned and pulled him tightly against her, so that he felt her soft breasts crushed against him. "Oh hold me, Ken, please. Hold me!"

The fresh smell of her newly washed hair was in his nostrils and her warm breath against his bare chest. As he held her against him he felt a greater peace than he had known since Kristin had left but, even more, a greater depression and sense of loss.

"Did you hear what people were saying in town?" she whispered so softly he could barely hear the words. "I heard it from some of the yachties."

"What?"

She giggled softly. "That these . . . flickermen give you a tremendous charge when you're fucking."

He sat up with a start. "What?" Had he heard her correctly? "Are you *crazy?*"

Her giggle seemed to verge on hysteria. "I guess if they don't *kill* you, that is."

"Jesus. . . ." he breathed. "For a moment there I thought you were *serious.*"

She suddenly pulled herself up and crushed her lips to his. "I am, for chrissake! Can't you see I'm going batty all alone on this dumb boat. Oh, Ken, *please. . . .*"

It was Alns, the onetime soulcompanion of Tre'ze, who was the first to discover that when the natives occasionally came together for what apparently was sexual coupling their combined fields yielded a pleasurable electromagnetic sensation. It was only faintly akin to what the Silumiut experienced while reproducing themselves when coalesced with one's soulcompanion and their joint symbiote, but nevertheless it was astonishingly agreeable. He eagerly reported that the peculiar combined field of two natives continued to build in intensity until it suddenly reached a series of sharp climaxes that splashed pleasurable energy out in disconcertingly powerful bursts. . . .

Oppressed and burdened, feeling himself to be almost without volition, he followed her silently down to the cramped stuffy cabin he had once known so well. What was it she had called those . . . things? Flickerers? No, flickermen. He wondered why. They flickered all right, but they looked a lot more like clouds than men.

He lay back in the total darkness of the small bunk and apathetically let her arouse him. It was not until he had rolled her beneath him and unceremoniously entered her that he began to feel again the eagerness and excitation he had become so accustomed to since meeting Kathie and then Kristin so many months before. He pulled her tight against him and thrust into her powerfully, mindlessly, conscious only of her warm sweaty body clutched around his own and of her harsh rhythmic breathing in his ears. He buried his face deeper into her soft hair that spread against the pillow and let his mind empty itself of all the fears and uncertainties that had stalked him since that terrible noon he had returned home to find his suitcase spread open on his small double bed.

Kathie's legs tightened around his hips, and he could feel her fingers digging into his back. "Look," she murmured into his ear. Reluctantly he opened his eyes and twisted his head over his shoulder. At first he saw nothing except the dark wooden bulkhead, but then with a start he realized she meant the faint glow that was now lighting the cabin as if by candle light. He gasped and raised his head. A few feet away, at the end of the bunk, a flickering network of pale blue and green luminescence hovered motionlessly, pulsating slightly. The bulkhead of the cabin was clearly visible through its insubstantial radiance.

"Oh god, it's here," whimpered Kathie, thrusting herself against him and pulling him ever deeper into her. "It's *here!*" He tried to wriggle away, but she clutched him desperately, and he heard her whimpering suddenly become the rhythmical moans of passion as she neared her climax. His own ardor was quickening rapidly and he hastened his movements to merge them with hers. The pale luminescence that gleamed beside them seemed to be growing brighter as he felt the familiar tingling in his arms and legs that presaged his orgasm.

Kathie began to tremble beneath him, and with a stifled cry he felt her suddenly grip him and then hold him immobile while she ground her hard pubic bone frenziedly against his own. The tingling in his limbs seemed to be pulsing in growing waves now, and he could feel it spreading to the rest of his body, as if an electric current were flowing from one side to the other and back again. He heard his own quick gasps for breath and felt Kathie's fingers claw into the tender flesh of his buttocks as she tried to pull him ever deeper within her. He was no longer conscious of himself and Kathie as separate entities, but only of a single merging of flesh and warmth and glowing blue light and the flowing of current and the unbearable mounting of tension and pressure. Suddenly it was too great to withstand and a moment later he shuddered and with great racking spasms felt himself and all the electrical charge that seemed to have accumulated within flowing in great bolts of sheer energy deep into the warm flesh that smothered him. From some great distance he heard a strangled cry and was dimly aware that Kathie too was still coming. . . .

Her long trembling moan of ecstacy abruptly cut off, to be replaced by a faint cry that it took him long moments to distinguish as one of terror. Still in the throes of his climax he pulled his eyes open to become vaguely aware that the flickering blue light had now moved around them to envelop Kathie's head and shoulders. The bunk in which they lay glowed in its pulsating light and he realized with sudden shock that his own arms and shoulders were deep within the faint blue glow.

He looked down to find Kathie's eyes glazed with fear, and as his last faint spasms gradually subsided he fell against her weakly, a single thought running through his mind: "Oh God, this is how I die. . . . Oh God, *Kristin!*"

They opened their eyes, to find that miraculously they were still alive. The glow was fading swiftly, losing both color and intensity, and they silently watched what remained of its flickering presence drift eerily through the paneled bulkhead and out into the night.

He became conscious of Kathie's wet sticky body against his and was thankful that the darkness masked the guilt and distaste he knew must be plain on his face. He could feel the warm wet flesh of her legs quivering against his thighs. Oh God, he thought, I actually forgot about Kristin while I was . . . Kristin, *forgive me!*

He pulled away from Kathie and silently groped about in the darkness until he found his shorts and left without a word.

None of the crew of the Riestu had ever encountered intelligent lifeforms before. It was only with the aid of the ship's memory banks and correlator that it was tentatively agreed that the natives of Water were divided into what the correlator assumed were the different sexes necessary for reproduction. It was pointed out that some biologists had speculated that the original Yas'elda may at one time have been divided in this fashion. In any case, it soon became easy enough to distinguish one so-called sex from another, though distinguishing individual members of each sex was another matter.

Tre'ze was one of the first to discover that the amount of pleasurable sexual activity engaged upon by these increasingly fascinating beings varied enormously from creature to creature. Since there were thousands of natives to choose from, it seemed only logical to him to seek out those who were the most active in this activity and to linger in their vicinity. A number of his crewmates, Alns among them, had become interested by the peculiar activities of the natives just around the Riestu, *and had begun to consider the possibility of attempting to establish communication with them.*

But Alns was a chief petty officer after all, and might be expected to take an interest in useless intellectual activities. As far as Tre'ze was concerned, since the rest of his days — and they promised to be few enough — would be spent here in the lonely exile of Water, he at least could find more satisfying activities than trying to talk with animals. . . .

Some days after the natives had entertained the ship's company by subjecting them to a entire day's bombardment with primitive chemical weapons Tre'ze drifted slowly by himself over the gently rolling ocean at least a dozen jumps from landfall. Ahead of him was one of the primitive sailing ships that the natives of Water apparently used for purposeful movement across the ocean's surface. He was in a contemplative mood that excluded the desire for companionship of his own kind, so he idly followed the small tossing boat for the rest of the day and throughout the night. The night after that he returned once again and as he approached it his sensitive field felt the faint traces of the now-familiar signals emanating from a pair of natives.

He was in luck, for this evening there was a couple already engaged in providing the mild but pleasurable stimulation his neural field so easily absorbed. But as a shipmate had recently told him, there was a way of sharply increasing the pleasure derived from these encounters. . . .

Cautiously, almost fearfully, he drifted over the busy couple so that their bodies were enveloped by his. Warily he kept from trying to merge their fields into his, but simply let himself passively absorb their radiations. Yes, it was as the venturesome Enamidir had said: by encompassing their field but not directly joining with it, a curious feedback seemed to be established. He felt their output intensifying and became aware of himself beginning to pulse and glow in rhythm with their quickening pace. Their surging discharge passed through him with a powerful shock and back again to them, then back once more to him in ever more pleasurable waves. . . .

Sated and exhausted by the strange sensations he let himself drift listlessly out into the night. What a curious experience! It was not at all like that of coalescing with a soulcompanion but . . . but in some peculiar fashion it was . . . it was almost more satisfying!

"That was scary," she said to him the next afternoon as they folded spare sails on the foredeck.

"Ummph," he grunted noncommitally, but shamefully feeling the sudden tingle of excitement course through him.

Her hand brushed against the sensitive white flesh of the inside of his wrist. "The flickerman. . . . You saw him."

"Yeah. Maybe. There was a light."

She turned her head, as if in shyness. "I . . . I don't think I . . . ever came like that before. That's what was scary . . . him there, and me coming like that, not even thinking about how he . . . might kill us."

The memories of the night before surged back, and he laid down the sail and slowly considered them. It *had* been more powerful than anything he could remember. Or at least since that night with Kristin at the Hungarian's when she and. . . . He shut his mind to the thought, and nodded grudging agreement. He drew a deep breath and slowly let it out, and with it his final guilt-laden misgivings about Kathie. Kristin would hate him for his weakness, he knew, and would surely punish him for it. But *she* was *there,* on one side of the flickermens' forcefield, and he was *here,* on the other. Someday they would be reunited, but in the meantime. . . .

As the Last One Left made its way slowly under sail to the haven of Rapa Iti at the very end of the lonely group of islands called the Australes some 800 miles to the southeast of Tahiti, they were unable to keep themselves from coupling frantically whenever the opportunity presented itself. From murmured conversations with Marti Fleischmann Kathie learned that the flickering wraith had appeared in the cabin of her father and that its effect had been as galvanizing on them as it was with Ken and her.

When the flickerman reappeared in her cabin two days later they left off their movements to appraise it warily. It seemed slightly smaller than before, but less diffuse and more clearly outlined in the darkness. Although blues and greens and grays danced and sparkled randomly within its form, it now seemed as if it were almost trying to mimic a semblance of human shape. A narrowing at the top could be a head, and there were occasional extensions of brightness that might be taken for a carelessly formed arm or leg.

"It's so *weird,* " whispered Ken. Slowly he withdrew from Kathie and stretched out beside her, pulling her warm back and buttocks against him. He entered her again from behind, and they lay together almost motionlessly, rocking pleasurably with the movement of the boat, staring curiously at the flickerman before them, wondering if once again the strange radiance would contribute whatever it was that had so heightened the ecstacy of their previous coupling. . . .

As the days passed the substantiality of the glassy gray sky seemed to intensify on the horizon before them. Occasional great bolts and flashes of yellow, white, and blue were seen beyond the prow of the ship, and it was apparent that the Last One Left was approaching the awesome juncture where the waters of the Pacific gave birth to the forcefield. Far ahead on the horizon could be seen a faint smudge that gradually grew in size until it became a long bank of low-lying clouds. Somewhere in the distance, concealed below them, was the island of Rapa Iti.

There was no sign of the flickerman that night, but when they awoke in the morning the dark mass of Rapa was clearly before them. As they approached it throughout the morning they watched the clouds begin to build up over the island, though not enough to hide the outlines of the dark green peaks. Through the binoculars some of them looked curiously like pyramids or fortifications now covered with vegetation.

The great wall of the forcefield itself could now be clearly seen, rising abruptly out of the horizon on either side of the island. Parts of the island, they saw, were cleanly sliced across by the awesome gray wall that reared so unimaginably above them.

Their charts showed Rapa to be surrounded by coral reefs, so they slowed their approach and debated whether to attempt landfall that afternoon or to wait for the clearer light of morning. It was the sight of a destroyer and corvette belonging to the French navy anchored outside the reef that decided Charles Leitner.

"Wherever there's those guys, there's nothing but trouble," he said. "They think they own everything. So we'll just go on in before they can think of any reasons to keep us out."

The auxiliary engine with its precious supply of fuel was started up, and with Peter Brooke at the prow giving hand signals to indicate the presence of the treacherous coral to either side, the *Last One Left* carefully picked its way through the winding narrow pass into the tranquil bay of Ahurei. Ken's eyes were supposed to be on the dark black shadows that lurked so menacingly in the slanting rays of late afternoon beneath the apparently inviting waters, ready to rip the bottom from the ship, but he was unable to keep them from lifting to the stupendous pearly wall that loomed so threatening above them, rippling and coruscating with a million shifting colors. Never had he been made so aware of his absolute puniness, his total nothingness in the scheme of things. How, he wondered, had the inhabitants of Rapa survived without becoming totally mad. . . ?

The small village of Aréa was at the entrance to the bay, behind a crumbling concrete quay crowded with launches from the warships beyond the reef and two wooden fishing boats. Several dozen French sailors and soldiers stood on the edge of the quay and watched their approach. "Surly looking bastards," muttered Charles Leitner. "Well, screw 'em." He turned the wheel hard over and maneuvered the ship 200 yards further down the shore, well away from the village. Twenty feet from shore the *Last One Left* was in ten feet of clear blue water over a pebbly bottom. Anchors were tossed out at either end and the ship came almost imperceptibly to a gentle halt.

They stood on the afterdeck, Charles Leitner's arm curled protectively around Marti Fleischmann's shoulders, and watched the rays of the setting sun glow briefly against the top of one of the odd pyramid-like peaks of the jagged mountains that surrounded the bay. Quickly the sun dropped behind a high dark ridge and the true glory of the shining forcefield was revealed for the first time.

"Jesus," muttered Peter Brooke reverently, awed by the glowing luminosity with its endless interplay of shifting, merging colors within the opaque pearly gray.

"A drink," murmured Charles Leitner softly, as if even he were partially daunted by the enormity of what loomed above them. "Get out the scotch. A celebration." But his voice seemed curiously muted. "Tomorrow we'll see about finding some way of getting out of this damn place."

Ken's eyes lifted to the dazzling splendor that now flooded the mountains and village with a cold gray light and dwarfed their tiny ship and their even tinier lives.

Did Charles Leitner *really* believe he was going to equip them all with shovels and tunnel his way out under *this?*

CHAPTER 9

It was only for Kristin that he had decided to walk up to Morongo Uta. This was the site of a fortified village the ancient inhabitants of Rapa Iti had built high in the interior of the island, accessible only by winding paths through the mountains. Millions of stones had been laboriously carried up from the deep valleys far below to build the houses and terraces at Morongo Uta and the dozen other settlements perched on dizzy mountain aeries where they were impervious to attack by the great war canoes that must at one time have been liable to suddenly appear over the ocean's vast horizon.

How long the Rapans had inhabited these villages nobody knew, for they had been overgrown with vegetation by the time the first Europeans had stopped briefly at Rapa, and their very existence was uncertain until the Norwegian explorer Thor Heyerdahl had excavated the site of one of the strangely terraced mountain tops to uncover the remains of Morongo Uta some four decades before. Thick vegetation had quickly recaptured the village after his departure, and it was only recently after the construction of an airstrip that the French government and the local community of 400 people had combined to clear it once again. Now it was maintained as a historical site and theoretically as a tourist attraction.

So much Ken had learned from the Mayor of Rapa Iti, a stout Polynesian woman with prematurely white hair pulled into a tight knot behind her head and with a impressive dignity that even Charles Leitner acknowledged. To Ken's relief, and probably that of Charles Leitner, *Madame le maire* Jeannine Teinuri had unexpectedly intervened the morning after their arrival just as the angry dispute between the French navy and the captain of the *Last One Left* was reaching its climax.

The dispute had had its ludicrous aspects, Ken saw, with Charles Leitner standing firmly on his dignity on the afterdeck, while three navy launches manned by ratings slowly circled the *Last One Left* as if preparing to mount an assault at any moment. Far from the dangers of the battle zone, a stocky officer in a white uniform liberally covered with braid stood on the rocky shoreline twenty feet away and hurled menaces in Oxford-accented English across the water.

"Who *says* these are interdicted waters?" yelled Charles Leitner disdainfully.

"I say so," shouted the furious officer, "I and the government of France. Now get those anchors up and that boat —"

"You should reread your international maritime law, sonny boy. Yachtsmen have free entry into any port in Polynesia once they have cleared customs and immigration in Papeete, as I have done and as my papers attest, except for ports clearly delineated as being in military zones, such as Mururoa. Rapa Iti is 600 nautical miles from Mururoa and by no stretch of the imagination a military zone. I am therefore absolutely within my rights to refuse to —"

"It is *now* a military zone," grated the officer, turning to gesture at the glittering forcefield that rose out of the jagged shards of the volcanic crater that formed the stupendous cliffs around the bay, "by edict of the High Commissioner. Or haven't you noticed that . . . that *thing* behind us?"

"And maybe *you* haven't noticed that I'm a United States citizen with —"

The French officer grinned unpleasantly at this misjudged sally. "And have *you* noticed that the United States is now somewhere behind that *thing?* Inaccessible to even its richest, staunchest, and most loudmouth citizens?" Sure now of his triumph, he smiled indulgently. "You have one hour to get that floating junkyard out of here. After which I'll have it towed to sea, whether there's anyone aboard or not."

"Be quiet, the both of you!" a sharp voice suddenly interrupted in French. Eyes turned to a white-haired woman sitting ramrod stiff in the back of a small skiff that had been unobtrusively rowed next to the *Last One Left* by a grinning Polynesian in the blue uniform of a village policeman.

"Madame *le maire,"* acknowledged the officer, saluting stiffly.

"It's the lady Mayor," whispered Ken to Charles Leitner.

"Hrmph. Well? Have you lost your wits? Ask her aboard."

Half an hour later Ken had accompanied them ashore to act as interpreter to Charles Leitner while he was formally presented by the Mayor to a number of those military officials and scientists whose disruptive presence in her small Commune Madame le maire Teinuri found every bit as irksome as Charles Leitner.

Under the guileful prompting of the Mayor it was eventually diplomatically conceded by a trio of naval officers without actually being explicitly stated that if the *Last One Left* had indeed put into harbor to undergo repairs for damages suffered at sea, she and her crew were free to stay until those repairs had been carried out. In return, it was, of course, hardly necessary to remind anyone as observant as Monsieur Leitner that Rapa Iti was, as he could readily see, something in the nature of a war zone, and that he and his crew, like everyone else on the island, were subject to the prevailing martial law.

"But of course," said Charles Leitner blandly, while Jeannine Teinuri scowled darkly at this crass reminder that in a world in which entire islands could be cut in half by mysterious forces from somewhere beyond the Earth the mayors of small Polynesian islands were of little consequence.

"War zone," snorted Charles Leitner contemptuously as they strolled down the pebbly shore towards where the *Last One Left* lay peacefully at anchor on a body of water as smooth as a pane of glass. "Some war zone!"

Ken pointed to the end of the bay, where the blue water and the jagged mountains on either side were suddenly cut across by the gray sweep of the forcefield, a grotesque and throat-clutching backdrop to what was otherwise a postcard-like scene of unspoiled South Seas beauty. "Just behind that forcefield there's another village called Ahurei," he said. "The Mayor was telling me about it. It's not as big as Aréa, only about seventy-five people, but . . . it's still a village."

Charles Leitner turned his scowl to Ken. "Well? What's that got to do with anything? Except for those seventy-five people being the luckiest sons of bitches in the world. Is *that* what you're trying to say? That they're on the *other* side of this fucking forcefield?"

Ken tried to stifle his sigh. "That too, I guess. What I was trying to say was all these people in Aréa, and now they've been cut off, just . . . just like they used to do in Russia or someplace. Maybe these people here aren't ever going to see them again. Maybe they're *dead*. We don't *know* what's out there beyond the forcefield. Maybe there's nothing at all any more. Maybe everybody *out* there is dead! Remember I told you about the guy in Tahiti who said that maybe we could communicate with the outside world by laser beams, or by bouncing sunlight off of mirrors? Well, I just asked one of these military scientists about that and he said that that was the very first thing they'd thought of trying to do. But that it didn't work. That the laser-beam light was polarized by the forcefield or something." Ken's voice had risen, and Charles Leitner turned to consider him thoughtfully. "The flickermen designed that thing to keep other people *out,* and us *in,* not to let us *talk* together, for chrissake! What's a crummy little laser beam to them, to someone who can build a forcefield 800 miles high? So how do we know about anyone out there being alive? *We may be the only people left alive in the whole goddam world!"*

He raised a hand that trembled with sudden rage and anguish to aim a finger like a gun at the impervious forcefield. "And there's the cause of it, right down there!" he shouted. "And you don't call *that* a fucking war zone?"

* * * *

Later that evening, after their new ally the Mayor and her husband and her two adjoints and their wives had been noisily waved goodby to following their dinner on board the Last One Left, Ken and Kathie found themselves alone in her cabin. The flickerman made its eerie appearance a few minutes after he had entered her, drifting slowly through the bulkhead against which their pillows rested, and enveloping them in its cool blue glow. It hovered around their naked bodies for a moment, then drifted on past to the end of the cabin, where it took up its accustomed station.

"Look," said Kathie. "Tonight it's a woman."

Ken strained to look behind him, without any great belief in her words. In the week since the flickerman had become an almost regular spectator to their bouts of lovemaking it had continued to evolve from little more than a generalized cloud of colored particles to something that was now in outline definitely human in shape. Ken was unable to distinguish features, but there were obvious arms and legs to go with what had previously been identified as a head and that now could almost be seen to be resting on a neck emanating from well-defined shoulders.

It was harder to see the point of all these newly acquired limbs, since they were just as transparent and insubstantial as the rest of the strange being. Even now the flickerman did nothing more than hover in the middle of the cabin, its glow deepening and intensifying as the activities on the bunk grew increasingly impassioned, then apparently joined them for their climax, after which it slowly faded away.

Ken turned his attention back to what he was doing with Kathie. If anyone had told him ten days ago that he wouldn't even pay attention to a flickerman while it watched him make love he would have called him crazy. He shook his head in wry forbearance. Now it was just part of the crazy new world in which he found himself.

For the flickerman — or flickerwoman as Kathie insisted it sometimes was — had apparently become in some way attached to the *Last One Left*. "It's all our good lovin'" grinned Kathie, "he just can't get enough of it."

Ken groaned in dismay at such an idiotic notion but couldn't get the perverse idea out of his head, any more than he could deny that for several days before reaching Rapa the flickerman had occasionally been seen drifting through the boat in the glaring light of day, or, even more disconcertingly, following across the tops of the waves as the *Last One Left* slowly cleaved through the water. It had caught at his nerves to look off to the side of the boat and see that *thing,* clearly now a human shape, fifty yards away and two feet above the water, calmly pacing the boat like a sheep dog herding a flock of docile sheep, gliding effortlessly forward on a smooth straight path that ignored the occasional wave washing through its flickering being.

But in the confines of their cabin Kathie had begun to insist that she could tell when the flickerman was male or female. "Maybe there's two them," joked Ken uneasily, "a male *and* a female, and they take turns watching us. Monday, Wednesday, and Friday for the man, Tuesday —"

"You're being silly. Anyway, just wait until the next time he comes. I'll *show* you." She leaned over to engulf him briefly with her mouth. "And we can pretend that we're the stars of that porno flick you *say* you didn't make, and the flickerman is just the director, or maybe one of the other actors waiting to join us." She giggled briefly. "That'll be *fun!*"

That evening the flickerman was clearly a flickerwoman, according to Kathie. "Look, Ken, can't you see?"

"I'm busy, can't *you* see?"

"Don't stop. Just look for a moment. Look: see those breasts? And the waist is narrower now, and the hips are wider." She sighed in exasperation. "Oh, Ken, can't you see it's a *woman?*"

"Women turn you on?" he muttered into her hair.

"Oh God, *anything* turns me on as long as it's you and that crazy flickerman," she moaned, and he felt her begin to thrust against him with increasing urgency. "I don't care *what* kind of a ghost it is!

By the time the natives' ship had reached the small island that was its destination Tre'ze had learned a number of things. Apparently the natives communicated with one another by movements of the same fleshy orifice in their head with which they consumed fuel. If this was indeed the case, then as far as he could see there was no sense in even attempting to communicate with them, for they would never be able to understand the Silumiuts' own subtle means of communication.

Another thing he had learned was to easily distinguish between the five creatures who made up the small ship's roster. Two of them were small, with long waving manes on their heads, and were the receptors into whom two of the three others thrust themselves. According to the correlator, these were the females, while the larger ones were known as males. One of the two couples was clearly more vigorous than the other, and enacted their mating ritual several times a day, as if they were consciously doing it for his pleasure. He found also that as he came to know them he could recognize their individual fields, but this was a useless distinction, for it was only when they merged their fields together that they became of real interest.

The most surprising thing of all was that as the days passed in their company he found himself slowly attaining a richness and fullness of body that had been absent for centuries now. In some peculiar way he didn't understand his field was charging itself from theirs almost as if they had been Yas'elda, and for the first time since he had been told that the ship's stock of symbiotes was dead he allowed himself a wary hope that his life might not be snatched from him in his early youth after all.

But more than that: he had come to realize that without conscious volition on his own part his body's normally amorphous shape had begun to mimic the strange primitive physical outlines of these exhilarating new creatures. His initial terror at this discovery faded as he could feel no dangerous side-effects from the mysterious process, and after a few days he no longer paid any attention to the phenomenon. But although he could see that his body was being twisted into a grotesque new shape, it was impossible to determine from his limited point of view more than that, and he wondered occasionally if he was slowly becoming a male or a female. . . ?

CHAPTER 10

Not everyone in the village of Aréa shared Kathie Leitner's sentiments. The arrival of a flickerman in their midst, already grief-stricken and panicky because of the massive intrusion of the gleaming forcefield a few hundred yards away, caused widespread terror the first night it appeared. The screams and shouts from the village carried across the dead calm of the bay and brought the inhabitants of the Last One Left cautiously up on deck.

The shining majesty of the forcefield cast its harsh pale light over the bay and mountains, making them look as gray and eerie as a cratered landscape of the moon. They saw the orange glow of kerosene lanterns begin to flicker in the dark shadows of the village, and then in the small prefabricated barracks the navy had hastily constructed at the entrance of the bay. Several sharp cracks, followed by a louder boom, suddenly echoed around them.

"A pistol?" muttered Charles Leitner. "And a shotgun?"

"Maybe they're revolting against the navy," yawned Kathie sleepily.

Bright yellow and white beams from powerful flashlights began to sweep through the village, and Ken could see a number of uniformed soldiers and sailors moving in and out of the shadows. Half an hour passed in which no further shots were heard and as the lights in the village began to slowly go out the crew of the *Last One Left* gradually made their way below deck.

It was not until the following morning that Ken learned the cause of the disturbance, and it took only a few hours more for the entire population of Rapa to become aware that the hideous ghost or *tupapau* that had come to haunt them had been brought by the Americans on their yacht.

He kicked angrily at a pebble in the middle of the path as he recalled the angry words he had exchanged with a dozen natives of Aréa half an hour ago before setting out on this footpath that would lead him up to the ancient site of Morongo Uta in the mountains behind the village. It was a problem that he had not foreseen when he had walked to town that morning, and that even now seemed more exasperating than rational.

But to these ignorant Rapans it was evidently a very real problem, even if they had ludicrously decided that *he* was to blame for all their troubles! The fact they he could argue with them in Tahitian had only seemed to make the situation worse. For it made him almost too accessible, someone akin to themselves, not one of these haughty *farani* soldiers with their imperfectly understood language and distant manners. *He* could be yelled at; they could not.

But in any case the whole thing was no concern of his. The flicker-men were now a part of everybody's lives, and the Rapans would have to accept it just as he and Kathie had done, although he could certainly sympathize with their shock at the initial sight of the glowing phantasm, especially if it had appeared a few feet away in the dark just as momma and poppa had settled down for a game of missionary's position.

But sooner or later the flickermen would have arrived at Rapa by one means or another. It was ridiculous to blame an individual boat for being the agency that had delivered the ghost to their midst. Couldn't they see for themselves that the flickerman floated over water just as easily as it floated over land? The flickerman didn't *need* the *Last One Left* to get to Rapa, for God's sake!

Ken had tried to point all this out, to no avail. The crowd around him had continued to swell and had started to jostle him as tempers rose. He had begun to feel distinctly scared before one of the Mayor's adjoints who had had dinner with them on the boat had been attracted by the din and had eventually dispersed the angry Rapans.

It was he who suggested that Ken walk on up to Morongo Uta, the site of the old fortified village the Mayor had told them about at dinner a few nights ago. It seemed like a boring way to pass the day, but after a moment's reflection he suddenly saw that it would be something to tell Kristin about, something that would please her, when eventually they . . . when. . . .

"How do I get there?" he asked.

Now he kicked a second pebble off the side of the path and watched it disappear somewhere in the brush that grew up the hillside far below. And even if this flickerman business *was* a problem, he told himself, it was Charles Leitner's problem, not his. After all, it was Leitner's boat, wasn't it?

With that he dismissed the subject, as he had tried to suppress any thought of Kristin as he made his way up the steep trail, although it was only for her sake that he would ever have bothered to walk up a mountainside to look at a bunch of old rocks piled together. He hoped she would recognize the gesture for what it was: a placatory offering to partially mitigate for . . . well, for whatever it was that he shouldn't be doing with Kathie. He sighed profoundly, and felt himself nearer to tears than he had since rejoining the crew of the *Last One Left* nearly two weeks ago. Why did he have to feel so *guilty* about everything?

Oh Kristin, why aren't you here?

* * * *

An hour later he stopped to wring the sweat from his soggy T-shirt. These jagged mountains that looked so lush and green and cool from below were actually harsh and desolate, with only scrawny knee-high shrubs growing on their volcanic sides. The winding path followed the open ridges and there was no respite from the blazing sun. He turned to look down at the faraway village on the cool blue bay and wondered if he should return. If that mountaintop far ahead that had been completely denuded was Morongo Uta, then he still had a long hike in front of him. Maybe he ought to return to the boat, and then he and Kathie could get a picnic lunch together sometime and come up here together, leaving early in the morning, when it was cool and —

Was he crazy? Bring Kathie to a place he was visiting for Kristin? He felt suddenly weak in the knees with trepidation at the idea that Kristin might somehow divine he had even entertained the notion. He let out a deep breath, appalled at how close an escape he had had.

Kathie was for one thing, he told himself, and one thing only. Fucking. Nothing more. Even Kristin would understand that.

As he neared Morongo Uta he saw that the great sweep of the forcefield would bring it near the very spot he was heading for. He stopped and turned to pensively survey the shining wall from its misty origins far beyond the distant horizon. It swept ruler-straight across the white-capped sea to arrive at Rapa, where it brutally chopped off the mountains and the far side of the Bay of Ahurei. Here it seemed to form a unimaginably gargantuan backdrop for the green peaks and ridges of the center of the island before once again shearing through the mountains to his right and eventually fading into the scattered clouds in the far distance. It was suddenly more than his mind could encompass, and he took refuge in asking himself why the Rapan from the Mayor's office hadn't warned him that the forcefield might run right across the middle of Morongo Uta?

He hesitated for another minute, then continued up the path. Maybe he hadn't known. With all the Rapans' other problems, why would any of them bother to walk all the way up here? And the French scientists who were here to study the forcefield could just step outside their doors at Aréa to do so. He was probably the first person to come up here since the forcefield had appeared.

He was even more disappointed by Morongo Uta than he had expected to be. He had harbored vague images of broken temples and columns, like pictures he'd seen of ancient Athens or Rome, with ruins that he could visualize as having once been buildings, no matter how broken down they now were. But this — this was just a lot of dirt terraces cut out of a jagged mountain top, with a bunch of little stones piled up here and there like foundations or maybe walls. *This* was the Morongo Uta he had spent all day getting to for Kristin?

But what *was* interesting was the forcefield. It ran up from a steep cliff to his left, then straight across a large mound dirt only twenty feet from where he was standing before receding over the side and then climbing yet another set of mountains over to his right. Seen from this close, it wasn't actually any more scary than it was from a distance. It seemed more like a great silent waterfall than anything else, with all its different colors rushing past him and disappearing into the earth so fast they were nothing but a long continuous blur.

He watched it spellbound, unable to tear his eyes away from its dazzling movement until he suddenly roused himself with a start. The damn thing had almost hypnotized him!

He was wondering if he dared approach it any closer, throw a rock into it perhaps, when there was the sound of footsteps behind him. Startled, he turned to see four large Rapans advancing on him rapidly, their faces set and grim. He felt a sudden surge of adrenaline race through him. Were these four of those same islanders who had harangued him so angrily earlier in the day?

"Hello," he said uneasily, forcing as much friendliness into his voice as he could. "Come up to see the site? Or do you work here? It must be a lot of work, keeping this —"

"You brought the *tupapau* with you," said one of them sullenly.

"Oh, not *that* again," he groaned, belatedly aware that this was perhaps not the tone to adopt. Here in the total stillness and isolation of Morongo Uta there was no Mayor's assistant to providentially come to his aid. He glanced nervously over their shoulders at the path he taken up the mountain. Could he run faster than them? They were all short and stocky, with enormously muscled thighs that looked as if they had spent a lifetime running up and down mountains. *Should* he start running? They'd think he was crazy. But maybe it was better to be crazy than — what?

He began to edge around them, but they stepped together to block his way. One of them laid a thick brown finger against his chest. "Why did you bring the *tupapau* with you?" he asked, staring at Ken with unblinking bloodshot eyes. Ken gulped, and backed away a step.

"Did you bring the *tupapau* to kill us?" asked another.

"Yes, why do you want to kill us?"

"For God's sake, of course I don't want to —"

"You must not invoke the name of God," admonished the eldest of the four. To Ken's astonishment he produced a tattered black bible no larger than his hand from somewhere within the baggy khaki shorts that were his only clothing and held it up before him, passing it back and forth slowly in front on Ken's face, as if by doing so he could ward off an imminent attack.

As if Ken was a werewolf?

And the bible was a clove of garlic or a silver cross or whatever it was that was used to ward off werewolves?

These people were crazy. *Crazy!*

The thought he had entertained as he stood on the deck of the *Last One Left* three days before as it slowly made its way into the Bay of Ahurei, suddenly returned to him.

How could the people of Rapa live in the face of such terrifying splendor without going mad?

But just as terrifying as the forcefield was a confrontation with naked madness, madness that glared at him through bloodshot eyes. Behind him, and to both sides, rushed the cascading colors of the forcefield. There was no retreat, no sanctuary from these pious madmen in any direction except forward.

"From the pits of Hell ye came, to the pits of Hell must ye return," intoned the madman in his old-fashioned sing-song Tahitian, raising his tiny bible high above him as if to smash it down on Ken's unprotected head.

"Amen," chanted one of the others, his eyes glazed and vacant.

Ken took a slow step backward, then stepped forward to kick the broadest and most dangerous looking of the four Rapans squarely between the legs with all the force that near-hysteria could lend him. The Rapan was lifted off his feet and cast backwards through the air by the terrible blow and sprawled bonelessly on the ground.

The shortest distance to the path down the mountains that was his only salvation was directly ahead. While the other three stood rooted in astonishment, he leaped forward, one dirty white sneaker landing pitilessly on the round brown belly of the Rapan who lay moaning in the dirt. "I'm going to make it," he thought exultantly — just as his other foot snagged against the outflung arm of the semi-conscious islander.

His body's momentum carried him forward faster and faster while he flailed his arms for balance and desperately willed his feet to somehow catch up with the rest of him. For a long timeless moment he thought he was going to make it, that his frantically churning legs had nearly regained their accustomed place beneath him, subject to his will, and then he was falling headlong into the warm brown dust.

While he lay half stunned, knowing that he had to get up and run whatever the cost, he heard voices around him, and then felt himself being lifted effortlessly into the air. He opened his eyes to see himself surrounded by brown bodies, to feel what seemed like a million callused hands clutching him with vise-like grips all over his body.

He was spun around and for a moment had to close his eyes from giddiness. When he opened them again he saw to his horror the tumbling colors of the forcefield nearly at his face, and then with grunts of effort sounding in his ears he felt himself being released from the grips that held him to soar effortlessly, dreamily through the air.

He had just the time to expel a single desperate scream before he watched his outthrust hand, and then his entire arm, be swallowed up by the tingling numbness of the swirling doom before him. He saw it rush up towards him and knew that in a fraction of a second he would be —

He had spent a part of the previous evening drifting through the dwellings in this small village of natives searching for new entertainment. But each couple he came upon had suddenly ceased their mating rituals and begun to rush about in erratic movements as if they were agitated by his presence. Soon the entire village was astir, and after watching a while in curiosity he finally jumped off to the horizon in exasperation. From there he eventually slowly drifted back to the ship in the course of the night, meditating on this strange new world and its even stranger inhabitants. Perhaps it was best after all to remain with a carefully chosen few, just as he had originally thought. . . .

Now in the bright sunlight of day he was aimlessly following his male creature with the pale, almost colorless mane up into the mountains. Almost certainly there would be no mating activities here, for the ship's forcefield was just ahead and it was unlikely there would be any other natives in such an isolated locale. But still, you never knew, for how could you predict the behavior of these bizarre animals?

He watched with interest as his male was joined by four other natives and his field began to pulse in a fashion Tre'ze had not previously encountered. Could this be the prelude to some mating ritual that was carried out only between males? His curiosity aroused, he drifted closer and was gratified to see that he had been right, for the five natives were now thrashing together and their neural fields were glowing intensely. He was wondering if he could risk joining this strange new coalescence when he saw his pale-maned native suddenly being slung through the air into the very face of the forcefield.

They were destroying his property!

"Stop!" he cried involuntarily, but it was far too late. The native — his native! — had just begun to penetrate its flowing colors, when the

entire forcefield wavered and then, incredibly, seemed to almost flicker out for an instant before re-establishing itself with a peculiar new quaver that was deeply frightening. He was moving away, wondering if the passage of his native into its terrible energies could have somehow been responsible for this extraordinary momentary failure, when Alns called to him urgently from the Riestu.

"Tre'ze!" his soulcompanion asked anxiously. "The natives have been detonating fusion devices against the ship and the screen! Are you all right? Tre'ze! Answer me!"

CHAPTER 11

"Dead?" repeated Ken.

He turned away from Vetea, the island chief. "I should be, I suppose. I don't know why I'm not." He raised his eyes to the shimmering gray sky beyond the fronds of the coconuts trees that were rustling softly in the gentle breeze. He could feel Vetea's gaze on him, both puzzled and concerned. Finally he spoke, almost as if to himself. "Perhaps I *am* dead." His lips twitched in a horrid travesty of a smile, and he moved slowly off in the direction of the lagoon where a dozen villagers were preparing their pirogues for an afternoon of fishing.

For unless everyone on this island was a most remarkable liar there was little discernable difference between himself and the very deadest of dead men.

All the things that had defined his life, had given it meaning, were now irretrievably gone — his culture, his few friends, his wife, his very *time,* all somehow torn away from him by the incomprehensible fury of the flickermen.

The flickermen.

The shadow of an ironic smile crossed his lips as helped load a bundle of laboriously woven nets into the largest of the pirogues. Perhaps that was the very point of the flickermens' macabre jest. He himself was now nothing more than a flickerman, a spectral being without substance, or purpose, or even reality.

He corrected himself. Without Kristin — he was *less* than nothing.

That was the thought that appalled him most. Kristin, dead these fifty years. Again and again he had turned the figures over in his mind, had even traced them carefully in the wet sand to study for some sign of error. But always the figures were the same. He had last seen her seven weeks ago skipping through the sunlight like a startled fawn as she bolted for the sanctuary of the shadowy forest. That was sometime in February of 2004, either the 7th or 8th, he'd somehow forgotten which.

Only seven weeks ago, but now he was in November of — what? 2090? 2100? No one on the island of Takaroa was even remotely interested in the question. Laboriously, one rainy afternoon when he had nothing else to occupy him, Vetea spent several hours talking his way through an elaborate family tree that spanned seven generations. The conclusion, which he stated as an absolute certainty, was that they were now living in the year 2093.

Intrigued by this strange new pastime, his half-brother Tupi began his own genealogy, incorporating within it most of the same relatives and forebears as Vetea's. His equally well-reasoned arguments showed irrefutably that the current date could only be 2107.

The one thing certain to Ken was that neither of them actually cared a whit one way or another. Keeping track of the seasons was easy enough, and even, if anyone wanted to bother, of the months, but here in the time-less state to which Takaroa had reverted, only a madman or a *popa'a* — a white man — could conceivably be concerned about some number as arcane as the theoretical date of a year.

The islanders themselves knew to the day whenever events of importance were due to occur, and from a century's close observance and experience they knew that on this particular evening, not far from the half-exposed coral reefs of Opaka several miles to the northeast of the village, schools of mahuri would be starting to swarm at dusk, easy takings for the next three days, until they vanished again until the following year.

This was the sort of calendar the Takaroans kept, and there was no provision in it for keeping track of irrelevancies such as how many years an unknown *popa'a* woman had been dead.

For dead she must be, even by the most optimistic reckoning. She was thirty-eight, no, thirty-nine, the day she fled into the woods seven weeks ago, and if a hundred years had passed, she would be 139 today. Assuming even that she had lived another fifty years to the age of eighty-nine, to somehow become — inconceivably — a feeble, gray-haired old woman, she must *still* have been dead these fifty years and more.

When he roused from his reverie he found without surprise that he was seated in the front of a small pirogue, his arms mechanically dipping a broad wooden paddle in and out of the clear waters of the lagoon, while behind him a voice droned on unheeded in Takaroan.

The fault, he knew, was clearly his.

No matter how he turned the matter around, it always came back to the same stark reality. Kristin was dead, and had been dead for fifty years now, simply because he, Ken Camden, had been derelict in his duty towards her. They had been married in a civil ceremony at the small mayor's office in Taiohae, and in French, but he knew the words that must have been spoken. "To love, honor, and protect."

Protect.

He had loved her, and had honored her, but how had he protected her? By letting her go back to Chicago. By letting them be separated.

By letting her *die!*

If only he had kept her from leaving, or had left together with her, he would have fulfilled his duty to her, and Kristin would still be young and alive, not a moldy corpse somewhere in a unknown graveyard.

Kristin.

Young and alive.

Her warm brown —

"Hey! Ho! You there, Skinny White Sea Serpent!"

Ken blinked his eyes in momentary bewilderment, then turned to look back over his shoulder at the dark brown islander in the rear of the tiny pirogue. He was grinning broadly and waving his paddle in admonition. "You're supposed to be moving that thing in your hands, not just sitting there with it trailing in the water like your long skinny snake."

Ken looked blankly for a moment at the paddle in his hands, then nodded guiltily. "Sorry," he murmured. "I must have been . . . somewhere else for a moment."

Months passed.

He stumbled through life on the atoll almost as a zombie, crushed by guilt and grief, consumed by loneliness and self-pity, barely able to tend to the most basic aspects of living. A small hut, little more than a lean-to, had been constructed of *bourau* branches and coconut fronds just behind Vetea's own solid coral-block house, and there he passed long quiet hours, staring blankly into the distance at the slowly changing colors of the lagoon and the gray sky above it. As far as they considered him competent, he was allowed to aid the islanders with their simple tasks of fishing, coconut harvesting, and planting. The jobs were all mindlessly repetitive, but he found that while he was engaged with them his mind was unable to wander off in other, more dangerous directions, just as his thoughts had always been narrowly focused when he had been working with his tools as a carpenter. For the job at hand, with its multitudes of small decisions and occasional frustrations, seemed to be all that his mind could encompass, and he knew that he was far happier for it.

Once convinced of the certainty that he was now alive a century after everything worth living for had vanished behind the mysteries of the flickermens' sky-curtain, he was totally without active curiosity about the world that so marginally impinged upon him. But as he politely answered Vetea's unending stream of questions about his life in all the storied riches of the glorious past, and half-listened to the other's endless chatter and reminiscing, he was unable to avoid absorbing a certain amount of knowledge in return.

Intercourse between the islands, he learned, those dozens, and perhaps hundreds, that fell within the great circle of the forcefield, was not much different now from what it had once been hundreds of years before. Surprisingly small pirogues still made the journeys between the nearer islands, and occasionally fetched up weeks later in unexpected destinations hundreds of miles off course. Enormous double-hulled canoes fitted with sails and carrying dozens of crew to paddle when necessary carried on an irregular trade between the half-dozen or so of the more populated islands.

But everything that he had always thought of as constituting the basics of civilized life before his stay in the Marquesas had vanished as definitively as if they had never been. Cars, jumbo pizzas, video cassettes, neatly packaged bottles of pills for whatever ailments trained doctors and technicians in white smocks diagnosed had long since disappeared, as well as all those things that had so recently begun to make life bearable on the atoll islands such as Takaroa.

Now there were no more motor-driven boats, or airplanes, or even radio communication between the islands. It was hard to believe that 200 thousand people who had been nearly as mechanized in their daily lives as most Americans could have allowed themselves to revert so quickly, and so complacently, to a way of life that could only be called primitive. The Polynesians he had met in the Marquesas had included engineers and airline pilots, as well as meteorologists and oceanographers and government administrators from the elite French schools for public officials. Surely when the forcefield had come down over Polynesia like an overturned bowl some of them must have been capable of applying their specialized knowledge to the rigors of their new life?

Not perhaps the bureaucrats, for who needed *them,* but what about the engineers and technicians who worked in the post office and ran the radio and telephone services? Was it conceivable that none of them had been able to ensure a functioning radio service between the islands? What did it take to make a radio work? Electricity of some sort, that much he knew. But, as he recalled, a local company even manufactured car batteries in Tahiti. If Tahitians could do *that,* couldn't they have found some way to generate the few watts of power it took to drive a small radio? Even if they could only transmit in Morse code, wouldn't that be better than nothing?

But perhaps, he finally told himself, they simply didn't care. Radio and television and drive-in movies and dental floss had only impinged upon them for a bare two generations. They had been happy enough and healthy enough for centuries without them. Perhaps as soon as it was clear there would be no more miracles of modern technology coming to them from across the seas they had thrown off all traces of the white man's civilization as easily as throwing away his tight-fitting leather shoes and long scratchy pants.

Or perhaps it had been simple indolence that kept them from trying to maintain some semblance of the life they had so briefly known.

Or a lack of raw materials.

Or the effects of cosmic rays passing through the glittering barrier of the forcefield. Maybe their very brain cells had been adversely affected. His own certainly seemed to be sluggish enough these days.

In any case, no one seemed to give a damn.

No more than he himself. . . .

Occasionally he saw the pitiful irony of his attitude, that of a man who was himself totally incapable of achieving any of the goals he so casually set for others. He shook his head bleakly at the sad folly of his white man's arrogance and returned to his contemplation of the billowing white rain clouds tinged with gray and blue that were moving in slowly across the breadth of the lagoon towards the village of Teavaroa and the fragile lean-to in which he sat, speckled by the pencil-thin shafts of golden sunshine that lanced through the roughly plaited leaves all around him.

But there were humble attributes to civilization that even he in his numbed state of consciousness was occasionally aware of missing. Items that he had never before paid attention to, because they had always simply *been* there, even in the tiny town of Hanavavé in the Marquesas, as remote a spot as anyone could hope to find on the face of the earth.

Toilet paper. Toothbrushes. Razor blades. Bath towels. Soap. Drinking glasses. Knifes, forks, spoons. Once embarked upon, the list was endless, and occasionally as he lay sleeplessly on his thin mat of plaited pandanus fronds he would try to enumerate them before sleep finally claimed him. But mostly he missed them only on those occasions when a lifetime's conditioning made him reach out automatically in search of one of them. For a startled moment, and sometimes even longer, he would be roused from his habitual state of apathy as he considered this particular small instance of his unending plight. But then with a faint sigh he would pick up whatever homemade artifact he was using in its place and the momentary spark of alertness would gutter and flicker out.

And yet Polynesians were far from being incompetent, he told himself, doggedly coming back to the question that continued to gnaw at him in spite of his general indifference to the circumstances of this strange new living death that held him in its thrall. Hadn't they conquered the vast distances of the Pacific, spreading across its thousands of miles of endless ocean and planting life on hundreds of its inhospitable islands, all within a few short generations?

Nor were they even particularly lazy, as they were so often characterized by exasperated outsiders. They could work tirelessly for days at a time at some job of physical labor such as chopping with homemade machetes at the encroaching jungle between their neat rows of coconut trees at a pace that would have left any manual laborer in Culver City gasping after a few minutes.

Perhaps, he told himself, haltingly trying to find the words in the befogged recesses of his mind, they were less indolent than merely apathetic. Perhaps they simply didn't care a hoot about all the lost glories of what they had once so briefly known.

It was only when he came to ask Vetea why he had been so ferociously threatened by what he now saw to be a community of eminently placid Polynesians that another dimension of the new reality in which he found himself began to unfold.

Like everything else, it was a consequence of the great sky-curtain that hung so inescapably above their lives.

"The French," said Vetea simply. "They're very bad. They want to kill all the Maohi, to make us their slaves. First they called the flickermen to Tahiti to make the sky-curtain, so that none of us could escape. Then they tried to keep us there as their slaves. When we resisted, they exiled us from Tahiti, which they keep to themselves and the flickermen. Who knows what marvels they retain for themselves? Perhaps the boats that fly and the boxes that talk. Someday they will attempt to use their marvels to enslave us all again. That is why we were angry when we first saw you. None of us have ever seen a white man, and it was only natural that we thought that you were a *farani,* come to do us some great harm."

"How very strange," murmured Ken. "You mean that all the Frenchmen inside the sky-curtain now live on Tahiti?"

Vetea nodded. "And all the Maohi have to live on the other islands. This is hardly fair. There are many, many islands, but there are many, many Maohi. There is only one Tahiti, but it is far larger and richer than all the other islands, and in any case the Frenchmen have stolen it away from us." He pursed his lips thoughtfully. "Someday we will take it back from them. And kill all the Frenchmen," he added equitably.

"Are there many Frenchmen, then?"

Vetea shrugged. "Who can say? No Maohi is allowed to set foot on Tahiti, on pain of death, or of being enslaved."

"That's hard to believe. When . . . where I . . . when I used to see Frenchmen and Tahitians, they were close friends. Many of them were married to one another. There were many —"

"Demis?" Vetea spat to one side. "Children of French and Maohi? Yes, I have heard there were many of them. They gave themselves airs and considered themselves superior to the Maohi." He smiled grimly. "Now there are only Maohi."

"Where are all the others? Or their descendants, I should say."

"Dead," said Vetea with simple satisfaction.

"You . . . killed all the *demis?*" Even for Ken the thought was troubling: there had been thousands of them, most of them as Westernized as himself; they were the officials who ran the government, the owners of the inter-island boats, the contractors who competed with the Chinese and French in the construction industry.

Vetea shrugged. "Who knows?" he said evasively. "Perhaps they all stayed on Tahiti with their friends the French when we Maohi were dispossessed and thrown into the ocean." He chuckled derisively. "If so, they have all had many years in which to repent their mistake."

"Why is that?"

"Who else could the French have made into their slaves? The Maohi refused, and left to live by themselves. Now we have a mighty empire, before which the French tremble and are unable to move from their pitiful refuge on Tahiti."

"An empire? We're part of an *empire,* here on *Takaroa?*" The notion seemed somehow comically absurd to Ken. Certainly there were no vestiges of imperial might or law here in the village of Teavaroa, where Vetea seemed to exercise what little authority obtained. Could a hundred kingdoms of Takaroa have banded together and proclaimed themselves an empire? For the first time in weeks he felt his oppression lighten at so ludicrous a notion.

Nor did Vetea seem overly impressed by the strictures of imperial sway. "It's called the Maohi Dominion" he said good-humoredly. "The capital, where the big chief lives, is the city of Uturoa, on Raiatea." He nodded his head indulgently. "I think."

There were so many contradictions and inconsistencies in Vetea's various accounts of the French devils and their fortress island that Ken's interest in the subject vanished once it had been clearly established there existed no miraculous gateway somewhere on the island of Tahiti through which one could step into the world beyond the sky-curtain.

For without such a gateway, of what conceivable interest was Tahiti and whatever the French slavers did there? He recalled the less than friendly attitude of the naval officers he had recently encountered in distant Rapa. As a man who had miraculously survived the furies of the sky-curtain, he might well be of interest to whatever scientists might now be living in Tahiti. As a rare specimen, he slowly told himself. Or a guinea pig. He remembered the fate of most guinea pigs.

No, it was far wiser to remain a discreet distance from whatever was going on in Tahiti. Here in Takaroa, at least, there was scant danger of the islanders cutting him to pieces to learn how his vital organs had survived their voyage through the forcefield and across the decades.

And even if he *could* move beyond the sky-curtain, he suddenly realized, what was there on the other side that would tempt him to make the effort?

Nothing but an unknown, desolate world in which Kristin had been dead for more than half a century.

He dismissed the half-considered notion as quickly as he had dismissed the garbled legends of Vetea and the other islanders. Kristin still existed, he knew, somewhere deep within himself, unchanging, ineradicable, eternally youthful, and would until the day he died. He did not have to travel beyond any sky-curtain to seek her out.

When the moment came to reclaim her he would know where to find her.

The Silumiuts' new home — or prison — had orbited Water's pale yellow sun more than a hundred times now since their arrival, and they were in little better shape than when they had arrived. Once they had learned the fatal dangers of trying to coalesce their fields with those of the Uglies their subsequent contacts had at first served to reinvigorate them almost as if the Uglies had been Yas'elda after all. But it soon became apparent that the effects were only transitory, and subsequent experimentation with the natives did nothing more than destroy a number of Uglies and hasten the decline of their own numbers. Already nineteen of the original company were in their last days, and seven had gone forever.

For years there had been constant talk of lifting the ship from Water and returning to the search for another world, but the same reasoning that had brought them to Water in the first place still obtained. There was no greater chance of salvation in further voyaging.

For a short while half-hearted attempts had been made to establish communication with the so aptly named Uglies, but the Silumiut could discover only incomprehension and hostility. It now seemed to have been a terrible mistake landing the ship on this tiny speck of land in the middle of the ocean instead of in some great urban center of obvious civilization. For obviously the natives of Home were incalculably more ferocious than those who inhabited the great landmasses they had earlier passed over. It had seemed logical at the time that there would be little to fear from the few inhabitants of an isolated island chain, but this logic was obviously faulty. The savage abruptness with which they had been attacked with the full fury of fusion arms had left them shaken. The forcefield itself had momentarily flickered and yielded before the totally unexpected blows, and it had taken years to restore it sufficiently to withstand any further attacks.

The natives had appeared far too primitive to possess such terrible weapons, but now the lesson was learned: grotesque and barbaric as they were, the Uglies must never again be underestimated. Before the attack it might have seemed feasible to lower the forcefield and make contact with those who inhabited the great cities of Water. Perhaps with them it would have been possible to establish communications and even bargain for their possible help.

But now the implacable hostility of the entire planet had to be assumed.

The Silumiuts' numbers continued to dwindle.

CHAPTER 12

It was many months before he saw a flickerman. That they still existed he knew from Vetea and the other islanders, who told long ribald stories concerning them and their spectacular roles in various of the Takaroans' erotic frolics. "Whatever they may be," said Vetea, "they appear to bring us no particular harm, unless the great sky-curtain itself is considered harmful in nature."

"Well, what good are they?" asked Ken irritably, shaken by this amiable dismissal of those hideous entities that had caused him such irreparable grief.

Vetea grinned slyly. "Best to ask the women of Teavaroa. They will tell you many tales of how the presence of a flickerman lent new vigor and rigidity to the wavering rods of the tired old men with whom they must seek to amuse themselves." His grin broadened and he laughed heartily, clearly excluding himself from the ranks of such fainthearted company.

Ken tried to smile, but a sharp pang of guilt shot through him as the words instantly recalled the long-repressed images of his own animal-like coupling with Kathie Leitner in the narrow bunk of the *Last One Left* while the twinkling glow of the flickerman danced in attendance. Seen now in the proper perspective, could anything have been more disgusting, more perverted even? And yet here was Vetea boasting of his encounters with the horrible phantasms! How could he bear to let them near him?

"So you say they do no harm then?" he demanded fiercely.

Vetea looked at him in surprise. "They do nothing but bring enhancement to some people's coupling. This can only be considered good. There are those who say that this is their way of encouraging the Maohi to couple more frequently and fervently, to bring forth great numbers of Maohi to populate the islands." He nodded sagely at the thought. "This would be in keeping with those who hold that the flickermen are the spirits of our former gods, come back to punish us for having once fallen into the ways of the *farani*."

"A strange sort of punishment," said Ken sourly.

Vetea acknowledged the justice of his comment. "The establishment of the sky-curtain was their initial punishment, that and our exile from Tahiti. Now they have decided the Maohi have suffered long enough and must reclaim their former lands. They are helping us by encouraging us to expand our numbers by much joyful coupling."

Ken sighed helplessly in the face of such subtle theological reasoning. "You say the flickermen visit Takaroa only rarely. What about all the flickermen that must be on Tahiti? Aren't they helping out the French with all *their* coupling? How do you know the French aren't producing many white children, to help them seize all *your* islands?"

Vetea frowned unhappily at this disturbing concept. "Certainly it is a joy to create children. Even without the flickermen it is no great difficulty. Perhaps on Tahiti it is the same." He reached down to choose a large green coconut from a pile of them beside Ken's shelter, and with three deft motions against a sharpened stake that protruded from the dirt ripped its thick husk from the hard brown nut inside. Several casual blows with a large stone broke open a neat round hole in the nut without spilling any of the cool clear liquid inside. He handed it to Ken, and began to open one for himself. "Or perhaps it is different. Nobody knows. Nobody has ever gone to Tahiti and returned to tell us what is there."

"Never?" repeated Ken skeptically.

Vetea's Adam's apple bobbed up and down as he drank deeply from the coconut. He cast it aside. "Never," he said firmly.

Within a few weeks he was vaguely aware of all the members of his new little world, the husky brown men and women, the toothless old grannies and grandpas, the hordes of swarming naked children. Within a few months he had names for all of them, and their individual characteristics were clear in his mind. His own identity varied. Sometimes he was Ken, a name easily pronounced in the local dialect, which happened to incorporate K's among its few consonants, and sometimes he was O Long White Sea Serpent, and its endless bawdy variations.

To the slight extent he was aware of the life of the community around him, he realized that as weeks and months passed he was becoming an object of even greater speculation than when he had first appeared so bizarrely among them. For his white skin and pale blond hair aroused far greater curiosity than he would have imagined possible, and he would occasionally start from a reverie to find to his discomfort one of the island girls or women running her hands dreamily through his hair.

The real object of their curiosity, he knew, was the Long White Sea Serpent, which had been discreetly kept from view since the initial moments of his arrival. Four or five times since he had moved into the tiny confines of his shelter behind Vetea's house he had had visitors during the night, giggling adolescent girls who were nothing more than dark shapes and questing hands and stifled entreaties in the darkness. The warmth of their smooth flesh was pleasant against his body, but the odor of coconut oil and homemade perfume was disagreeably strong in his nostrils. It was impossible to keep his mind from turning to the long-dead girls of

Fatu Hiva in the Marquesas and their still mysterious uses of fruits and flowers. And behind them, somewhere in the darkness, Kristin hovered like a vengeful living presence, so as he might shoo away overly frolicsome kittens, he would gently push the venturesome girls out into the night.

Two or three of their mothers came to try their luck, far more insistent in their use of hands and mouth, but after a few minutes in which he politely let them discover for themselves the impossibility of rousing his torpid sea serpent they too were expelled from his little home, disappointed and even more curious about the nature of this strange *popa'a* from beyond the sky-curtain.

"Did it unman you then, your journey from Rapa through the sky-curtain?" whispered a disappointed matron in the course of her second visit to his thin pandanus pallet, as she rubbed his unresponsive flesh between her hands. "You do not appear to be a *mahu* or *raerae*, although in this domain looks are sometimes deceptive."

Ken shook his head in the darkness. "No. I don't prefer boys. It's just that. . . ." A strange inspiration suddenly came to him. "It's just that the flickermen have stolen my manhood from me." He heard the soft intake of her breath. "How else do you imagine that they can so greatly augment pleasure, and stiffen the rods of those they watch and mingle with as they dally with beautiful Maohi women? How else except by stealing it from unfortunates such as myself?"

A soft moan of pity came from the woman who crouched beside him. She bent to fervently kiss his sea snake. "Will it ever come back?" she whispered. "Will the flickermen ever restore your manhood?"

"I don't know," he said, gently pulling her away from him. "It is painful for me to contemplate such a beautiful woman as you while I am reduced to such a state. This is why you must not return until I am well again." He squeezed her softly on the shoulder. "I will tell you when the time has come." As he heard the rustle of her tapa-cloth pareo being pulled around her, he murmured sleepily, "And tell all the others, would you? Tell them that they'll know when the time comes."

After that he was left to himself, and was scarcely aware of the hushed voices in his presence, and of the pitying looks that were occasionally directed at him by the sympathetic Takaroans. The next woman who attempted to entice him did so far more directly than any of the discreet islanders. This was Mama Tito, an enormously robust woman who could have posed for a portrait of any of the ancient queens of Hawaii or Tahiti. He was not surprised to learn that she was, in fact, descended from the last kings of Tahiti, the Pomarés, who formally ceded what little remained of their power to the French in the waning years of the nineteenth century.

She arrived by boat with a retinue of family and loyal followers, the first visitor to the island community since his own arrival so many blurry months before. The boat was a large doubled-hulled canoe that had something of the hand-carved appearance of the ancient war canoes Ken had seen pictures of in Kristin's books, but that owed its low sleek lines and carefully rigged sails to the long gleaming catamarans and tri-marans he had once seen crowding the yacht harbor in Papeete. A sturdy wooden cabin with a thatched roof was set squarely in the middle of the platform that joined the two hulls, half-hidden by a welter of naked children, squawking livestock in small bamboo cages, and great stores of food and water.

A dozen adult Polynesians improbably descended from the craft, like the endless sequence of clowns from the tiny car in the circus, and a like number from the two less-imposing single-hulled sailing craft that had accompanied it through the pass and into the sheltered waters of the lagoon.

Ken watched in awe as the great bulk of Mama Tito waddled down the gangplank and across the beach, where she enfolded first Vetea and then the other elders to the vastness of her bosom. She was draped in an enormous billowing robe of spotless white tapa cloth and had a round brown face that gleamed in the bright sunlight. Her jet-black hair was tied into a single long braid that fell down her back. As he watched her from the shadows of his little hut he thought that her loud joviality as she greeted the Takaroans and hugged them to her was mainly superficial. He had seen too many politicians on television before leaving the States to be greatly impressed, but as she moved slowly about the village he reluctantly admitted to himself that there was something about her pres-ence that was both commanding and regal. Could this, he wondered, be the queen of that shadowy Maohi Dominion of which the islanders were only dimly aware? For in spite of her great moon face, and the great bulges of flesh that heaved and rolled beneath her all-concealing white robes, she *looked* in all fairness a proper queen.

Another stupendous feast was ordained for that afternoon, in which most of the provisions that had painstakingly replenished since the dep-redations of his own were once again joyously depleted. Ken was no longer able to avoid meeting this redoubtable presence and her trailing retinue. As the man from beyond the sky-curtain he possessed in the Takaroans' eyes a prestige and importance far surpassing that of Mama Tito, and so was seated directly across from her on the long array of banana leaves that served as both table and seats.

As the interminable meal wore on and the torches began to glitter in the darkness Ken watched her stuff improbable amounts of food into her constantly moving jaws and learned little about her except of her royal descent from the line of Pomarés, and that she lived on the island of Raiatea, not far from where Tihoti Baxter sat as self-styled king and ruler of the Maohi Dominion.

As she conversed with Ken she constantly interrupted her remarks to shout jovial asides up and down the table, but her glittering little brown eyes were never far from his. He sipped his pineapple beer and coconut toddy cautiously while attempting to satisfy her curiosity about his life in the Polynesia that had existed in the days before the flickermen had so totaled disrupted it. Her questions were sharp and penetrating and, unlike those of Vetea and the other genial islanders, reflected an analytic intelligence that was sorting and categorizing, using the answer to one question to lead logically to the next as she tried to arrange everything he said into a single comprehensible sequence. "The French," she said. "Tell me about the French." He told her about the French until the torches guttered and the music was loud and raucous and he had to go off to relieve himself in the bushes.

As he stepped out of the concealment of the bushes another dark mass at his elbow suddenly moved towards him, startling him until he realized it had been the great bulk of Mama Tito standing motionlessly in the darkness. She reached out with her curiously small hand to grip him around the upper arm. "Come to my quarters on the ship," she said. "There we shall be alone. The others will be spending the night ashore."

The thought of being enfolded in those enormous arms, of being smothered between the great globes of those improbable breasts left him momentarily speechless. He knew that Polynesian men seemed to prefer their women plump, or even fat, but surely there must be limits! Was it possible that so gross a creature could harbor the same desires as more normal beings? Women such as —

He shook his head brusquely. "I'm sorry," he muttered. "I've been sick. There's . . . nothing I can do for you. It has to do with being thrown through the sky-curtain." He stepped back a pace, away from her small damp hand. "Someday when I . . . regain my forces perhaps."

He could feel the intensity of her gaze on him, even in the darkness. "There is a flickerman on board," she cajoled softly. "My personal flickerman. He will restore —"

"I think your personal flickerman has decided it's time to go exploring." Ken turned to point at a luminescent glow that was moving steadily across the beach and into the inky shadows of the houses beyond. Even from here he could see that in the century that had passed since he had last seen one of these creatures they had continued to evolve. Poor long-dead Kathie Leitner must have been right after all. The ghostly flickerman he had glimpsed passing in and out of the houses of the village was now obviously male. Limbs and torso were distinct, the proportions of the body were clearly masculine, and there even appeared to a blurry bulge at the junction of his thighs, like that of a ballet dancer in his skin-hugging tights.

"He will return when he sees us together," insisted Mama Tito. "Come. It will be like nothing you have ever known." She reached out to pull him against her.

Angrily he jerked away from her grasp. "Some other time, I said!"

"You really don't want to make love, you, me, and the flickerman?" she asked in tones of genuine surprise.

"No!" He started to turn away. "I can't!"

"Wait!" Her voice was still insistent, but its tone had suddenly changed. Now it was cordial, but business-like. "We have much to discuss, you and I . You are unique in all the world. Would you waste your time here among the numbskulls of Takaroa, whose only thoughts are of eating, fishing, and mindlessly coupling? Come with me to —"

There were muted giggles in the darkness just behind them, followed by the sounds of snapping branches and scampering feet. Mama Tito's attempt at seduction had been affording amusement to unknown numbers of Takaroa's youthful numskulls. By tomorrow, Ken knew, their conversation would be known to everybody in the village.

He smiled faintly and moved off into the shadows, leaving Mama Tito speechless behind him.

In the days that followed, Mama Tito spoke to him graciously whenever their paths chanced to cross, though impersonally and regally. Twice she asked him to share a meal with her party of voyagers so that they could further discuss the puzzles of the world he had left behind, and twice he reluctantly accepted. Three times he was asked, and at last frankly implored, by intermediaries to accompany her little group in their wanderings among the islands. "Mama Tito is a great woman," whispered the last of them softly. "Someday she will be the greatest in all of the Dominion. All of those who help her now will surely benefit!"

Ken smiled listlessly. "I see. Tell her I will consider the offer."

As the weeks passed Mama Tito and her crowd gathered with each of the islanders in turn, seeking — what? Votes? Allegiance? Religious converts? Political contributions? Ken was uninterested. The politics and dynastic struggles of the Maohi Dominion were affairs to be left to others. What did interest him though, after all these months of numbed half-consciousness, was what Mama Tito had called her personal flickerman.

Clearly it was no such thing, for though it may well have been her companion on her voyage, just as he and Kathie Leitner might once have been said to possess their own flickerman, now it was apparently content to remain ashore among the happily ruttish natives of Takaroa.

During the day, as the ghostly presence drifted serenely through the village, passing in and out of the walls of the buildings, all of the islanders frankly shied away from it. But as night fell and couples began to drift off to their homes or into the darkened bushes or the endless forest of coconuts, the flickerman's slow comings and goings provoked nothing but soft whispers and excited giggles.

It passed through his own hut one evening while he lay restlessly on his hard pallet, moving slowly through one of his low plaited walls and directly over his stomach on its way out the other. Tonight in the confines of his little hut it seemed more of a pale translucent gray than the blue he had remembered, flicked with streaks of what might be electrical discharges. Fear, hatred, and curiosity mingled in almost equal parts as he shrank back from its sedate progression over his outstretched body. Before it slowly vanished, leaving him once again in darkness, he noticed that its face was blurrily shaped in the form of human features, and that a distinct outline of male genitals hung between its legs.

Roused from any further hopes of sleep, he climbed to his feet, and, as naked as the flickerman, stepped out into the night. The pale glow was not far away, drifting slowly into the black mass of the forest. The moon was low in the sky, and there were no villagers about that he could see. He followed a dozen yards behind without trying to analyze his motives for his strange behavior.

The flickerman moved with impunity through bushes and trees, while Ken had to stumble around them as best he could with only the faint cold light cast by the flickerman to aid him. As it moved deeper into the forest it appeared to be taking on a deeper intensity, in which the gray was first shot through with elements of blue, and then nearly eclipsed by it. Fascinated now by the progress of this glowing blue creature a stately eighteen inches from the ground, he walked suddenly into a coconut trunk, smashing his forehead painfully.

He reeled back, with bright stars and circles and colored motes of light dancing in his vision. A patch of dazzling violet moved across his eyes and as his head whirled in his hands he unexpectedly recalled what Kristin had once told him about a discredited madman named Reich and his bizarre theory of orgasm energy. No, *orgone* energy, though it was hard to remember the difference. Orgone energy, if he had understood Kristin right, was the basis of all sexual energy, and, although this part was harder to understand, it somehow possessed a color. The color of an orgone was blue, the same blue that colored the ocean, and thunderheads, and the very sky itself. Ken had never understood how a color could also be responsible for sexual energy as well as such things as static electricity, but Kristin had told him there were still a surprising number of people who believed in Reich's zany concept.

As his eyes cleared, and he looked ahead to find the flickerman motionless among the trees some distance ahead, its clear blue glow now pulsing and throbbing distinctly, he asked himself if old Reich might not have been correct all along. For as he moved silently through the undergrowth he knew what he would find: the flickerman in attendance to a couple making love.

He knew that was he was doing was shameful, but he felt himself pulled forward by the same urgency that seemed to propel the flickerman. It was only when he heard the grunts of pleasure and effort that he stopped and concealed himself behind a coconut tree. Before him, in a tiny clearing lit only by the illumination of the flickerman, three of the island's pimply youths were taking their turns with a plump laughing matron at least three times their age. The hovering flickerman was glowing intensely now, and had moved forward to position himself directly over the couple on the ground, as apparently intent on their activity as the two naked boys who stood to either side of the woman's outspread hair, erect organs in their hands.

The youth who knelt between her uplifted knees was making hoarse gasping noises now, and, at last abashed, Ken backed cautiously away from the clearing, then turned and made his way slowly through the night to his hut. His loins were tingling for the first time in months, and his mind was filled with grotesque images of Kristin coupling in a frenzy with a half a dozen Marquesan youths. What would *she* have made of the flickermen and their extraordinary ability to enhance the act of love?

He reached his shelter and stretched out on his mat of plaited pandanus. His eyes closed, and he clearly saw Kristin's naked form, and then himself naked, and thrusting into her. And then the two of them bathed in the glow of a hovering flickerman, throbbing and expanding, a bright sparkling blue, augmenting and intensifying the already almost overwhelming glory of their lovemaking.

He felt his body begin to stir, and hesitantly reached down to touch his stiffening flesh.

Unhappily, almost against his will, he knew that he had at last rejoined the living.

CHAPTER 13

Only two weeks after the departure of Mama Tito and her entourage a number of sails were spotted on the horizon far to the west. Several hours later three large trimarans glided cautiously through the pass in front of the village of Teavaroa and anchored a few feet off shore in the sheltered lagoon. To Ken's astonishment, the villagers were nearly frantic with excitement at the sight of the three boats. They gathered along the shore and shouted and waved until the boats were stationary, then waded out through the shallow water until they could pull themselves on board. Could this be the almost legendary king, Tihoti Baxter, come to visit to his loyal subjects? he wondered. If so, his full name must surely be Tihoti the Well-Beloved.

The answer was initially less dramatic. "Arioi!" cried a young girl who was leaning against Ken's leg, her pudgy little hand wrapped around his index finger. "It's the Arioi!"

As he watched the crew of the three boats slowly disembark, he turned the word over in his mind. Arioi, Arioi. . . . Dimly he remembered something about the Arioi from one of Kristin's books. What could it be. . . ?

At least a hundred people eventually came ashore from the ships, all of them with fine bodies and of striking allure. Ken was struck by the almost uniform beauty of the women, whatever their size and age, and by the careful grooming and clean-cut looks of all the men. The Arioi were loud and boisterous and given to quick banter and easy laughter. There were a dozen or so small naked children among them, but after a while he noticed that unlike Mama Tito's entourage there was no one among them who was old, or even middle-aged.

Each trimaran had a large central structure, with the same jumble of animals and goods around it as on Mama Tito's craft. Grinning, he watched half a dozen dogs of mixed ancestry leap into the warm waters of the lagoon and frantically paddle ashore, where they quickly began to dispute the rights of the territory with the startled dogs of Teavaroa. The sleek feline forms of black and white cats stalked angrily back and forth across the boats, ignoring both the squawks and cries of the caged chickens and pigs and the three or four roosters that perched above them in the rigging.

While the islanders gathered around eagerly and the level of noise rose quickly, the Arioi began to spread out brightly colored tapa cloths on the smooth green lawn in the center of the little village. Bundles of tied-up banana leaves and baskets of woven pandanus were brought ashore and a small assortment of trade goods produced from within. These were laid out on the tapa cloth and the handsome men and women from the ships were soon exhorting the villagers to examine their wares.

Ken stepped forward and moved slowly through the crowd, wonderingly examining the strange miscellany that was offered by the Arioi. There were hundreds of multi-colored shells — cowries, augers, and conches, all neatly laid out in semi-circles, in ascending orders of color and size. There was a single leather boot, cracked and moldy and looking as if it might be five centuries old rather than merely one, but nevertheless a man's left boot. There was a pair of gleaming stainless-steel scissors carefully mounted in black mother-of-pearl shell handles. There was a portable Hitachi television with a cracked nine-inch screen, a number of moldering books in French, English, and Spanish, four metal balls for playing *pétanque,* a double-breasted blue serge suit that must have already been ancient when the sky-curtain descended, and several dozen rusty mechanic's wrenches.

Ken smiled and moved on to the next display. This was more practical, consisting of hundreds of fishhooks and knives made from various bones, shells, and teeth, all carefully crafted and murderously sharp. The three Polynesian men and two plump women who were tending the display looked up in astonishment. He half-turned to peer over his shoulder before he remembered the apparent uniqueness of his appearance.

A great cry went up from two of the men, and in a few seconds he had become the center of attention for all the Arioi. Hands fondled his arms and shoulders, now tanned a soft honey color but still far lighter than those of any who surrounded him, and reached out to touch the locks of hair that tumbled to his shoulders, bleached almost white by the sun and salt water.

Among the dozens of chattering women he noticed three or four who were tall and slim, two of them with a hint of the almond eyes that denoted a mingling of Chinese blood. They were all lovely, but far too skinny he supposed for the tastes of most of his Polynesian compatriots. They smiled flirtatiously when they saw his eyes on them, and he smiled back involuntarily. They were really awfully young, he saw now, sixteen or seventeen at the most. Perhaps they simply hadn't had the time to grow fat yet. . . .

For a moment a bizarre thought came to him: what would it be like to love such a beautiful young creature, living aboard a boat and traveling slowly from island to island in a timeless and endless process of bartering goods and gossip?

The bizarre notion was somehow so disturbing that to banish it he abruptly pushed his way through the crowd that still surrounded him and stalked off half-angrily into the plantation of coconut trees that crowded against the village's edge. But why should I be angry? he asked himself wonderingly, as he reached the cool shade of the gently swaying trees.

And at whom?

Myself?

Those pretty girls?

Why should the sight of a pretty face so upset him?

Oh Kristin, can't I even *look* at another face?

There was no communal feast to celebrate the arrival of the Arioi, for the island's larders had not yet begun to recover from the ravages incurred by the party in honor of Mama Tito, and to suddenly feed a hundred additional mouths would be to strain the limits of even Polynesian hospitality. So the Arioi slaughtered some of the livestock they had brought with them, and some they had traded for only a few hours before, and joined their cooking pots to those that the Takaroans were stirring on the fires scattered throughout the village.

While the women tended to the cooking, the men, aided by Vetea and fifty of the villagers, had quickly demolished a number of *bourau* trees for their long straight branches, and had begun to construct a startling number of small shelters in the shade of the coconut trees. Fresh green coconut fronds were floated down from the towering trees and swiftly plaited into flimsy but effective roofs and walls. From where he sat hunkered in his own tiny shelter, Ken shook his head in admiration at their quickness and dexterity: within a few hours an entire little village had been constructed.

The final meal of the day was finished by late afternoon and now the Arioi became busy with a different set of preparations. Against the edge of the coconut trees they began to construct from already prepared sections what appeared to be the backdrop and wings of a wide open-air stage. Large light panels of painted tapa cloth and plaited pandanus were moved back and forth, and torches carefully arranged. The panels were painted with stylized representations of tikis, flowers, animals, and fish in the midst of intricate networks of flowing lines. Fresh flowers and bright green banana leaves and coconut fronds were draped around the flambeaux posts and hung to the side wings. As he watched the Arioi carefully unpack costumes from great wooden trunks, he gradually began to recall vague memories of what he had read about them so long a lifetime before.

There had been much about the Arioi in Kristin's books, but all that he now remembered was that they were a strange mixture of traveling minstrel show combined with religious sect. They moved freely about the islands of the archipelago, independent of all local castes and tabus, carrying out elaborate religious ceremonies and putting on equally elaborate shows of dancing and singing. What was intriguing about the Arioi, he now recalled, was that the shows they put on, evidently for entire communities, were universally called by the European writers of the times grossly indecent or even outrageously obscene.

He scratched the rough stubble of his chin that he seldom bothered to shave more often than once a week, given the nature of the homemade implements he was forced to use. Arioi had long since disappeared when he first came to the Marquesas. In fact, he supposed, they must have been among the first of the local customs to be suppressed by the various missionaries who had descended on Tahiti like a cloud of vultures during the nineteenth century. It was hard to imagine what could be more distasteful to a dedicated missionary than a pagan sect that incorporated explicit sex into its cavorting. He grinned faintly. Was it possible that this revised traveling carnival that called itself Arioi might in any way be like its long-suppressed ancestors?

He rose to his feet. The Graumann's Chinese Theater of Takaroa was about to put on its initial evening performance. As he strolled across the village he remembered what he thought he might have glimpsed for a moment in the angry blaze of the midday sun — two or three almost imperceptible forms of transparent flickermen fluttering like heat waves above the motionless trimarans of the Arioi. Was it likely there would flickermen accompanying the Arioi unless there was something unusual enough to hold their interest? He felt the now familiar tingle begin to spread though his thighs and abdomen. It looked like it might be a surprising evening.

It was even more surprising than he had expected. For there was nothing at all about the ensuing three-hour spectacle except for an abundance of gleaming bare breasts that could have offended the sensibilities of even the most straitlaced Baptist. Overhead the moon glimmered blurrily through the faint gray glow of the sky, while around the makeshift stage dozens of torches burned yellow and orange, casting dark black shadows across the dimly lighted backdrop. To a great beating of tom-toms and wooden drums a long procession of female dancers began to wind their way through the crowd. Long grass skirts bleached a delicate white hung from the sides of their wildly rotating hips. Their gleaming brown torsos and breasts were bare, and their arms were held straight before them as they snaked across the grass to the pounding rhythms. Straight black hair dangled down their bare backs, circled by broad headbands of shell and tapa that held fluffy red and white plumes that towered far above their heads.

They were followed by the men of the troupe carrying musical instruments and wearing nothing more than a garland of flowers about their heads and clean white pareos knotted about their hips. The ear-splitting racket of their wooden drums — logs of varying sizes carved into what looked like miniature canoes and pounded with a variety of implements — seemed to throb to the primitive beat of something deep within him, and he felt his loins stir in response.

For the rest of the evening the troupe danced, sang, and pranced while the islanders clapped loudly and roared their approval. The women darted back and forth for frequent changes of costume, while the men remained clad in their skimpy loincloths. None of their subsequent dances were any more overtly erotic than the free-wheeling *tamuré* at which Kristin had been so expert, and most were sedate and stylized movements that involved much slow swaying of hips and arms while a hundred voices joined in sweet song. The music was often that of the old church hymns or *himénés* he had enjoyed listening to in Fatu Hiva, with great swelling rhythms that surged and receded like the ocean's waves.

In mid-performance a dimly glowing flickerman drifted slowly out of the night to hover motionlessly in the midst of the dancers while the Takaroans whispered and pointed. Five of the muscular Arioi musicians immediately surrounded the flickerman, jumping wildly as they grimaced menacingly and thrust their carved wooden drums at it in gestures of scorn and derision. The flickerman ignored their antics and was shortly joined by a second, and then a third. These, Ken could see at once, were females, smaller, rounder, and with swelling hips and breasts.

With great whoops and terrible faces the Arioi leapt forward to swing their improvised clubs through their insubstantial bodies as if they were dealing deadly karate blows. The three flickermen remained apparently unheedful even as they suffered countless decapitations, but at last they moved off as sedately as they had entered, disappearing through the backdrop to the accompaniment of hoots and jeers. The musicians shook their fists at the departed specters, and gleefully invited the Takaroans to applaud them for their courage and expertise in dispatching these fearsome monsters. . . .

It was, reflected Ken later, quite a show for the price, which in his case had been negotiated down to three small shells, two white augers and a shiny green trochus. The aftermath had been also been amusing to watch for a short spell, as the islanders brought forth beer and coconut toddy and, male and female alike, openly attempted to woo the handsome half-naked Arioi, whose gleaming skins glittered like ancient gold in the orange glow of the flaming torches. Playfully but artfully the Arioi resisted their advances, thirstily gulping the proffered enticements, but coquettishly declining any invitation to move into the shadows or darkened houses. Ken had only watched from the sidelines, but he understood the islanders' impulses — during the show it had been hard to keep his eyes from two or three of the tall svelte dancers and their high conical breasts and small dark nipples.

The next day he took a small pirogue and paddled alone far into the center of the lagoon, where he cast a line unsuccessfully for fish. Behind him he could barely see the tops of the coconut trees that skirted the village of Teavaroa where the Arioi had once again set up their display of goods. He shook his head. What would Kristin give to be able to see this strange new world!

What *he* would give to have her present. . . .

When he returned that afternoon he found the Arioi at work setting up their stage again, this time with backdrops that were painted to represent definite scenes: the inside of a stylized Tahitian home; a beach with several pirogues drawn up on it; what might have been the inside of a passenger jet. And a tall bamboo fence was being unrolled in a semi-circle around the area the audience had occupied the night before. He raised his eyebrows. Last night must have the preliminaries; tonight was the main event. But what was so special about tonight's show that it needed a fence around it? Hype to jack up the price of admission, he told himself.

He was at least right about the price. It was definitely more expensive. Ken shrugged good-naturedly — he had nothing left to barter in any case — and turned away. There was nothing to prevent him from at least listening to the music from a few dozen yards away. He was stopped by Vetea, who handed him a bunch of large taros tied together. "Here," he said. "A gift for my friend the Skinny White Sea Serpent. Use it to watch the entertainment. Tonight you will find it different."

Different it was. There were short skits of comedy and buffoonery, some in pantomime, some in dance, others with dialogue that reminded him of television situation comedies. The slapstick was broad and rowdy, and provoked great roars of laughter from the islanders, who appeared to be there in their entirety, along with all of their infants and children. The comedy skits were interspersed by acrobats and jugglers who were surprisingly skillful, particularly two bare-breasted girls who tossed a dozen flaming torches back and forth so quickly that it looked as if a burning chariot wheel was turning in the air.

These were songs and dances of a livelier, earthier nature than those of the night before. As the evening wore on he noticed that bare breasts were more and more prominent in the sketches, that the skirts the girls wore were becoming shorter and less concealing, and that round na-ked behinds were occasionally visible as the Arioi leaped and cavorted through their routines.

At last the backdrops representing the interior of a Maohi household were pulled into place. A short skit ensued in which one of the lovely young girls he had admired the night before vainly attempted to escape from her parents' vigilance to meet her boyfriend, who implored her with broad gestures through the open windows. At last the parents fell asleep and as the girl lay pretending to sleep her boyfriend climbed stealthily in through a window.

Ha! thought Ken, *motoro,* the national sport of Polynesia, as Kristin had called it. Evidently it hadn't changed in the last century. But as the boy sneaked cautiously across the stage, Ken felt his heart give a sudden lurch: the boy was entirely naked, and possessed of an large erection.

He glanced around at the audience of Takaroans. They were whistling and clapping, and shouting good-natured remarks. Whatever the Arioi were up to, it seemed to be acceptable to the islanders. He turned back to the skit, to watch the boy slowly caress the sleeping girl until she awoke and sat up to seductively remove the small skirt she wore. He had just begun to couple with her, kneeling before her with her long slender legs raised against his thighs, when the girl's father awoke and with an angry shout leaped at the boy with an ornately carved wooden club. His organ waving frantically, the boy ran across the stage and leapt through an open window, closely followed by the furious father. A moment later the abandoned daughter, weeping loudly, climbed out through the window too, leaving her plump but attractive mother sitting on her sleeping mat, shaking her head in bewilderment.

To enormous roars of approval from the Takaroans the handsome young boy reappeared from the other side of the stage, his organ as rigid as when he had so precipitously jumped through the window. A finger held to his lips, he carefully tiptoed across the stage until he had reached the wide-eyed matron. A moment later she had pulled away her pareo and was kneeling on her mat while he thrust into her powerfully from behind.

The rest of the show was just as blatantly sexual, and it was not long before Ken noticed that first one, and then another, of the flickermen had unobtrusively drifted into the corners of the stage. His eyes moved from them back to the two couples who were now demonstrating complex and unlikely positions of love-making. These were obviously the same couples who had earlier appeared as acrobats, and with a wistful sigh Ken realized that he would never be able to contort himself into such improbable positions as they were modeling with such ease.

The wooden drums and tom-toms were beating faster now, in a steadily mounting rhythm that was keeping time to the quickening thrusts of the two males. The two flickermen were now joined by two others, and the four of them slowly drifted across the stage, their forms pulsing and sparkling with blue light. The drums had reached a frenzy and Ken felt his own stiffness pressing uncomfortably against his coarse tapa pareo. The harsh strident drums seemed to be pounding directly upon his brain, so fast there was hardly a pause between beats. The two couples on stage writhed and twisted in passion, their hips a blur of violent movement, their gleaming bodies an eerie cold blue in the glow of the flickermen who had converged around them. At last, just as Ken thought he could stand it no longer, there was tremendous crash of drums and then a sudden dead silence, broken only by the ecstatic wail of one of the girls on stage. The flickermen, two males and two females, glowed even more brightly, while sparks of miniature lightning seemed to ripple and flash throughout their forms. A few moments longer and the two couples broke apart, the men still massively rigid, and with happy waves to the audience ran quickly to the wings. The show was over.

Now began the real bartering, as the items of genuine value the islanders had cached away were brought forth: an intricately carved narwhal's tooth, a small pearl, a cracked shaving mirror, a length of stainless steel radio antenna, a stunningly complex headband of thousands of colored shells painstakingly arranged to imitate a dozen different flowers. All of these, and dozens of other items ranging from a small blue glass jar to a superbly crafted piece of ironwood for pounding tapa cloth, were offered to the grinning men and women of the Arioi. As one by one they disappeared into the night with the islanders Ken began to hear loud cries of passion from the depths of the forest and the islanders' modest homes. The blue glow of the flickermen was everywhere now as the four of them separated and moved quickly in and out of the shadows, disappearing through walls and reappearing a few minutes later on the other side of the building in quest of yet another couple.

His mind a tortured jumble of conflicting emotions, Ken watched the lively bargaining for a quarter of an hour, then despondently began to make his way slowly back to what must now be considered his home. Perhaps in the morning, he told himself, he would see to building himself better lodgings. Now that he had finally shaken off his months-long lethargy, he could no longer —

He felt a hand tug at his elbow, and he turned to find himself looking into the eyes of one of the lithe young Arioi who had so captivated him. A powerful surge of lust coursed through him as he saw that it was the same girl who had appeared in the first of the pornographic skits. She wore only a small skirt, and the dark nipples of her firm conical breasts were only inches away from his own bare chest. She was tall, he saw, nearly as tall as Kristin, but with swelling hips, and her large dark eyes were warm and inviting. She smiled, and pulled him towards her. "Come," she said softly.

He moved involuntarily towards her, unable to keep his hands from impulsively grasping the smooth mounds of her breasts. But as he touched her flesh the images of his terrible coupling with Kathie Leitner suddenly flooded him, that mindless fucking that had led so directly to his catastrophic removal to this island and the subsequent death of Kristin. He stood rooted in an agony of indecision, unable to tear his hands from the girl's yielding flesh and return to his shack. She made no move to remove his hands.

"I have nothing to offer you," he muttered at last.

"Your chief has told us about you." She raised her right hand to clasp it against his, and push it hard against her breast. "You are the chosen one of the flickermen, who are the special mentors and companions of the Arioi." Her hand squeezed his. "Come, let us see what manner of man you are."

He felt great beads of sweat breaking out on his forehead. He had opened his mouth to at last repulse her, for Kristin's sake, when the image of Kristin's own animal-like coupling with her Marquesan lovers, so totally like the behavior of the Arioi themselves, suddenly raised him to such a pitch of erotic fervor that his knees began to tremble. He raised his quivering hand to her face and ran it across the warm smooth skin of her cheeks. Her lips half-opened to gently mouth the side of his index finger.

"Yes," he whispered at last, hoping that Kristin, wherever she might be, was unable to hear him.

She drew him into the forest and they coupled beneath the trees, with the ghostly forms of flickermen coming and going about them. He had never made love to a Polynesian before and so was a stranger to their ways, but she was supremely adroit, and after he had flooded her with a sudden initial outpouring that was torn from him almost the moment he entered her and she had clenched him with her incredible muscles she led him on to climax after climax until at last with a female flickerman pulsing and glowing all about them they came together with an intensity so all-embracing and overwhelming that as he lay gasping, his entire body as taut and rigid as if he had been flooded with high voltage current, he felt his head swirl and his limbs begin to melt, and for the first time in his life he tumbled unconscious in a dead faint.

When he opened his eyes sometime later he felt the soft warmth of the girl lying against his chest. Her large almond eyes were inches away from his.

"Yes," whispered Hina gravely. "The flickermen approve of you. Perhaps you are their son after all."

It was Tre'ze who first came across the Ugly whose entire field was somehow different. For decades now he had been wandering listlessly between the outlying islands, preferring the relative solitude of the lives of the islanders to the more complex patterns of life that existed on Home, where the Riestu still remained high in the mountains.

At first glance the Ugly seemed startlingly like the pale-maned native he had known shortly after they had come to Water, but a moment's thought showed this to be clearly impossible. That Ugly had long since been terminated, thrown for unknown reasons by his fellow Uglies into the deadly furies of the forcefield. Could he possibly have survived? Of course not. But there was, he supposed, no reason why this present Ugly might not be a descendant of that other one — that might explain the striking resemblance.

Even when the Ugly was not engaged in the mating ritual the pattern of his spectrum was not only different — it was also startlingly powerful. There was an almost tangible quality of reassurance and spiritual balm about it, an overall sense of tightly controlled energy that seemed almost . . . almost . . . purposeful? Nothing like this had ever been encountered in any of the other Uglies, and it was certainly far different from the field possessed by a healthy symbiote. But strange as this one was, somehow it almost smelled right.

CHAPTER 14

A timeless year or more passed as Ken Camden and the Arioi meandered languidly from island to island in their great trimarans, entertaining, edifying, trading their goods, bartering their sexual favors. Twice they recruited new members from among the young and particularly beautiful; three times they left behind one of their own. For male or female, any former Arioi was instantly welcomed into the community of any of the small islands they visited.

Ken himself had been enlisted because he was reasonably handsome, white without being *farani,* endowed with his startling blond hair, and in all probability either crazy or possessed of a superior type of mana. Either eventuality made him an interesting addition to the troupe.

Or so he told himself as at last his final inhibitions sloughed off like a discarded snake's skin to join all those other vanished customs and attitudes that had once defined his life. He awoke one day to take stock of his situation and clearly saw there was now no longer anything at all to distinguish him from any of the other members of this strange community he had chosen to join.

Ken Camden an Arioi? He shook his head at the wonder of the notion. Never had it been his intention to efface the inner core of his being, to transform the essential Ken Camden that was himself, rather than merely accompanying the Arioi on their endless round of travels. . . .

But what else could you call someone who lived with them, slept with them, spoke their language and followed their customs, and even, finally, joined them in their shows and orgies of commercialized sex?

That had been the hardest part, learning to barter his favors among the island women for trifling objects that once he would have laughingly spurned. Though he was probably far too skinny by local standards, he realized soon enough that he was avidly sought after by a surprising number of women of all ages. He sometimes wondered if the few he chose to actually couple with ever felt an obscure disappointment at the performance of this son of the flickermen, for though he was frequently joined by one or another of the four flickermen who seemed a permanent part of their floating community, he knew that however vigorously he discharged his side of the bargain he could never surmount a reserved detachment that seemed to make him as much a spectator as a participant. But still, he told himself, he heard no complaints, from either the complaisant islanders or the more demanding Arioi with whom he sometimes shared his body. But then — who would dare address a grievance to a supposed son of the flickermen?

He sighed unhappily. Pretentious sentiments, he knew, for someone who had chosen the path of whoredom, whatever else his new companions the unfettered Arioi might choose to call it. . . .

It was, surprisingly, far easier participating in their X-rated shows than coldly selling himself to the highest bidder. Although he now cavorted in ways he would have once have thought impossible, he discovered he enjoyed the innocent fun of the good-natured comedy skits, however bawdy or even obscene they eventually became. Deprived of so much else of what the world could offer, this was how Polynesians now chose to order their lives, and it seemed harmless enough in comparison to what he remembered of most of the outside world before the sky-curtain had suddenly fallen. And in any case, although he had certainly been implored to often enough, he had still not sunk to the point of actually making love on stage before hundreds of people. To do that, he supposed, it was not enough to *be* Arioi, you had to be *born* Arioi.

Or was he merely being hypocritical? he wondered. What was the difference between selling himself in private and displaying himself in public? It didn't seem to offend him to declaim nonsense in English, or lead the audience in a sing-along, or even to play the role of a French buffoon stupefied by the superior sexual prowess of Maohi men in a new skit that quickly became an audience favorite. In fact, he hardly noticed any longer that as he mouthed his lines and mugged and grimaced and capered about the stage, as many as six handsome couples might be making love practically beneath his feet.

Perhaps one day he too would find himself among them. For hadn't *he* once wanted to be an actor, beloved by millions? Hadn't he at least *once* considered participating in a porno flick, back in that part of his life which now seemed like a dream? He grimaced wryly. Perhaps it was here, a hundred years in his future, and 4,000 miles away, that he was at last ready to fulfill his *true* destiny.

As he lay on deck staring up at the eternal pearly gray that had replaced the dark starry skies of his earlier life he asked himself with a pang what Kristin would have made of it all. . . .

"But where do you live?" he had asked, even as he made up his mind to bid farewell to Vetea and the island community of Takaroa forever.

The Arioi had looked at him in astonishment. "Live? Why, here on our boats! Where else would Arioi live?"

That was true, of course, but it was equally true they spent at least as much time, or even more, ashore on the various islands to which their leisurely journeying carried them. For the past two or three years now they had been making their way randomly up and down the long chain of atoll islands that composed the Tuamotus. These varied in size from tiny islets of a few acres in extent and incapable of supporting more than the most marginal of existence for a handful of people, to the great circular reefs such as Rangiroa, in whose enormous central lagoon all of Tahiti could have been submerged.

He learned that of the hundreds of islands in an archipelago that stretched for nearly a thousand miles from east to west there were only three or four dozen that were populated, though even this was more than in the final days before the coming of the flickermen and the sky-curtain.

"Many, many of these islands were reinhabited after the *faranis* seized Tahiti," explained Tamuela, a wiry curly-haired Arioi not much older than Ken who in rank seemed at least the equal of any of the other half dozen men and women who composed the governing council that ruled the three boats.

"Is it true that the French tried to turn all the Maohi into slaves?"

"Is that what you learned on — where did we find you, Takaroa?"

"It was never made very clear. The only thing that *was* clear was that Takaroans didn't like the French."

Tamuela laughed condescendingly. He had a seafarer's traditional scorn for the ignorance and backwardness of all landlubbers. "I'm sure none of them could tell you *why* they dislike the French."

"Can *you?*"

"Ah!" Tamuela grinned broadly, proud of his cunning in avoiding so wily a trap. "But I *don't* dislike the French." He sketched an airy gesture. "After all, I'm Arioi. What are the French to *me?*" He snapped his fingers loudly. "Nothing. Less than nothing. How can I be bothered to dislike them?" And laughing loudly at his own cleverness he sauntered forward to where the prow of the central hull was cleaving smoothly through the gently rolling waves that separated the islands of Taenga and Raroia.

Ken shook his head at his own foolishness. Tamuela was right. Why should he care about the French, and the reasons for their enmity with the other Polynesians? Wasn't he now an Arioi, far above all such pedestrian concerns?

But Tamuela and the other Arioi were not always as unhelpful, and as the islands drifted by one after the other with the same languid monotony as the days and weeks and months, he learned a little here, a little more there, until he had at last built up a general picture that, he was surprised to see, more or less coincided with what Vetea had once told him in so many contradictory ways.

He himself, he knew, had witnessed the last days of the islands' brief fling with the Western way of life, as well as the harbingers of what was to come. For however strict the rationing of whatever stocks of gas and aviation fuel were on hand when the forcefield had suddenly appeared, sooner or later they would have been expended, by simple evaporation if nothing else. So no more cars, no more planes.

Could the French navy have managed to fire up its oil-burning boilers with charcoal or dried coconut husks? He snorted at the image. It seemed highly unlikely. So no more navy.

Which would have left several thousand French soldiers, sailors, and civilian technicians little more to do than eat their way through those supplies they had stored away and guard whatever nuclear devices might have been stockpiled on Mururoa for testing.

Had those weapons finally been used against the flickermen's screen or the mother ship in the mountains high above Papeete? he wondered. None of the Arioi knew. Yes, almost certainly they would have been eventually exploded, he decided, as the months passed and the supplies of imported food and wine finally dwindled to nothing, and the government stopped issuing paychecks to the many thousands of people, both Tahitian and French, who depended on Paris one way or another for their income, and mounting fear and desperation more than outweighed any lingering caution.

For in any case the military were now the rulers of Tahiti, and to the military mind an obstacle existed only to be blasted at until it finally ceased to be an obstacle.

So Ken was certain that whatever horrendous weapons Mururoa was capable of supplying must at last have been used, with no more discernable effect upon the flickermen and their sky-curtain than the Arioi's mugging and grimacing when they were fortunate enough to have a flickerman drift on stage during the course of their performances.

And having once laid its heavy hand upon the islands, it now seemed as if the military and its generations of descendants had ever after refused to lift it.

And in a few short years after Ken Camden had disappeared into the maelstrom of the forcefield high in the mountains of Rapa, they had acted to turn Tahiti into their private fiefdom.

The Chinese, he gathered, had been the first to go. Originally they had been brought to Tahiti as coolie labor during the American Civil War to work in the cotton fields that a few incorrigible optimists had planted as supplies of Southern cotton began to dwindle. In the years that followed the collapse of the cotton boom they first became the island's truck gardeners and then little by little its merchant class.

He tried to imagine what all of the shops and boutiques in downtown Papeete, as well as the grocery stores that circled the island, had done when at last their stocks of imported goods were exhausted and there were no more to come. Ten thousand suddenly idle Chinese must have looked increasingly superfluous to the 200 thousand Tahitians who had always harbored distinctly mixed feelings about the clannish, ambitious strangers from the Celestial Empire. Did the Tahitians join the French in gathering up all those Chinese who refused to docilely pick up their spades and hoes and return to the fertile soil of the valleys and mountain slopes? Or had they only acquiesced in a decision made by others more ruthless than themselves?

He would probably never know. But in any case the Chinese were herded together and eventually resettled on the island of Makatea 130 miles to the north of Tahiti. A mesa-like island with sheer cliffs that thrust suddenly out of thousands of fathoms of water, its flat hot surface had once been mined for rich deposits of phosphate. When the phosphate had played out some years before the arrival of the flickermen, the mines had been abandoned as well as the settlements of wooden barracks that had housed the workers and their families. Now, he imagined, they must be teeming with whatever was left of the descendants of those French citizens unfortunate enough to have born with a different shape of eye.

"Do you ever go to Makatea?" he asked the Arioi girl who had singled him out on Takaroa with such devastating effect.

Hina shook her lovely head and stared at him with that expression of baffled exasperation she used when he proved himself more ignorant than might be expected even of a *popa'a* from beyond the sky-curtain. "To sleep with *tinitos?*" she said distastefully. "Never!"

"Tinitos used to be very rich," he teased, remembering the streets of Papeete clogged with Mercedes driven by chic young Chinese men and women.

Offended, she rose petulantly to her feet and stalked angrily away, her firm round bottom swaying gracefully as she walked. Ruefully he watched her slim brown back disappear around the side of the trimaran's central structure. Tahitians really had very little sense of humor, he reminded himself.

Nor did it seem they had very much of their island either. With the Chinese removed from the picture the French and Tahitians were now free to work out their grievances upon each other. A large number of Tahitians had been agitating for independence even as the forcefield descended, he remembered, mostly the impoverished and dispossessed. Now that the weight of the fifty million Frenchmen who so cruelly oppressed them could no longer be brought to bear in the form of planeloads of additional gendarmes, had the *indépendantistes* thought the moment propitious to demand their legitimate rights as the sole masters of their archipelago's fate?

If so, they had seriously misjudged the moment. In the decades of the sixties and seventies, thousands of Polynesians had flocked in from the outer islands to share in the great prosperity that was washing over Tahiti as the army and the Atomic Energy Commission dispensed their bottomless fund of francs. Many of them had ended up living in shabby shantytowns, their new lives far removed from the land and sea that had so bountifully supported them for generations. Now they were in the same predicament as all those Tahitians and half-Tahitians who had been employed by the ever-expanding bureaucracies of the island until the catastrophic coming of the flickermen.

What was to be done with these fifty or sixty thousand urbanites who were dependant on jobs that no longer existed?

It was easy enough for the rulers of Tahiti to look back upon the quiet days before the arrival of the army and the subsequent social upheavals, when the sleepy colonial island of Tahiti and its forty thousand people had been almost entirely self-sufficient, when the outer islands had been populated by natives who lived not much differently than their ancestors had before the arrival of the first Europeans.

So any Polynesians rash enough to have ever spoken in favor of independence, or even to have harbored kind thoughts about local autonomy, soon found themselves being shepherded by heavily armed legionnaires and gendarmes onto whatever craft could stay afloat long enough to bear them to some distant island. If they were extremely lucky, they might even have been transported back to the hot waterless atoll from which they had once escaped. . . .

Eventually, Ken judged, some three-quarters of the island's population was dispersed in this way, leaving only the French and those Tahitians sufficiently docile to tend to the farming and fishing and domestic chores necessary to support their overlords in a way of life that probably wasn't much different from what Paul Gauguin had witnessed a century before in the 1890s.

"Did the Maohi really kill all the half-Tahitians?" Ken wondered. "Vetea seemed to say they did."

Tamuela shrugged. "A few perhaps. The *demis* evidently thought of themselves as being more *farani* than Maohi. That would have angered the Maohi of the time."

"But where are they then? There used to be *thousands* of them!" Ken shook his head in vexation. "That's what's so *stupid* about all of this business. Almost everyone on Tahiti had French blood or Chinese blood or missionary blood or whaler blood in them. There *weren't* any pure Tahitians anymore, except maybe in some of the outer islands. Look at the name of this so-called king of yours on Raiatea — Tihoti *Baxter,* for chrissake! Baxter, that's Maohi?"

Tamuela smiled tolerantly. "Not *our* so-called king. Somebody else's, perhaps. He could be a flickerman for all it concerns us. But you yourself know far more about these matters than any of us. So why do you ask these endless questions?"

Ken stared out at the crests of the passing waves. "I don't know. I just like to know, I guess."

Tamuela drew himself up, puffing out his smooth broad chest. "We are Arioi," he said roguishly. "We are uninterested in knowing. We are interested only in *doing.*"

Amused, Ken could only shake his head. "Do this then: tell me what happened to all the *demis.*"

"What! You are as insatiable as a *farani* virgin confronted with the mighty instruments of six lusty young Arioi. *Still* you ask your questions! Very well, I will answer. I don't *know* what happened to all your precious *demis!* I imagine they are on Tahiti, serving their masters the French, whom they so long sought to imitate. Certainly I know of no great bloodletting in which they were all massacred."

"You relieve me. Once you start killing people because of their blood it's hard to know where to draw the line. First the halfs, then the quarters, then the eighths, then the —"

"Spare me!" cried Tamuela, jumping to his feet. "I am Arioi, I have no concern with such things!"

"Even if the French chose to move out of Tahiti and retake all of the other islands they handed back to the Maohi?"

Tamuela waved a hand dismissively. "Pah! Talk to frighten children. They are far too feeble, far too few in numbers."

"That's not what you told me the last time we talked."

With a great sigh, Tamuela sank to the deck, to rock back and forth on his haunches. "Perhaps. I may merely have been repeating what I am told that Tihoti Baxter and his circle of lickspittles on Raiatea are apparently fond of spouting."

"And what is that?"

"That the French have amassed great stocks of weapons, many of them like those magical kinds they formerly possessed, which we thought had fallen into disuse and disrepair. That their numbers are swelling so rapidly that soon they will have over-crowded Tahiti and will need to establish their dominion over all the other islands within the sky-curtain, as once before they ruled. That they need great numbers of new slaves to tend their fields and serve them in their homes. That we Maohi must prepare to battle them, to drive them back into the sea, to kill them all, to retake Tahiti for our own."

"That's what Tihoti Baxter is saying?"

"Perhaps. Perhaps not. That is what certain people, many of them ignorant, *say* that he is saying."

"And do you believe it?"

Tamuela shrugged his bare shoulders. "Yes."

"What! That the French are —"

"No, no, no. I believe that Tihoti Baxter is *saying* all those things. Not that they are true. I believe that the magic weapons of the Frenchmen long ago melted into rust, that the French are content to perhaps occasionally march about in their old moth-eaten uniforms, and then sit in the shade of their cool houses while their Tahitian slaves labor for them, that they are perfectly content to let the Maohi do whatever they like on the islands on which they live — even to let a fool like Tihoti Baxter govern them if they choose."

"But if it's not true, why would this Baxter —"

Tamuela sighed again, but this time clearly at the dull-wittedness of his strange blond companion. "How else could a man like Baxter, a *demi* with skin not much darker than yours, hope to remain as chief of his so-called Maohi Dominion? You, O White Skinny Sea Serpent! You have now lived among the Maohi. You have seen the Maohi of the numerous islands we have visited. You have even coupled with many Maohi women. What then have you remarked about the Maohi?"

Ken frowned. In this mood Tamuela reminded him of no one so much as Kristin, posing infuriating questions, the answers to which any schoolchild except Ken Camden was supposed to know. "I don't know," he said at last. "Lots of things, I guess."

Tamuela raised his hand before him. "I will tell you then, O Stranger to Our Ways," he said sardonically. "The Maohi are in many ways no different than the Arioi. That is to say, they are interested in precisely five things. I will enumerate them for you." He began to count them off on his fingers.

"One: eating.

"Two: drinking.

"Three: coupling.

"Four: sleeping.

"Five: being left quietly to themselves to indulge in items One through Four."

"That's all?"

"Isn't it enough? That's why no Maohi will pay any attention to Tihoti Baxter and his so-called Dominion unless they're sufficiently frightened into believing he might save them from being made into slaves by the French. What do they care about the French, unless they think the French are coming to take their land and women?"

"You're very cynical."

"Cynical?" Tamuela scowled. "That is not a word I know. I am merely telling you what I thought you wanted to know, why I and the Arioi are not concerned about the French."

"I see. And the Arioi never visit Tahiti?"

"I will tell you frankly, since you yourself are now Arioi, and one of us. We have discussed the matter. Yes, for many years now. The French must still have great amounts of treasure that would be of use in our travels. But always the conclusion we come to is the same: some other time, perhaps. Who would want to couple with skinny white *farani* women, or with their hairy white men, all furry with curly black pelts on their backs and buttocks, like the monkeys that live in the jungle and climb through the trees?"

"Not because they're a menace?"

Tamuela snorted disdainfully. "A menace? To the Arioi? To Tihoti Baxter and timid children of that nature, perhaps yes. To anyone else, no." He rose to his feet once again. "I tell you: the French have no ships, nothing more than small sailboats that they occasionally still sail about for the pleasure of it. Aside from knives they have no weapons that will work after a hundred years' exposure to the corrosion of the salt air. They have no ships that sail magically through the sky. They have nothing but their scrawny white women and their dreams of ancient glory."

And their flickermen, thought Ken as Tamuela made his way forward through the clutter that littered the deck from the trading at their last island. A UFO that may still be glowing somewhere up in the mountains of Tahiti, and God knows how many flickermen.

But it seemed to him as he tried to sort out it all out that it might be more accurate to think of the remaining French, however ruthless and authoritarian their ancestors might once have been, as castaways like himself, marooned on their single island, stranded in the midst of a sea of enemies, rather than as the fearsome ogres of Maohi legend. . . .

CHAPTER 15

Slowly, almost imperceptibly, Ken found himself being drawn more and more closely to Hina, the tall lithe Arioi girl with whom he had broken his long months of abstinence under the now-distant skies of Takaroa. After the catastrophic consequences of his mindless dalliance with Kathie Leitner had become so starkly apparent, he had sworn bitterly to himself that never again would he become a victim of those terrible hungers that women seemed to be able to arouse within him. For also abiding deep inside him was whatever remained of Kristin, and that would be sufficient for him until the time came in which she would in some way make herself known to him.

But until that day arrived he could allow himself nothing more than the simple easing of the demands of the physical body with an occasional islander or Arioi woman, a union that was sometimes crassly commercial, but even with the Arioi always impersonal and merely transitory. For wasn't it Kristin herself who had shown him how it was possible to couple with numerous others and yet still retain her own integrity, her single-minded devotion to one person? It had taken him some time, and the total destruction of nearly everything he had once known, to learn this lesson, but it was now indelibly etched on his soul.

So although his eyes at first had seemed eager to seek out Hina and linger on the long sleek lines of her smooth brown body and the seductive beauty of her delicate face with its exotic hint of the orient in her dark eyes, he had firmly stifled any notion that she was in any way prettier or a better lover or of a more pleasing personality than any of the other equally lovely girls among the Arioi.

It might have been easier, he admitted, if she had lived on one of the boats other than that which he had joined, the *Porpoise of the Waves,* but once he was aboard and discovered that he would be constantly in her proximity, rather than create a disturbance that might be misunderstood, he told himself that in this there was an opportunity to test his character and resolve.

His relations with Hina thereafter were always amiable and open, as it was impossible to avoid her company on a ship that was astonishingly large for a trimaran but still excruciatingly small for thirty-five adults and a full complement of squalling children and noisy animals.

The large central cabin was used primarily to shelter the children, and as a refuge in bad weather. Otherwise the Arioi lived, cooked, and slept on the open deck in all except the heaviest storms. Then everyone aboard except those on watch would huddle against one another on the finely plaited mats that covered the cabin flooring and in the midst of loud talk and louder music those who wanted to would close their eyes and instantly drift off to sleep. Ken had never served in the army and learned this useful trick, but after a few months of troubled sleep on the open deck he gradually acquired it from sheer fatigue, and eventually took more no notice than any of his Polynesian shipmates of whatever commotion was going on around him.

The four flickermen, two females and two male, were generally unobtrusive, drifting at random from one ship to the next in no discernable pattern, as much a part of the Arioi's lives as the noisy roosters and smelly pigs that accompanied them on their travels. So much had the flickermen been integrated into their lovemaking that even here they were hardly noticed except occasionally when their colors intensified and brightened beyond the usual, and whatever couple they were merging with in their ecstacy burst forth with particularly noisy cries and groans of release. At which any Arioi within earshot might look up and direct some bawdy jest to the glowing nimbus that bathed the sweaty couple in its cold blue light.

Occasionally, to put his resolve to the sternest test he could devise, Ken would seek out Hina and for a few brief minutes seek to merge his body with hers. He had been surprised to discover upon joining the *Porpoise of the Waves* that the lovemaking of the Arioi between themselves was generally just as brisk and unexotic as what most of the ordinary Polynesians usually engaged in, the male kneeling before the female and raising her buttocks to allow him to penetrate, then a few minutes of powerful uninterrupted strokes until the sudden climax. The exotic refinements the Arioi so zestfully demonstrated during their island entertainments were mostly just that: demonstrations.

There was little permanent pairing of couples, and the occasional children who were born were raised collectively until they were three or four, at which point they were left behind with happy foster parents on one of the islands they came to in their never-ending wanderings. Eventually some of them might be gathered up on some future visit ten or twelve years later to rejoin the company of the Arioi, but only if they fulfilled the Ariois' demanding standards of grace and beauty.

Partial nudity was common enough on the ships, but among themselves the Arioi were somewhat more modest in their behavior than their public entertainments might have led him to believe. Although it was not unheard of for a lusty couple to suddenly drop whatever they were doing and suddenly join their bodies without regard to whoever was around them, generally there was little sexual activity except in quiet corners of the darkened cabin or under the evening sky, the lovers' bodies often modestly half-shrouded from view by a light pareo thrown discreetly about their hips. Certainly there was none of the orgiastic behavior they indulged in during their shows, nor did he observe even small groups of three or four lovers entwined.

No, their private sex lives were all very brisk and straightforward, a textbook illustration of what he had already concluded his own life must now be, a vivid example of how a carefully maintained detachment towards sex was both feasible and natural.

Likewise, he was surprised as well as relieved by the banality of their general method of kneeling between the girl's upraised legs. It was, he discovered, far easier to retain a certain impersonality about the lovely girls he now occasionally coupled with if his sole point of contact was at the joining of their frantically twisting thighs.

But as he looked down at Hina's glistening body moving against his it was impossible to restrain himself from reaching forward to cup those lovely firm breasts between his hands, or from reliving those moments of frenzy and overpowering spasms that had seized them both that night in Takaroa. . . .

That's why you have to test yourself, he repeated as he grimly counted the weeks and months since his last coupling with her. Another week, and then he could join her again. That would be six full weeks since the last time, conclusive proof that he was in no way in love with her, or even particularly partial to her. For even Kristin couldn't object to his making love to the same girl only once every other month or so. She should, in fact, admire how he successfully resisted the occasional natural temptation to visit Hina more often, given the obvious fact that she was so much prettier than any of the island women he was occasionally obliged to couple with, or even than any of the —

Stop that! he told himself. Hina's just another girl. Just another Maohi. No different from any of the islanders. And probably no different from the voracious Kathie Leitner herself if you were ever unwary enough to let her ensnare you. No, never forget that. A little prettier perhaps, but *no different from any other girl.*

He could almost see Kristin's face before him, her pale thin lips twitching in an icy smile of approval.

In a way, he knew, it was Kristin who was responsible for what followed. For it was obviously impossible to entirely avoid Hina's company given the circumstances of their lives, and the more he saw of her and came to know her, the more he slowly began to see in her the many similarities and resemblances to Kristin.

At first he told himself that this was only a wistful trick of a still troubled mind, and tried to make light of his own foolishness. But as the months drifted by and merged with the different islands and their different women, he found himself increasingly intrigued by this strange notion, and finally realized that in order to refute it he was almost obliged to study Hina and her ways ever more closely.

Physically, he saw, they were much alike, tall and slim and dark. Kristin's breasts were whiter, he remembered, and Hina's were possibly a little higher and firmer, but that was only because she was some twenty years younger. At first he had thought that Hina's hips and behind might be somewhat rounder and fuller, and her shoulders a trifle narrower and more smoothly fleshed, but it was impossible to conceive of anyone lovelier or more feminine than Kristin, so he knew that in this he was obviously mistaken, that in the months and years he had now been bereft of Kristin his mind had begun to suffer inexplicable lapses.

All the more reason then to proceed with this dispassionate analysis of the Arioi girl, for in doing so it would only serve to fix the image of Kristin more firmly in his mind. . . .

It was harder to decide what he saw in Hina's eyes and mouth and the way she used them. Her face was not as expressive as Kristin's, but then most Polynesian faces, even those of the Arioi, simply didn't reveal much more than the most elemental outpourings of rage and grief and joy. For all their occasional loveliness, their faces were stolid and lacking in character, even as their owners chattered and gossiped and made love.

But Hina, if you took the trouble to regard her carefully, simply didn't stare back at him through great bovine eyes that reflected the dullness and lack of curiosity of so many Polynesians. No, hers sparkled and twinkled, with the same merriment and intelligence in them that he had instantly seen in Kristin's that far-off day on the Hungarian's terrace. It was only because for so long he had tried to avoid looking into these eyes that he been able to delude himself that she was in no way different from all the other amiable but essentially childlike girls and women of the islands.

Her mouth too was Kristin's, broad, mobile, expressive, a charming and unfailing guide to the mercurial shifts of her moods. For like Kristin she was utterly without guile or artifice, a woman of obvious, well-defined appetites and pleasures who unhesitatingly tried to satisfy them in as straightforward a manner as possible. Even in the constrained, and to Ken, vaguely unsatisfactory, Polynesian method of coupling that they used between them, her orgasms were sharp and frenzied, obviously far more passionately experienced than those of the other women he knew, whose brief sweaty spasms were little different in intensity or significance from a fit of sneezing.

And, of course, there was Hina's attachment to Ken itself. True, she could hardly be said to be flinging herself at him, but her eyes were constantly meeting his from whatever ends of the boat they might happen to be. And even when she was coupling in front of hundreds of cheering islanders he could feel them sometimes seek him out, and she would grin cheerfully at him, as if asking him to admire just how beautiful she was and how cleverly she was playing her role before all these silly islanders. . . .

And finally: why else had she singled him out that night on Takaroa, when any man on the island was hers for the taking? Merely because he was white and a novelty? Because he was the supposed favorite of the flickermen? Because of simple curiosity?

The more he considered it the more unlikely this seemed.

There was obviously something about Hina, and about *him* in relation to Hina, that was not as simple as it first appeared.

Even the flickermen were somehow aware of it, for it was incontestable that they were more in evidence and far more radiant whenever he and Hina joined themselves together than during any of his coupling with the faceless women of the islands. And this was no mere delusion on his part. Hadn't two of the Arioi women told Hina they had never seen the flickermen pulse and throb with such powerful intensity as when Hina and the flickermen's peculiar son, the Skinny White Sea Snake, were coupling in some darkened cranny of the boat? These Arioi had now had decades to study the ways of the flickermen from close proximity — could any judgment in such a matter be more expert than theirs?

Knowing now that he was no longer alone in noticing this, he could see that his own orgasms with Hina were far more overwhelming in their intensity than he had previously allowed himself to admit. He wondered if it could be because of the flickermen? Did the Arioi attract flickermen of some special potency? He considered this notion, then rejected it. From everything he had ever heard, flickermen were flickermen, with no discernable individual differences between one and the other, whether they lived ashore on an island such as Takaroa or accompanied a troupe of Arioi whose main purpose in life was making love.

No, sickly gray or lusty blue, male or female, one flickerman was just like another.

The true explanation obviously lay not in the fact that these flickermen were different, but that *he and Hina were different!*

He recoiled before this deeply troubling concept, for on the surface of things it appeared to clearly contradict his sworn resolve to hold himself apart precisely from any personal involvement that could conceivably make his relationship with a woman in any way distinctive or individual. The resumption of his affair with Kathie Leitner had proved disastrous. He knew that Kristin had forgiven him for that monstrous folly that had cost them her very life, but he could not afford to count on her generosity a second time. . . .

For three days he brooded on the matter, slumped inertly under a corner of the roof, oblivious to all that went on about him, much as he had spent those first months of his life on Takaroa before the strange flickerman-imposed lethargy had finally worn off. From time to time he nibbled listlessly at whatever a solicitous Arioi might offer him to eat, but to their quizzical efforts at conversation or companionship he could only murmur beneath his breath and turn his eyes out to sea.

But on the fourth day everything was suddenly revealed to him with such startling clarity that after his initial elation had passed, he wondered numbly if he could be in actual danger of losing his faculties for not having seen it from the very first.

He laughed softly to himself and climbed wearily to his feet. Impossible! Never had his thoughts sparkled and darted off in so many enticing directions with such zest and clarity! He began to make his way forward. The racing winds at the front of the ship would be as brisk and invigorating as he himself now felt. It had been an inexplicably difficult route that he had been obliged to take, but now he had reached its end and the path before him was straight and well defined. He smiled faintly, and clapped a startled Arioi on the back in sudden exhilaration. In a while he would seek out Hina, and, buoyed by the glow of this inner peace that seemed to radiate throughout his body, would begin the joyous process of her education.

For after marrying Kristin, hadn't *she* devoted herself to educating and instructing *him,* to pulling him up to her own superior standards and expectations? In her efforts to make him worthy of her, hadn't she actually been molding him into someone not unlike herself, so that in a sense he could almost be said to have become an extension of Kristin? This was obviously so, and now he clearly recognized it. The Ken Camden who had challenged the incomprehensible forces of the flickermen's mighty sky-curtain and had bested them, who stood now on the prow of this plunging catamaran with the wind and salt spray whipping against his bare body, that Ken Camden was far more truly the descendant of Kristin Dellinger than of that vacuous blond beachboy who had embarked so heedlessly from Newport Beach for the South Pacific so many years before.

And what Kristin had done for him, it was now his plain duty to do for Hina, who already had so much of Kristin in her. The capabilities were clearly there. It would be intolerable selfishness on his part not to guide her steps towards her full potential, a potential of which she herself was totally unaware. Yes, it would be nothing less than active malice not to help her discover what wonders existed within her and what joys life could hold beyond bestial couplings before slack-jawed communities of ignorant Polynesians.

So anything that served to reshape her more closely in the image of Kristin, he reflected, was nothing less than a creative act of positive devotion to those memories of Kristin that still lived within him and that guided him in all his waking moments. For there could be no greater expression of his love than to recapture in the pliant clay of the Arioi girl whatever of his beloved Kristin he was capable of recreating.

He ran his hands through his damp tangled hair. He would have to make himself presentable before he approached Hina. He turned and took the first steps towards the new life that lay before him.

He could feel a great warmth and joy welling up inside him. Somewhere, he knew, Kristin approved.

CHAPTER 16

"I will going to the beach."

"I *was* going."

"I *was* going to the beach."

"That's perfect."

"Really? I really speaking English well?"

"I *am* really."

"I *am* really speaking English well?"

"Yes. Very, very well. There's no one around for a thousand miles who speaks it any better."

Hina clapped her hands together and laughed happily. Her bare breasts jiggled enticingly as she rocked up and down on her heels with merriment. Ken reached out and with the tip of his finger traced a feathery circle around one of her small dark nipples. It stiffened immediately, while the smooth brown skin of her breasts and arms became pebbled with gooseflesh. She pushed his hand away. "Don't," she said in Tahitian, darting quick looks around the boat. "Someone might see."

"They see you doing lots of other things every time we have a show."

"But that's different."

He shrugged, unwilling to continue the argument. He would never understand these Arioi, but in a sense it no longer mattered, for as Hina increasingly took on the ways of Kristin he would no longer be dealing with an almost cartoon image of the beautiful but naked girl of the South Seas islands, but with an educated, Westernized woman. She couldn't be expected to discard her entire Arioi upbringing in a few short weeks or even months, of course, for it would take time and patience, but already he had made immense progress with her.

He bluffed a playful gesture towards her still rigid nipple and smiled fondly. "Tonight," he said slowly in English, "I'm going to take that in my mouth and suck it until you cry and moan. Then I'm going to put your other one —"

She giggled softly and ran her hand over the tips of her nipples, looking down at them as if seeing them for the first time. She was enchanted by their own secret language that he was teaching her, and when they made love they now did so in English. By speaking English she was temporarily no longer Arioi and they both greedily availed themselves of all the pleasures and the subtleties of love-play that the Arioi ran through in their skits and shows, and of which Kristin had been such a master. No more hasty couplings while he crouched over her briefly and then stalked away as casually as one of the boat's roosters after servicing a clucking hen. Now it was *love* they made together, long, slow, and tender, although she was always cautious that none of their fellow Arioi should watch them. They did, he knew, but as long as her peculiar behavior was confined to O Strange White Sea Snake a polite convention had sprung up to pretend it wasn't happening. But the fact that she could now step outside the boundaries of traditional Arioi ways even temporarily was all that really counted, for it revealed the new Hina, the Hina who was being molded by his hands, the Hina who someday would be as much like Kristin as he could made her. . . .

"What else you do me?" she asked coquettishly, looking up at him from under hooded eyes.

"What else *will* you do with me."

"Yes. What else? Tell."

He told her until he felt his own flesh begin to stir, and then with some difficulty turned back to their English lesson. Their lovemaking would, in any case, have to wait until dark. If only they were ashore on one of the islands, perhaps with their own little shelter, or with the entire wilderness of the island at their disposal. . . .

But at the thought of their island stopovers his ardor began to cool. It didn't really bother him to watch her in the make-believe love-play of the Arioi during the show, and he had now come to realize that in some peculiar way this even served to excite him, but he was increasingly less reconciled to the thought of what she did after the shows to earn the assorted jumble of goods that the Arioi considered wealth.

Of course *she* didn't think of herself as being a whore, only as an Arioi, so in that case she probably wasn't really a whore. But it still made him uneasy, and after she returned to him in the night from the sweaty embrace of some fat grunting islander any thoughts of love were impossible to entertain.

"But you do it yourself," she chided him whenever he brought the subject up. "Your Long Rigid Sea Serpent, all those ugly Maohi women offer whatever they can steal from their boyfriends to feel it in them. *That's* not wrong. So how can what I —"

He would wave the argument away before it started, because he really had no answer to it, except to say that what he was doing *was* wrong, and he shouldn't be doing it any more than she, and he never would be if it hadn't been for —

But that too was so complex and tangled a subject that to become involved with it would serve no useful purpose except to needlessly confuse Hina. Already she was having difficulty enough in absorbing everything that he was trying to teach her, and he knew that he was attempting too much, too quickly. This, after all, was a girl who had never been to school, who literally didn't know how to add two and two!

But that was all too easy to forget as he marveled at her intelligence. Listening to her, it was impossible to believe that she hadn't studied English for years, or perhaps learned to speak it in California. Once she had a word, its pronunciation thereafter was perfect, and she could repeat long strings of words, entire sentences even, without a mistake.

He himself was shy about singing before others with his own slightly reedy voice, so when he discovered that she could sing entire songs within a few minutes of first hearing them he eagerly began to teach her everything he could remember. For to his surprise he still heard Polynesians singing songs with music that was readily identifiable as antedating even his own long-lost era. *Red River Valley* was one, *She'll Be Coming 'Round the Mountain* another.

The words were now in Tahitian, of course, but whenever he heard the old familiar tunes he was instantly transported back to childhood and dim memories of his first school years in Springfield, Illinois. But it was only after he had taught Hina a number of his own sentimental favorites like *Bridge Over Troubled Waters* and *Help Me Make It Through the Night* that he realized what a mistake he might have made. His intention had been to find her a more enjoyable way of learning English, and to develop someone who could perhaps replace him, or at least assist him, in doing the American songs he occasionally sang during their shows.

But to hear her sweet clear voice singing the melancholy songs in the soft hush of early evening while the sun was disappearing over the rim of the restless gray ocean or silhouetting the stark forms of waving palm trees against the sky was something more than he could bear, as all the grief and despair he had known since being cast alone into this terrible new world welled up inside him, and he would sink into a numbed paralysis while tears rolled unheeded down his cheeks. . . .

After that he taught her only resolutely cheerful songs that could also be learned by other members of the troupe, so they could be sung together by a group, accompanied by their banjos and guitars and drums and even an occasional flute. *Ta Rah Rah Boom De A,* was a great favorite of the audiences, who had no idea that the words he had provided made no sense whatsoever. Others were *This Land Is Your Land, Deep in the Heart of Texas, Clementine,* and *The Yellow Rose of Texas,* as well as whatever country and western songs he could recall.

The Arioi all seemed to have perfect ears as well as being great improvisers, and all he had to do was hum a tune a single time for them. If it pleased them, by the following day they had a entire set of lyrics for it, generally bawdy, often totally obscene. There was still a nostalgic melancholy in listening to these songs, no matter how lively they were, but at least none of them had the power to completely incapacitate him as the haunting verses of *The Last Thing on My Mind* sung by Hina in the purest of American accents had done until he had forbidden her to sing it within his hearing.

If she could learn to speak English and sing American songs with such facility, he knew, she could learn anything else once her mind had been sufficiently oriented in the right direction. How keenly he now regretted that he himself had wasted so many years of his own schooling, those years he had almost actively refused to learn whatever was offered. And even with Kristin — he had resisted *her* efforts, and it was only subconsciously that he had finally absorbed much of what she had tried to teach him.

Now he was experiencing the same reaction from Hina. As he struggled to teach her whatever he could recall of history, geography, anthropology, ethnology, all the bits and snatches of his vanished culture, and in particular everything he had learned from Kristin, she would become sulky and balky, and her eyes would take on that dull Polynesian opaqueness he found so irritating in everyone else. At first he was baffled by her stubbornness, then angered by it, just as he remembered he had vexed Kristin by his own loathsome stupidity.

But Hina wasn't stupid! That was what he couldn't understand. How could she be, she who had so much of Kristin in her?

When he finally realized what she was up to, he could only smile in delighted relief at her playfulness. How obvious it now was! Her physical beauty and almost depraved adult sexuality had blinded him to the fact that she was still little more than a child. And she still took a child's joy in playing games, especially those games that were incomprehensible to adults. Child-like, bound by the rules of some game that only she recognized, Hina was actually only *pretending* that his efforts to tear her away from the happy but mindless existence she led with the Arioi were being totally ignored.

Just as *he* had with Kristin, he knew, secretly Hina was storing up everything he taught her.

From the atoll of Makemo the three ships of the Arioi moved south to Motutunga, then west to Anaa. North to Ananea, then east again to Marutea, Nihiru, Rekareka, Tauere, and Haraiki. From there to Hikueru, which in Ken's vanished past had been renowned for the quality of its black mother-of-pearl shell. Here they found large numbers of Chinese, descendants of those who decades before had owned those ubiquitous general stores and bakeries that had furnished livings to Chinese on every island of Polynesia.

Here and there in his travels with the Arioi Ken had seen families of Chinese scattered among the islanders, most of them raising crops and livestock that they must then barter to their Polynesian neighbors for — what? he wondered. Pearls? Coconuts? Additional land to grow even more crops? Could even a Chinese make himself rich in a society without money, without anything to spend it on?

It was not a question that he dwell upon. He was only amused to note that in spite of their loud denigration of the Chinese, the Arioi women were quick enough to disappear into the darkness with the occasional Chinese who came by to barter with them after one of their shows. But never did he see a Chinese woman or girl negotiating with one of the handsome young Arioi men. . . .

On Hikueru there were now two separate communities, a largely Maohi one on the north side of the lagoon, and a largely Chinese one to the south. The Arioi anchored their ships in the north and set up their stage and usual temporary community among the 700 Maohi who lived in the village of Tupapati. From there a number of them sailed one of the ships southeast across the smooth waters of the lagoon to the smaller Chinese village that had grown up around what had once been one of the richest shelling areas. Ken accompanied the fifteen men who made the journey. None of the Arioi women went along, for it was strictly a trading mission. Occasional *tinitos* they might dally with discreetly and pretend they hadn't; a village of them they disdainfully ignored.

Ken found a small ramshackle village that was desperately makeshift and tawdry compared to Tupapati and to most of the other Maohi communities he had seen, for the Chinese had obviously had to build theirs from scratch, with what bits and pieces of leftover materials they could scrounge.

The population was pale and scrawny and unhealthy looking, far more like the pictures he had seen of the half-starved peasants of ancient China than the prosperous well-fed Chinese he remembered from 2003 Tahiti. The villagers had little to trade beyond great baskets of curious Chinese vegetables and innumerable quacking ducks, but both of these were avidly snatched up by the Arioi. It was impossible to keep them from eventually learning something of the nature of Ken's improbable story, and then they clustered around him with the same eager curiosity as any group of Maohi.

A ancient Chinese woman dressed in even more ancient shapeless black rags tugged at his arm. She was bent nearly double with age, and her toothless face was as wizened and spotted as a dried apple. To his wonder, she began to address him in the halting French she had learned eighty years before from her long-dead mother, who had been a small girl when the forcefield had worked its malevolent destiny on the Chinese of Polynesia. Until recently, when old age had forced her to retire, she had been the sole teacher in the small school that the community still maintained.

"Your story is very strange," she said, laying a trembling hand the color and texture of a faded leaf on his arm. "I'm not sure I entirely understand it, but I imagine that you must be the loneliest man in the entire world."

Ken felt tears unexpectedly well in his eyes at these words of compassion from a total stranger — the first he had heard in the two years since being spun out of the sky onto his back in the sands of Takaroa. "Yes," he murmured. "I've sometimes felt alone."

"Come," she said, tugging again at his arm. "There is no one else for me to give them to. I would hate the thought of them being thrown away after my death."

Her mother, she said, had spoken fluent English, and she herself had initially taught French to her students for well over three decades, until she had at last bowed to the demands of the younger generations and had abandoned it in favor of a strictly Chinese curriculum. When the present teacher, herself a lady well into her sixties, had replaced her, the old woman had taken home with her whatever remained of the crumbling books in French and English that she had slowly accumulated over the years. Now her eyes were too poor to allow her to read them, and there was no longer anyone else on the island to whom they could be of any use.

So Ken acquired several dozen ancient books that had miraculously weathered the decades squirreled away in a Chinese community in the middle of the Tuamotus. When the voyagers returned the following day to Tupapati and the rest of the troupe, he stubbornly refused to join them in that evening's entertainment. A number of the more rakish Chinese had accompanied their ship in their own pirogues, and even if they hadn't been there to bear witness, he knew there was something totally indecent in cavorting in the Ariois' lewd frolics on the same island as that wonderfully decent old lady from almost the same era as himself. She would be rightly dismayed and insulted to think she had given her precious books to such a shameless monster of depravity.

The Arioi shook their heads in bewilderment and hastily began to reorganize their show, muttering loudly about the peculiarities of Strange White Sea Serpents. . . .

* * * *

A hundred miles further to the east Ken found that a message awaited him. Tihoti Baxter, chief of the Maohi Dominion, had come to hear of the strange white man from beyond the sky-curtain of the flickermen, and had sent messages radiating from Raiatea in all directions, directing that the Arioi bring this person before him with all due speed.

Tamuela and the other members of the ruling council were more amused by such presumption than impressed. "In due course," shrugged Tamuela. "Tihoti Baxter has lived this long without the company of Our Illustrious and Personal White Sea Snake. It will do him no harm to wait a while longer."

Ken did not try to hide the relief he felt. He had no desire to come under the scrutiny of Tihoti Baxter and his so-called Dominion, at least at the present time.

"Do you ever visit Raiatea?" he asked uneasily.

"Of course. As a matter of fact, we're on our way there right now."

"We are?" Raiatea, Ken knew, was on the other side of Tahiti, and at least five or six hundred miles from where they now found themselves on the eastern edge of the Tuamotu archipelago.

"Yes. First we must finish visiting another six islands here in the Tuamotus, then we continue southeast to Nukutavake and those islands of the Gambiers that have not fallen behind the sky-curtain. It is at least seventeen years since the Arioi have visited them, and they must be eager to receive us. Think of the treasure they will have accumulated during that time, with nothing to do with it except save it for our coming!"

"I see," said Ken, smiling wanly. "And after the Gambiers?"

"We may well come back by way of Raivavae and the Australes. They too have been too long bereft of the Arioi." He tapped a knuckle against Ken's hard biceps. "You will enjoy the women of the Australes. They are big, fat, *powerful.* Not like these scrawny little chickens you seem to prefer in your perverted Sea Serpent fashion."

Ken grinned back at him. "And how long you do estimate all this to take? It is certainly a very direct route you plan from here to Tihoti Baxter and the Maohi Dominion."

Tamuela turned to squint up thoughtfully at the pale moon that hung over the western sky nearly in the direction where Raiatea might be found, as if doing a long series of calculations in his head. "Yes," he at last in solemn tones. "Tihoti Baxter exhorts us to all due speed. We must be careful to obey. I estimate that we shall therefore be in Raiatea in not less than two to three years."

CHAPTER 17

Not long after leaving Hikueru Ken began the tedious business of teaching Hina to read and write. She giggled happily when he showed her the books and clapped her hands in excitement. Within a few minutes of opening the first book the initial excitement had worn off and she was looking at him in hurt bewilderment. "But why do I have to read?" she asked plaintively.

"To make you like Kristin." The words formed instantly in his mind, but he was able to stop himself from actually uttering them. "You'll see," he reassured her with a smile. "You'll wonder what you did all your life before you could."

"I don't *want* to be like some *farani popa'a* woman who spends all day reading and writing," she said sullenly, as if she were somehow reading his mind.

Ken turned away to keep her from seeing the bewilderment and hurt, as well as the unavoidable anger, that the words had provoked. Kristin, he muttered to himself, Kristin. . . . For a long moment he was seized by a overwhelming sense of doubt and dismay such as he had not experienced since first finding himself on Takaroa, and he stared bleakly into an long empty future.

But then he drew a deep breath and turned back to her a broad smile. "Well, we'll see. Why don't we put the books away for today and just concentrate on your English. How about a song?"

Her face cleared instantly. "Oh yes! Let's *sing . . . Glory, Glory, Hallelujah.*"

"Why not? *Mine eyes have seen the glory of the coming of the Lord. . . .*"

That was what his lips were mouthing. But *stupid fucking ignorant bitch* were the awful words that had suddenly sprung unbidden into his mind, and he sat petrified, his outstretched arm motionless, his thoughts in turmoil. No, I didn't think that! he cried silently. I didn't! Oh, Kristin, *I didn't!*

It was after sailing from Hikueru to Marokau, on the way from Marokau to Amanu and Hao, that the extraordinary gathering of the flickermen took place. Until that time he had never seen more than five gathered together, and even that was rare, for the four that accompanied their ships were seldom glimpsed together, and when the Arioi went ashore whatever flickerman might be hovering about the island apparently paid no more attention to their own flickerman than did the island cats to the cats on the three nearby ships.

He later remembered that it was a beautiful warm evening in which the wind had suddenly died, and the ships were lying almost motionless on the slowly rolling sea. Everyone except the sleeping children was on the outside deck, and he and Hina had taken the opportunity to move their sleeping mats into the darkness of the cabin. They had been hungrily wrapped around each other for only a few blissful moments it seemed when they became vaguely aware of the general chatter and music from the deck slowly subsiding, and then of a loud series of cries and shouts. They looked up to find a flickerman hovering above them, a male, while a second one came drifting through the bamboo plaiting of the walls. Grinning, he thrust deep within her, and she squeezed him playfully in return. *Two* flickermen in attendance — the evening promised to be a spectacular one!

A third female flickerwoman drifted through the far wall, followed by another, and then still another. The inside of the cabin was now clearly lighted by their cold blue illumination, and still they continued to arrive. Uneasily, Ken turned his head from one side to the other, but Hina, brought up among them since infancy, paid little attention except to thrust her hips against Ken's with increasing urgency. The flickering light was becoming almost disturbingly bright as perhaps two dozen of the glowing nimbuses converged around their sweating bodies. Through their transparent bodies he could see that an equal number of noisy Arioi were peering in at them through the open doors and windows. Modestly he reached to pull the pareo more carefully over his pumping buttocks, but in an instant it had been kicked away by Hina, and her arms had clasped him tightly against her damp sticky chest. Now they were in the very midst of a hellish glow of sparkling and dancing electrical discharges and flashes, and he felt the onrushing surge of his climax beginning to grip his limbs. Oblivious to the hooting Arioi and the burning of impalpable flames, he gave himself up entirely to the waves of sensation that had him in their grip.

The great meeting of the flickerman was the main topic of conversation aboard the three ships for the next week. Twenty-seven or twenty-eight of them had been counted during the two days they remained with the little fleet, floating sedately from ship to ship to ship, but coming back time and again to hover closely around Ken.

After first trying to ignore them, he had yelled and raged at them futilely, and had finally returned to going about his affairs as if unaware of their presence. But whatever his reactions, the flickermen paid them no discernable heed, drifting aimlessly about in their own deliberate way.

Much of the Ariois' bawdy speculation dwelt in loving detail on the lusty cries and thrashing of that awesome first climax he and Hina had reached in apparent conjunction with twenty-eight flickermen, and he was badgered until he had to shyly admit that it had indeed been far beyond the ordinary. In the days before the flickermen disappeared as suddenly as they had appeared, he and Hina made semi-public love three more times in the eerie presence of the assembled flickermen and flickerwomen. These were almost command performances demanded by their curious shipmates, who at least watched quietly from a discreet distance, but he felt nonetheless as if he had been performing on stage. But though it hardly seemed possible to him, the intensity of their climaxes continued to increase with each encounter, until at last he felt himself almost a discorporate being, rendered apart from his ordinary earthly body, so dazzling and grandiose were the sensations that tossed him about as if he were a leaf in the midst of a swirling maelstrom.

Hina too must have been experiencing the same overpowering ecstacy, for afterwards she volubly conveyed a vivid account of each experience to the enthralled audience of Arioi. Numerous other couples were soon flailing noisily together on the three boats in hopes of duplicating the same spectacular results. To their disappointment they generally attracted five or six flickermen in a short period of time, but after a few minutes most of the glowing wraiths soon drifted off, leaving the sweating couple to the company of one or two of the luminescence beings at the most.

Ken now felt a resurgence of the initial awe with which he had once been regarded. It was impossible to move about the boat without the curious stares of the Arioi following him, and what had long since become only a sardonic form of address akin to the jocular variations on Lengthy White Sea Serpent now took on new solemnity when the Arioi referred to their unfathomable white shipmate as the Son of the Flickermen.

But as the next island appeared over the horizon, other concerns became gradually more pressing, and soon he and Hina were being left more and more to themselves, and finally within a few more weeks it was almost as if nothing out of the ordinary had ever occurred.

It was not long before the curious traits of the new male were noticed by the other three Silumiut who for decades now had trailed along with these Uglies whose sole purpose in life appeared to be traveling from island to island to mate with the local inhabitants. But this exciting new Ugly had been his discovery, and he was insistent that he had the primary right to him for as long as he wanted. The others who had experienced the Ugly's extraordinary field objected vehemently, so that finally a council was convoked in order to deal with this strange phenomenon.

Twenty-four Silumiut converged on the three native ships as they sailed slowly between islands, the largest gathering of crew members in nearly five decades. Several times they all mingled together cautiously as the Ugly mated with his customary female, and it was instantly apparent there was something quite out of the ordinary about him. It was decided that he was most probably a chance mutation, one of the rare ones to survive and flourish.

If that were the case, suggested Yrem, why not try the procedure that Bylangu had once proposed? They now had an idea of how extraordinarily short the life-span of the Uglies was, and how quick their reproductive cycle. Perhaps this Ugly's traits could be passed along to another generation and even augmented. Why had they allowed themselves to sink into brooding despair by their initial failures on Water? Centuries of life remained to them — plenty of time in terms of the short-lived Uglies to breed themselves a herd of fine new Yas'elda. . . .

Although the mutineers of the Riestu were members of the most advanced species in the galaxy, individually they were little more than simple crewmen, trained only in the specific duties necessary to running a scoutship. The few intellectuals aboard had all been cast adrift when the ship's officers had been hurled away in the lifeboat. Both the veterinarian and the geneticist had long since been dissolved to nothingness. Had Gon'ut and Aroto been with them here on Water, almost certainly they would have had procedures for isolating the Ugly from any possible external dangers that threatened his survival. Then in the tranquility of their laboratory they would have done whatever was necessary to breed him to other Uglies.

But now. . . .

Eventually it was agreed there was little more to be done than watch over the native with the strangely appealing field. He already appeared to be a more than averagely vigorous male, and it had long been taken for granted by the Silumiut that the Uglies experienced a pleasurable augmentation to their neural field when coupling in the presence of themselves. Now the Ugly who was the object of their hopes must be encouraged to breed by careful mingling with his neural field to augment his sexual drive as much as possible.

After much rancorous arguing it was finally decided that the only way to avoid further dispute was to give the coveted assignment of watching over the Ugly to Tre'ze, for it was undeniable that it was he who had *made the initial discovery. Besides Tre'ze there were three other Silumiut who normally followed these ships. That number would remain at three, but henceforward those Silumiut who wanted to share in watching over this exciting new discovery would have to rotate the three posts among themselves.*

Only Tre'ze was completely pleased by this compromise. . . .

Although it was no more possible to distinguish between the two female flickermen than it was between the two males, Ken had the uneasy feeling that even after the other two dozen flickermen had departed he was now more persistently attended by one of the female flickerman than were any of the other crew of the three ships. Certainly she seemed to be constantly present whenever he and Hina sought to enjoy themselves together, although at other times she drifted unobtrusively back and forth between the three ships. Hina was also aware of this, as were the other Arioi, and for a while she basked in the glow of envy tinged with wonder that came from possessing her own personal flickerman.

But even the novelty of this wore off as the months stretched out to become a year while the *Porpoise of the Waves* moved slowly south-eastward through the far end of the Tuamotu archipelago and into the Gambiers. Suppose he *did* have a flickerman, a female one at that, who seemed to be dogging his steps? Ken occasionally asked himself. What could he *do* about it? Nothing. It seemed to do no harm, and when he and Hina were together, as they often were, it certainly added to their sex life.

But then — even more rarely — he would recall the arrival of the flickermen in the Papeete of 2004, and the grim memory of the fleeing Korean sailor would be as horribly vivid as when he had watched the pursuing flickerman suddenly merge with the terrified little man and cast him lifeless at Ken's feet. With a shudder he would try to suppress the thought, for according to the Arioi nothing so horrifying had ever happened within living memory. Certainly *they* had never had any reason to be wary of the strange beings.

So his fears would pass, and he would return to the ordinary routine of daily existence in which he devoted as much time as he could to the person who more and more clearly now was revealing what there was of Kristin within her. Thanks to endless patience on his part, she had finally mastered both the alphabet and the numbers as far as 100. That was a far step from possessing two PhDs, but even Kristin had started somewhere, and *she* had started without the terrible burden of being born into a world of illiterates. Someday, he knew, he would be able to sit down with Kristin on a flowered terrace, and they would once again lift tall cool ice-filled glasses to their lips, and they would look back on these preposterous days of her origins and —

Kristin? No. Hina. He and *Hina* would sit down —

Ice-filled glasses? he asked himself. A daydream.

Like everything else?

No! *Nothing* in life was a daydream. *Anything* was possible. Hadn't *he* proven that with the very fact of his existence, here in this world a hundred years after he should have been dead?

And after all, he whispered to himself, he wasn't asking for much.

Only Kristin.

For years Tre'ze had let his outward shape shift randomly from male to female and back to male, its form apparently determined by whichever of the mating natives possessed the more powerful field. A dominant male Ugly would cause a Silumiut to mimic a female Ugly. Why this should be so was more than Tre'ze could imagine, but it was undeniably the case, and so now it appeared that she would remain a female as long as she remained with her Ugly. . . .

Her Ugly! How peculiar to think of Uglies in that way. The last time she had, it had been . . . yes, when she had followed that other *pale-maned Ugly, the one who had been thrown into the forcefield! How extraordinary. . . . Why had she never had the same feeling of possessiveness about the myriad of other Uglies she had briefly encountered in all the time that had passed since then?*

She hesitated. It seemed somehow wrong *to refer to the creature whom she was going to watch over as simply* Ugly. *Uglies* were *ugly, of course, hence the name. But this particular one . . . surely his form was marginally more pleasing than that of any of the others. The fact that he mated so frequently with his Ugly companion — wasn't that proof of his special nature, even of a special Ugly handsomeness? Yes, obviously.*

It was equally obvious that so handsome a creature needed a name.

Silumiut were straightforward to the point of inanity when it came to bestowing descriptive names on material objects. It took Tre'ze only a few seconds to name her splendid new creature.

Henceforward her Ugly would be known as Mine.

There was a girl in the troupe named Moea who was as tall as Hina, and nearly as beautiful. He had made love with her twice in the days before coming to realize the true purpose of his existence among these peculiar folk, and although he had always afterwards been as amiable with her as he was with anyone else, he had been obliged to make it clear that for the moment he had time for teaching the ways of the past to only one person. Once Hina had been fully educated, he would be glad to help any others in the same way. Eventually Moea had given up pestering him and had seemed to accept what everyone else already had — that strange as it might seem, their Peculiar White Sea Serpent preferred to devote himself exclusively to one woman.

Now Moea came to him with startling news. Hina had confided to her that she was pregnant. And not by Ken, but by one of the seven nameless fishermen she had coupled with on the island of Tureia. Later, she had whispered to Moea, she would tell Ken that he was the father of the child, in the hopes that the flickermen would look as attentively upon him as they did upon Ken.

Ken sat staring at her silently. With a faint smile of commiseration, Moea reached out to touch him lightly on the knee. "I thought you should know," she said, and raised her eyes to his. His gaze never left her until at last she rose uneasily to her feet and sauntered away, her pert behind swaying enticingly.

Ken was initially stunned, then angered. Pregnancy was no part of his plans. Never had the possibility of fathering a child occurred to him, even with —

Even with. . . .

Kristin.

He scowled, and felt the fingernails of his clenched fists digging deep into his palms. He suddenly felt an overpowering urge to lash out at someone, to sink his fists deep —

But —

But. . . . He felt the tension slowly begin to drain away.

Was *this* the sign he had been waiting for these long years since their terrible separation? Now that Hina's education was well underway, could *she* have decided that this was the moment to reveal herself at last, initially at least in the person of this Polynesian girl who more and more had come to resemble her? Could a *child* be the long-awaited auspice, a symbol of the permanency of their union, a signal that now was the time to put the ways of the Arioi behind him and devote himself exclusively to his Kristin?

He smiled, his face radiant with sudden happiness. No matter that for the moment the girl called Hina was little more than a public whore. Whose baby *could* it be but his? He jumped lightly to his feet. Someday he might twist the neck of that trouble-making bitch Moea for her jealous lies, but not today — today was a day to celebrate!

* * * *

For the next week he talked both earnestly and joyously to Hina. In a year's time the Arioi would have completed their long swing through the Australe islands to the south of Tahiti. The baby would have been born by then and would need the security of life ashore. The first stop after the Australes would be Huahine. This was a rich fertile island of mountains and rivers and numerous villages, almost within sight of Raiatea. Here they would leave the Porpoise of the Waves and settle down to raise their family.

"Settle down in *Huahine? Us?"* Hina looked at him in perplexity, but Ken's attention was on green hills and valleys far beyond the white-capped waves that were rolling slowly by on either side. Already he could see something the sort of life they would lead. It would be just as if Kristin had come to join him. He would continue to instruct Hina, while returning to his trade as a carpenter to earn a living. Whatever tools the inhabitants of Huahine were now working with, he would improve. But even if he had to work with clam shells and rocks, he was still, and forever, a master carpenter. After he had built a house for themselves and they were well settled down, he could then start on his plans to open a little school and museum, to preserve the heritage of the past and pass on whatever knowledge he could recall. Hina would join him in this as more and more she became that person from the past who was all he needed to complete his happiness. Together they would be a beacon of learning and —

"That's crazy," interrupted Hina, rubbing her hand nervously around and around the smooth brown skin of her hard flat belly, as if marveling that all these absurd speculations could be growing out of a single tiny node that had not yet begun to stir. "I can't go and live on Huahine. I'm an *Arioi,* not a Chinese farmer!"

Ken heard her as if from a great distance. "You'll see how pleasant it will be," he said mildly, his eyes already on the small thatched house in the middle of a sunlit clearing with bright bougainvillaea and hibiscus growing all about it. A tall slim woman with long black hair that fell in two braids over her firm breasts was stepping down from the house, a golden-headed baby in her arms. Even the fine breasts were no longer naked and exposed — now they were covered by a shirt of white and green checks. . . .

His happiness was nearly fulfilled. Soon all the degrading practices of the Arioi would be a forgotten thing of the past, along with the strange and terrifying events that had befallen him since that disastrous day a villager of Hanavavé had casually informed them of the authentic UFO that had come to visit the far-off cities of the world. Now he and Kristin would build their new life together in the quiet peace of some small village in Huahine and never again would they be parted.

Hina was both baffled and vexed by Ken's totally incomprehensible stubbornness and wrongheadedness. At last, after lengthy consultations with the other Arioi, she did the only thing possible to redress the situation: on the eighth day she aborted the foetus. Informed too late of what she was doing, he arrived just in time to watch aghast as she casually dropped what must have been his child into the blue-green waves to float away on the current. Numbed, he fought against a terrible impulse to leap into the surging waves and with his child find an eternal peace, then turned without a word and stumbled into the cool shade of the cabin, where he cast himself into its darkest corner to stare sightlessly at the plaited wall.

Late that night, when he had at last fallen into a tortured sleep, Kristin came to him briefly in his dreams. She was just as he had recalled her, tall and slim with sparkling hazel eyes and broad pale lips and a pale white bathing suit around her breasts and hips that melted away to become the pale white flesh he had always loved, and he asked himself in his dream as she approached how he could ever have confounded this, the *real* Kristin, with that totally different being who was only pretending to be Kristin. "Ken," she beseeched him, throwing out her arms but somehow being unable to wrap them around him even though he stood just before her, "Oh Ken, I long for you . . . I long for you." Her eyes were wild and anguished. "Oh save me, Ken, *save me!"*

Two days later, while Ken still lay in a corner of the cabin, one of the female flickermen hovered briefly about Hina, who was sulkily cleaning fish on deck, then moved off to one of the other two ships. The Arioi aboard the Porpoise of the Waves watched it reappear a short time later with the three others, floating serenely across the waves, to once again seek out Hina. The Arioi girl looked up without interest at the four pale luminescences that surrounded her, then turned back to the fish.

Ten minutes later they were still there and she began to feel a trifle unsettled by their constant presence. "Stupid ghosts," she shouted irritably, "be off with you! Do you think I'm going to make love with these stupid fish for your stupid pleasure?" Angrily she splashed a gourd full of sea water at them.

A long moment later the four palely glowing forms unexpectedly converged to envelop her where she sat. Petrified, the Arioi watched

Hina's hunched-over brown form begin to flicker within the shapeless glow of the four merged beings. Her body arched nearly backwards, and they heard a terrible scream start to rise, only to suddenly choke off. For a timeless moment Hina's rigid body quivered slightly, then toppled backwards to the deck, where she lay with mouth agape and eyes staring blankly upwards. The deep blue the flickermen had momentarily assumed was already fading, and slowly the four of them were now moving about their separate ways. Half a dozen still-living fish from the overturned basket flapped spasmodically against Hina's motionless feet.

Tre'ze had completely attuned herself to the highly individual pattern of Mine's field, and after she had realized that he appeared to mate with but a single female, to that of the female Ugly as well. It was well that she did so, for otherwise she would not have noticed the faint, almost imperceptible variation in the female's pattern that appeared one day and gradually grew stronger. She and the other three Silumiut who were accompanying the ships consulted together and jubilantly decided that this was what they had been so devoutly hoping for: a newly conceived Ugly, one who would inherit his father's unique characteristics. Already, they felt, they could distinguish in the foetus's feeble spectrum something of the pattern that so clearly set Mine apart.

After that, her primary attention swung from Mine to his pregnant female, for it was with her now that their interest lay. Unfortunately most of the Ugly's daily activities and patterns of behavior were still as incomprehensible to Tre'ze as when she had first come to Water. That was why Tre'ze had no way of knowing what was happening to the tiny creature within the Ugly's belly until suddenly its field began to flicker and then suddenly snuffed out.

Two days later Tre'ze and the others were still unable to decide whether the termination of the foetus's life had been deliberate or simply one of the many accidents that befell this primitive species. But whatever the case, it was clear that this particular Ugly could not be entrusted to bear any future offspring of Mine. They considered briefly the means of making her unavailable to him, and then moved off purposefully to do what had to be done. Perhaps it would also serve as an object lesson to the other female Uglies. . . .

CHAPTER 18

Ken's initial shock quickly gave way to relief, and he thrust the unpleasant memory of Hina from his mind. Soon she was as wraithlike to him as the flickermen, and far less real. Only Kristin now mattered, and he could clearly see that she was not to be found among the Arioi, no matter how alluring any of them might seem. Once again he shrouded himself behind the impersonal detachment he had sworn to maintain before he had inexplicably allowed himself to be ensorcelled by that malevolent being whom the flickermen had so providently removed from his life.

The Arioi, however, were appalled. Was it to punish their association with the white man from beyond the sky-curtain that the flickermen had suddenly struck down one of their number? Or even more chilling: was it Ken himself who had called upon the flickermen to take a terrible revenge upon Hina for whatever girlish slights she might have thoughtlessly inflicted? If so, he was truly the Son of the Flickermen, and possessed, perhaps, of too powerful a mana for even the Arioi to withstand.

But Ken was unmoved by the initial hostility that emanated from the Arioi after Hina's death. Hadn't *they* encouraged her to . . . to do that deed that was so abominable that even the flickermen could no longer bear her presence among them? Obviously! So now they must share the responsibility. . . .

And if they wouldn't?

Would they simply throw him overboard, some dark night when the waves were high and the winds were howling? How convenient that would be. . . .

Or would they dare? His flickerwoman trailed in Ken's wake with far more persistence than could be explained by random chance. Would the Arioi note her glowing blue presence and heed the lesson of what had become of the only one of their number to ever grievously displease the Son of the Flickermen? It would be interesting to find out, he told himself bleakly. In the meantime, he would be wary of stepping near the edge of the boat late at night when the cold sparkle of no flickermen could be seen.

But the Ariois' initial hostility gradually gave way to a distant coldness, which in turn became a cautious reserve, which finally seemed to peter out as it became apparent that the flickermen were not about to strike down any more of their number. Perhaps the whole sad affair had nothing to do with their Strange White Wiggly Snake after all. Perhaps for reasons that would never be understood, the four flickerman had been displeased by the girl Hina splashing them with seawater while they meditated above her. Perhaps. Perhaps. But in the future it might be best to accede to the Son of the Flickerman's desires whenever they were at all within the realm of the possible. . . .

Ken's desires were as modest as they had ever been. The only important ones, those concerning Kristin, were never spoken of to anyone except Kristin herself when she came to visit him occasionally in his dreams. Outwardly his relationship with the Arioi was unchanged from what it had been. He ate with them, slept among them, participated in their shows, helped them keep their boats in good repair. Was there now an unavowed and intangible barrier of caution and reserve that was never entirely breached, even in their most intimate moments? Ken shrugged the notion off. If there was, it was the Ariois' doing, not his.

Slowly the three ships worked their way through those isles of the Gambiers that had been trapped within the sky-curtain, then began the long voyage that would take them westward to Raivavae and the other islands of the Australes. If the ships had turned far to the south on their present journey, he knew, they would come eventually to Rapa Iti, assuming the Arioi were the navigators they claimed to be. But Ken had no desire to see what might have transpired in the hundred years since his last memorable encounter with the natives of that isolated speck of land, and none of the Arioi were eager to sail so far south for whatever might be gained from the visit to a single small island.

The islands of the Australes all resembled Rapa, green and mountainous and far cooler than the torrid atolls of the Tuamotus. They were densely populated, with far more inhabitants than had lived there even in pre-European times, for the islands were temperate and fertile and supported many kinds of agriculture. Surprising numbers of the natives rode about on horses in the course of their daily lives, and there were small herds of cattle on some of the lush upland plateaus. For the first time in years Ken tasted beef and carrots and — most wonderful of all — potatoes roasted in ashes and eaten with enormous portions of luscious home-made butter. Perhaps, he thought, as he reached for yet another potato, *this* is where I should leave the Arioi and spend the rest of my life.

But the very words *spend the rest of my life* had ominous and depressing overtones, however agreeable the prospects of occasional steaks and baked potatoes might be, and on balance the idea was not an agreeable one. He was barely thirty years old, yet already his life had taken many bizarre turns. Who was to say that even stranger — and conceivably more pleasant — ones might not be waiting for him somewhere in the miles and islands that lay ahead?

So as the Arioi moved slowly from village to village, and then on the next island in the chain, Ken remained aboard. As Tamuela had warned him, the women of the Australes were big and powerful and many of them were as fat as he recalled the half-forgotten Mama Tito as being. A smattering of religion seemed to have survived in many of the villages as well, so the Arioi were far more discreet in the shows they put on. They could occasionally be as uninhibited as in the Tuamotus, but far more often they presented little more than their formal dancing and musical programs of old-time *himénés*. If they did put on a second show, it was apt to be more bawdy than obscene, and even then there was noisy trouble with some of the stricter churchgoers who were descendants of the Protestants, Catholics, Mormons, and Adventists who seemed to have come en masse from Tahiti during the great migrations of a century before.

Except for attending the wedding services of two of his friends, Ken had never been to church in his life and had paid no heed to whatever role religion had played in his village in the Marquesas so long ago. Certainly it had not been in evidence in the lives of the islanders of Takaroa. So now he marveled that here in the Australes the Maohi seemed by and large to have maintained their diverse beliefs, while in the atoll islands to the north no trace of Christianity remained that he could see. Perhaps Kristin would have seen at a glance why this was so, but in any case it was no interest to him except as how it affected the fortunes of the Arioi and himself.

But he quickly realized that religion made a convenient excuse for refraining entirely from the distasteful business of mingling with the stout Australe women who were so little to his taste. Instead, as the months passed after the disappearance of Hina, he gradually began to turn his brief attentions to the other Arioi girls and women. Their initial nervousness had mostly faded by now, and he used them as unceremoniously and as dispassionately as they themselves used one another.

So this is what it might be like for a rooster in a farmyard, he thought, as he one day realized he had now coupled with nearly every female aboard the *Porpoise of the Waves,* as well as many of those on the other two ships. But at least the willing *vahinés* of the Arioi appeared to take more notice of the proceedings than did the average chicken, and with one or more of the troupe's flickermen always in attendance during their love-play it was the women who sought him out as often as the contrary.

"Fortunate for you that your Skinny White Sea Snake is so puny and easily satisfied," teased Tamuela as they sat idly one day watching the distant twinkling of three of the flickermen hovering over one of the other ships. "Hardly exerting itself, it is never greatly tired, and so is readily available for the convenience of all these undiscriminating women."

Ken could only grin and shrug non-committally.

"Note," said Tamuela holding up a finger, "your incessant activity frees the men of the ship from all this tiresome business, and permits them to reserve their forces for those charming ladies of the islands who are so rightly enamored of our manly attributes that they eagerly offer us their most precious goods in return for their momentary accommodation."

"You're saying that I'm a benefactor to the ship."

"Exactly."

Ken could feel his body shaking all over with silent laughter. Was it he who thought that Tahitians had no sense of humor? "I fear it has more to do with the flickermen than anything I myself have to offer."

"That may well be, O Noble Son of the Flickerman. You have noted there is nearly always one of the female flickermen hovering about you? Is she there to help you entice young girls and ancient matrons to your arms? Or merely as a fond mother, hovering about her only child?"

Ken laughed aloud, something he did so rarely that the sound of it in his ears startled him. "I will consider your question attentively," he replied, rising to his feet, "and answer you in due course." As he strolled off he said to himself that there was something very different about thinking and talking in Tahitian — could he ever had said anything as unnatural as that in English?

Just as there was something different about the flickerman, or flickerwoman really, who seemed to have become his semi-permanent companion. The thought had been gnawing at him for some time now, at first idly, and then with more insistence. Perhaps he should have mentioned to Tamuela. Or conceivably Tamuela was also aware of it and had been attempting to broach the subject in a roundabout fashion.

Ridiculous! Why would Tamuela bother to be so subtle?

No, it was probably only Ken who was coming to believe that he could now distinguish one wraith from the other, that he did indeed have a particular flickerwoman who had singled him out for her attentions.

But was the notion really so absurd? Hadn't he laughed at Kathie Leitner when she had suggested she could distinguish between male and female flickermen? And hadn't the initially shapeless beings continued to evolve, until they were now either clearly males or females? Why shouldn't they now take the next step and cast themselves into distinct individuals?

* * * *

There was a long pause after the disposal of the female Ugly, and then one day Mine suddenly resumed his mating activities. Tre'ze was pleased to see that now they were spread among a wide variety of partners, and she eagerly joined herself to their pleasurable games. As the months passed his neural radiation seemed to be constantly gaining in strength, increasing Tre'ze's own pleasure far beyond what she had ever considered possible.

As the positive feedback between the two of them continued to grow, she found herself being tugged in some unfathomable way into a curiously heightened state of tension from which she was unable to find any easy release. Her limbs continued to gain definition, and now she was aware of them as separate parts of her body that occasionally moved back and forth in unconscious imitation of the female Uglies. Just about the time she discovered that first one, and then another, and then a third of Mine's partners were pregnant with his offspring an appallingly bizarre idea slowly began to suggest itself to her: that some horrible compulsion was building up within her very body that demanded an increasingly material form. . . .

That evening he sought out one of the older and more agile of the Arioi women. His flickerwoman was already present when he pulled themselves over so that Maeva was now straddling him from above, a position that most of the Arioi disliked. Maeva however grinned down cheerfully at him, then tossed her long hair over her shoulder and with her eyes closed began to rotate her hips slowly around his rigid flesh. Hardly conscious of what she was doing, Ken lay back to examine the flickerwoman — his flickerwoman? — that hovered just to the left of Maeva.

Even at nighttime it was hard to be certain, given the insubstantiality of the flickermen, but this one seemed marginally less tenuous, a trifle more distinct, indefinably different in both color and texture from the other flickerwoman. The shape of her face was clearly that of a woman's, and as her coruscating lights and twinkling sparkled and glowed without ever holding a fixed shape, there were tantalizing glimpses of what might conceivably be the rudimentary forms of cheekbones, eye-sockets and a nose. A single braid of long hair was occasionally hinted at against her back, while her breasts were plump and well-formed. To Ken there was no doubt at all that she was distinctly different from the other flickerwoman. Even her hands and feet more closely resembled those of a human being. Was he really the only person aboard to see this? Even as he considered this, the flickerwoman began to slowly merge her glowing nimbus around Maeva's gleaming body, and he gave himself up to the passions of the moment.

By the time the troupe reached Rimatara, the last of the Australe island chain, the already dim memory of Hina seemed to have faded entirely from the consciousness of the Arioi. He learned now to his considerable surprise that one of the girls with whom he had made love was pregnant, and then a second, and then a third. He had no knowledge of their means of avoiding it, but he knew it was rare for an Arioi to conceive unless she wanted to. Was there some significance in this burst of sudden pregnancies, or was it simple coincidence?

"Your Great White Sea Monster possesses enormous mana of its own," said Tamuela after Ken had posed the question. "At least, so these foolish girls seem to think. Or perhaps they are all so overcome by ecstacy at the intrusion of your flickerwoman that they no longer think to take their regular precautions."

"Do *you* think I'm . . . the father of all these babies?"

"Perhaps. Perhaps not." He looked at Ken keenly. "Does it matter to you who is the father?"

Ken looked deep within himself. "Not at all," he said at last. He gestured to indicate all the other members of the boat. "Suppose the babies *were* all mine? None of *them* would mind?"

Tamuela looked surprised. "Mind? That the Son of the Flickermen is the father of new Arioi? Why should they mind? On the contrary, it can only bring good fortune to all of us."

"I see."

"And this time," said Tamuela grimly, "there will be no . . . accidents with the unborn babies. You may assure yourself of that. And your friends the flickermen," he added so softly that Ken could barely make out the words.

"Ummph," said Ken uneasily, and turned the subject to what Tamuela and the Arioi knew of the flickermen, for as the weeks passed it seemed to him that more and more the glowing phantasms were encroaching on his life. In all probability he was completely helpless to resist their purposes, but it could do no harm to try to comprehend them as fully as possible.

To his surprise he learned that in Tamuela's opinion there might not be more than a few hundred of the unfathomable beings for all the myriad islands of Polynesia.

"No one has ever bothered to count them, you understand," said Tamuela, "and how could they? But after observing them and their ways for many generations now, that is the conclusion that must be reached. You will find, for instance, that in the great city of Uturoa on Raiatea with its many thousands of inhabitants there are no more than ten or twenty at the most."

"And yet we have four."

"Exactly!" said Tamuela proudly. "Now you know what it means to be Arioi!"

Equally surprising was Tamuela's conviction that the flickermen who drifted about today's primitive Polynesian world were the same as those whom Ken had initially seen in Papeete a century before, however much their superficial outlines might have changed.

"A hundred years old!"

"What is a hundred years to a flickerman?"

Ken had never before considered the flickermen in terms of age. What *was* a hundred years to a flickerman? Perhaps less than the span of a single week to a human being. . . . Could that be why it had always proven impossible to communicate with them in any meaningful fashion? With the best intentions in the world, how could human beings communicate with some of the varieties of gnats that were born, lived, and died within a matter of hours?

"It is said that the *farani* soldiers long ago learned to talk to them," ventured Tamuela. "Not long after they appeared, and before the French banished the Maohi from Tahiti."

"It doesn't seem to have brought them any great advantages."

"Unless they helped the *farani* expel the Maohi from their homeland."

But that was of little concern to Ken. "And in all this time none of you Arioi have ever distinguished between individual flickermen, you who have had them as permanent companions for many generations now?"

"Never," said Tamuela with absolute conviction. "When we go ashore, on most islands our flickermen mingle briefly with those already ashore. Afterwards we travel on with four flickermen. But who is to say whether these are the same four we arrived with? No, even the fish in the ocean, the grains of sand on the beach, have more individuality than the flickermen. Although it appears to please them to float slowly alongside our ships, moving at the same pace as we do, they are known to be able to cover vast distances in a single instant, as when the twenty-four came to . . . visit us some time ago. For all we know, every morning we awake to find a different three or four flickermen attending us."

"I see," said Ken, and turned the conversation to other matters without asking if the eerie wraiths had ever been known to attach themselves to a single person. Was it really wise to let Tamuela and the Arioi know that he possessed what he now knew to be his own particular flickerwoman?

Was it possible that for inscrutable reasons of their own the Arioi were only *pretending* that they didn't recognize her individuality? Or was it merely a case of over-familiarity? Having had the flickermen about them for generations now, were the Arioi no longer capable of seeing them as they actually were?

But now that *he* had identified a particular flickerwoman, was it his imagination or were his orgasms, even with a multitude of partners, becoming even more transcendent than they had been with Hi . . . with that girl who had once so cruelly deceived him? Connoisseurs of wine, he knew, had elaborate standards by which they graded and classified fine vintages. But had anyone ever drawn up a scale of comparison to judge the relative excellence of orgasms?

He grinned wanly. Perhaps even now, in laboratories far beyond the confines of this forcefield, a Nobel-prize-winning team of French scientists was working on the matter.

His grin quickly faded at the thought of what lay beyond the flickermens' sky-curtain, for that was where Kristin had gone and where it seemed she must have remained. Once he had thought he had regained her, but that had been proven a tragic illusion. Now his life seemed to be little more than a plaything in the hands of the flickermen. If so, there was nothing he could do about it. But oh! if only he could share the transcendent joys of the flickerwoman's fiery presence in a relationship of mutual commitment and absolute love such as he had known with Kristin. . . .

What then would their love be like?

CHAPTER 19

Before them loomed the forbidding mass of Raiatea, nearly hidden by the heavy black clouds gathering along the summit of the great mountain that dominated its skyline. Unlike the soaring peaks of the Marquesas this mountain was a single monolith of flattened gray stone like an enormous gravestone lying on its side. The perpendicular cliff it presented to the sea was shrouded in shadows, as were the smaller peaks that ran into the distance from either side of its depressing facade.

On the horizon to one side of the *Porpoise of the Waves* was the pale blue outline of the island of Bora-Bora, while on the other side the even fainter shape of Huahine could be seen. Behind the ship were the green peaks of Raiatea's small sister island of Tahaa, tenuously joined to Raiatea by several miles of coral reef that enclosed a shallow lagoon whose white sand bottom sparkled a brilliant green in the bright sunlight. Only the gloomy mass of Raiatea, wrapped in clouds and shadows, was impervious to the cheerfulness of the day.

And somewhere in that dark band of vegetation that clustered at the base of the enormous cliff, Ken knew, was the town of Uturoa, capital of the Maohi Dominion and seat of the *Métua*, Tihoti Baxter. Could there really be many thousands of people huddled there in the shadows of that gloomy mountain, as Tamuela had said?

He had his answer a short time later as their ships sailed carefully through the pass between the pounding surf on either side and into the shelter of the quiet harbor. As the three ships drew closer Ken could see what appeared to be every one of those many thousands gathered on the crumbling concrete quay that ran for several hundred yards along the waterfront. Beyond them, mostly hidden in the shade of towering mango and breadfruit trees was the town of Uturoa, looking as if some long-ago war had once been fought there.

The noisy crowd cheering their arrival at the dock ignored the heavy gray rain clouds that hung ponderously against the mountainside, casting a mournful gloom over what should have been a joyful entrance into a picturebook village of the South Seas. But probably they didn't have much else to cheer about, thought Ken, inexpressibly depressed by his initial view of Uturoa.

Everywhere he saw blackened ruins of one- and two-story concrete buildings, their roofs collapsed, their walls broken and shattered. Most of them were now little more than piles of rubble, almost totally hidden by the ubiquitous vines and vegetation of the islands that could so quickly obliterate the traces of everything manmade. Scattered among the ruins, and as far to either side as he could see, were the small thatched-roof homes of plaited bamboo or coconut fronds that he had seen everywhere in his travels throughout the archipelago.

Each Arioi was crowned by an enormous garland of sweet-smelling flowers as he stepped ashore, and the crowds jostled one another for the privilege of draping flower leis around their necks. A thousand lips seemed to smack wetly against Ken's cheeks and mouth. Feeling almost invisible behind the enormous depth of flowers that nearly masked his face, Ken marched with the others in a long procession along the muddy thoroughfare through the center of town to the rhythmic accompaniment of drums and wooden *toérés*. Everyone who had been at dockside seemed to be accompanying them, joined now by a thousand scrawny dogs that ran in and out of their legs, yelping and growling.

The procession wound through what must have been the pre-flickerman city, and Ken could see now that all of the ruins were the result of fire rather than warfare. When he turned his eyes to the thousands of people who swarmed around them he could see that many of them were as clear-skinned as himself. So much for the Takaroans' stout affirmation that all the *demis* had been long ago liquidated by vengeful Maohis of untainted blood. . . .

Their destination was on the far side of town, where a small park had been hacked out of the thick growth of trees and underbrush that blanketed the island. Here was a spacious green lawn instead of the tramped-down dirt that surrounded all of the hundreds of huts that jostled against one another in the town. Three large structures of traditional Tahitian design and of graceful proportions nestled in the shade of towering ironwood trees. Two enormous stone tikis stood guard at the entrance of the largest of the long, low buildings, and the varnished coconut trunks that served as posts and beams had been carved into a multitude of shapes. The low walls of the semi-open buildings were of glossy bamboo, and the steeply-pitched roofs were of fresh new pandanus. Beyond the buildings Ken could catch glimpses of the blue of the open ocean and the faint outline of Huahine on the distant horizon.

Gradually the park filled with people while the drums and *toérés* kept up their incessant beat. Ken had purposely tried to lose himself somewhere in the middle of the procession, so it was now with some difficulty that he watched the ceremony that took place at the steps of the central building.

The drumbeats reached a noisy crescendo, then came to their usual sudden halt. From where he stood he could see little more than Tamuela and the other leaders of the Arioi exchanging formal greetings with seven Tahitians males who had stepped from the interior of the building. The seven wore sparkling white tapa-cloth pareos and long red cloaks of some bright red material that descended in thick folds around their otherwise naked torsos. Large glossy necklaces of mother-of-pearl shell and sharks' teeth lay on their chests, while their heads were nearly concealed by elaborate ceremonial headdresses of pandanus, shells, and feathers.

Six of them, Ken could see, were broad, powerful Tahitians with thick brown arms and legs and enormous round bellies. In the midst of these six stood a small clear-skinned man of indeterminate age who appeared to be nearly swallowed up by the costume in which he found himself. The men beside him carried long wooden javelins with glossy white tips that might have been carved from ivory. He himself held beside him a ceremonial warclub carved with elaborate intricacy from some dark brown wood. The little man shrank into insignificance in the midst of the massive Polynesians who surrounded him, but Ken had little doubt that this was the titular leader of the supposedly far-flung Maohi Dominion, the *Métua* of the Polynesian people, that almost mythical creature, Tihoti Baxter.

There were speeches by various of the Arioi and the locals, all of which Ken ignored, followed by dancing and songs performed by well-rehearsed groups of Raiateans. The ceremonies were far too elaborate to have been improvised, and he knew that the natives of Uturoa must have been preparing for their arrival for some time now. Which, of course, was not particularly surprising, as the three ships had just come from a two months' stay on Huahine, an easy day's crossing to Raiatea. As the interminable ceremonies dragged on he spent more and more time looking up at the ominous black clouds clinging to the mountainside nearby, expecting a terrible downpour at any moment. But though the sky grew darker and darker the rain refused to come, and presently the long procession began to make its way back to their ships.

The following day the Arioi were led to a somewhat swampy clearing in the midst of a dank grove of towering bamboo and shady green chestnut trees and began to prepare their customary quarters for the rest of their stay ashore. Two days after that they put on the first of a number of shows in a theater that was far more elaborately constructed than anything Ken had seen to date.

The first performance was of their ceremonial dancing and singing, and was witnessed by the gorgeously clad men and women of what Tamuela told him was the local aristocracy. A caste system had been slowly developing on Raiatea and its neighboring islands for several generations now, and here in Uturoa, the dominant city in the Maohi world since the mass expulsions from Tahiti a century before, society was far more stratified than anywhere else.

This was easy enough to believe, thought Ken, as he watched the performance through a chink in the bamboo backdrop and contrasted the sleek men and women of the audience with the bedraggled and impoverished Polynesians of the hundreds of small huts that made up the city of Uturoa. Nowhere else in his voyaging had he encountered such disparity between rich and poor, and he wondered what there was in Uturoa to keep so many people living there under its perpetually dark and gloomy skies.

Tihoti Baxter was seated inconspicuously in the middle of the audience, hardly recognizable without his elaborate ceremonial costume as the *Métua,* or leader, of all the Maohi people. There seemed to be a certain cleverness about his thin, pinched face, decided Ken, but even that might be reading too much into it. Certainly he seemed no more charismatic a leader than the junior-high shop teacher of Ken's he so closely resembled. And, of course, it might only be in Tihoti Baxter's own imagination that he was the leader of anything more than a small clique of eccentrics here in the town of Uturoa. . . .

But that was not quite the truth, he learned in the weeks that followed. There had once been fourteen islands in the east-to-west archipelago known as the Society Islands. Four of them now were in the hands of the French: the most important of them all, Tahiti; its sister island of Moorea; and the two nearby islets of Tetiaroa and Mehetia.

The remaining ten now comprised what Tihoti Baxter was pleased to call his Maohi Dominion. Raiatea, which had traditionally been the second island in importance after Tahiti, was its capital. To the east was the populous island of Huahine and the smaller, low-lying island of Maiao. To the northwest were Tahaa, Bora-Bora and Tupai. Further west was Maupiti, and beyond that the three insignificant islets of Mopelia, Manuae, and Motu Oné. As the distances grew from Tihoti Baxter's center of power in Uturoa, so did the influence of the Maohi Dominion wane. Judging by what he had seen in Huahine, Ken reckoned it must be close to non-existent by the time it reached Motu Oné. The nearest islands in the Tuamotu group, Mataiva, Tikehau, and Rangiroa were also under the nominal sway of the Dominion, but most of the inhabitants of those islands would have been astonished to learn it. . . .

"The Dominion extends as far east as the Gambiers, as far south as Rapa, as far west as Aitutaki, as far north as the Marquesas," said Tihoti Baxter grandly.

"I see," said Ken non-committally, who knew from personal experience that this was not the case in at least three of the four instances. Aitutaki he had never heard of.

"Or at least," said the ruler of the Maohi Dominion with a rueful smile, "it is supposed to."

Ken found it impossible not to return the smile. It was difficult not to find something likable in the absurd spectacle of this small pale-skinned creature loudly proclaiming his leadership of all the enormous brown-skinned Polynesians he called his own. Just how seriously Tihoti Baxter himself took it all, Ken found impossible to judge.

They were seated on uncomfortable wooden chairs of *tau* wood on a slightly raised dais in the far end of the smaller of the three buildings that served as the center of the Dominion's government. The dais was made of highly polished wood that glowed almost golden in the long shafts of sunlight that slanted in beneath the overhanging thatched roof, while the floor of the rest of the building was of carefully raked white sand.

Great sprays of flowers were set throughout the room and on the small tables and chairs that were scattered incongruously across the sand. A dozen large Tahitians idled at the far end, talking and laughing raucously. Three bare-breasted girls in their middle teens sat behind Tihoti Baxter languidly cooling themselves with what appeared to be Chinese fans and giggling softly amongst themselves. Ken and the ruler of the Maohi Dominion were sipping tepid limeade from genuine glasses, tall heavy water tumblers that had somehow survived the ravages of the past century.

"You were asking earlier about the date," said Tihoti Baxter, smoothly changing the subject. "Today is the 27th of August, 2108. I'm afraid that you had the misfortune to fall initially upon those who have been too long deprived of the benefits of our civilization. Not *every* island in Polynesia has reverted to semi-barbarism, you know."

"So I see," said Ken. Tihoti Baxter himself spoke the same educated Tahitian that his old Mormon teacher in Hanavavé had once taught him. "Raiatea is . . . well —"

"Not what you imagined it to be, eh? You mustn't believe everything you hear from the Arioi, you know. You have spent a considerable time amongst them, I believe?"

Ken shrugged. "Two, three, four years. No one kept a calendar."

"Here we keep calendars," said Tihoti Baxter firmly. "Among other things. Here we also keep the heritage of the Maohi safeguarded, and we keep the French in check on Tahiti. As the Dominion expands and its influence grows, the French become more and more intransigent on those islands that they have stolen from us and that it is our solemn duty to reclaim. To this I am sworn, and in this I am certain you will prove invaluable."

"I ?" said Ken in astonishment.

"Are you not the Son of the Flickerman? So the Arioi have assured me." Tihoti Baxter leaned forward, and gestured delicately with the motion of a single finger. "Is not that your own flickerman who hovers in the far corner of the room?"

"You mustn't believe everything you hear," evaded Ken.

"Particularly from the Arioi, eh?" All the good nature had suddenly vanished from his face. "The Arioi have come to believe that they are a law apart, exempt from any obligations to the Maohi Dominion of which they are actually no more than court jesters. Let us hope that *you* are not entirely Arioi in your conceptions of this matter. For sometime soon now they will almost certainly have to be taught a sharp lesson. No longer can we permit them to encourage defiance and challenges to our authority among those ignorant islanders on whose gullibility they batten."

Ken bristled at the hostility in the *Métua's* voice, but responded mildly enough. "I'm nothing more than a carpenter who —"

"— has been miraculously transported to us from out of the past. We will speak of this soon at great length, and carefully evaluate everything you have to tell us. You, Ken Camden, with or without your supposed flickerman, are almost certainly the most important man in the world today."

"Important?" scoffed Ken, more annoyed than amused. "In what ways? I can't design a better boat, or grow a better tomato, or build a printing press, or produce gasoline from mangos to power an electric generator built from scrap metal." He glanced around at the cunningly-designed joists and beams of the high-roofed long-house in which they conferred. "Even as a builder I doubt if I could improve on the workmanship or design shown here. Nothing I know is of any great use."

"You are an educated man from a great civilization. The least bits of your knowledge will be of significance. More than that," said Tihoti Baxter softly, glancing cautiously over his shoulder at the three chattering girls, "you come from an epoch of great warriors. You will teach us the art of war, and you will help us retake Tahiti from the French."

It was hard to keep from laughing. "I was a carpenter, not a soldier."

Tihoti Baxter scowled. "You seem to glory in your uselessness. How then should we distinguish you from a *farani?* We have only your own word for this preposterous story of your origins. Where is the proof that you are not actually a cunning French spy? The Arioi may be gullible, but *I . . . .*" With a soft sigh he sat back and signaled for one of the girls to refill their glasses. "Very well," he said presently. "We shall reflect on the matter. Perhaps you can be of use. Perhaps not. If not. . . ." He sighed again, more loudly this time, and his long cold stare, Ken knew, was the last warning he would receive.

Tamuela was concerned, but not overly surprised, when told of Tihoti Baxter's comments regarding the Arioi. He in turn sighed. "Loyalty to himself and his follies — what else does any princeling ever demand? It has been the same for many generations now. Whenever some would-be ruler sets himself above the ordinary folk of any of the islands, the first thought that comes to mind is that henceforth the Arioi must heed his every petty command." He snorted. "But princelings come and go, and the Arioi continue as they please, beholden to no man and no princeling."

"There are many thousands here in Raiatea, and at most a hundred Arioi," pointed out Ken. "If only a few of his supposed subjects chose to obey Tihoti Baxter, they could still overwhelm us by sheer numbers."

"Yes," said Tamuela sadly. "We have already considered this at length. We are still the Arioi, but it is perhaps best that we give this latest princeling no undue cause to move against us." He stepped forward to clasp Ken's bare shoulders with his powerful brown hands. "I fear, my friend the Great Wiggly Sea Snake and Enchanter of Maidens, that now we must take our leave of you. The man Baxter has made it quite clear that above all else he desires your continued presence in Uturoa."

Ken felt his heart lurch in the sudden shock. "You'd leave me here in —"

Tamuela's hands tightened on his shoulders and he smiled wanly. "I am afraid it must be. Mighty Arioi that we are, none of us possess a personal flickerwoman to mete implacable justice to our enemies. You, my dear friend, most manifestly do." His smile broadened. "Instead of being sorrowful, why not cast your mind upon those thousands of delectable maidens already maddened for the merest glimpse of your Celebrated White Sea Serpent? And whatever the consequences might be to us, we would never leave you here unless we were convinced that your flicker-woman will protect you from whatever schemes of Tihoti Baxter you may wish to be protected."

His fingers tightened a final time, and he stepped back. "I told you that we have considered this matter at some length. And we are convinced that it is Tihoti Baxter who will need protection — from *you.*"

CHAPTER 20

In the weeks that followed, Ken found that the population of Uturoa was far smaller than he had initially supposed. Tihoti Baxter's Maohi Dominion was a government of sorts, but it had little in common with the elaborate structure of what Ken had been brought up to think of as constituting a government, and there seemed no real reason for his subjects to huddle together in a city for services that didn't exist. There was no mail delivery or fire department, no city hall or department of public works, no hall of justice, no social security office, no state department, no Congress, no Pentagon.

There was, in fact, very little except Tihoti Baxter and his court of several hundred self-proclaimed nobles, most of whom were his relatives to one degree or another. By shrewd manipulation of their constant intrigues and rivalries the nondescript little man had first become leader of their family councils and had then gradually extended his influence throughout the neighboring islands. He was said to be quietly lobbying for the establishment of a royal bloodline with himself as the founding father, but up till now had been forced to remain content with the less satisfying title of *Métua* — the Leader.

He maintained himself in a precarious power with the support of an unknown number of strutting tattooed warriors who presumably enforced whatever decisions might be handed down from time to time. The only government agents that Ken recognized as such were the tax collectors, but aside from the tithes that were irregularly levied on the fruits of their labors, the small farmers and fishermen who made up the bulk of the population lived almost totally unmindful of Tihoti Baxter and his court.

There was a lively food market in the center of town, but most of the natives subsisted solely on what they themselves could grow or fish from the ocean, and in consequence the population was broadly scattered for several miles on either side of Uturoa. Only for rare events such as the coming of the Arioi did the outlying Raiateans come into town in any numbers.

So much Ken learned during his gloomy rambles through town and the surrounding countryside on those days he was not summoned to the court of Tihoti Baxter for intensive questioning concerning everything he could recall of his vanished past. The Maohi who worked the land were as hospitable and eager to meet him as any of those he had met in the other islands, and it was rare that he could stroll further than a hundred paces without hearing the standard Tahitian greeting of "Haéré mai tama'a!" "Come and eat!" Frequently he did, sharing their humble food of taro and plantains dipped into bowls of *mitihué* or *fafaru*, while crowds of naked children stared in wonder at the white man who walked about with his own flickerwoman.

One home several miles to the west of Raiatea at which he stopped to accept an impromptu invitation was surprisingly substantial, and the muscular young man who shared his copious meal of baked fish and grilled lobster was obviously far more prosperous than his neighbors. Two serving girls attended them during the meal, and Ken could glimpse other workers in the extensive vegetable gardens and plantations around the house. "A fascinating story," said Opatia when the meal had ended. "What I would give to have lived your life!"

"You're quite welcome to it," said Ken drily. "I can think of many others I would have preferred."

Opatia's handsome face smiled in disbelief. "Can you ride horse-back? Of course! I imagine there is nothing you are incapable of doing! Come." He winked slyly. "A little exercise to help our digestion while we travel a few miles to introduce you to someone whom I am certain would enjoy meeting you. And then we might return to tumble a couple of these charming girls together, eh?" He clapped Ken tentatively on the back. "What do you say?"

"All things in due course. Let me see the horses first. I would hate to leave you feeling responsible for my death."

Opatia darted an uneasy glance at the nearly invisible flickerwoman hovering in the sunlight just outside the house. "Perhaps we could walk. It is not —"

"Nonsense," said Ken heartily, suddenly enjoying his teasing of this inoffensive young man. "I adore horseback riding. Who would care if I broke my neck?"

A few minutes' ride through a broad field of gently waving sugarcane brought them to a shady grove of trees nearly at the base of the great mountain that loomed so ominously over the island. The house was even more substantial than Opatia's, with a number of large outbuildings around it. Several dozen people of both sexes lazed at their ease in the cool shade or worked at a pace that made them almost indistinguishable from the others.

As they stepped into the obscurity of the house Ken was startled by the sudden movement out of the shadows of an enormous dark silhouette that enfolded him in a smothering embrace of warm flesh. Even fatter and more regal than before, Mama Tito clasped Ken against her hard round belly and the soft pillows of her breasts and kissed him moistly on the mouth.

The rest of the day and most of the evening was spent in earnest discussion with Mama Tito and her son Opatia. It was easy enough to gather that she constituted the loyal opposition to Tihoti Baxter, but the degree of her loyalty was not one that Ken thought he would like to subject to a very severe test. Wearily he answered many of the same questions that Tihoti Baxter had already asked and politely refused an invitation to move his affairs to her estate for an indefinite stay.

"I think our *Métua* prefers I remain within hailing distance of the palace. He is still making up his mind as to whether I am a French spy or not."

Mama Tito's entire body shook with her rumbling laughter. "It is late. At least spend the night."

"Thank you. Another time perhaps."

Mama Tito nodded curtly, and Ken rode back to his small bungalow, escorted by Opatia and his glowing flickerwoman.

"You've been talking to that so-called Mama Tito creature," said Tihoti Baxter reproachfully.

"Yes."

"What does she want?"

"To sleep with me."

Disconcerted, Tihoti Baxter blinked in surprise. "That gross creature? Hah! Nothing would surprise me about her." He puckered up his lips. "Is that all? Of course not. Tell me everything about your visit."

Ken told him, adding, "She is like you: interested in learning what my world was like."

"So she says. She also has certain other interests. You would do well to be wary of her, for she is a woman of almost insensate appetite." He smiled bleakly. "In ways other than a craving for handsome young men."

Ken nodded politely.

"Now then," said Tihoti Baxter briskly. "You were telling me about these so-called hot-air balloons that could fly through the air carrying a number of men aboard them. Now suppose we procured great quantities of the finest tapa cloth —"

A month later as he left the palace in the early dusk after a particularly grueling session of explaining to a skeptical Tihoti Baxter why he knew nothing about the manufacture of poison gas, his heart suddenly leaped. Across the lawn, coming towards him was what could only be a white woman! Even from here he could see that she was tall and slim, with long dark hair. Could . . . could it be at last . . . come to rescue him . . . Kristin?

"Kristin?" he muttered, hardly daring to breathe as he numbly watched her approach, tightly flanked by two of Tihoti Baxter's muscular tattooed warriors. As she slowly passed, shoulders slumped and head bowed, her large dark eyes lifted to meet his, and he saw them widen in astonishment. Her lips parted, but before she could speak she was roughly shoved into the shadows of the long-house. Ken stood motionless for a long time after she had passed, his heart pounding in his chest, the image of her face as she had turned to look back wonderingly over her shoulder graven in his mind. . . .

A long sleepless night eventually passed. Trembling with eagerness and anxiety, he paced the trash-strewn streets of Uturoa throughout the morning while the hour of his meeting with Tihoti Baxter slowly approached. At last he was within the palace and impatiently waiting for the Métua to conclude his rambling discourse on what it would mean for the well-being of the entire Dominion if only he were to possess even the smallest of quantities of the mildest of poison gases. Finally he could restrain himself no longer. Nearly five years he had waited. But now even another few minutes was intolerable. . . .

"The . . . *popa'a* woman," he murmured in a half-strangled voice. "What is . . . who *is* she?"

"White woman?" Tihoti Baxter looked at him in surprise. "What — Ah, that one! You must have seen her last evening." He smiled sourly. "Extremely recalcitrant. If all white women are like her, then I can almost feel sorry for their *farani* men."

"She's . . . French?" Why had this startling concept never occurred to him?

"Of course, what else could be that white and that skinny?"

"But . . . what. . . ."

"Is she doing in the midst of the Maohi Dominion? Actually she has been here some little time now, several months I believe."

"Months?"

"As a prisoner. She was captured on one of our raids of Tahiti."

His heart was beating faster now and he could almost hear the blood pounding in his ears as he looked away and softly asked, "May . . . may I meet her?"

Tihoti Baxter stared at him, opened his mouth to draw in a deep breath, then closed it again. He grunted once and turned around to consider the two half-naked Tahitian girls who sat patiently plaiting pandanus hats in a corner of the room. After a long moment his eyes moved around the ceiling, as if seeking the faint outline of the flickerwoman, then returned to Ken. He grunted again, and a sardonic smile slowly crossed his lips.

"The rape of a *farani* woman is no great sport," he said offhandedly. "When one rapes a Maohi she fucks back with a will. This one lies there as if dead. Nothing arouses her, no matter how strenuous the effort."

He leaned forward to tap a fingernail against Ken's knee. His smile had faded and his eyes were cold and unyielding. "This *farani* woman is of no interest to me, even as a novelty. But many of my nobles and warriors have urged me to give her to them, that they might teach her the ways of a Maohi."

Ken could hear the hiss of his breath as sudden terrible images formed in his mind.

"But," said Tihoti Baxter, his voice falling to a whisper. "I see now that you have been too long without a woman of your own. Even your flickerwoman appears to have deserted you. I will *give* you this *farani* woman, Ken Camden, to do with as you choose — on the following condition."

"You'll give. . . ." he breathed, hardly daring to believe the words.

"I said there's a condition." His eyes met Ken's. "That from this moment on you will devote yourself exclusively, and wholeheartedly, with every resource at your command, to me, my welfare, and my projects."

Ken's heart welled up with elation and joy. Before the startled *Métua* could move Ken had embraced him formally and kissed him on both cheeks. "I accept your condition," he said softly. "I am forever yours."

Tre'ze and the other three Silumiut were puzzled when Mine came ashore with his tribe of Uglies one day and simply remained there, while the others rejoined their ships and sailed away. Was this the prelude to some possibly dangerous turn in Mine's life, or was it merely normal Ugly behavior?

But now the question was less urgent than it once might have been, for Mine had given positive proof that he bred true. Among the Uglies who had resumed their journeying were two small infants, a male and a female, both of whom had clearly inherited the pattern of Mine's extraordinary field. Two others would be born in the coming months, and it seemed increasingly hopeful that Mine's characteristics could be spread rapidly throughout the Uglies' genetic pool.

A second conclave was held, this time in the Riestu *on Home, and it was agreed that if Tre'ze wanted she could continue to watch over her prize Ugly, while his four offspring would now be permanently guarded by at least eight Silumiut.*

The meeting at the ship was the first time in many years Tre'ze had encountered her former soulcompanion Alns, who was surprised and disturbed by the many changes he found in her. "You're taking this business of breeding Uglies far too seriously," he chided. "Look at you! Even here, among your own kind, you still retain their shape." He flicked a tiny extension of his field against her in a light caress. Even before she could protest the coarseness of his gesture, he had withdrawn in distaste. "You're even beginning to smell *like them!" he said in astonishment. "Tre'ze, what's* happening *to you?"*

CHAPTER 21

"I've never heard anybody speak French like you," said Leilah Beaudenon disdainfully. She spoke with the thick slurred accent of Mediterranean France and rattled her words off at a pace like a machine-gun from between barely moving lips. It was nearly impossible for Ken to follow her speech. "I suppose it comes from becoming a savage."

Ken smiled. "It's just an American accent."

"You think I'm one of these ignorant savages, gullible enough to believe anything I'm told?"

"You don't *have* to believe me, you know," he said soothingly. "What difference does it make where I come from?"

"What *difference?*" The sharp, almost angular features of her face twisted contemptuously. "You think because these . . . these" — she burst forth with a harsh volley of words he couldn't understand — "monkeys have been taking turns fucking me that I've become like one of *them?*" She stared at him with appalling hatred, the lips of her thin hard mouth drawn back in a snarl. Her black eyes glittered dangerously. "That I'm no longer *French?*"

Disbelievingly, he felt the entire structure of the fine new world he had so elaborately constructed in his mind since Tihoti Baxter had spoken his magical words coming apart in his hands. "You misunderstand what I —"

"Misunderstand? *Merde!* That you want to fuck me too? Well, go ahead! Do whatever you like, you turncoat, you traitor, you. . . ." Her small breasts heaved beneath the rough brown pareo that covered her thin wiry body as her breath hissed in and out. She leaned forward in a sudden harsh movement, and for an instant Ken thought she was about to spit on him. "Just be certain you have six men to help you! And someday, you bastard," she whispered hoarsely, "I'll have the pleasure of cutting off your balls and throwing them to the fish!"

Ken fell back, chilled by the venom in her voice. "That's *not* what I meant!" he cried plaintively. He waved his hand despairingly in a broad circle. "There's a *million* girls out there I can . . . do that with." He looked at her helplessly, then turned away with downcast eyes. How different this meeting was from what he had so ardently envisioned! "That's not what I want," he murmured almost to himself.

She snorted loudly. "Then what *do* you want?"

Love. Affection. *Kristin.* But how could he tell her all that? "I don't know," he said mournfully. "Perhaps . . . perhaps just that you don't hate me."

"A Frenchman who's gone over to these monkeys, these terrorists, and you think I won't hate you? Are you a total lackwit? You must have picked up some of their stupidity also!"

"I'm not a Frenchman, I tell you!" He shook his head in despair. "I fall into a crowd of Tahitians, and *they* want to kill me because they think I'm a Frenchman. Then I meet a Frenchwoman, and *she* wants to kill me because she thinks I'm a Frenchman." His lips twisted into a ghastly effort at a smile. "What happens when I meet a Frenchman? Will *he* want to kill me because he thinks I'm a Frenchman?"

She seemed to choke for a moment on a stifled laugh, and then he watched in wonder as the tension in her pale white face slowly drained away, leaving only a wary suspicion. "You're *really* not French?" she asked hesitantly. "I'd have to kill you if you were, you know," she added quickly in perfect seriousness, and Ken could feel his heart melting at the absurdity of their conversation.

He shook his head. "I'm really, really not French," he said with all the conviction he could muster. "Honest."

"You're . . . *American?"*

He nodded.

She bit her lip. "Not French. And not one of these . . . savages." She raised her glittering eyes to his. "I don't know which one would be worse."

Ken shrugged unhappily, helpless in the face of the implacable hatreds that seemed to drive her. "All I want to do is . . . well, protect you, I guess." He brushed his hand across his eyes, at a loss for what to say next. "If . . . if you don't want to stay . . . I . . . I guess you can . . . well, go back to —"

She turned her head slowly, cautiously, as if seeing for the first time the small but well-built Tahitian dwelling with its fresh new pandanus roof and clean white sand floor. Thick clusters of leafy banana plants screened it from its neighbors. In the midst of the bananas was a small cookhouse where an old woman stood, deftly carving the skin from a fresh pineapple. On the other side of the bungalow was a clean airy structure that housed a shower, and yet another for a toilet.

She shuddered visibly, as if recalling some dreadful memory, and her face hardened. "I could," she said defiantly, "I could go back to . . . whatever . . . and I will if I have to." She challenged him with her glittering black eyes until he nodded, acknowledging her indomitability, then sighed softly. "But . . . prove to me you're not French and . . . and I'll stay."

The barest of grins tugged at Ken's mouth. "Once before I was in exactly the same position as I am now." His grin broadened. "But I don't think I ought to show you how I proved then I wasn't French."

She stared at him haughtily. "I don't understand what you're talking about."

"Neither do I sometimes," he said almost gaily, gripped by a sudden soaring elation. Wasn't *this* the same tough, brassy independence that had animated Kristin, the same go-to-hell attitude that was as much a part of her as the sudden smiles that dazzled like sunbursts from the depths of her terrible black angers? Kristin, he implored silently, oh *Kristin*. Just be patient. Just be patient a little while longer. . . .

He turned his attention back to the tall, almost gaunt French girl who stood before him, her arms crossed defiantly across her chest. Leilah. Leilah. Leilah. What a beautiful name. Almost as beautiful as —

He looked deep into her unfathomable black eyes, and tentatively held out his hand. "But . . . why don't you sit down, and I'll tell you about it."

She reminded Ken of a hurt and angry cat who had been deserted by the family with whom it had lived for many years, to be forced now to wrest a living from garbage cans and wild prey. Her experiences had been worse than that, of course, but she never spoke of them, and he was fearful of raising the subject, realizing how easily he could be equated with her tormentors. He watched her stalk cautiously through his small house and its surroundings, looking into every corner and behind every bush, her eyes darting rapidly back and forth, as if her semi-freedom was a terrible joke and at any moment now she might spot the tattooed warriors of Tihoti Baxter, come to take her back to whatever bleak destiny life in the Maohi Dominion might hold.

When the old woman served their first meal she pushed the fish suspiciously around the folded banana leaf that was her plate and sniffed the fresh *mitihué* with repugnance before dipping her finger carefully into the thick white liquid and tentatively poking at it with the tip of her tongue.

If she wasn't moving warily about the house, she sat huddled in a corner, her arms around her knees, her eyes fixed unblinkingly on Ken or the old woman or on the flickerwoman. The first evening, she watched Ken arranging the pillows and bedclothes on the sleeping pallet that covered nearly all of the slightly raised dais at one end of the room and spoke her first words in hours. "You want to fuck me, I suppose."

Ken grimaced at the harshness of the words, saddened and hurt that she could so misread his intentions. He smiled as reassuringly as he could. "Another time perhaps. Don't let that concern you. Please. It's no problem. Come sleep? This is the only place that's comfortable, I'm afraid."

She stared at him from out of the shadows. At last her head nodded minutely. "Later, perhaps. I won't disturb you." Ken nodded in turn and tried to arrange himself for sleep. It was a long time in coming, but before he drifted off he knew he was still alone on the pallet.

In two weeks her frame had begun to fill out, and her face had lost its pallor. She was still almost a milky white, far lighter in complexion than Ken, but that was how he recalled Kristin as being around her breasts and hips. She washed her long black hair daily in the rainwater that dripped down from the backyard shower, and cautiously accepted the gift of some scented oil from the old woman, so that soon her hair was as soft and glossy as Kristin's had been.

It was rare that she responded to his cheerful flow of idle chatter, though when she did her comments were always as sharp and pungent as a gourd of *fafaru*. But at last her curiosity was stirred by the constant presence of the flickerwoman. "That flickerman," she barked in her rapid, mumbled French that still now caused him difficulties. "She's *yours?* That's what the monkeys say."

Ken smiled quizzically. "That's a hard question. Maybe she thinks I'm *hers.* "

Leilah snorted scornfully, and returned her attention to the greasy piece of baked pig before her. Five minutes later she looked up again. "Why? Why do you say that?"

"It's a long story. The last time I tried to tell you you got bored."

"I'm bored just sitting here, just waiting for —"

"What?"

"I don't know. That's why I'm bored, I suppose. Bore me some more. Tell me about the flickermen."

A few days later she suddenly stopped him as he prepared to leave for his afternoon session with Tihoti Baxter in the nearby palace. "Why do you spend so much time with that dwarf who's the king of the monkeys" she demanded. "Neither of you appears to be queer."

Ken hesitated. Was there any particular secret to Tihoti Baxter's various projects? None that he could see. "At the moment his dearest ambition is the construction of a enormous new palace somewhere in the mountains where he will be able to look down upon all his happy subjects."

"A palace? For that . . . that banana-eating monkey?"

Ken shrugged. "I think he's really quite intelligent. He just wants something that will . . . oh, symbolize his power, his leadership over all these other Tahitians who would love to take his place. How long can one of these local-style buildings last? He thinks I can design and build him something more substantial, something more . . . kingly."

Leilah snorted contemptuously. "And can you?"

"The design might not be very kingly, but I can build it."

"And will you?" she demanded. "Why should you?"

He shrugged again. "He's given me this house, that old woman who takes care it. I've got to do something to —"

"And me," she said angrily. "Don't forget he's given you *me!*" She turned away. "Go on! Go build your palace for the monkeys!"

He shook his head sorrowfully. How blind she could be! "While he's busy building palaces," he said softly, "he's not training armies to invade Tahiti and kill your friends and relatives."

"Very well: you're not French," she said unexpectedly a few days later. "And you don't seem to be one of these monkeys."

"I *am* practically one by now. But I started out just as I told you — an American."

She stepped closer, and he could almost feel her warm breath against his face. "Then . . . there's no reason to . . . keep me here, is there?"

It was impossible to meet her eyes. "No," he admitted, looking up at a large ripening stalk of bananas.

"So now you'll let me go back to my home?"

He let his eyes move in the direction of Tihoti Baxter's palace. "Do you really think that's possible?" he asked softly.

Her eyes followed his, then came back to study his apologetic but determined face. "No," she said harshly. "I suppose it isn't."

CHAPTER 22

"Well, how is the monkey palace progressing?" demanded Leilah a few days later. "Is that all you do over there?"

Ken smiled as he considered the hours spent with Tihoti Baxter. "I'm also his Leonardo da Vinci. He thinks I might invent the submarine for him."

"I know what a submarine is. Did this Leonardo invent it?"

"About 300 years too soon — I think."

"What does *that* mean?"

"He was a genius who was way ahead of his time in almost everything. I heard someone say once he was like me — a time traveler, but one who was stuck in the past instead of the future."

"Hrmph." Like a large nervous cat wandering at random, she moved slowly around the room in ever-narrowing circles until as if by accident she found herself next to the sleeping pallet on which Ken sat. She sank to her knees on the far end, her eyes avoiding his. "Leonardo," she muttered. "Is that American? Tell me about him."

"The little I can." Ken bit his lip to hide the elation that surged through him. "I don't really —"

"And then you can tell me about time-travelers. And submarines. And what it was like in Tahiti in the year 2000, and in France, and in America."

"That's a lot to tell about in one afternoon."

"And . . . and anything else you've been telling that monster Baxter," she ran on breathlessly as she suddenly swung about to face him. For the first time since coming to live with him, she reached out to touch him, gripping his bare knee with her long powerful fingers. "Tell me everything you tell Baxter." And now her glittering black eyes pierced him directly. "And tell me everything you *don't* tell Tihoti Baxter. That's what I really want to know."

After that the mornings and evenings were spent answering her questions and recounting in the minutest detail everything he could recall of his previous life and the world in which it had passed. Her questions were as sharp and as to the point as anything Tihoti Baxter or Mama Tito had ever asked, and even more wide-ranging. In return she would occasionally answer a few of the questions he interjected about Tahiti, and gradually he began to build up a picture of the society in which she lived.

"Of course we have schools!" she said irritably "How do you think I learned to read and write? You really think Tahiti is anything at all like this island of savages?"

"That's why I was asking."

"Well, *don't!* I don't want to think about it!"

But gradually he learned of a carefree life growing up among small landowners and artisans in a society that probably wasn't much different from that of a sleepy sixteenth-century provincial town in southern France. They still had books and musical instruments as well as houses and furniture and dishes and tools left over from the days before the forcefield. Horse and buggies had replaced the vanished autos, and no one seemed concerned that a trip to visit friends on the far end of the island was now a full day's journey instead of a one-hour drive. Though the long-proposed hydroelectric project always seemed to be postponed from one year to the next, there were small schools to attend, and occasional concerts, and plenty of good food to eat, and even second homes in Moorea for those lucky enough to own a sailboat. As Leilah lost herself in her descriptions her harsh voice would gradually soften and her eyes would grow moist and shiny and it seemed to Ken as if she had led a truly idyllic existence. She had married young, and after a few unhappy years had left to live by herself in a small hut on the wild coast far to the southwest of Papeete, where she had unexpectedly been taken by a small contingent of Tihoti Baxter's warriors, who had been on more of a scouting mission than a raid. His relief was enormous. What would he have done if somewhere she had possessed a husband and children who longed for her as he still ached for Kristin?

"What about the Tahitians?"

"What about them?"

"What do they do?"

"Do? They work for us, of course. And live by themselves. What else would they do?"

Ken had once heard of serfdom, but now was uncertain as to what distinguished it from slavery. Perhaps nothing. But it was clear enough that those Chinese and Tahitians permitted to live on Tahiti were either serfs or slaves. He knew that he should be angry and horrified, but the more he became habituated to Leilah and her casual assumption of total superiority to all Polynesians the less it came to disturb him. She was wrong, of course, and someday would realize it, but in the meantime there were a hundred thousand or so of *them* out there and probably not more than ten thousand French. Let *them* do something about it if they didn't like it.

"What is this anthropology you're always mentioning?" she demanded irritably one day. "And ethnology? Why would anyone want to bother studying *Tahitians?* There must be something more to it that you're not telling me. Otherwise it wouldn't make sense."

How marvelous she was! That was just the sort of question Kristin would have asked if she had had the misfortune to have been brought up among the French racists of Tahiti instead of the genteel liberals of Bucks County. But she was learning. My god, how quickly she was learning! Everything a Kristin should know, everything a Kristin would *want* to know, she was absorbing like a giant sponge. No! Like a giant *computer!* For a day, a week, a month later the information would still be there, only now it had been sorted and correlated and placed in context with everything else she had so greedily devoured, and could be used to ask the next series of questions that he was more and more unable to answer.

Occasionally he looked back, abashed and appalled, at the memories of his aberrant behavior with that half-forgotten Arioi girl. How could he ever have shown such a lack of discernment and judgment in trying to shape such a . . . well, monkey was a harsh word, but sometimes a fitting one, into something she so obviously was never intended to be? But how different it was with Leilah, a genuinely questing intelligence that was as obviously superior to his own as his had been to . . . that other person. He saw now that his quest would someday be rewarded and that soon his years of despair and anguish would be at an end. Even now his happiness was almost complete. If only, he thought, there wasn't that one last thing which with Kristin. . . .

And even that lingering strain vanished one rainy afternoon while thunder rumbled in the mountains just behind, and long flashes of sheet lightning lit up the dark confines of their bungalow with startling brightness. As apparently oblivious to the storm as to everything else, the flickerwoman hovered motionless at the far end, indifferent to the drumming of the rain on the heavy thatch of the roof. Leilah's eyes moved from the flickerwoman to Ken and back to the flickerwoman.

"Is it true?" she demanded suddenly with her usual brusqueness. "What they say about . . . you and that flickerwoman?"

"God knows. They probably say a lot of things."

"About when you fu . . . make love. They say . . . well. . . ."

Ken shrugged. "She's just there. That's all I know."

"Hrmph." Leilah rose to her feet and without ceremony began to remove her skirt. "Well?" She looked down at him sharply. "You've put your flickerwoman through her paces for every other woman in the

Maohi Dominion, or so they say." Her lips twitched peculiarly. *Could that be a* smile? he asked himself wonderingly, while his legs began to tremble and butterflies filled his stomach. "Why don't you show me what you've shown everyone else." Her hands cupped her small white breasts and her thumbs flicked teasingly over the ends of the rosy nipples, while her eyes met his and held them. "Well?"

"You're so . . . gentle," she said later. "You make love like . . . like a woman would, I suppose."

"You don't like it?" he asked, astonished. This was certainly the last comment he had expected to hear.

"It's . . . different." She rose briskly from the tousled pallet. "I suppose I'll get used to it." She grimaced distastefully. "At least it isn't like Tihoti Baxter and his menagerie of savages."

He watched her wrap a pareo around her slim hips and start towards the showerhouse. He felt baffled and hurt. What did she want him to do — *hit* her? "I'm . . . sorry. I thought —"

"That I'm a piece of old porcelain, perhaps?" She hesitated, then deliberately let the pareo drop to the sand floor. Naked, she walked back to where he still lay, and placed her feet to either side of his chest. He raised his eyes to the fleshy lips of her sex unconcealed by her sparse black triangle, then up to the taut lines of her face as she struggled to find words for her emotions. "I . . . don't dislike you, Ken," she said at last, as if confessing to some shameful act. She dropped to her knees so that her soft breasts dangled against his smooth chest, and her arms tightened around his neck. "And I've never known anything like your flickerwoman." As her lips sought his, he heard her murmur, "I want to see if it's like that every time. . . ."

Their sex together thereafter was infrequent but of an intensity and a fervor that was as great as anything he had ever known. They would lie gasping and trembling for long minutes afterwards while the sweat slowly dried on their bodies. The flickerwoman's normal hue now seemed to be deepening and brightening, and Leilah, who had spend many months in contemplation of the glowing nimbus, was quick to note the difference. "She's almost beginning to look like a person," she said irritably. "Look at those boobs — are those nipples that are starting to stick out?" Her lips tightened in the same familiar way as Kristin's. "If she decides to grow a pussy, don't ever let me find you using it — not if you want to keep on using mine."

Ken grimaced but was tolerant of her little foibles. It was so obvious that she was trying to use her sex as a weapon, an instrument of persuasion and coercion, just as the ordinary run of women were accustomed to doing, that he wanted to laugh. But if that was how she chose to act, what was to be his response? To rape her from time to time? No, it was best to let time take its course. He had learned from his abortive experience with the Arioi girl that nothing could be rushed. Leilah had come to his bed of her own volition. Because of the flickerwoman she was drawn back to it time after time, apparently almost against her will, but enough to keep him on the thin edge of satisfaction.

Eventually she would surely come to learn how Kristin must act. . . .

He was radiant with happiness.

She didn't know what was happening to her. Her secret fear that Mine was somehow drawing her closer and closer to actual materiality she had never dared to speak of to the others. Their reaction would almost certainly be that of horror, and they might well move to terminate her on the spot, for even the hint of such a grotesque transformation would be considered outright bestiality. At the very least, they would prohibit her from ever again attending Mine. And, to her secret shame, Mine was now the one thing in all of Water that sustained her interest in living. . . .

Leilah would go nowhere except in the company of Ken, not even as far as the town's marketplace only a few hundred yards away. "There's no need to be afraid," he began maladroitly.

"Afraid?" she flared viciously. "Afraid of a tribe of monkeys? I'm afraid I'll *spit* on them, that's what I'm afraid of!"

There was little he could find to say in reply, so he turned away with a soft sigh. But she would accompany him through the untended streets of the town, stalking angrily by his side, darting defiant looks of scorn at everything about her while Ken beamed and exchanged cheerful greetings with most of the people they crossed. Her look of contempt would broaden to encompass him as well, but as the weeks passed she gradually allowed him to lead her further and further away from town, until one day he realized that she was clearly anxious to be out of the bungalow and off on one of their long rambling walks.

A few days later as they strolled along the single dusty road that ran around the island they looked up at the sudden clatter of hoofbeats to see a bare-torsoed rider approaching them rapidly. Two other horses ran behind, their tethers held in his hand. "Ho!" he cried loudly. "I've been looking for you. Why walk when you can ride?"

Ken sighed. "It's Opatia," he said. "Mama Tito's son."

Leilah was aloof and cold with Opatia, who could hardly contain his enthusiasm at the sight of her exotic beauty, but to Ken's enormous astonishment she seemed captivated by Mama Tito. The four of them sat in the shade of an ancient banyan tree whose branches extended over nearly an acre of meticulously maintained grounds behind her main house. It was near the end of the afternoon, when most Polynesians ate their main meal of the day, and enormous quantities of food were being placed on the ironwood table before them. At first Leilah said nothing, and Ken was content to let Mama Tito make the conversation, but soon he was startled to hear Leilah, who had apparently been ignoring the discussion, comment to Mama Tito in tentative, broken Tahitian.

Mama Tito's moon-like face broke into an enormous grin and she replied in equally broken French. The name of Tihoti Baxter's eventually came up, and Leilah's face instantly grew cold and rigid. Mama Tito's shrewd brown eyes studied her for a moment and then she waved imperiously at Opatia and Ken. "Be off with you," she growled. "Go discuss your many conquests by yourselves. There are matters of discussion that concern only women." And she wrapped an enormous arm around Leilah's shoulders and pulled her against her mountainous body.

Ken was only too pleased to escape Mama Tito's somewhat compromising company, and gratefully allowed himself to be led by Opatia to a small rock-lined pool that had been created in the middle of a narrow stream that burbled down from the mountains. There he sank into the cool deep water and resigned himself to a flow of eager questions about the intimate behavior of Arioi girls.

CHAPTER 23

"I have been reconsidering," said Tihoti Baxter. "If we were to build a fine new palace here in Raiatea it would only serve to confirm that this is now the permanent capital of the Maohi Dominion." He cocked his head to consider Ken thoughtfully. "Such, however, is not the case. Uturoa is clearly the . . . what is that word you used yesterday?"

"Provisional?"

"Uturoa is clearly the *provisional* capital. The true and rightful capital of the Maohi Dominion is Papeete. A new palace here would only harden the French in their obduracy. Regard! they would say. Tihoti Baxter, the so-called king of the monkeys, has resigned himself to staying in Raiatea for the rest of his life. To encourage him in this wise decision, and to celebrate the end of hostilities, let us dispatch a squadron of soldiers to Huahine to procure a few hundred additional slaves for our gardens and farms."

Ken rubbed the bristly end of his chin. "You really think that would be their likely reaction?"

Tihoti Baxter shrugged. "It seems possible. But you are my advisor in all *popa'a* matters. What is *your* opinion?"

"As you know by now, I am a builder by trade. I am far more competent advising you in the ways of building a new palace than in the means of recovering Tahiti from your enemies."

"Hah! Enemies only because they *choose* to make themselves our enemies. We Maohi are only too willing to live in peace with the *farani* — it is only necessary that they restore our lands."

"That's asking a lot after a hundred years."

"Then we must take them from them as they took them from us!" The set of his mouth was grim. "Our resources are limited. They must not be squandered on such absurdities as a new palace. We have but a single objective: Tahiti!"

Ken hoped he had suppressed the faint sigh that dealing with the *Métua* so frequently evoked. He was still as wary of Tihoti Baxter as the leader of the Maohi Dominion was of him, but his commitment to him was perfectly sincere. It was Baxter who had restored him fully to life by his overwhelming gift of the only thing that now mattered to him, and for that he had pledged his eternal loyalty. Up till now it had been a pledge that was easy to fulfill. If only Baxter could be weaned away from his obsession of liberating Tahiti from the *faranis*. . . .

For the *Métua* was obviously a man of wit and cunning, which had been further honed by the scramble to the top of the local political heap despite all the obvious handicaps he labored under. And in spite of his occasional petty angers and cruelties he was by nature a man of good will and cheery disposition. All things being equal, he genuinely seemed to wish his subjects well. Was it really the *Métua's* fault that being born into this strange kingdom of the flickermen had left him with all those attitudes and prejudices of the Polynesians whom he now supposedly ruled? He *was* a Polynesian after all. What more could you expect?

Well, why not a benevolent dictatorship? Or an enlightened despotism? With judicious advice and lucid argument perhaps Tihoti Baxter could be molded into —

He snorted at his foolishness. He, Ken Camden, had barely finished high school. What did he know about benevolent dictators or enlightened despots? Far better to find some simple means of guiding the Métua back to his elaborate dreams of a great palace in the mountains. . . .

In the early evening he returned from the long-house that served as Tihoti Baxter's palace with a large role of tapa cloth on which he had been sketching designs for a new one. The one he would propose would be no larger, but would be built for the ages in a variety of local woods and small slabs of the brittle local stone. To his surprise, and then alarm, he found Leilah gone. "She left this morning by herself," said the old woman. "Just walked on into town."

It was well after dark when she returned. She raised her eyebrows when she saw the anger and relief on Ken's face. "I've been out for a stroll," she said. "Isn't that what you've been wanting me to do?"

"But you've been gone all day! You don't know what I thought when I saw —"

"That I was gone? That I'd decided to swim back to Tahiti?"

He pulled her unresisting body against his and held her tightly. "Don't ever joke like that," he murmured into her fragrant hair. "Please."

"I'm hungry," she said, pushing herself away. "What is there to eat?"

"But where have you *been?* It's dange —"

"With my lover of course," she said over her shoulder, on her way to the cookhouse. "Where else would I be all day?"

"Your . . . lover?" he repeated numbly, unable to move while he watched her slice a grapefruit in half and peel two bananas.

She sauntered back to the bungalow, a half smile on her face. "Would it matter to you?" she asked.

"Oh *Leilah,"* he cried in anguish.

She snorted derisively and bit off half a banana. She cocked her head and regarded him with the same little taunting smile. "Very well," she said at last. "I have no lover. You may *hear* that I do, but I don't. Is that clear?"

He shook his head slowly. "I don't understand."

"Poor little Ken," she cooed, stepping forward to take his hands and place them against her soft breasts. She looked up at him with her deep glittering eyes. "Do you trust me?" she whispered, and her arms encircled his bare back. He could feel the hard bone of her pubis grinding against his sensitive flesh.

He squeezed her tightly against him. "Yes," he murmured, "I trust you, I love you, I love you. . . ."

Above them the glowing nimbus of the flickerwoman moved nearer.

After that she moved as freely about the town as if she had been back in her native Papeete, and began to exchange conversation with the old woman who took care of the house. Her Tahitian improved rapidly and there was a new sparkle in her eyes and even an occasional snatch of song on her breath. To any questions he posed she would either scowl angrily or smile mysteriously, so eventually he gave up asking them, and within a short time her independence seemed as natural to him as her morose gloom had a while before.

It was, he now realized, exactly how Kristin would be expected to behave. Had he become so absorbed by Tihoti Baxter and his half-baked projects that he had completely forgotten Kristin? Memories of last night's fervent lovemaking suddenly flooded him, and with a light step he set off for the daily audience at the palace. He had been too much concerned with the trivial aspects of her regular absences to realize how quickly time was passing, and how much had already been accomplished in guiding Leilah to her ultimate destiny. Soon now, *very* soon now, his beloved Kristin would come to join him.

When she was urgently summoned back to the Riestu yet again, not long after Mine had apparently settled down to living with but a single new mate, she was nearly panic-stricken. Her body was now clearly that of an Ugly female, and its strange demands were growing daily more insistent. Had the others at last decided to deal with the monstrosity that had sprung up amidst them?

As she entered the ship her fears increased sharply, for she could instantly feel an overwhelming aura of panic and hostility. Hesitantly she passed into the general council room where long ago Bylangu had been so horribly executed. Once again what must have been the ship's entire company was already assembled. There were Silumiut she hadn't seen in over a century and who had grown dim in her memory.

The sense of fearful agitation was almost more than she could bear. But to her enormous relief none of the others took any notice of her at all, not even Alns. For there was far more important news to concern them: against incalculable odds the ship's officers in their lifeboat had been rescued by another ship of the Continuum and were even now bearing down on the mutineers in righteous fury.

Unknown to any of the Riestu's crewmen, all ships of the Continuum carried within their propulsion systems a complex code that could be triggered by a simple communication from a line officer of the Continuum. It must have been conceived of to deal with cases of mutiny such as this one, for upon receiving the proper signal the propulsion system rendered itself inoperative.

So now, while Captain Hippelon taunted them with sardonic gibes from a year's journey beyond the solar system, the crew were trapped here on their chosen sanctuary of Water, totally unable to escape their rapidly approaching nemesis.

"Tihoti Baxter told me today that you have a lover," he said to Leilah with a forced smile.

"Did he now? Did he tell you who the unfortunate man is?"

"No," said Ken uneasily, recalling the Métua's cold eyes and curt warning. "He just told me to . . . be careful. And to tell you to be careful."

"He's a fool," she said harshly, then sighed. "Very well, I suppose I'd better tell you. I've been seeing Opatia."

"Mama Tito's son?" he gasped. "He's your —"

"Of course he isn't! You think I've taken to fucking monkeys? How else do you think I can meet Mama Tito without Tihoti Baxter and his spies learning about it?"

He sat in shock as she unfolded her appalling story. Meeting secretly for many months now, she and Mama Tito had come to terms and concluded an alliance between them. Ever since encountering Ken years before on Takaroa, Mama Tito had been fascinated by his enormous mana, even before he had added the almost incomprehensible boon of his own flickerwoman. For many years Mama Tito and her kinsmen had been preparing the way and at last the time was judged propitious. Now Ken would secretly ally himself with Mama Tito, and together they would have little trouble in overthrowing Tihoti Baxter. Her kinsmen and supporters were numerous throughout the islands, and if she succeeded in toppling this petty princeling, she, Mama Tito, the genuine descendant of the Pomarés, would take her rightful place as the first queen of a new dynastic order.

"But *why?*" protested Ken, "why should *we —*"

Leilah's eyes glinted. "Once *she* is on the throne, who do you think will be behind it, telling her —"

"Madness!" groaned Ken, terrified at the mortal danger Leilah had created for herself. "This is folly! Even if we somehow survive this, what makes you think she'd listen to you, or to me? What makes you think she'd be a better ruler than —"

"Who *cares* if she's a better ruler?" hissed Leilah viciously. "She'd be *our* ruler, is the important thing!"

"But Baxter's been *good* to me," cried Ken in anguish. "He's . . . he's not such a bad ruler as you think. And . . . and I owe him my loyalty." He grasped her hands and tried to pull her to him. "He brought you and me together," he whispered, "that's —"

Leilah's face contorted with rage. "The monkey who kidnaped me from my home, who raped me, who watched his *friends* rape me, who keeps me a prisoner on this island of monkeys, *this* is the man you owe your loyalty to?" She snatched her hands away and slapped him viciously across the face. "This is the man you want to *thank* — for bringing us *together?*"

Most of the mutineers had long since forgotten that this was what they actually were, and the sudden shock of reality was devastating. Most of them were racked by sheer hopelessness and lapsed into total apathy, but a smaller number were galvanized into a furious urgency. While the others drifted listlessly back through the island chain, they threw themselves upon the Riestu in a frenzy. It was inconceivable that a silent command, hurled from light-days away, could so irreparably doom them to certain obliteration. What Captain Hippelon could do, they could undo!

"If you ever betray Mama Tito to Baxter I'll kill myself." The horrifying words had echoed through his mind for days after she had first spoken them in a flat, emotionless voice from which there was no appeal. Aghast, Ken asked himself if it was conceivably possible that —

Impossible to put it to the test! With a silent apology to Tihoti Baxter, Ken sadly redefined the limits of his loyalty. He would never seek to actively betray the *Métua,* but henceforth he would remain silent and let the rival Maohi factions settle matters between themselves. His gratitude to Tihoti Baxter was great; his need for Leilah Beaudenon was far greater.

And growing greater all the time. Her supposedly clandestine meetings with Opatia were things of the past now and how she communicated with Mama Tito he dared not ask, for fear that he might inadvertently reveal the secret to Tihoti Baxter. Whatever their plans were, she kept them to herself, just as she now jealously hoarded the most secret core of her being. It was as if the last six months had never been, he thought dismally as he lay alone night after night while Leilah slept in a bed of her own devising on the sand in the far end of the bungalow.

How different she had become! It was as if she took a grim pleasure in taunting him with all those little gestures of love and familiarity that once she had denied him. She had begun to cook his meals, tend to his clothing, trim his hair, talk earnestly about the still nebulous plans for the palace in the hills. She went shopping now in the marketplace, and paddled her own small pirogue around the harbor and nearby lagoons. A docile brown horse appeared in the garden one day, and Ken was obliged to add a stable to the other outbuildings.

More startling yet, she accompanied Ken to a great feast Tihoti Baxter had decreed in honor of a visiting chief from Huahine, and smiled and chatted amiably with the groups of curious Maohi who clustered around them. On the *Métua* himself she bestowed a small curtsy and a benign nod of the head. Then she squeezed Ken's hand ostentatiously and with a fond smile led him off to join a group of plump Maohi ladies dressed in splendid robes that glittered with improbable quantities of multi-colored shells. Her first public appearance was a triumph that left Ken both elated and saddened, for only he was aware of the subtle mockery in even the slightest of her gestures.

What did Kris — Leilah do to keep herself so outwardly serene and cheerful? he wondered as he twisted in torment in the darkness. For months now he had been in a constant state of tension and hyper-awareness, as if his very nerve-endings had been sandpapered raw and even the dancing molecules in the air grated against them. She who was once so lusty and ardent — could she somehow turn off her need for sex as simply as if it were a faucet? The thought of Kristin in the arms of another man was painful enough; but Kristin on a tiny sleeping mat alone by herself was not Kristin at all. . . . Did she have a lover, a real one this time, far more carefully concealed than the scapegoat Opatia? Or did she masturbate quietly in the darkness, or under the trickling water of the shower, her hands parting the soft flesh to —

Miserably he climbed to his feet and shuffled across the cold sand of the bungalow to the cool dampness of the grass outside. The glowing night sky cast a harsh illumination on the inky silhouettes of the banana plants that surrounded him. He looked up at its cold gray radiance and asked himself if ever again he would see the stars.

What star had the flickermen come from, he wondered, and for what inscrutable purpose? Had they traveled a million light years just to place a forcefield in the middle of the ocean and spend the next two centuries watching the natives fuck? The universe was said to be a strange, incomprehensible place. But could it be *that* strange?

But what else could the flickermen be doing here then? His own flickerwoman seemed bewildered and agitated by what now passed between Ken and Leilah. For several weeks she had floated restlessly between them, as if urging them to once again merge in that joyful fervor she shared with them. Her presence had been so constant in the past few years that he had come to think of her as almost an extension of himself, but now she would vanish for weeks at time. She had been gone now for over three weeks, and as he paced slowly up and down the dark garden he wondered with a sudden surprising pang if this time she might not be gone for good?

The thought was a startling one, and somehow peculiarly disturbing. He stopped and stared blindly into the inky blackness of the bungalow where Leilah lay sleeping. Could he actually be . . . *missing* his flickerwoman? he asked himself wonderingly, not so much for the sexual enhancement she brought to all their lovemaking — but for her somehow reassuring presence?

He moaned softly in the stillness of the night as the appalling nature of his existence was now starkly revealed. He was a virtual prisoner in the hands of Tihoti Baxter. And a prisoner even more shackled to the whims of Leilah Beaudenon. And though somewhere nearby, just at the corner of his vision, Kristin still waited patiently, she was growing less and less apparent.

He shook his head despairingly.

How would he manage without his flickerwoman?

For a week Tre'ze joined them in their attack on the inner workings of the propulsion system, then returned in a series of quick leaps to Mine's dwelling for the release from her body's tensions that she could only achieve in his presence. But to her dismay Mine and his female appeared to have abandoned their mating rituals. For two weeks she hovered restlessly, hoping this was only temporary, while tension and anguish continued to build in her. At last she could stand it no longer and returned despairingly to the Riestu. Here at least she might be able to contribute something that conceivably could lead to her salvation.

CHAPTER 24

For three days Ken was turned back at the entrance to the palace by two of the Dominion's tattooed warriors. They shrugged when asked the reason. "Many kinsmen from the other islands. Much talk-talk." They shifted their ceremonial spears from one hand to the other, then sat down in the shade of the roof's overhang, for Maohis did not adapt easily to ceremonial guard duty. "When they're through fighting and eating maybe he'll have time for his white Arioi again."

"I see," said Ken, and strolled slowly home. Later there were numerous rumors, each more elaborately authenticated than the previous, that Tihoti Baxter, founder and erstwhile *Métua* of the Maohi Dominion, had been deposed. Sometimes it was as the result of a bloody coup, others by a quiet family vote, or still again for reasons of health. Whatever, he was gone. . . . Ken and Leilah stared at each other in silent speculation, and waited for the next item of misinformation from the old woman, who seemed to somehow procure it from the trees and bushes around her.

On the fourth day he returned to the palace and passed through the unguarded portals to find Tihoti Baxter seated at the far end of the chamber, looking much as usual. They exchanged tired smiles. "The news of your death appears to be somewhat exaggerated," said Ken.

The *Métua's* eyebrows shot up. "Is that what they were saying in town? Interesting. It's only in the vicinity of the *Métua* that the coconut radio ceases to function." He pinched his thin cheeks between his fingers and pursed his lips thoughtfully. "Do you *really* think the French have no radios?"

Ken shrugged. "It seems hard to believe that several thousand army technicians and civilian scientists could have let their . . . civilization collapse so much in only a century that they don't even have radios, but that's only because I don't know anything about radios and how they work. And I keep forgetting that everything that existed on the Tahiti I knew was imported. Once your radio stops working, and you've run out of spare parts, then there just aren't any more radios."

"Why couldn't they build them?" demanded the *Métua*.

"Out of what? The only materials are what you can get from melting down something else — you know better than I that these volcanic islands don't have any ores or minerals. And then you'd have to have electricity to make them work. You'd think they might be able to get a generating plant going, but Leilah says they're unable to. You know how everything rusts here — they probably don't have anything left to make one out of."

"They still have at least a few guns that supposedly work."

"I guess that's possible. I think the army used to pack their rifles in some kind of grease. That would preserve them for a long time — unless the cockroaches ate the grease!" Tihoti Baxter smiled wanly, for he knew as well as Ken the voracity of the island's cockroaches. "But I'd be astonished if any of their bullets still worked. I don't think you can pack *them* in grease. I think they'd just be balls of rust by now. In any case, I wouldn't want to be the one to try firing one of them."

Tihoti Baxter lifted his eyes thoughtfully to the closely aligned rows of pandanus in the high ceiling of the long-house. "The French are greatly outnumbered. Without radios and guns they would have to fight basically on our terms. Therefore," he smiled slyly, "you are saying there is no reason why we cannot successfully invade Tahiti and drive the *faranis* into the sea?"

"Let him go and be killed," urged Leilah. "That's not being disloyal to him — you're just letting him do what he wants to. You said you wouldn't interfere with —"

"No," said Ken coldly, his duty clear before him. "I didn't say I'd just let him be killed without —"

Her lips tightened and for a moment he thought she was going to fall into one of her terrible rages, but to his surprise she suddenly smiled thinly. "What are we arguing about?" she asked gaily. "It's not as if you *can* dissuade him from this . . . this project of his."

Ken sighed, and with a weary nod acknowledged the truth of her argument. The *Métua* seemed to have come under concerted attack for a variety of differing motives from those allies and kinsmen who kept him in power. He had temporarily held them off by once again promising the long-awaited redemption of Tahiti from the French, but now all of his cunning and sly maneuvering was of little use. He was going to have to produce something spectacular in the near future or risk losing his position. Unless Ken could graphically show why he would face certain defeat, the beleaguered *Métua* would now have to lead his troops against whatever remained of the French army. Ken shook his head sadly. Even if Tihoti Baxter *knew* he was sailing to defeat and death he might still carry on with his plans, for what were the alternatives that eventually awaited him in Uturoa?

He looked up to find Leilah grinning at him triumphantly, and had to turn away from the hard glitter of the cold black eyes.

* * * *

"So you have nothing to contribute that can guarantee me success in my venture?" asked Tihoti Baxter. "Suggestions, tactics, strategies, weapons, inventions, nothing at all?"

"Nothing," echoed Ken.

"But if you did, you would of course share your thoughts with me."

Ken stared at him coldly. "Reluctantly, but I would."

The *Métua* looked at him with interest. "Why reluctantly?"

"I hate the idea of killing. Of you killing Frenchmen, of Frenchmen killing you. Here in . . . these beautiful islands it . . . just doesn't seem right."

"Is it right that the French should have Tahiti?"

Ken waved that argument away irritably. "I *told* you I'd help if I could. I just don't know how. Can't you understand that I'm just a simple-minded carpenter?"

To his surprise the *Métua* only smiled at his outburst. "Perhaps, perhaps. We shall see." He nodded several times as if to himself. "Yes, I really think we shall see."

It was appalling how easily he had let himself be outmaneuvered. And Leilah — she who fancied herself the great conspirator! — why hadn't she foreseen something of this nature? What they might have done to forestall it short of stealing an pirogue and paddling off into the night he didn't know. But at least they might have had a chance. And now there was none.

"When your mind turns itself to my affairs," Tihoti Baxter had said two days later, "it seems to occasionally lack . . . concentration. That is the single reproach that might be made of you."

"I'm sorry," replied Ken uneasily, wondering what this was leading to. "It's hard to concentrate on command."

"Is it now?" A peculiar smile hovered on the *Métua's* lips. "Turn your mind to this: Your . . . companion, Beaudenon *vahiné,* has graciously accepted my invitation to return to Tahiti."

"What!" Ken felt as if he had been hit by a physical blow. "Return to —"

"Yes." Tihoti Baxter's face was suddenly cold and set. "In my company. She will be on the same ship from which I will lead the attack." He turned away, then stopped to add over his shoulder, "Perhaps you will find your powers of concentration improving."

But Ken was running out of the palace.

At home he found that Leilah had already been marched away by four of the Maohi Dominion's tattooed warriors.

* * * *

"No harm will come to her." The words of Tihoti Baxter still rang in his mind. "Unless through some negligence of your own. She is presently safe and comfortable. It is up to you to see that she remains that way."

"Very well," he replied, somehow stifling the rage that threatened to burst forth like exploding lava. His eyes sought the familiar comfort of the hovering flickerwoman but it was months now since he had last seen her. If only she had been beside him! Would even Tihoti Baxter have dared this outrage in her presence?

Oh! if only he could call her down with her companions to heed his commands! Tihoti Baxter would even now be a dead man lying at his feet!

But he couldn't, so now he must try to ensure that Leilah, and the hateful Tihoti Baxter, returned safely from this insane project of invading Tahiti.

"Very well," he said wearily. "Tell me what your plans are."

"Ahhh," said the *Métua* with a faint smile. "I knew you'd be interested once I commanded your full attention."

Perhaps chief among Tihoti Baxter's varied qualities, Ken had discovered, was patience. This was an attribute so rare among the Polynesians in this world of the flickermen that it constituted for its possessor an almost supernatural power, and it might have been one of the principal reasons that the diminutive Métua had risen to his present position. Now it permitted him to reluctantly appreciate the virtues of Ken's plans and to eventually decide to set them in motion. They were not so dramatic as what he himself had initially conceived, and far less bloodcurdling than what his principal chieftains were urging, but the path to leadership of the Maohi Dominion had also been a series of single small steps. And Ken's overall strategy was sufficiently devious to appeal to his own innate sense of slyness and cunning. "Very well," he said at last. "My chiefs will detest this plan, but they will carry it out." He shook his head in mock admiration. "It's marvelous how complicated you are prepared to make life for everyone else just to keep one farani popa'a woman out of harm's way."

"Yes," said Ken with a tight smile, "isn't it?" His eyes had a hard glitter to them, and after staring into them for a long moment Tihoti Baxter turned uneasily away.

"You will be joining us when we sail?" asked the Métua.

"Why should I ? It's your war, not mine. I've done my part. You do yours."

Tihoti Baxter stared at him in genuine surprise. "You don't want to see . . . well. . . ."

"When I see Tahiti it won't be from a fleet of warships."

The *Métua* shook his head in dismay. "This is hardly gallant behavior! It never occurred to me that —"

Ken permitted himself a cold smile. "As the expert on twentieth century warfare, I can assure you that General Eisenhower did not personally accompany the fleet on D-Day."

"So you say, so you say. . . ." He scowled fiercely. "This changes the complexion of everything. How can I be certain that all this is not a gigantic trap prepared by you to —"

Ken's face was equally grim. "Have you forgotten my companion Beaudenon *vahiné* so quickly? *She* is the certainty that all this is not a gigantic trap designed to snare a *Métua.*" He shrugged."In any case. . . ."

Tihoti Baxter grimaced in sad acknowledgment. "As you say. In any case it is now far too late to do anything about it." He stared at Ken with grudging respect. "You seem to have an answer for everything."

Everything except my flickerwoman to strike you down, you treacherous little bastard, murmured Ken inaudibly as he turned disdainfully away.

Three weeks earlier a fleet of twelve catamarans and war canoes had put to sea with a full complement of warriors. Tahiti was to the southeast of Raiatea, but they sailed almost due south for nearly a hundred miles before finally turning to the east. In this way they passed far to the south of Tahiti's large sister island of Moorea. Once past Moorea, the fleet turned north, and late one afternoon suddenly came out of the setting sun in the channel between Moorea and Tahiti, heading directly for Papeete. A few small sailboats fled before them, and as the fleet lay to several miles offshore of Papeete they had the satisfaction of watching flickering orange lights burning throughout the night in the capital of the French-held islands.

At sunrise a small fleet of French sailboats came forth tentatively from Papeete's protective harbor and immediately split into two groups, as if to encircle the intruders. The Maohi fleet immediately turned and made at full speed at the southernmost of the two groups. The French hesitated, then turned and ran for shelter in Faaa where a century before the two-mile-long jet strip had been built in the shallow waters of the lagoon.

With disdainful cries of contempt at the cowardly *farani,* the Maohi ships turned about and with equal dispatch chased the remaining half of the French fleet back through the pass and into the harbor of Papeete. A faint rattle of small arms could be heard, and a few bullets tore through the fleet's sails, but none of the Polynesians were hit as they hunched over their paddles and quickly moved out of range. Shortly afterwards loud booms could be heard ashore and some moments later large geysers of water began to spurt up harmlessly far from the ships.

Still crying their taunts, the Dominion warriors turned west and moved quickly along the southern coast of Tahiti in the direction of the grand estates on the white sand beaches of Punaauia. With their binoculars the commanders of the ships could occasionally spot groups of Frenchmen galloping hastily through the trees in the same direction. They smiled to themselves, and urged their crews to even greater speed.

All afternoon the Maohi sailed back and forth along the coast of Punaauia without venturing near the crashing surf that pounded against the offshore reef or the rushing waters of the pass, as if fearful of finding themselves bottled up in the confines of the lagoon. Frenchmen followed their movements along the shore, a few of them waving rifles, most of them with nothing more lethal than spears and knives.

That night, while fires burnt along the beaches, half a dozen small pirogues made their way silently into the lagoon from passes at either end and paddled unseen for several miles along the coast. Oily torches were suddenly lit, and flaming arrows began to trace glowing arcs across the sky. There were several dozen large Tahitian-style residences in the area, and nine of their dry thatched roofs were soon on fire. Minutes later great red and orange flames were jumping towards the sky as the raiders paddled unmolested back to the waiting fleet.

The following day the warriors of the Maohi Dominion sailed back to Papeete, feinted again in the direction of Punaauia, where dark trails of smoke could still be seen against the sky, and then turned towards Arue and Point Venus, where the ancient lighthouse commemorating the arrival of Captain Cook still stood. Here they were greeted by the spectacle of thousands of resolute French, both men and women, grouped along the black sand beach of Matavai Bay that ran out to the lighthouse. Apparently unwilling to face such overwhelming odds, the fleet lingered indecisively just beyond the pass for the rest of the day, and when the sun rose the following morning all trace of it was gone.

It returned to Raiatea three days later, where a triumphant feast awaited the warriors. Their shouts and roars of laughter were joined by those who had sailed the four ships that had approached Tahiti from the north during the memorable night on which Punaauia had been so easily laid waste. For while the island's population was rallying to the defense of besieged Punaauia, 250 hand-picked warriors had slipped quietly ashore on the rugged shoreline of the sparsely populated district of Mahaena and within minutes had disappeared into the foothills that came down to the ocean's edge.

As far as Ken and Tihoti Baxter could determine, the successful dispersal of the commandos had gone entirely unnoticed. . . .

Now, three weeks later, it was time for the *Métua* of the Maohi Dominion to personally lead his attack on the vile French presence in Tahiti. Ken had been permitted short visits once a week to the small bungalow outside of town where Leilah was under careful guard, and it was with leaden footsteps that he made his way slowly back to town after his final visit. Would he ever see her again? he wondered in black despair. Almost certainly so, for in theory she should be far from danger, but what then would the future hold? Two months of captivity at the hands of Tihoti Baxter while Ken struggled to further the *Métua's* goals at the expense of her countrymen had done little to brighten her disposition or draw her nearer Ken. If anything, the love and rapport he had so carefully nurtured for so many months now seemed almost irretrievably shattered. For a moment he had hesitated, and then finally not even tried to kiss her farewell, for there was a grimness to her face that absolutely precluded it. Now he turned his face up to the glowing night sky. Kristin, he cried silently, oh, Kristin, where are you?

CHAPTER 25

Leilah stood before him, pale, dirty, and haggard, her face contorted by such hatred and rage that he was unable to move from the table at which he sat eating his evening meal. A roughly woven basket dangled from her right hand. Eight days of fearful speculation had passed since he had last seen her, but already his surge of elation had died as quickly as it had leaped up in him.

With a sudden gesture she threw the basket in his direction. It hit the sand beside him with a muffled thud and a dark round object rolled forth. Puzzled, he raised his eyes from the bowling ball to Leilah, then back to the dark sphere in the sand. Why on earth would she be carrying a bowl —

He suddenly saw the head of a human being staring up at him with lifeless eyes. The head of a young dark-haired woman.

When he eventually returned from the darkness of the banana trees, his stomach still tied in painful knots and the harsh taste of acid in his throat and mouth, he saw that Leilah had placed the horrible object in the middle of the table and was seated before it, staring at it with apparent calm. She must have seen his shadow, for without turning she spoke softly. "This . . . thing you see before you is what remains of a woman named Isabelle Chaumette. We grew up together in Papeete, and went to school together. Her boyfriend tried to seduce me and she blamed me. After that didn't we see each other very often, but when we did we still said hello. Now . . . here she is, sitting in the middle of Ken Camden's table in Uturoa. Thanks to Ken Camden. Is that what you'd like to say, Isabelle? Thank you, Ken Camden."

He stumbled across to the other side of the room, unable to look at the ghastly object on the table. "Put it away," he pleaded, "please."

Leilah turned to him with a terrible caricature of a smile. "You don't think she's nice looking? You don't want a closer look —"

Numbly he shook his head. "Is this what. . . ? I mean, what did. . . ? I didn't *mean* for —"

"Ah!" she cried. "You didn't mean it? Is that what you're trying to say? You thought all of your pretty war-making was just like the stories in one of your books, that no one was going to get hurt, that —"

"Don't say that!" he shouted. "I was just trying to keep you safe from —"

"Tihoti Baxter? My family? The French army?" She laughed, a ghastly hollow sound. "Your plans worked perfectly, just the way you told

Tihoti Baxter they would. He's busy right now getting drunk with all his chiefs and nobles but he'll probably send someone over to get you soon so he can congratulate his genius in person." She turned her eyes back to the head on the table. "His plans worked, Isabelle. Wasn't that clever of him? And he saved his little Leilah. Wasn't *that* clever of him?"

His plans. A grandiose word for a simple scheme to keep Leilah out of harm's way. First he had convinced Tihoti Baxter that the Dominion forces would need further information about the French and their military readiness before launching a final all-out assault. An apparent full-scale attack on Papeete would provide them with the information, but only if it were properly prepared.

First they would launch a diversionary attack by a small fleet on Punaauia, that would allow the surreptitious landing of raiders on the other side to the island. After the commandos had disappeared into the mountainous interior, a second, more imposing war fleet could be prepared. This one, with Tihoti Baxter himself in command, would sail directly for Papeete with no attempt at deception, as if to launch an all-out attack. By the time the fleet reached Tahiti the French would be waiting for it with everything at their command.

And as the French faced the sea, ready to destroy the invaders, those 250 warriors already ashore would sweep down from the mountains and take the city from behind. The element of surprise would be devastating. Depending on the ensuing circumstances, the Maohi fleet could continue to stand off shore, still acting as a decoy, or it could send elements ashore to join the commandos.

Whenever it was feasible to make their escape, the raiders would be paddled back to the waiting ships and the fleet would return to Raiatea without further engaging the enemy. What would eventually follow after that would depend on their assessment of the raid and of the information that the commando party had gathered during their attack.

For a carpenter who had never seen death more closely than on a television screen it had seemed like a reasonable enough plan. . . .

And Leilah said everything had worked just as he had hoped. Her very presence was proof enough of that. He should be exultant. But here in the middle of his table, sitting in the middle of his unfinished *meal,* was one of those horrible consequences from which he had hoped to be forever sheltered.

"If I get rid of it, can we talk seriously?" asked Leilah.

"Yes, oh God, yes. Just . . . please . . . get rid of it."

When he finally dared to raise his eyes the dreadful thing was gone, but he found himself nearly retching again at the memory. Leilah sat on one of their two chairs, glaring at him with terrible eyes that he found himself unable to meet.

"So you think you're Leonardo da Vinci," she said softly. "You think you're turning this Tihoti Baxter of yours into a philosopher king, don't you?" Her lips twisted in disgust and her voice rose to a sudden shout. "But this Tihoti Baxter is nothing but a barbarian monkey, and he's the one who's turning *you* into a murderous savage!"

Ken could only grimace, unable to find words to express the agonizing emotions that struggled within him.

Leilah leaned forward and spoke with quiet intensity. "Can't you see that this terrible fighting between our races must *stop?* Before you and your Tihoti Baxter expand it to the point where it's unstoppable?"

Numbly, he felt himself nodding. "You and I ," he heard her saying, "are the only ones who *can* stop it. Do you understand that? *Look at me!*" she suddenly shouted. "Do you understand that?"

"I understand," he murmured in a broken whisper.

"Because if you *don't,*" she warned, "there's only one thing left for me to do."

"Do?" he echoed.

"Yes, *do!* And I'll do it tonight! I'll jump in the ocean and start swimming back to Tahiti. I'll die of course, but at least I'll die trying to *stop* a war instead of dying in one that my . . . my husband is starting."

"Husband?" he echoed incredulously.

"Well, that's what you are, aren't you?" she said almost defiantly. "At least as long as I'm caught on this island of savages."

He looked up at her. Gaunt, exhausted, and bitter, she had never seemed more desirable. It was many months now since he had felt more than the occasional touch of her hand against him. He felt his loins stirring in sudden excitement. He began to rise to his feet, but she waved him abruptly to a halt.

"I'll . . . I'll be a . . . wife again to you," she said softly, her eyes dark and unfathomable, "when Mama Tito is on the throne." She climbed wearily from the chair. "Until then I'll be sleeping where I did before. Over there." Suddenly she swung around. "Well? Do you agree? Do I sleep here tonight or do I start swimming?"

He shook his head in sad bewilderment. Is this the way the lusty, the almost insatiable, Kristin acts? But he was forgetting, he must be too tired to think clearly. This wasn't Kristin, this was —

"Yes," he murmured. "I agree. Just . . . just please don't . . . go away."

By his treachery in taking Leilah hostage, Tihoti Baxter had forfeited any right to respect. Otherwise it would have been almost possible to feel sorry for him, so easily did he let himself be snared in the tangles of the net that Ken and Leilah were weaving for him with occasional suggestions from the third party to the conspiracy, Mama Tito.

But Ken was appalled by the nature of the plot and the lengths to which Leilah and Mama Tito were prepared to go to ensure its success. "I can't believe it," he whispered, unable to keep the dismay from his voice. "This will kill hundreds of people."

"They're only monkeys," she said stonily. "Anyway, isn't *that* what they want to do to *my* people?" She suddenly grinned viciously. "Is that really what's troubling you? Or the fact that now I have to sleep with that monkey Tihoti Baxter? You knew he'd been raping me when he so kindly made a gift of me to you. You didn't seem very squeamish about it then. Why should you be now?"

As always, he was helpless in the face of her arguments. "That was different," he protested, "that was —"

"Because now I have to pretend to enjoy it?" she taunted. She looked at him from hooded eyes. "How do you know I'm *not* enjoying it?" A sardonic smile crossed her lips. "I'm certainly not having any fun from *you.*"

Her cruelty was devastating. How much she had in common with Kristin! "Please," he implored softly, reaching for her hand. "You're forgetting how much I love you. Just once? Please? It's been —"

She let her hand linger in his before pulling it away. "When Mama Tito is on the throne. Not before." She smiled teasingly. "I'd let you watch us while I'm with his excellency the monkey king, but he thinks it's a secret that only the two of us are sharing." She laughed harshly. "Until I become his queen, no one's supposed to know. Not even my loving husband."

One more attack on Tahiti, orchestrated by Ken and carried out with all the resources at his command, and Tihoti Baxter would have at last demonstrated to the French that it was useless trying to resist the Dominion's power.

Such was the message that Leilah brought to the *Métua's* private quarters whenever she was able to join him for their brief, illicit meetings. "They'll understand that, because *I'll* be able to convince them of it. But first you'll need one more attack. I know my people — they're stubborn. But they're not foolish. If they have to live under a Maohi leader in order to live in peace, they will. But they'll need to deal with someone they can trust, and there's only one way to assure that. After the next attack I'll leave Ken, and you'll make me your queen."

"Queen?" Tihoti Baxter muttered softly.

"Of course. You'll be the king, or emperor, or whatever you choose to call yourself. After all, you'll be the ruler of *everybody*. . . ."

"And you'll be my queen?"

She laughed lightly. "You can keep all the little concubines you want. *They* won't bother me. But you'll have to offer *something* to my people. What better than a Frenchwoman on the throne beside you." She snuggled closer. "And our children. They will truly unite our races."

"Perhaps," muttered Tihoti Baxter cautiously, "perhaps," but she could see the glitter in his eyes, and she knew that he would never be able to resist the dictates of his ambition. "What further use then do we have of Ken Camden, now that you mention the matter? Perhaps it would be best if —"

"Not yet," she cautioned softly. "He may still be useful. You can always get rid of him when you want. But once you've gotten rid of him, you won't be able to get him back."

"I suppose you're right," he agreed reluctantly. "But —"

Her lips hesitated inches above the soft flesh she was softly stroking. "As soon as you have carried out the attack," she whispered. "Then you get rid of him."

With even greater reluctance than before Ken allowed himself to be drafted into organizing the attack. "But only because of Leilah," he said, yielding at last. "She's convinced me this is the only way to finally put a stop to all this fighting and killing."

"Indeed?" murmured Tihoti Baxter. "How very wise of her. I didn't realize a *farani* woman could be so sensible."

"After . . . after this is all over," said Ken haltingly, "she and I . . . well, we're going to be married. . . ."

"Are you now?" The *Métua's* eyebrows lifted slightly, and he smiled benevolently. "How much each of us will have to celebrate."

"You . . . you will let us, won't you?"

Tihoti Baxter stared at him guilelessly. "Why on earth would I have any objections? I personally will arrange for the feast to celebrate the happy occasion."

Encouraged by the success of the last raid on Tahiti, most of Tihoti Baxter's chieftains eagerly began the preparations for a final attack that would prove decisive. It was impossible to keep the news of it from quickly spreading around the island, and it was not long before Mama Tito and her powerful kinsmen began to raise loud objections. The Métua now found himself in a delicate position. Much as he would like to rid himself of the enormous woman and her kinsmen, it was clearly impossible to do so just as he was attempting to unite all of the islands of the Dominion in this single vast undertaking. A discreet murder was impossible, for Mama Tito was far too well protected on her great estate, and the only alternative, a minor civil war, was clearly out of the question.

"Kill her," advised Ken stonily, "or she'll ruin everything. She's telling everyone who will listen that we should stick to small hit-and-run raids, wearing them down gradually. A lot of people are going to believe her."

"Maohi are courageous, straightforward, and direct," counseled Leilah at one of her secret meetings with the Métua. "It isn't possible to keep them fighting sneaky little raids for the next twenty years. They'll get bored and go home first. Or they'll get themselves a new Métua. They *want* a single big battle that will determine matters once and for all. All you have to do is appeal to their sense of courage. Mama Tito is just a cowardly old woman, and anyone who listens to her is equally as cowardly. *That's* the line to take with Mama Tito. Don't ever treat her seriously. Just laugh at her and call her a coward. *That* will deflate her quickly enough."

"Your Ken Camden suggests I should . . . kill her."

Leilah snorted. "What does Ken Camden know about anything? Why do you think I'm with you right now, instead of him? There are *some* people who are men without having to have a flickerman around them all the time." Her nostrils flared scornfully. "Without his flickerwoman Ken Camden is *nothing*. And now even his flickerwoman has left him. So he's *really* nothing."

"You really think it will be safe to. . . ?" For once Tihoti Baxter seemed curiously indecisive. "There *is* that story about the Arioi girl who was —"

Leilah grimaced in disgust. "My Métua is afraid? I'll do it myself then. Just give me a sharp enough knife and I'll bring you his head in person!"

"He really is a bloodthirsty savage," said Leilah. "After I said that, he was all over me in a flash. He must have fucked me another three times." She directed a cool smile at Ken, who was twisting in torment in his chair. "That excites you, doesn't it, the idea of that savage little monkey fucking me?" She ran her tongue teasingly around her lips and leaned forward across the table. "We're almost there," she whispered, letting her finger trace small circles on the back of his hand, "we're almost on the throne."Maybe I'll be nice to you." Hardly daring to breath, he watched her lean back and begin to caress her breasts inside her white and brown pareo. Her lips parted. "I'll let you take out your cock and jack off while I tell you about what I did this afternoon with Ti —"

But with a soft cry of anguish Ken had knocked the chair to the floor and rushed out into the sanctuary of the night.

CHAPTER 26

This time when the fleet of nearly ninety ships finally sailed, Leilah stayed behind in Uturoa, for she had a very special duty to attend to. A dozen warriors from the island of Maupiti had been selected and solemnly sworn to unquestioning obedience. Four days hence, coinciding with the great battle that would have been joined a hundred miles to the east, she was to lead them to Mama Tito's, many of whose warriors had been obliged to accompany the war party, and to forever rid Tihoti Baxter of her troublesome presence. "And I ," said Tihoti Baxter, "will take Ken Camden with me, and after he has been permitted to exult in the joys of our victory there will be a grave acci —"

"Too dangerous," warned Leilah. "Suppose he were captured by my people? Think of the knowledge they could wring from him. You yourself have said his worth is that of fifty boatloads of warriors." Her voice sank to a whisper. "And . . . there are many flickermen in Tahiti. He may still attract them. It might be well to be . . . prudent . . . when the time comes to. . . ."

"You *do* fear the flickermen!"

Leilah shrugged. "It costs nothing to be cautious. Leave him here. His . . . demise can be a part of our victory celebration."

But Tihoti Baxter, Métua of the Maohi Dominion, never lived to see the mournful feast in honor the ascension of Mama Tito to the newly created throne as Queen Vaiariti Itia Tevahine Pomaré, first ruler of the Maohi Empire.

For five months now the island of Tahiti had been preparing for the arrival of the Dominion's fleet, guided by the intelligence transmitted by Leilah Beaudenon through intermediaries sent by Mama Tito. As Tihoti Baxter's ninety ships sailed serenely past the island of Moorea with their destination of Papeete already visible at the base of the blue-gray mass of Tahiti, six peculiar craft moved out of the shadowy enclave of Cook's Bay and drove directly for the Polynesian fleet. Gleefully Tihoti Baxter gave the order for the fleet to turn and encircle these insolent marauders.

Ten minutes later the intruders were amidst them, strange catamarans driven at improbable speeds by paddlewheels powered by what could only be steam boilers set in the middle of their decks. They were, in fact, little more than floating gun platforms, with their hulls protected down to the waterline by skirts of rusty scrap aluminum, while six-foot barricades of the same material shielded their crews. Each ship was equipped with twenty riflemen and an eclectic variety of small artillery. The fire from the large guns was erratic and uncertain, but the homemade shrapnel quickly ripped away the Maohi sails and cut down the unlucky Polynesian crews like giant scythes.

Thirty seconds after the battle had been so unwisely joined, Tihoti Baxter himself lay dead, a shredded piece of unrecognizable meat, the target of the fifty nearest rifles. When the terrified Maohi survivors of the first ghastly onslaught looked around to see another ten ships of the same design bearing down on them from Papeete they turned and fled as best they could.

The two French fleets chased them for a dozen miles, disabling or destroying another thirty ships, and left the surviving crewmen floundering helplessly in the blue seas. By the end of the morning the remains of the once-imposing fleet had been scattered in every direction, while the nearly unscathed units of the French navy were steaming triumphantly back to Tahiti.

Of the 3,600 men who had sailed a week before, a bare 800 straggled back to Raiatea. It was a disaster of such unimaginable magnitude as to be incomprehensible to the grief-stricken Polynesians. In the midst of their lamentations appeared the grim but regal figure of Mama Tito, quivering with a terrible anger. "It was Tihoti Baxter who led our men to this gruesome slaughter," she cried, "Tihoti Baxter and his wicked court. I urged them, I begged them, I *pleaded* with them not to risk this disastrous venture. All of you will recall that I did so." She raised an enormous arm and pointed it with awful wrath in the direction of the dead *Métua's* palace. "Even now, the evil kinsmen of this foolish chief are conspiring to choose yet another of their company to carry on the insanities of this most evil of all men. Is *that* what those brave warriors who died so nobly but so uselessly for the Maohi people would have wanted?"

Within a few hours a howling mob had fallen upon the unlucky survivors of Tihoti Baxter's court and quickly hacked most of them to pieces. A dozen or more were carried away to an uncertain fate as prisoners, and later that same day Mama Tito was prevailed upon by the same clamorous mob to accept the crown.

Leilah and Ken, late advisors to the now-despised *Métua,* had been hidden away in the safety of a small bungalow on the new Queen's estate while the mob rampaged through the town. Early that evening a jubilant Opatia came to tell them the news. Ken was disheartened and downcast as he contemplated the terrible loss of life incurred for the sake of supplanting one small Polynesian ruler by a rather larger one, and found it impossible to convince himself that the slaughtered Polynesians had only brought it on themselves by wantonly seeking to attack the unoffending French.

But Leilah was transformed. Her black eyes sparkled exultantly as she hugged first Opatia and then Ken. A glow of purposefulness and energy seemed to radiate from her, and she paced the confines of the bungalow with the impatience of an imprisoned tigress, occasionally flashing enormous toothy grins at the two men. At last she ushered Opatia out and turned to Ken. At the sight of her flushed face and parted lips he felt his loins and thighs begin to tingle. The deaths of thousands of men lay heavy upon him. Much of the guilt, he knew, was his. But still it was impossible to keep from hoping that now she had achieved what she had so single-mindedly worked for, she might at last relent from her harsh denial of her —

"Come here," she ordered, and his heart raced.

As Ken moved towards her she pulled her pareo free of her hips and sank back on the room's single chair, the nipples of her small breasts already protruding, her long slim legs spread wide. Trembling, he bent to kiss her, but she caught his head in her hands and pushed it down between her breasts. A moment later he was on his knees as she guided his face along the smooth flesh of her taut stomach and into the moist warmth between her outspread thighs.

As his lips and tongue lashed her with the pent-up hunger of a year of anguished privation her breath began to catch in her throat. Suddenly she gasped and pulled him roughly against her. Her trembling legs clamped about his head as her body stiffened, and she came with a long piercing wail. Forcing her still quivering thighs apart, Ken lurched to his feet and pulled her unresisting body forward, to thrust into her with a single movement. As she wailed a second time, he scooped her up beneath her thighs and still impaled on him carried her across the room, where they tumbled to the sleeping mat.

Sometime during their frantic coupling the glowing blue form of the flickerwoman drifted out of the darkness and merged with their frenzy. At their moment of orgasm, as Leilah scratched and thrashed and screeched in his arms, it seemed as if the room had suddenly burst into light. In the midst of a timeless eternity in which his entire body quivered in the tension of a single great galvanic spasm, he was jolted by wave after wave of searing energy that seemed to catch him up in a swirling torrent of dazzling brightness and then to cast him into an utter blackness.

When he slowly came to himself he saw that the flickerwoman now hung motionless in the far corner of the bungalow, glowing a deep radiant blue that cast long black shadows across the room. Leilah was as shaken and unnerved as he had ever known her. She wrapped herself tightly around his body, her warm breath fluttering against his bare chest, until slowly her trembling subsided and her labored breathing became inaudible. "Was that the flickerwoman?" she whispered wonderingly. "That did. . . ?"

"I don't know," he whispered in turn, "but I love you."

"Hold me," she murmured. "Hold me tight."

"I love —"

"Tighter," she ordered harshly, as her hips began to move rhythmically against his thigh, the hard bone of her pubis grinding imperiously against his taut muscles. The radiance of the flickerwoman swooped across the room to engulf them, and her breath caught suddenly in her throat. "Tighter," she gasped, "tighter, tighter, *tighter!*"

But as the days and nights passed and the propulsion system remained totally inert in spite of their frantic efforts, a growing lethargy began to settle over them. The other ship must now be only a matter of months away. Captain Hippelon had informed them that it was massively armed. Was there anything more they could do except prepare themselves to meet their fate with dignified acceptance? One by one the remaining crewman began to drift away until only a dozen of them were left aboard.

Tre'ze was wondering if it might not be preferable to find some subtle means of terminating her existence rather than let herself suffer the agonies of execution that Second Officer Bylangu had undergone, when a faint tingling in her field brought her out of her morose reverie. Across all these miles — could that be . . . Mine and his mate?

Calling Tre'ze?

With Leilah as her councillor, the new Queen quickly began the consolidation of her power. What remained of Tihoti Baxter's former palace after the bloody purge of his court was pulled to pieces and burned, and Queen Vaiariti now held court in the quarters of her own estate. During the day Leilah would disappear to spend long hours with the enormous woman Ken still thought of as Mama Tito, while he himself worked happily and peacefully in an airy new structure he jokingly called his office.

Here, with the aid of two elderly master builders, he had begun the plans for a new palace, one that Queen Vaiariti had decreed must be worthy of the great dynasty that at long last had regained its rightful place among the Maohi people. Like the aborted project of Tihoti Baxter's, this too would be constructed in the mountains of Raiatea, but on a far grander scale than anything the unfortunate *Métua* had dreamed of.

Leilah had little to say about her duties with the new Queen, but it was soon evident to Ken that Mama Tito's consolidation of power consisted primarily of the systematic destruction of her enemies, real or imagined. He was both shocked and sickened, for although he knew the Polynesians of centuries before could be fierce and bloody warriors, he still thought of them as the peaceful, pleasure-loving islanders among whom he had spent so many years. It was frightening now to realize that among these apparently carefree people there were human beings capable of inflicting the same terrible suffering on others that he had once seen on television as happening in far-off countries in central Europe and blackest Africa.

But Leilah found it only natural that Queen Vaiariti should move to liquidate the remaining kinsmen of Tihoti Baxter. "They'd only to the same to her."

"But they *didn't*! They just let her sit out there on her farm, plotting against them and getting fatter!"

Leilah stared at him coldly. "I don't think you should let Mama Tito hear you talking that way: she might decide that flickerwoman over your shoulder isn't as dangerous as all that after all."

"So now I can't even talk in my own house! Where I came from there were lots of people like Mama Tito all over the world. They were called dicta —"

"She's a *queen* who's only trying to protect herself!" shouted Leilah, exasperated by his willful stupidity. "You think Tihoti Baxter was so wonderful — have you forgotten what I was supposed to do to Mama Tito while he was invading Tahiti?" She glared angrily. "And have you forgotten what was going to happen to *you?* You should thank God that Mama Tito *is* on the throne — it's the only reason you're still alive!"

CHAPTER 27

This was an argument that was difficult to counter, so he immersed himself in his work, and exchanged little conversation with Leilah beyond cursory discussion of the progress of his plans. But to his surprise and gratification he soon discovered that this strange new Leilah was now no longer content with the former two or three amorous encounters per week. Now she pulled him to her in the gray light of dawn and in the long evenings after their early meal. They took long siestas in the heat of the afternoon that were devoted more to lovemaking than to napping. With the flickerwoman glowing exultantly and immersing them in her magical spell Leilah cried and moaned and thrashed until she came time after time, clutching him greedily until she had wrung the last possible pleasure from his exhausted body. Was it the flickerwoman who was responsible, he wondered occasionally during their first week of frantic coupling, or had he at last awakened in her the true nature of Kristin that had for so long been lying dormant? But soon it was difficult to remember that it had ever been any different and he went cheerfully about his daily routine, knowing that in a few short hours he would once again be in Kristin's arms.

The extraordinary idea came to her even as her field flickered and pulsed in joyous absorption of Mine's incredible radiation. Inevitable doom awaited her in any case — why not gamble what little remained of her life in a final attempt at salvation?

She would attempt to merge with her native!

The torrential downpours of the rainy season came and went, and as soon as it was dry enough a narrow road to lead to the site of the new palace began to be laboriously dug out of the mountainside. The building site was only a hundred yards above sea level, but commanded a magnificent view of the turquoise green and blue waters of the shallow lagoon that stretched between Raiatea and its sister island of Tahaa. Teams of sweating Polynesians worked for five months to cut three levels out of the sticky red clay, and as Ken directed them he felt he could now literally turn his back to whatever distasteful activities were going on in those small, unreal dollhouses far below him. For up here it was easy to repress the lingering memories of whatever he himself might once have contributed to the success of Kristin's and Mama Tito's bloody grasp for power.

But he was unforgettably reminded of it on the day decreed by Queen Vaiariti for the ceremonial laying of the cornerstone of her grandiose new palace. A thousand elaborately costumed dancers and musicians snaked their way up the mountain road, loudly pounding their drums and *toérés,* their shiny brown bodies glistening with sweat in the brilliant sun. Enormous pits had been glowing since the day before for the roasting of dozens of pigs, and an equal number of calves had been slaughtered and dressed. These had been spitted and were already turning slowly over a great bed of glowing charcoal when the vast bulk of Queen Vaiariti came into view, riding regally by herself in a small black carriage drawn slowly up the hillside by two white horses.

A dozen deep holes had been prepared on the three levels of the site and a large ceremonial stone laid beside each of them. While Ken and Leilah followed a few paces behind in the midst of the notables who constituted the new royal court, Queen Vaiariti waddled ponderously across the dirt to the nearest hole. Four priests dressed in the ceremonial costumes of centuries before gestured ponderously with their carved warclubs and began to declaim loudly. After ten long minutes had crept by Ken turned his thoughts inward in hopes of shutting out their steady droning. Sometime later Leilah prodded him sharply — it was time to step forward to assist in the actual placement of the cornerstone.

He bowed his head courteously to Queen Vaiariti, who rewarded him with a distant smile and a thoughtful glance at the flickerwoman just behind his left shoulder, glowing brightly even in the direct sunlight. Six husky Maohis stood beside the queen, ready to manhandle the roughly shaped cube into the hole, and Ken moved forward to direct the procedure.

"One moment," said Queen Vaiariti in a soft voice. "There is a final part of the ceremony that must be carried out." She turned her small brown eyes to his and smiled benignly. "It was, we have been informed, a tradition among our ancestors at dedications of a similar nature, which we are now pleased to reestablish."

To his stunned horror Ken watched as the trembling form of one of Tihoti Baxter's former retinue was led forth from the crowd, his arms bound tightly behind him. The noisy crowd grew deathly silent at the sight of the naked man, and before Ken could fully realize what was happening the Polynesian had been thrust into the hole, where he lay moaning in a crumbled heap. At the queen's command the stone was pushed to the side of the hole, then tumbled in to crush his chest with a terrible crunching sound that would echo in Ken's mind during the dark hours of the night for the rest of his life.

A lusty cheer arose from the crowd and Ken turned away, sickened. Were *these* the same friendly people with whom he had lived on Takaroa and celebrated the joyous pleasures of the body among the Arioi? Could it be that Kristin was right after all, that they really *were* nothing more than cunningly dissimulated savages? His eyes found hers in the midst of the notables, and he was chilled by the grim smile that crossed her lips.

He pulled her to one side as the procession moved on. "What's going on?" he whispered harshly.

"There are another eleven holes," she answered. "You aren't going to watch?"

"Eleven. . . ? It's going to be the same at —"

She smiled faintly, as if amused by his squeamishness. "But she's saving the best for last. Look over there."

His gaze traveled in the direction of her finger to the cooking area, where two dozen sweating Tahitians turned the crisp brown calves over the smoking coals. "I don't see what you —"

"To the left. That other spit. The one they haven't put on the fire yet."

At first it looked like just another calf prepared for cooking, its innards removed and its hooves and head lopped off. But then his mind refocused on the long, *long* legs, the two arms bound to the torso, the fingers on the hands and the toes on the —

He turned to stare at her in horror. "But that's. . . ."

She turned her great black eyes up to him. "Yes, it is, isn't it?" Her eyes glinted with amusement. "It's Mama Tito's idea. There will be a ceremonial . . . tasting. It will bind all of her followers to her forever."

He felt himself ready to gag. "You . . . you and I will . . . not . . . will *not!*" His hand tightened on hers until he could feel her bones nearly ready to snap. "Is that clear?" he hissed with a fury he had never before felt. "Is that *clear?*"

She nodded. "If you say so." Her cold, bleak smile broadened and her eyes glittered. "But I really don't see why you're so concerned. . . . After all — they're only monkeys. And one of these days all the rest will follow."

Ken was chilled and terrified. He pushed his way through the happy crowd and ran swiftly down the mountain, conscious only of the cool wind against his hot flushed face, and of the labored pounding of his heart against his ribs.

The idea had came to her full-blown, but without precise definition, and she was never able to clearly decide exactly what it was she hoped for. Could she actually become a part of Mine, a Silumiut consciousness sharing Mine's body and persona? Or could she perhaps even exclude his own persona and somehow take over his body for herself? Or should the apparent yearning for substantiality with which her own body had been increasingly tormented be the focus of her efforts? All she really knew was that something was pulling her towards a union of some unimaginable sort with her native lover. Now all she could hope for was a union that would not destroy her . . . and her host.

That night he could hear the faint sounds of far-off music and revelry, borne to his darkened bungalow by the breeze out of the mountains, and it was with profound relief that he settled by himself onto his sleeping mat.

But sleep was a long time in coming, and it was a restless and troubled one, tormented by strange dreams and abrupt awakenings. At last, sometime towards morning, Kristin again appeared to him. Once again he realized that this was the *true* Kristin, just as she had always been, just as she always would be.

"You're confusing me with somebody else," she told him reproachfully, her long black braids dangling over her shirt of white and green plaids, her eyes hurt and bewildered. "She is not me, she is not me, she is not me!"

There was movement on the mat, and he turned to see Leilah's naked form sprawled out next to him. Her hard angular features were softened by sleep and the harsh lines of anger that were now sometimes visible in her face had been smoothed away. *She is not me.* It was suddenly all so apparent — oh God! how terribly apparent! — that *she* was not Kristin.

He felt the foundations of his life crumbling away beneath him as he stared blindly at her small naked breasts, his eyes and mind struggling to make sense of what he was seeing. It was as if he had suddenly had a divine revelation.

For if *she* was not Kristin, then who *was?*

It was at this moment, as he lay numbed by the impact of this devastating question, that the woman beside him stirred sleepily and pulled herself against him. Even a few minutes earlier, he knew, he would have shied away in revulsion from her gruesome touch, that hand that was the hand of the murderer and cannibal. But now he was strangely indifferent as he let her hands move slowly across his body.

As if from a great distance he watched as she aroused him to a state of urgency and then eagerly straddled him with hungry loins. Though she twisted and thrust herself frantically against his rigid flesh, her face remained serene, lips half parted and eyes still closed, as if lost in some profound meditation. And now the flickerwoman grew visible just behind her, her glowing blue form in the cool gray light of early morning more substantial than it had ever been before.

The flickerwoman drifted closer, her outline beginning to merge with Leilah's, and he irritably wrapped his arms around the softly moaning woman and pulled her tightly against him so that his view of the flickerwoman was unobstructed. As Leilah writhed and ground herself against him, he strained to flesh in the spectral outline, to make out those tantalizingly illusive features. She was drifting lower now, her transparent blue legs spreading out in human fashion as she draped herself over their two outstretched bodies. Leilah gasped loudly, and for a long moment the flickerwoman seemed to be lying gracefully on top of Leilah's long slim back, her insubstantial arms and legs wrapped around their solid bodies. Her face was just inches away from his own now, and he stared unblinkingly into half-glimpsed eyes that gleamed and sparkled and danced with a million twinkling lights, flickering in and out of perception and perhaps of reality.

And then her body drifted still lower, enveloping them both in its cool electric luminescence, and the familiar pounding rhythms seized him relentlessly. Leilah was straining against him, a soft keening coming from between her lips, and suddenly he felt their orgasms approaching with a rush. As the spasms gripped him and the rhythmic pulsing of the flickerwoman's blue radiance flashed and dazzled, he felt himself being swept away in the surging flux of their combined energies. And staring once again deep into the coruscating eyes of the flickerwoman, he experienced the most profound revelation of all.

The flickerwoman was Kristin!

The months passed and the impulsion towards physical materiality grew greater and greater as the feedback between their neural systems steadily built up and the bonds between herself and Mine seemed to tighten daily. It was now obvious that Mine's unwitting volition was increasingly drawing her towards substantiality and that even if she was to escape the wrath of Captain Hippelon and the Continuum Navy it would only be in the guise of a short-lived Ugly.

But already she had begun to think of herself not as an Ugly, but as a Beautiful, for there was something pleasing and yes, beautiful, *about the contours and shape of this body she now terrifyingly felt herself on the very threshold of achieving. There was something about it that had increasingly begun to feel* right, *and she could see how someday it might harmonize with the smooth clean lines of Mine's. . . .*

CHAPTER 28

Leilah came into the bungalow in late afternoon whistling a sprightly tune. He looked up from his meal of yams and grilled fish, considered her briefly, and returned to his dinner. She pulled the other chair close to him and sat so that their knees were nearly touching. With a soft sigh he returned his piece of yam to the chipped blue and white plate. What would it be now? he wondered. Couldn't she see that he needed to be left in peace to sort things out? Why couldn't she find someone else on whom to inflict her interminable accounts of incessant plotting and counterplotting?

She tapped the back of his hand with a long slim finger, as if to be certain of his attention. "You recall the late *Métua?*" she began archly. "Yes? You really do? One would hardly credit it, you sit there looking so slack-jawed these days. . . ."

"I recall him," he said impatiently.

"You may also recall his strange scheme to somehow create a union of our two peoples by marrying . . . me!" Her face puckered in a delicate moue of amused derision. "That monkey!" She laughed, and squeezed his inert hand playfully. "Just because I was letting him fuck me. What a *typical* monkey!" She cocked her head and grinned at him quizzically as she waited for his reaction, but he remained expressionless, unmoved by her childish taunts. "Now there's another one," she said at last.

"Another what?" he asked, anxious to have her finish whatever absurd story she seemed so set on telling.

"Another monkey, of course. Who wants to fuck me. And marry me. In order to unite our races!"

"Well? Are you going to?"

"You're not even interested in who he is?"

His sigh was louder this time, and his eyes moved to where Kristin hovered motionlessly high against the ceiling. If only he could be free of these endless ridiculous distractions. . . . Be patient, he told her. Now that we're found each other, it won't be much longer. . . . "If you think I should be." He glanced at her fleetingly, and reluctantly turned his mind to those matters that appeared to concern her so. "It's . . . oh, Opatia, I suppose."

She stared at him suspiciously, all pleasure instantly wiped from her face. "How did you know that?" she asked sullenly.

His eyes widened in surprise. "Who else could it be?"

Stung by the absence of surprise or anger, she grimly forced him to listen to the entire story in all its excruciating detail. Devoid of all her elaborate trappings, its outline was simple enough by her torturous standards. The straightforward lust that the jolly, rather likeable, Opatia had always felt for Leilah had been further inflamed by her constant proximity to him as they acted as Queen Vaiariti's two privy councilors. As she wearily evaded his heavy-handed advances for what seemed the thousandth time it finally occurred to her that this simple-minded monkey was, after all, the eldest son of the reigning monarch. . . .

"The French may have won a single great victory," she told Queen Vaiariti a few days later, "but they are still realists." In twenty years' time the Maohi people would have more than replaced the numbers lost, while the bitterness of the defeat would only serve to incite the Polynesians to greater resolve. And never again could the French count on facing an enemy led by so obvious a lunatic as Tihoti Baxter. Sooner or later, they knew, they must eventually be overwhelmed by the sheer numbers of the Polynesian people.

A union of the two races such as the *Métua* had been encouraged to envision was clearly unfeasible for the moment. But a union between Leilah and the queen's appointed successor could be a first step towards a peaceful solution of their problems, for it was obvious that measures must be taken by Queen Vaiariti to ward off a possible French counter-attack on the seriously weakened Maohi Empire. Suitably presented, a large formal wedding would give the French a graceful means of recognizing the legitimacy of the Maohi Empire's sphere of interest and of Queen Vaiariti's restored dynasty. And recognition by the French could only serve to strengthen the Pomaré dynasty's still tentative grip on the many scattered islands of the Empire.

Mama Tito's liquid brown eyes stared past Leilah, her moon-like face unreadable.

"And now the flickerwoman is equally mine," added Leilah slyly. "Ken has shared his mana with me. If you permit, I will be able to share it eventually with your son." Queen Vaiariti blinked, and pursed her lips thoughtfully. Leilah leaned forward and spoke with all the earnestness at her command. "You *know* that without his flickerwoman, without *me*, Ken Camden is nothing."

By guile, duplicity, and ruthlessness Mama Tito had clawed her way to the top of a patriarchal society. It was easy enough for her to discern these same traits in another woman, and easier still to believe that Leilah would have naturally sought to wrest the powerful mana of the radiant flickerwoman from an unwary male.

After three days of careful thought she gave her approval to the union.

"So one day soon I'll have to fuck our monkey friend," said Leilah deliberately, with that tiny smile of anticipation he had come to recognize whenever it was her intention to humiliate him in some dreadful way. "You do like that, don't you, your wife being fucked by a monkey? It's just like all those merry games people tell me you used to play with the Arioi."

"Merry games?" he murmured. "Oh." He shrugged. "I suppose so."

"But don't you *care?*" she cried, stung by his maddening refusal to react as she had hoped.

"About you marrying Opatia?" He turned his gaze to the infinitely patient Kristin and wondered if she was somehow listening to this absurd discussion and what she could be making of it.

"Yes!" she shouted. "About me fucking him. About me marrying him! About . . . about *everything.*"

"Should I ?"

"But can't you see I'm doing it all for *you?*"

For the first time he looked at her with genuine interest. "For *me?*" Could she have become completely deranged by her association with Mama Tito?

She bent forward so that her lips were only inches from his, and her nostrils flared. Her shining black eyes glittered hypnotically. "Don't you see?" she whispered. "We'll negotiate a peace with Tahiti, and to ratify it the French will be invited from Tahiti for the wedding and all the ceremonial functions we can think of." She glanced quickly around the deepening shadows in the bungalow and lowered her voice even further. "At least, that's the way Mama Tito *thinks* it's going to be."

"But of course it isn't."

She grinned ferociously. "What will actually happen is that when they come for the wedding my people will fall upon Mama Tito and her cannibals and destroy them forever. And then you and I will rule over any of those who are left!" Her breasts were rising and falling with her quickened breathing, and her hand slid beneath his pareo to grasp his limp flesh. "And you and I will rule. . . ." she echoed dreamily.

But Ken had lapsed once again into his infuriating abstraction. "Whatever you say," he murmured indifferently, "whatever makes you happy." With a sharp snort of anger she pushed back the chair and stalked furiously out into the early evening.

He watched without interest until she had disappeared, then raised his eyes again to where Kristin waited for him to resume their silence communion. After a long soothing interval in which he slowly cleared his mind of all of Leilah's strange passions he smiled fleetingly and returned his attention to his interrupted meal.

I've been sick for many years now, he thought as he raised a piece of cold yam to his mouth and began to chew. I can see that clearly. It must have been some side-effect of going through the forcefield, one that took time to heal. But now I'm well. I've recovered my senses.

He swallowed the rest of the yam and looked up longingly at Kristin. And I've recovered Kristin. I've recovered Kristin. As he lingered over the sound of these pleasing words, a strange corollary suddenly suggested itself. Or . . . could it be that *she* had recovered *him?*

He pushed the rest of his meal away and sat gnawing at his knuckles as he tried to make sense of the notion. Did it, finally, make any difference? She was here — that was all that mattered. Just as he himself had been inexplicably cast by the forcefield into this future world he now inhabited, so must Kristin have found some means outside the flickermens' sky-curtain to channel its incomprehensible forces into flinging her across all the years that had passed to rejoin him here in the form of this flickerwoman.

In the *form* of this flickerwoman?

Or through the *intermediary* of this flickerwoman?

Surely there was a difference?

For in one case Kristin would —

He shook his head fretfully, and tried to turn his thoughts to less baffling speculations. Kristin was here. That much he knew. But only in the insubstantial form of a glowing blue nimbus that merely aped the outline of her lovely body.

How was he to regain her completely?

For it had to be reluctantly acknowledged that once the first great joy of recognition had passed, their relationship was, as it now existed, like Kristin herself, far too insubstantial to be fully satisfying.

Only at the ecstatic moment of sexual climax was their union fully realized. Was the sexual factor the essential catalyst needed to fully restore Kristin to life?

The more he considered it the more probable it seemed. He himself had been . . . impaired . . . for many years by his passage through the forcefield. Likewise, something about the way it functioned must have prevented Kristin from being able to return immediately to her corporeal body. Instead she had been forced to assume the intangible being of a flickerman's ghostlike form. . . .

It was easy now to look back and see her gradual transformation over the passage of the years from that initially wraith-like apparition on Takaroa to the radiant Kristin who was now only so short a step from that final transformation that would restore her to him in all her physical beauty.

But it seemed clear that it was only through the . . . energies. . . ? that were created and discharged by the sexual act that this slow evolution had been taking place. By themselves, his unceasing love and yearning had simply not been enough.

For in spite of them, hadn't Kristin been forced to disappear for months at a time when Leilah had refused to share his sleeping mat? But as soon as Leilah had returned to it, so had Kristin. And it was obvious now that it was these last months of feverish coupling with Leilah that had brought Kristin to her present state of tantalizing near-substantiality.

All that remained was to complete the transformation. . . .

To restore Kristin to life.

But. . . .

He winced in dismay at the distasteful thought.

But for *that* — Leilah was necessary. . . .

CHAPTER 29

"I've done it," said Leilah defiantly.

"Done it? What's that?"

"Fucked Opatia."

There was a long silence while Ken looked up from their sleeping mat to where the radiant blue form of Kristin so patiently waited for him to complete her final transformation. "He must have enjoyed that," he observed at last.

"He did," she said stonily. "The monkey! But *I* didn't."

"But are you really supposed to?" he teased. "I thought that what counted in these affairs of statecraft was —"

"Stop being tiresome! I've told you and told you and *told* you that I'm doing this for *both* of us."

"So very self-sacrificing of you."

"Well, it *is!*" she shouted in sudden fury, sitting upright beside him and clenching her fists. He could hear her breath hissing between her teeth. "And I don't see why *you* can't do something to help!"

"Me?" he asked in astonishment. "You think Opatia is —"

"Of course he isn't!" Her lips narrowed into a thin pinched line and her next words almost indistinguishable. "Why can't . . . can't you . . . send that *thing* along to help?"

"Thing? What thing?"

"That thing up there in the ceiling you spend all your time mooning over! What *other* thing do you think I'd be talking about?"

"Send Kris — Send the flickerwoman to help you fuck *Opatia?*" He wondered if he could be hearing her correctly.

She turned away from his astonished gaze. "Why not?" she asked sullenly, her eyes lowered. "All the other flickermen float around from couple to couple. Why can't this one?"

He shook his head in dismay. How could you even begin to talk to someone as crazy as Leilah had become lately? "I don't know," he sighed. "Why don't you ask her?"

"Ask her? Ask her what?"

"Ask her to follow you. Isn't that what you want her to do?"

"I don't want to ask her. I want *you* to *tell* her!"

"You think I can tell a *flickerwoman* to do something?"

"But you *have* to!" she wailed. "I *told* you I promised Opatia that. . . . Well. . . ."

"That you'd share your flickerwoman with her?" He stared at her in exasperation. "I'm afraid you're going to have to work that out on your own." He grinned at her sardonically. "Why don't you try offering her a bowl of milk? She might follow you like a cat."

"But this is *important,* can't you see that?" Her eyes suddenly glistened with tears. Of vexation? Of thwarted fury? How astonishing she was!

Even more astonishingly, she fell against him and buried her head against his bare chest, and he listened to her begin to weep. "It's just not *fair,*" she sobbed weakly. "It's . . . it's so . . . normal now with . . . you and the flickerwoman. Why can't I . . . . It's *awful* with him. It's just like doing it with a monkey. If only I could have the flicker —"

Ken was saddened and repelled by this whining caricature of the woman he had once been deluded into believing he loved. Even the touch of her damp sweaty skin against his was distasteful. His fingers tightened on her bare shoulders and his impulse was to push her away from him and out of his life forever. But for the moment that was still impossible, for Leilah was still the vital link between himself and Kristin. Without Leilah . . . there could be no Kristin.

He grimaced, and rolled to his side, so that his lips could find her small brown nipple. She gasped with pleasure and her arms tightened around his neck. Oh Kristin, he thought, hurry . . . Please, Kristin — hurry, Kristin, hurry!

As the other ship came into the solar system and began to pass through the orbits of the outer planets it was almost as if Mine and his female had begun to catch some sense of the desperation that gripped her. Just as she was being shaped by the unspoken volition of her native lover, could he in some way be half-aware of the imminent doom that loomed for Tre'ze? If not, then why was Mine now in almost constant activity with his mate, as if he knew that each exchange of forces between them was bringing Tre'ze closer and closer to substantiality?

Could it be, she asked herself in growing wonder, that she and Mine were in some strange way becoming . . . soulcompanions? She shuddered at the thought, but at the same time found herself gripped by an almost unbearable excitation and exhilaration.

Soulcompanion to a . . . Beautiful?
Tre'ze and Mine, soulcompanions?
Yes!
Soulcompanions!

* * * *

The days and weeks became months and once again the rainy season was upon them. Originally Mama Tito had shown the same far-ranging inquisitiveness as Tihoti Baxter about the potentially valuable knowledge Ken might put to her use. But apparently her interest in him and the strange marvels of the twentieth century had extended only to how they might be of use to her in her single-minded drive for power. Now that she had achieved the Maohi throne Queen Vaiariti seemed to have lost all interest in him beyond his work on her palace. So every day he rode his docile black mare dutifully but contentedly between his bungalow and the building site in the mountains. In the late morning he returned home for lunch and often enough a joyless but lusty coupling with Leilah on their rumpled sleeping mat.

Kristin was ever-present, so in spite of the disdain and even muted hatred he now felt for the obsessed Frenchwoman with whom he was obliged to live, their physical couplings were of an intensity that was sometimes almost unbearable. As the three of them coalesced into a single glowing nexus of mutually reinforcing energies the tensions generated by their unions daily seemed to grow greater and greater, and their electrifying discharges increasingly frenzied. It was common now for Ken and Leilah to be simultaneously jolted into unconsciousness, and as he put his hand to his chest afterwards to feel his still racing heart he wondered how many more times either of them could survive the intensity of Kristin's emotions.

But their couplings now seemed to be Leilah's sole interest beyond her obsessive plotting, and more often than not it was she who pulled Ken down to their sleeping mat. After each exchange he could almost see Kristin taking on a deeper and richer substance, and at last even Leilah came to notice that the traits of the flickerwoman were now those of a specific woman.

To Ken it was self-evident that they were those of the Kristin he had met and married a century before. But to Leilah they were merely those of a broad-shouldered woman with long slim legs and features nearly as angular as her own. "I wonder why she has two braids?" she muttered one day. She jerked her head so that her own long braid jumped across her shoulder and dangled down between her breasts. "I only have one."

"What do you mean?" asked Ken uneasily.

"I mean that she has two braids and I only have one. You'd think that if she's trying to look like me she'd be able to count how many braids I have."

Ken stared at her in dismay. "You think that . . . the flickerwoman . . . is trying to look like *you?*"

"Well, who else would it be? She's spent the last two years living with me, hasn't she?" She grinned unexpectedly. "She certainly isn't starting to look like *you!*"

Ken shook his head slowly. "No, I suppose not. You *really* think she looks like you?"

Leilah looked up at the radiant Kristin, so beautiful and so obviously Kristin. "She's bonier, I suppose, and her breasts are bigger. I wonder what her pussy's like? It's like her eyes: you know they're there, you can see the outline, but you can't really *see* them."

What was it about himself that attracted crazy people? Ken wondered sadly. First that Arioi girl on the boat, Hina, Hinano, whatever her name was, the one the flickermen had finally mercifully taken away. And even the other girl before that, the one on the yacht, the one who had brought him here from Los Angeles, *she* had been more than just a little weird too. And now Leilah.

But Leilah was clearly more peculiar than either of the others.

Leilah was *crazy!*

He grimaced angrily, then without a word pulled her roughly to the mat and jerked fiercely at her pareo. So she thought that Kristin was trying to look like *her,* did she? Open your eyes, bitch! He'd show her what Kristin *really* looked like!

When Alns unexpectedly turned up in a listless parody of Mine's fine male form she was both troubled and angered by his presence. But Alns seemed equally uncertain and wary in the face of the enormous vitality that she so exuberantly radiated, though he was unable to conceal his dismay at the monstrous abnormality of her field. "You think it's monstrous?" she flared. "I think it's beautiful. Why don't you go away and leave me alone? Go find a . . . an Ugly of your own!"

It was almost impossible to get out the word Ugly, and in a sudden fury she leapt menacingly at him, ready to slash his field to shreds. But he retreated in a panic, and pulsing in agitation she returned to take up her position just behind Mine. Already she was regretting her terrible anger, for though she knew she could now easily overwhelm Alns, suppose he were to attack her with a number of the others? Now that she was so close to her goal? No! That would be utter, criminal stupidity!

"You may stay," she told him coldly, "as long as you keep both your distance and your opinions to yourself. If you approach me, I shall. . . ." She said no more, but let an ominous burst of power radiate for a bare instant. "Is that clear?"

He glowered sullenly, but made no reply, and after that his gloomy presence soon became commonplace and finally nearly unnoticeable.

But suddenly Leilah's craziness was no longer the sole problem he had to contend with. The pale gray radiance of a flickerman had come to watch over one of their afternoon couplings, apparently without participating, and then had returned that evening and the following morning. After that he was a near-constant presence in their bungalow, drifting slowly about in no discernable pattern. In contrast to the rich glowing blue of Kristin and the sharply defined features that made her so beautiful a woman, the intruder was pale and insubstantial, a feeble nimbus of washed-out gray with hardly more than a tinge of blue. Even in the darkness he was difficult to clearly focus upon, so incohesive was his flickering outline, and all that could be seen was that he was definitely a male.

"I don't like that . . . *thing,*" said Leilah plaintively, for once echoing his own thoughts. "There's something about it that . . . I just don't like. Why doesn't she send it away?"

Yes, thought Ken. Why *doesn't* she send it away?

The more he studied the intrusive presence as the weeks wore on, the more he came to feel that for all its apparent indifference to both themselves and Kristin there was nonetheless something distinctly ominous about the wispy gray being.

Was *ominous* the correct word? he asked himself one rainy evening as his eyes moved back and forth from the lovely smooth form of Kristin to the tenuous outline of the flickerman. No, somehow the new flickerman was indefinably *menacing*. . . .

But how could an ill-defined flickerman be menacing? It was something about its attitude, its very posture. . . .

As if he was a policeman!

What a peculiar notion. . . . But one that refused to leave his mind, and that began to suggest other possibilities.

A spy?

Some sort of guardian of flickerman morals and customs?

A spurned lover?

At the thought, it was as if a giant hand had suddenly clutched his heart. A moment later he could feel it pounding violently in his chest.

A lover? A *jealous* lover?

But when you examined it, what could be more probable? Someone as beautiful and desirable as Kristin — hadn't she always been surrounded by would-be lovers?

He could hear his breathing now, whistling in and out of his parted lips.

This lover — another human being? One who had somehow managed to follow Kristin out of the past?

Or — even worse — a flickerman? Who somehow imagined that he could perhaps take her for his own?

Aghast at the possibilities that suddenly confronted him he climbed to his feet in a burst of motion and ran heavily through the sand to the other end of the room, where the flickerman hovered against the bamboo wall. As Ken approached, its outline became blurred, and by the time he was at the wall, actually standing partially inside the flickerman, it was impossible to distinguish it except as a faint glow in the air around him.

Slowly he forced his clenched fists relax. How could he harm a flickerman? It was ridiculous to even try. If even *Kristin* couldn't get rid of him, how could *he* ever hope to?

Slowly he walked back through the cold sand, head bowed in thought. Policeman, or lover, or spy, it no longer mattered who or what the new flickerman actually was. It was enough to know that he was a menace that stood between Kristin and him. And he knew too in some undefinable but absolutely certain way that the time remaining was perilously short — that if he and Kristin were ever to merge in total union, or if her flesh-and-blood body was ever to be restored to her, it would have to be accomplished before this ominous flickerman could prevent it.

Soon, Kristin, he promised fervently, soon. . . .

CHAPTER 30

He was still musing on this unhappy situation three months later when Leilah came to babble to him of her foolish intrigues. The new addition to their household had so far made no overt gesture of hostility, but he continued to feel wary and apprehensive in its presence. And now here was Leilah to listen to, full of her absurd plots and bloody betrayals.

Vaguely he recalled that there had been a crisis not many weeks before. Queen Vaiariti had been incensed to learn that the radiant blue flickerwoman whom Ken had brought with him from the islands disdained to grace the sexual activities of Leilah and her son Opatia. Contrary to what Leilah had so solemnly assured her, then, the flickerwoman was not a commodity to be passed around at will after all. . . .

And so it seemed that all of Leilah's artful planning and plotting had come to nothing, for without the flickerwoman what else was there to set her above any other scrawny white Frenchwoman? But apparently Leilah had found some means to surmount these objections, for her babble today was of the plans for the actual wedding, and whether or not the first part of the Queen's new palace would be completed in time for the ceremonies. Secret negotiations, she said, had been proceeding between the islands on several levels for many months now, and a large delegation of French leaders had tentatively committed themselves to coming to Raiatea.

The only question of any importance that remained was: who was going to betray whom?

"I thought that was easy enough," said Ken distastefully. "You and your friends from Tahiti are going to get rid of Mama Tito and then, as I recall, you and I are going to rule happily ever after as Ken the Kind and Leilah the Lenient."

She nodded slightly, her eyes wary as always when he lapsed into unaccustomed sarcasm.

"Just when is all of this butchery supposed to happen?" he asked. "Before the wedding, or after?"

"Whenever it's feasible. Is there a difference?"

"I was wondering about Opatia — your royal husband-to-be. What lies in store for him?"

Leilah looked down at her long slim fingers. "What do you mean?"

"You've never really explained to me why you think that you and I , two *popa'as,* are going to be allowed to rule over an empire of Polynesians. Even if one of us has a private flickerwoman."

"I've *told* you: the French will install us, they'll —"

"They'd be much better off with someone like you married to some-one like Opatia. A royal couple like that might even make sense."

She looked at him with wide, guileless eyes. "You don't . . . don't think that . . . that . . . I'd — "

"Wait until you'd been married to Opatia before you gave the signal for the massacre?" He smiled sardonically. "A massacre in which your . . . former friend just *happened* to be —"

"Ken!" Her breath caught in her throat. "You *know* I wouldn't!" She reached forward to catch him by the hand. "That's what I wanted to talk to you about." She glanced fearfully over her shoulder. "You're saying that perhaps *I'd* betray *you*," she murmured softly. "You don't under-stand the *real* danger. What I'm *really* afraid of is that Mama Tito is going to betray *me!*"

. . . .the shrill cry from the Riestu *was an outpouring of despair and terror. "They're nearly here! They're already trying to knock down the field. . . ."*

"How do you mean?" he asked slowly.

Her glittering black eyes bored into his. "I think this wedding is just a pretext for her to lure as many Frenchmen to Raiatea as she can. Once they're here she'll try to take them hostage." She squeezed his hand tightly. "Or — try to kill them!"

He stared at her impassively, but already his thoughts had begun to wander away from her tedious fantasies. Did Leilah any longer have any grip at all on reality? Just enough, probably, with all her obsessive plot-ting, to get them both killed and barbecued by Mama Tito just in time for her next housewarming party. . . .

His eyes sought and found the cool glowing comfort of Kristin, hov-ering just behind his right shoulder. She seemed to be looking down at him and waggling her head in pity. Impulsively he reached out to take her hand in his, so real did she seem. It was only as his hand closed on the emptiness of the air that his mind refocused and became aware of the bamboo wall and the bougainvillaea outside the bungalow so clearly visible through the infinity of dancing lights and tiny flashes of lightning that defined Kristin's body.

Once again the terrible reality had to be faced — for all his wishful thinking and cheery optimism about gradually liberating Kristin from the bonds of her insubstantiality she was still, in essence, little more than an illusory will o' the wisp, a nebulous blue flickerwoman. . . .

With a sound that was half-sob, half-gasp, he rose to his feet in de-spair and grasped Leilah by the shoulders. She broke off from whatever she was muttering to look up at him in surprise. For a moment he held her gaze as he probed the depths of her gleaming black eyes, wondering what tortured thoughts actually passed through that alien mind, and then he realized that her head was snapping back and forth. He looked down and saw that his fingers had clawed deep into the flesh of her shoulders and that he was shaking her violently. Her eyes were wide with sudden fear, and as he saw the dim outline of the wispy gray flickerman drift slowly into view just behind her he realized that the time for contemplation had finally passed. He felt his chest heaving, and the sound of his harsh breathing was loud in his ears. It was time to act.

He had to bring Kristin to life *now!*

. . . .there was nothing Tre'ze could do to aid those who had chosen to remain with the Riestu *to desperately battle with what few resources remained to them. She had perhaps only minutes left to her life! Her radiation output welled in a great burst of uncontrollable fear, and as if he felt the unspeakable urgency of her demands, Mine's own field suddenly flared, and a moment later his mate was beneath him on the floor of their dwelling. . . .*

Without a word he pulled the pareo from Leilah and flung it across the room. A moment later he had tumbled her roughly to the sleeping pallet and had straddled her, clasping her breasts around his already stiffening flesh to arouse himself against her smooth warm body. The fear he had seen in her glittering eyes vanished as she was caught up by his feverish urgency, and she pulled him forward to take him greedily into her mouth. The pulsating blue radiance of Kristin drifted down over his legs and Leilah's head so that he could see himself engulfed by Leilah's lips only through the flickering obscurity of her translucent body. Leilah's hands were digging into his buttocks as she writhed beneath him, trying to pull all of him into her mouth, but with a stifled moan he wrenched away to thrust himself deep into the soft wet flesh between her outspread legs.

She gasped loudly and hooked her legs around his, locking him in her grasp. Their hips ground in furious rhythm against each other as he tried to merge his entire being with hers, for this he told himself was now his only hope of liberating Kristin from the flickering confines of her spectral prison.

. . . .as they joined together Tre'ze merged her field with theirs and as quickly as she dared began to channel her own energy into their joined field in constantly growing increments, as if finally coalescing with a true soulcompanion. . . .

As their rhythms grew more frenzied Kristin's glowing nimbus settled over them like a cool blue mist. But its coolness was illusory, for almost instantly they were stunned by an explosion of electrical outpouring more overwhelming than any they had ever known. It fused their bodies together into a single bond of raw nerve endings that tingled and burned and shrieked with unimaginable pain and pleasure. As Ken's entire being was slammed and torn and stunned by wave after wave like the mightiest orgasm ever conceived it was as if the sun itself had burst apart and was spraying its incandescent fury through him.

He shuddered wrackingly as the terrible current subsided slowly, and he opened his eyes to find that Kristin no longer enveloped them, but was standing now just by their heads, her radiant blue feet only inches from Leilah's outspread hair. Still half-numbed, his reeling mind could barely comprehend the smooth blue feet he saw resting firmly on the polished wooden floor. With a terrible effort he focused on those feet and realized with a swelling exultation that these were real toes with real toenails he was staring at and that the gleaming floor was now only barely visible through the nearly total opaqueness of her body!

Fearfully, hardly daring to hope, he managed to raise his head and saw the lovely mobile features of Kristin looking down at him wonderingly with the eyes he had once known so well, eyes that had lids and lashes and dark purple irises in place of hazel. . . .

"Kristin," he muttered hoarsely, and extricated his arm from beneath Leilah's head to reach out to touch the long smooth calf of her glistening blue leg. He touched it —

— and felt his hand slowly sinking within it, as if it were pushing against a yielding blue jelly.

He moaned with agonized disappointment, then stiffened in sudden rigidity as another wave of the same tremendous current shot through him to seize his entire body. There was a brief cry from Leilah as the surge of forces emanating from Kristin radiated through him to her, and then he felt her twisting desperately against his own still body. Her arms tightened convulsively around his back, and she reached what he knew would be the first of many climaxes.

. . . .*she could feel them shudder as her energy surged through them and returned to her in the curious circuit of their combined field, and suddenly she found herself no longer enveloping them within her all-embracing body but standing beside them, looking down at their straining bodies. And there was Mine's hand . . . slowly sinking into the half-formed flesh of her own leg. . . . She could actually feel his hand upon her! An uncontrollable spasm gripped her very being and she shuddered as great waves of pure energy burst forth from her inner core and into that extension of flesh that was so terrifyingly buried within her. . . .*

As she shuddered and writhed he could feel her supercharged energies flowing up through his outstretched arm to mingle with those of Kristin, raising them to ever greater intensity. Leilah's mouth twisted convulsively in a long silent scream, and he realized that his own breath had long since been caught in his chest. Desperately he tried to pull air into the starving lungs of his rigid body, and as his chest reluctantly began to respond he felt his hand slipping away from where it had been gripped in the center of Kristin's translucent calf. A moment later she had moved out of his vision, but as his breath returned with a rush he felt a ghostly hand brush along his back. . . .

. . . .*she could feel the sudden surge in the field around Mine when his mate began to discharge her own stored-up forces in sharp, intense spasms, and somehow tore herself away from his outstretched arm. But now she found herself staggering waveringly about the room, the strange texture of the floor against her feet, the very molecules of the air imping-ing upon her skin. Was this what it was like to have a physical body? But why couldn't she control it? Why didn't it go where she wanted it to? She lurched and stumbled, and felt herself falling against her lover's back. . . .*

His head swam drunkenly a surge of delirious joy.

Kristin was nearly solid!

Suddenly he could contain himself no longer, he knew he was about to come, with all the pent-up forces that had been generated by this desperate encounter. But how to effect the final liberation of Kristin, to channel *all* of their energies to this single goal? She was now almost restored to reality — what tiny bit more was needed?

He gasped at the clutching spasms of Leilah's tight flesh and at the electrifying touch of Kristin's warm arms wrapping themselves around his back. He could feel himself now teetering on the edge of the impend-ing explosion. . . .

. . . .hardly aware of what he was seeing, his mind registered the sight of a bright gray flickerman pulsing vividly in the corner of his vision, then suddenly flaring across the bungalow as if to intervene — too late!

. . . .for the room was spinning dizzily. . . .

. . . .he gasped. . . .

. . . .waves of energy burst forth from Kristin in great pulsing surg-es. . . .

. . . .he was transported, swept away. . . .

. . . .Leilah was screaming now in mindless release and as his first overwhelming spasm shook him Ken could feel his very being pouring out into Leilah and Kristin, merging, coalescing, rising, transcending. . . .

. . . .*as Tre'ze felt herself assuming material form and for the first time experienced the terrifyingly strange solidity of Ken pressing against her, she looked up to see her soulcompanion Alns suddenly surging for-ward. . . .*

. . . .he clutched at Leilah, and as his senses reeled and he was whirled by forces beyond his comprehension his arms tightened around her sinewy frame and squeezed it so tightly against his own torso that he was dimly aware of the sound of her breath being expelled in a mindless gasp....

. . . .*apparently releasing a last mighty surge of energy that caught the unwary Alns and sucked him instantly into the depths of the vortex that swirled around them. . . .*

. . . .as her powerful life-force flowed around and into and through him and Ken and was swallowed up by the desperately striving Tre'ze. . . .

. . . .just as the weapons of the Silumiut Dominion began to batter down the forcefield maintained by the ship high in the mountains of Tahiti, splashing a tiny scattering of their unthinkable energies into the locus of the *Riestu* and from there out into the remaining flickermen wherever they had hoped for shelter from the awful retribution that had come down upon them. . . .

. . . .*and as the flux of the four beings merged into a single overpowering field she felt herself being simultaneously torn apart and being enveloped by Ken Camden. . . .*

. . . .who tore himself away from the damp, thrashing body beneath him and joyfully turned to pull Kristin's firm smooth body against him, a naked, living, flesh-and-blood Kristin just as he had loved her a century before. Even as they were engulfed by a sudden blinding flash of dazzling brilliance his arms had tightened around her and as their lips met savagely he knew a peace and happiness that would never end. . . .

. . . .*as her lips touched his she realized in a last ecstatic moment that the overload of uncontrollable forces was about to destroy them all, and she pulled herself against the burning flesh of the only man she would ever know. . . .*

EPILOGUE

Mama Tito — now Queen Vaiariti Itia Tevahine Pomaré — raised her eyes from the mid-afternoon meal she was taking in the cool shade of a ironwood tree and stared open-mouthed at the streaming colors and flickering sheets of lightning that suddenly flashed across the eastern sky. Long seconds of anguish stretched out as she wondered if that biblical end of the world that some of the more credulous of her subjects still believed in could actually be coming to pass, and as a hot damp sweat broke out on her she asked herself if it was too late to learn to pray. . . .

The vast manifestations of pulsing reds and oranges became a clear pale yellow and then a coruscating blue and green, and then she heard screams of terror coming from the servants around her, for the entire heavens were in motion now. The opalescent pearl gray of the great sky-curtain that hung over her entire empire had begun to ripple with bright blues and greens and yellows that streamed across the sky like tremendous ocean currents, gathering up all the colors that before had only glinted and flickered half-glimpsed in the glowing sky-curtain.

Her eyes widened, and just as she felt that she could no longer contain the terrible knot of abject fear that burned within her, the seething movements overhead suddenly slowed and the glowing colors began to fade rapidly. A few minutes later all trace of them was gone and all that remained was the great arch of the clear blue tropical sky, a marvel unseen now for more than a hundred years.

She gaped at it in stunned astonishment and then fell back in the vast chair that held her while her mind began to work with frenzied calculation. At last she climbed laboriously to her feet and waddled off slowly to where a cluster of warriors pointed and gestured with loud cries of speculation.

Clearly the flickermen's sky-curtain was gone, she told herself, and soon now what remained of the world beyond would be coming forth to learn what had become of the Maohi Empire and its peoples. . . .

"Ho!" she cried to the tattooed warriors. "Go and fetch me the blond-haired *popa'a* and . . . and his flickerwoman." If she still exists, she added to herself thoughtfully, for when the sky-curtain that had imprisoned them for so long had vanished as abruptly as it had come, might not the strange flickermen have vanished with it as well? Fretfully she turned and made her way back to her interrupted meal. If indeed the outer world was about to intrude on her peaceable kingdom, who better than the man from beyond the sky-curtain to advise her in her preparations for that delicate and potentially dangerous encounter?

The entity that had once called himself Ken Camden looked down at the still trembling form of Leilah Beaudenon. Her eyes were closed and her breasts heaved as she panted raucously for breath. "I've been stupid," he thought, as the memories of everything that had happened since being flung through the sky-curtain flashed through his mind with painful clarity, along with every other memory his brain had recorded since birth. It was a process that took no more than a few seconds. When he had reviewed it and sorted everything into order, he took a further moment to evaluate the totality of his previous existence, then summed it up dispassionately. "Sick, of course, for a number of years, but also very, very stupid."

The pale red aura that was now clearly visible around the French-woman's body pulsed erratically as her body quivered and her breath continued to come in ragged gasps. "At least I didn't kill her," he thought, "there at the very end. And I was certainly crazy enough to if it had been needed to restore Kristin."

Poor long-dead Kristin, gone now forever....

And poor Tre'ze....

At least *she* had had a joyous moment of flesh and blood reality, just as poor sick, stupid Ken Camden had had a final moment of bliss as he once again held in his arms his beloved Kristin.

But now there was nothing left of Kristin/Tre'ze except this translu-cent blue lump of jelly-like substance that lay on the white sand floor of the bungalow just beyond Leilah's disheveled black hair. The size of a mongrel dog, it was shrinking away rapidly, melting into air like the last remnants of a forgotten dream slinking away at daylight. When it was no larger than a coconut he raised his eyes to the far side of the bungalow.

Yes, the forcefield *was* gone, just as he knew it was. Had *felt* that it was. And there, between the leaves of the great ironwood trees, for the first time in years, was a glimpse of that beautiful blue sky he had once taken so much for granted.

Soon the outside world would be intruding....

"K... *Ken?* Are you... are you all *right?*"

"Yes, I'm fine."

Leilah was sitting up now, her arms crossed protectively across her small breasts, her eyes wary and still half-mad. The red nimbus around her head was pulsing rhythmically, like the visual representation of the thudding of a mighty drum. Whatever had once remained of Kristin/Tre'ze had now completely vanished, leaving only a formless imprint in the sand.

"I'm sorry that I--" he began, then saw her eyes widen in fear. It was then that he realized that no sound was coming from his mouth. "Oh," he said, raising his hand instinctively to his mouth. The golden aura that enveloped his hand and arm as well as the rest of his body was pale but clearly discernable. "Is it this that frightens you?"

There was still no sound that passed his lips and he frowned for a moment, concentrating. He did a brief mental inventory of everything that now comprised his body, first down to the molecular level, then the atomic, and finally the subatomic. It was *weird*, he told himself, seeing himself in this way, or at least it would have been weird to that poor simpleton Ken Camden, but to him it all made perfect sense. "Thank you, Tre'ze," he murmured, "for liberating me...."

Now that he understood what went into the composition of his body, it was easy enough to make a few minor adjustments.

"I'm sorry," he repeated, and this time he could feel the physical muscles in his throat working as the clearly audible words issued from his mouth. "I didn't mean to frighten you."

"But... but why have you got that... that golden haze around you? And... and where's the flickerwoman? I don't understand...." Leilah's voice trailed off as her eyes moved jerkily around the confines of the bungalow.

"This seems to be what I've become," he said. "Not precisely what I was before. And this... golden aura seems to be part of it. Perhaps if I work at it I can turn it off, at least to keep people like you from seeing it. As for the flickerwoman, she's gone. They're all gone, all of the flicker-men, forever. They won't ever be coming back. And the forcefield is gone, too, the sky-curtain."

Once again her eyes grew wide. "They're... gone? Forever? Did *you* have something to do with that? Did you *kill* them?" Her hands flew to her mouth in dismay. "What will Mama Tito say— what will she *do* when she learns that you've...."

"I didn't kill them, Leilah. They killed themselves, in a sense, poor creatures. But now they're gone, and the sky-curtain is gone, and the outside world will be returning. And Mama Tito will be nothing but a petty chieftainess on a tiny speck in the middle of the Pacific Ocean."

"The French... the *French* will be returning?" she whispered.

"If they still exist outside what used to be the forcefield. And the Americans too, I imagine. Whoever can get here first."

"But Mama Tito. She'll...."

He stretched out his glowing hand, paused for an instant to fully substantiate it, then reached down to take Leilah gently by her left hand. "Come. We'll go have a word or two with Mama Tito. I promise you that she won't hurt you. Or anyone else, for that matter."

"No!" Leilah twisted as violently as a terrified cat as she tried to jerk her hand away. The nimbus that encircled her head flared a fiery red. "She'll *kill* us! She'll— Let me *go*! *I'll* kill you, you and all the rest of the monkeys, everyone who ever wanted to kill me, and fuck me, and— The French will do it for me when they get here! I'll *tell* them to! I'll tell them to kill *all* of you! You, and— Let me *go*, I tell you! Let me go!"

"Poor Leilah." He considered her thoughtfully for a few moments, evaluating her from all aspects, then reached out mentally with an invisible hand and ran it gently into her angry red aura. The fingers ran across her forehead and scalp, caressing and calming, then through her skull into the seat of her being, where he continued to soothe and compose, easing a stricture here, releasing a blockage there, alleviating all the bottled-up rage and madness that had followed her kidnaping from Tahiti at the hands of Tihoti Baxter. As he probed and untangled, the fires in the aura that surrounded her gradually died, moving by imperceptible degrees from red to orange to yellow to pale green to dark green to pale blue. As the colors changed, her physical struggles lessened until at last she sat comfortably before him, the once taut features of her tormented face relaxed into the greatest expression of serenity he had ever seen.

He lingered a moment longer, until the pale blue of her aura had become a rich, deep blue that matched that of the sub-tropical sky, and then he stepped back, his work completed. So that old madman William Reich that Kristin had told him about was right after all, he marveled. Organic energy, with its attendant color blue, really *was* the basis of all mental health. It just needed to be released in order to perform its natural functions....

His restraining hand slipped down to Leilah's elbow, and he helped her rise to her feet. "Put on whatever's appropriate to visit a Polynesian Queen," he said, "and we'll be on our way. I'm sure that one way or another Mama Tito already has us in mind."

Leilah gave him a saucy grin. "Yes, I imagine so, poor foolish woman. You really think you can keep her from hurting us."

"I think so. You'll have to trust me."

She reached out to take his hand. "I don't *feel* anything different about your body, I just see this... whatever it is around you. Does it make you feel different?"

"Not in itself, no. It's just a... manifestation, like the color of a person's skin."

"Oh." Leilah considered this carefully. "Then you haven't... become a flickerman?"

"Perhaps a little bit, in a sense. We were in the center of incomprehensibly powerful forces — we're extremely lucky to have survived at all. But I'm still relatively human. I think."

"Hmmm. Does this mean we can still... well...?" She smiled shyly in a way she had never done before..

"Perhaps. We'll have to see."

"See if... *you* want to?"

"Perhaps. Life is starting all over again, for all of us. Some things are not yet entirely clear."

"Yes. Yes, I can see that." Suddenly she threw herself again him and wrapped her arms tightly around his body. "Thank you, Ken," she murmured softly into his chest, "thank you. For everything you've ever done for me. I don't think I've ever told you that before. But I mean it. I really do."

"Yes, I know. And I appreciate that. Now put on your pareo and sandals and let's go visit royalty."

She stepped back and studied his body carefully, from toes to hair. "And you? Are you going like that? With no clothes on at all? Nothing about you has shrunk, you know. You'll drive the poor old woman crazy!"

He smiled faintly. "Yes, I think I will go like this. A nice golden glow will make me even more impressive if it emanates from *all* over. She's seen naked men before. And I don't think that the Healer *has* to wear clothes. Come."

Leilah watched wordlessly as her golden companion walked effortlessly through the pleated bamboo wall of the bungalow and out to the garden. A moment later she ran to the stable for the horses. "Do you really *need* a horse?"

"I'm not entirely sure yet. For the moment, I'll use one." He substantiated himself enough to swing easily onto his mount's back.

Leilah had just climbed onto her own horse when four of Mama Tito's tattooed warriors galloped up. The being that had been Ken Camden studied their auras with interest. One was a neutral, pale blue, another a bluish green, but the other two, as befit their warrior status, glowed the same angry red as Leilah's had been a few minutes before.

The larger of the two warriors with a red aura gestured imperiously. "The Queen commands your presence at once."

"We will follow you if you don't ride too quickly."

"Very well." The warrior now examined the others more carefully. "Where are your clothes? Make yourself suitable at once! You would take yourself into the presence of the Queen like that?" He gestured angrily with his ceremonial but still deadly warclub. "Quickly now!"

The golden aura that enveloped the Healer's body intensified until it rivaled the overhead sun in intensity. The warriors drew back, their eyes wide.

"I think this will be sufficient," said the Healer in a mild tone. "You may lead the way." He nudged his mount forward, then turned to smile at Leilah. "I think that much work awaits me in this new life. Perhaps you would care to share it with me."

Her black eyes considered him gravely. "Perhaps. We will see." She turned her mount and began to ride towards Mama Tito's.

A moment later the Healer followed. "Yes," he said aloud in English. "I will have a whole world of work to do."

Mama Tito sighed gustily in enormous discontent and impatience as she waited for her warriors to return. Such a *handsome* young man! It had rankled increasingly that she had never been able to entice him to her sleeping quarters for even a few moments of passing pleasure. If nothing else, a decent respect — or a even righteous fear — for her elevated position ought to have shown him his clear duty and led him to submit to her occasional idle whims of the moment. Surely there was no other man in her kingdom whom she would have permitted to disdain her regal favors so openly. If only he weren't so obsessed with that strange Frenchwoman and that even stranger flickerwoman. . . .

But now the sky-curtain was gone, and all the world must surely change. Many of the changes were certain to be unwelcome. The French, for instance: would they return in great numbers from their far-off homeland with their soldiers and magic weapons, to once again subject the entire Maohi Empire to their tyranny?

She raised a bright orange plantain to her lips and began to chew it thoughtfully.

It was not impossible there could also be more pleasant changes. If in fact the flickermen had at last departed, a minor consequence would be a Ken Camden suddenly bereft of his invulnerable guardian. Perhaps *now* the golden blond youth might be coaxed into showing a more decent respect for his superiors and their keenly felt desires. . . .

She swallowed noisily, and dreamily reached for a soft pulpy mango as the erotic images of their forthcoming encounter tumbled pleasurably through her mind.

How fortunate, she thought wistfully, were those women lucky enough to be held and loved by such a man as Ken Camden. . . .